George Bernard Shaw

Love Among the Artists
(An Autobiographical Novel of G. B. Shaw)

George Bernard Shaw
LOVE AMONG THE ARTISTS

(An Autobiographical Novel of G. B. Shaw)

A Story With a Purpose

Published by
MUSAICUM
Books

- Advanced Digital Solutions & High-Quality book Formatting -

musaicumbooks@okpublishing.info

2021 OK Publishing

ISBN 978-80-272-7464-2

Contents

George Bernard Shaw by G. K. Chesterton	11
Introduction to the First Edition	11
The Problem of a Preface	11
The Irishman	13
The Puritan	17
The Progressive	22
The Critic	30
The Dramatist	37
The Philosopher	50
Love Among The Artists	73
The Author to the Reader	74
BOOK I	75
CHAPTER I	75
CHAPTER II	79
CHAPTER III	84
CHAPTER IV	93
CHAPTER V	100
CHAPTER VI	111
CHAPTER VII	118
CHAPTER VIII	123
CHAPTER IX	135
CHAPTER X	142
CHAPTER XI	148
CHAPTER XII	159
CHAPTER XIII	169
CHAPTER XIV	180
BOOK II	191
CHAPTER I	191
CHAPTER II	201
CHAPTER III	214
CHAPTER IV	228

George Bernard Shaw by G. K. Chesterton

Introduction to the First Edition

Most people either say that they agree with Bernard Shaw or that they do not understand him. I am the only person who understands him, and I do not agree with him.

G. K. C.

The Problem of a Preface

A peculiar difficulty arrests the writer of this rough study at the very start. Many people know Mr. Bernard Shaw chiefly as a man who would write a very long preface even to a very short play. And there is truth in the idea; he is indeed a very prefatory sort of person. He always gives the explanation before the incident; but so, for the matter of that, does the Gospel of St. John. For Bernard Shaw, as for the mystics, Christian and heathen (and Shaw is best described as a heathen mystic), the philosophy of facts is anterior to the facts themselves. In due time we come to the fact, the incarnation; but in the beginning was the Word.

This produces upon many minds an impression of needless preparation and a kind of bustling prolixity. But the truth is that the very rapidity of such a man's mind makes him seem slow in getting to the point. It is positively because he is quick-witted that he is long-winded. A quick eye for ideas may actually make a writer slow in reaching his goal, just as a quick eye for landscapes might make a motorist slow in reaching Brighton. An original man has to pause at every allusion or simile to re-explain historical parallels, to re-shape distorted words. Any ordinary leader-writer (let us say) might write swiftly and smoothly something like this: "The element of religion in the Puritan rebellion, if hostile to art, yet saved the movement from some of the evils in which the French Revolution involved morality." Now a man like Mr. Shaw, who has his own views on everything, would be forced to make the sentence long and broken instead of swift and smooth. He would say something like: "The element of religion, as I explain religion, in the Puritan rebellion (which you wholly misunderstand) if hostile to art — that is what I mean by art — may have saved it from some evils (remember my definition of evil) in which the French Revolution — of which I have my own opinion — involved morality, which I will define for you in a minute." That is the worst of being a really universal sceptic and philosopher; it is such slow work. The very forest of the man's thoughts chokes up his thoroughfare. A man must be orthodox upon most things, or he will never even have time to preach his own heresy.

Now the same difficulty which affects the work of Bernard Shaw affects also any book about him. There is an unavoidable artistic necessity to put the preface before the play; that is, there is a necessity to say something of what Bernard Shaw's experience means before one even says what it was. We have to mention what he did when we have already explained why he did it. Viewed superficially, his life consists of fairly conventional incidents, and might easily fall under fairly conventional phrases. It might be the life of any Dublin clerk or Manchester Socialist or London author. If I touch on the man's life before his work, it will seem trivial; yet taken with his work it is most important. In short, one could scarcely know what Shaw's doings meant unless one knew what he meant by them. This difficulty in mere order and construction has puzzled me very much. I am going to overcome it, clumsily perhaps, but in the way which affects me as most sincere. Before I write even a slight suggestion of his relation to the stage, I am going to write of three soils or atmospheres out of which that relation grew. In other words, before I write of Shaw I will write of the three great influences upon Shaw. They were all three there before he was born, yet each one of them is himself and a very vivid portrait of him from one point of view. I have called these three traditions: "The Irishman," "The Puritan," and "The Progressive." I do not see how this prefatory theorising is to be avoided; for if I simply said, for instance, that Bernard Shaw was an Irishman, the impression produced on the reader might be remote from my thought and, what is more important, from Shaw's. People might think, for instance, that I meant that he was "irresponsible." That would throw out the whole plan of these pages, for if there is one thing that Shaw is not, it is irresponsible. The responsibility in him rings like steel. Or, again, if I simply called him a Puritan, it might mean something about nude statues or "prudes on the prowl." Or if I called him a Progressive, it might be supposed to mean that he votes for Progressives at the County Council election, which I very much doubt. I have no other course but this: of briefly explaining such matters as Shaw himself might explain them. Some fastidious persons may object to my thus putting the moral in front of the fable. Some may imagine in their innocence that they already understand the word Puritan or the yet more mysterious word Irishman. The only person, indeed, of whose approval I feel fairly certain is Mr. Bernard Shaw himself, the man of many introductions.

The Irishman

The English public has commonly professed, with a kind of pride, that it cannot understand Mr. Bernard Shaw. There are many reasons for it which ought to be adequately considered in such a book as this. But the first and most obvious reason is the mere statement that George Bernard Shaw was born in Dublin in 1856. At least one reason why Englishmen cannot understand Mr. Shaw is that Englishmen have never taken the trouble to understand Irishmen. They will sometimes be generous to Ireland; but never just to Ireland. They will speak to Ireland; they will speak for Ireland; but they will not hear Ireland speak. All the real amiability which most Englishmen undoubtedly feel towards Irishmen is lavished upon a class of Irishmen which unfortunately does not exist. The Irishman of the English farce, with his brogue, his buoyancy, and his tenderhearted irresponsibility, is a man who ought to have been thoroughly pampered with praise and sympathy, if he had only existed to receive them. Unfortunately, all the time that we were creating a comic Irishman in fiction, we were creating a tragic Irishman in fact. Never perhaps has there been a situation of such excruciating cross-purposes even in the three-act farce. The more we saw in the Irishman a sort of warm and weak fidelity, the more he regarded us with a sort of icy anger. The more the oppressor looked down with an amiable pity, the more did the oppressed look down with a somewhat unamiable contempt. But, indeed, it is needless to say that such comic cross-purposes could be put into a play; they have been put into a play. They have been put into what is perhaps the most real of Mr. Bernard Shaw's plays, *John Bull's Other Island* .

It is somewhat absurd to imagine that any one who has not read a play by Mr. Shaw will be reading a book about him. But if it comes to that it is (as I clearly perceive) absurd to be writing a book about Mr. Bernard Shaw at all. It is indefensibly foolish to attempt to explain a man whose whole object through life has been to explain himself. But even in nonsense there is a need for logic and consistency; therefore let us proceed on the assumption that when I say that all Mr. Shaw's blood and origin may be found in *John Bull's Other Island* , some reader may answer that he does not know the play. Besides, it is more important to put the reader right about England and Ireland even than to put him right about Shaw. If he reminds me that this is a book about Shaw, I can only assure him that I will reasonably, and at proper intervals, remember the fact.

Mr. Shaw himself said once, "I am a typical Irishman; my family came from Yorkshire." Scarcely anyone but a typical Irishman could have made the remark. It is in fact a bull, a conscious bull. A bull is only a paradox which people are too stupid to understand. It is the rapid summary of something which is at once so true and so complex that the speaker who has the swift intelligence to perceive it, has not the slow patience to explain it. Mystical dogmas are much of this kind. Dogmas are often spoken of as if they were signs of the slowness or endurance of the human mind. As a matter of fact, they are marks of mental promptitude and lucid impatience. A man will put his meaning mystically because he cannot waste time in putting it rationally. Dogmas are not dark and mysterious; rather a dogma is like a flash of lightning — an instantaneous lucidity that opens across a whole landscape. Of the same nature are Irish bulls; they are summaries which are too true to be consistent. The Irish make Irish bulls for the same reason that they accept Papal bulls. It is because it is better to speak wisdom foolishly, like the Saints, rather than to speak folly wisely, like the Dons.

This is the truth about mystical dogmas and the truth about Irish bulls; it is also the truth about the paradoxes of Bernard Shaw. Each of them is an argument impatiently shortened into an epigram. Each of them represents a truth hammered and hardened, with an almost disdainful violence until it is compressed into a small space, until it is made brief and almost incomprehensible. The case of that curt remark about Ireland and Yorkshire is a very typical one. If Mr. Shaw had really attempted to set out all the sensible stages of his joke, the sentence would have run something like this: "That I am an Irishman is a fact of psychology which I can trace in many of the things that come out of me, my fastidiousness, my frigid fierceness and my distrust of mere pleasure. But the thing must be tested by what comes from me; do not try on me the dodge of asking where I came from, how many batches of three hundred and sixty-five days my family was in Ireland. Do not play any games on me about whether I am a Celt, a word that is dim to the anthropologist and utterly unmeaning to anybody else. Do not start any drivelling discussions about whether the word Shaw is German or Scandinavian or Iberian or Basque. You know you are human; I know I am Irish. I know I belong to a certain type and temper of society; and I know that all sorts of people of all sorts of blood live in that society and by that society; and are therefore Irish. You can take your books of anthropology to hell or to Oxford." Thus gently, elaborately and at length, Mr. Shaw would have explained his meaning, if he had thought it worth his while. As he did not he merely flung the symbolic, but very complete sentence, "I am a typical Irishman; my family came from Yorkshire."

What then is the colour of this Irish society of which Bernard Shaw, with all his individual oddity, is yet an essential type? One generalisation, I think, may at least be made. Ireland has in it a quality which caused it (in the most ascetic age of Christianity) to be called the "Land of Saints"; and which still might give it a claim to be called the Land of Virgins. An Irish Catholic priest once said to me, "There is in our people a fear of the passions which is older even than Christianity." Everyone who has read Shaw's play upon Ireland will remember the thing in the horror of the Irish girl at being kissed in the public streets. But anyone who knows Shaw's work will recognize it in Shaw himself. There exists by accident an early and beardless portrait of him which really suggests in the severity and purity of its lines some of the early ascetic pictures of the beardless Christ. However he may shout profanities or seek to shatter the shrines, there is always something about him which suggests that in a sweeter and more solid civilisation he would have been a great saint. He would have been a saint of a sternly ascetic, perhaps of a sternly negative type. But he has this strange note of the saint in him: that he is literally unworldly. Worldliness has no human magic for him; he is not bewitched by rank nor drawn on by conviviality at all. He could not understand the intellectual surrender of the snob. He is perhaps a defective character; but he is not a mixed one. All the virtues he has are heroic virtues. Shaw is like the Venus of Milo; all that there is of him is admirable.

But in any case this Irish innocence is peculiar and fundamental in him; and strange as it may sound, I think that his innocence has a great deal to do with his suggestions of sexual revolution. Such a man is comparatively audacious in theory because he is comparatively clean in thought. Powerful men who have powerful passions use much of their strength in forging chains for themselves; they alone know how strong the chains need to be. But there are other souls who walk the woods like Diana, with a sort of wild chastity. I confess I think that this Irish purity a little disables a critic in dealing, as Mr. Shaw has dealt, with the roots and reality of the marriage law. He forgets that those fierce and elementary functions which drive the universe have an impetus which goes beyond itself and cannot always easily be recovered. So the healthiest men may often erect a law to watch them, just as the healthiest sleepers may want an alarum clock to wake them up. However this may be, Bernard Shaw certainly has all the virtues and all the powers that go with this original quality in Ireland. One of them is a sort of awful elegance; a dangerous and somewhat inhuman daintiness of taste which sometimes seems to shrink from matter itself, as though it were mud. Of the many sincere things Mr. Shaw has said he never said a more sincere one than when he stated he was a vegetarian, not because eating meat was bad morality, but because it was bad taste. It would be fanciful to say that Mr. Shaw is a vegetarian because he comes of a race of vegetarians, of peasants who are compelled to accept the simple life in the shape of potatoes. But I am sure that his fierce fastidiousness in such matters is one of the allotropic forms of the Irish purity; it is to the virtue of Father Matthew what a coal is to a diamond. It has, of course, the quality common to all special and unbalanced types of virtue, that you never know where it will stop. I can feel what Mr. Shaw probably means when he says that it is disgusting to feast off dead bodies, or to cut lumps off what was once a living thing. But I can never know at what moment he may not feel in the same way that it is disgusting to mutilate a pear-tree, or to root out of the earth those miserable mandrakes which cannot even groan. There is no natural limit to this rush and riotous gallop of refinement.

But it is not this physical and fantastic purity which I should chiefly count among the legacies of the old Irish morality. A much more important gift is that which all the saints declared to be the reward of chastity: a queer clearness of the intellect, like the hard clearness of a crystal. This certainly Mr. Shaw possesses; in such degree that at certain times the hardness seems rather clearer than the clearness. But so it does in all the most typical Irish characters and Irish attitudes of mind. This is probably why Irishmen succeed so much in such professions as require a certain crystalline realism, especially about results. Such professions are the soldier and the lawyer; these give ample opportunity for crimes but not much for mere illusions. If you have composed a bad opera you may persuade yourself that it is a good one; if you have carved a bad statue you can think yourself better than Michael Angelo. But if you have lost a battle you cannot believe you have won it; if your client is hanged you cannot pretend that you have got him off.

There must be some sense in every popular prejudice, even about foreigners. And the English people certainly have somehow got an impression and a tradition that the Irishman is genial, unreasonable, and sentimental. This legend of the tender, irresponsible Paddy has two roots; there are two elements in the Irish which made the mistake possible. First, the very logic of the Irishman makes him regard war or revolution as extra-logical, an *ultima ratio* which is beyond reason. When fighting a powerful enemy he no more worries whether all his charges are exact or all his attitudes dignified than a soldier worries whether a cannon-ball is shapely or a plan of campaign picturesque. He is aggressive; he attacks. He seems merely to be rowdy in Ireland when he is really carrying the war into Africa — or England. A Dublin tradesman printed his name and trade in archaic Erse on his cart. He knew that hardly anybody could read it; he did it to annoy. In his position I think he was quite right. When one is oppressed it is a mark of chivalry to hurt oneself in order to hurt the oppressor. But the English (never having had a real revolution since the Middle Ages) find it very hard to understand this steady passion for being a nuisance, and mistake it for mere whimsical impulsiveness and folly. When an Irish member holds up the whole business of the House of Commons by talking of his bleeding country for five or six hours, the simple English members suppose that he is a sentimentalist. The truth is that he is a scornful realist who alone remains unaffected by the sentimentalism of the House of Commons. The Irishman is neither poet enough nor snob enough to be swept away by those smooth social and historical tides and tendencies which carry Radicals and Labour members comfortably off their feet. He goes on asking for a thing because he wants it; and he tries really to hurt his enemies because they are his enemies. This is the first of the queer confusions which make the hard Irishman look soft. He seems to us wild and unreasonable because he is really much too reasonable to be anything but fierce when he is fighting.

In all this it will not be difficult to see the Irishman in Bernard Shaw. Though personally one of the kindest men in the world, he has often written really in order to hurt; not because he hated any particular men (he is hardly hot and animal enough for that), but because he really hated certain ideas even unto slaying. He provokes; he will not let people alone. One might even say that he bullies, only that this would be unfair, because he always wishes the other man to hit back. At least he always challenges, like a true Green Islander. An even stronger instance of this national trait can be found in another eminent Irishman, Oscar Wilde. His philosophy (which was vile) was a philosophy of ease, of acceptance, and luxurious illusion; yet, being Irish, he could not help putting it in pugnacious and propagandist epigrams. He preached his softness with hard decision; he praised pleasure in the words most calculated to give pain. This armed insolence, which was the noblest thing about him, was also the Irish thing; he challenged all comers. It is a good instance of how right popular tradition is even when it is most wrong, that the English have perceived and preserved this essential trait of Ireland in a proverbial phrase. It *is* true that the Irishman says, "Who will tread on the tail of my coat?"

But there is a second cause which creates the English fallacy that the Irish are weak and emotional. This again springs from the very fact that the Irish are lucid and logical. For being logical they strictly separate poetry from prose; and as in prose they are strictly prosaic, so in poetry they are purely poetical. In this, as in one or two other things, they resemble the French, who make their gardens beautiful because they are gardens, but their fields ugly because they are only fields. An Irishman may like romance, but he will say, to use a frequent Shavian phrase, that it is "only romance." A great part of the English energy in fiction arises from the very fact that their fiction half deceives them. If Rudyard Kipling, for instance, had written his short stories in France, they would have been praised as cool, clever little works of art, rather cruel, and very nervous and feminine; Kipling's short stories would have been appreciated like Maupassant's short stories. In England they were not appreciated but believed. They were taken seriously by a startled nation as a true picture of the empire and the universe. The English people made haste to abandon England in favour of Mr. Kipling and his imaginary colonies; they made haste to abandon Christianity in favour of Mr. Kipling's rather morbid version of Judaism. Such a moral boom of a book would be almost impossible in Ireland, because the Irish mind distinguishes between life and literature. Mr. Bernard Shaw himself summed this up as he sums up so many things in a compact sentence which he uttered in conversation with the present writer, "An Irishman has two eyes." He meant that with one eye an Irishman saw that a dream was inspiring, bewitching, or sublime, and with the other eye that after all it was a dream. Both the humour and the sentiment of an Englishman cause him to wink the other eye. Two other small examples will illustrate the English mistake. Take, for instance, that noble survival from a nobler age of politics — I mean Irish oratory. The English imagine that Irish politicians are so hotheaded and poetical that they have to pour out a torrent of burning words. The truth is that the Irish are so clearheaded and critical that they still regard rhetoric as a distinct art, as the ancients did. Thus a man makes a speech as a man plays a violin, not necessarily without feeling, but chiefly because he knows how to do it. Another instance of the same thing is that quality which is always called the Irish charm. The Irish are agreeable, not because they are particularly emotional, but because they are very highly civilised. Blarney is a ritual; as much of a ritual as kissing the Blarney Stone.

Lastly, there is one general truth about Ireland which may very well have influenced Bernard Shaw from the first; and almost certainly influenced him for good. Ireland is a country in which the political conflicts are at least genuine; they are about something. They are about patriotism, about religion, or about money: the three great realities. In other words, they are concerned with what commonwealth a man lives in or with what universe a man lives in or with how he is to manage to live in either. But they are not concerned with which of two wealthy cousins in the same governing class shall be allowed to bring in the same Parish Councils Bill; there is no party system in Ireland. The party system in England is an enormous and most efficient machine for preventing political conflicts. The party system is arranged on the same principle as a three-legged race: the principle that union is not always strength and is never activity. Nobody asks for what he really wants. But in Ireland the loyalist is just as ready to throw over the King as the Fenian to throw over Mr. Gladstone; each will throw over anything except the thing that he wants. Hence it happens that even the follies or the frauds of Irish politics are more genuine as symptoms and more honourable as symbols than the lumbering hypocrisies of the prosperous Parliamentarian. The very lies of Dublin and Belfast are truer than the truisms of Westminster. They have an object; they refer to a state of things. There was more honesty, in the sense of actuality, about Piggott's letters than about the *Times'* leading articles on them. When Parnell said calmly before the Royal Commission that he had made a certain remark "in order to mislead the House" he proved himself to be one of the few truthful men of his time. An ordinary British statesman would never have made the confession, because he would have grown quite accustomed to committing the crime. The party system itself implies a habit of stating something other than the actual truth. A Leader of the House means a Misleader of the House.

Bernard Shaw was born outside all this; and he carries that freedom upon his face. Whether what he heard in boyhood was violent Nationalism or virulent Unionism, it was at least something which wanted a certain principle to be in force, not a certain clique to be in office. Of him the great Gilbertian generalisation is untrue; he was not born either a little Liberal or else a little Conservative. He did not, like most of us, pass through the stage of being a good party man on his way to the difficult business of being a good man. He came to stare at our general elections as a Red Indian might stare at the Oxford and Cambridge boat-race, blind to all its irrelevant sentimentalities and to some of its legitimate sentiments. Bernard Shaw entered England as an alien, as an invader, as a conqueror. In other words, he entered England as an Irishman.

The Puritan

It has been said in the first section that Bernard Shaw draws from his own nation two unquestionable qualities, a kind of intellectual chastity, and the fighting spirit. He is so much of an idealist about his ideals that he can be a ruthless realist in his methods. His soul has (in short) the virginity and the violence of Ireland. But Bernard Shaw is not merely an Irishman; he is not even a typical one. He is a certain separated and peculiar kind of Irishman, which is not easy to describe. Some Nationalist Irishmen have referred to him contemptuously as a "West Briton." But this is really unfair; for whatever Mr. Shaw's mental faults may be, the easy adoption of an unmeaning phrase like "Briton" is certainly not one of them. It would be much nearer the truth to put the thing in the bold and bald terms of the old Irish song, and to call him "The anti-Irish Irishman." But it is only fair to say that the description is far less of a monstrosity than the anti-English Englishman would be; because the Irish are so much stronger in self-criticism. Compared with the constant self-flattery of the English, nearly every Irishman is an anti-Irish Irishman. But here again popular phraseology hits the right word. This fairly educated and fairly wealthy Protestant wedge which is driven into the country at Dublin and elsewhere is a thing not easy superficially to summarise in any term. It cannot be described merely as a minority; for a minority means the part of a nation which is conquered. But this thing means something that conquers, and is not entirely part of a nation. Nor can one even fall back on the phrase of aristocracy. For an aristocracy implies at least some chorus of snobbish enthusiasm; it implies that some at least are willingly led by the leaders, if only towards vulgarity and vice. There is only one word for the minority in Ireland, and that is the word that public phraseology has found; I mean the word "Garrison." The Irish are essentially right when they talk as if all Protestant Unionists lived inside "The Castle." They have all the virtues and limitations of a literal garrison in a fort. That is, they are valiant, consistent, reliable in an obvious public sense; but their curse is that they can only tread the flagstones of the courtyard or the cold rock of the ramparts; they have never so much as set their foot upon their native soil.

We have considered Bernard Shaw as an Irishman. The next step is to consider him as an exile from Ireland living in Ireland; that, some people would say, is a paradox after his own heart. But, indeed, such a complication is not really difficult to expound. The great religion and the great national tradition which have persisted for so many centuries in Ireland have encouraged these clean and cutting elements; but they have encouraged many other things which serve to balance them. The Irish peasant has these qualities which are somewhat peculiar to Ireland, a strange purity and a strange pugnacity. But the Irish peasant also has qualities which are common to all peasants, and his nation has qualities that are common to all healthy nations. I mean chiefly the things that most of us absorb in childhood; especially the sense of the supernatural and the sense of the natural; the love of the sky with its infinity of vision, and the love of the soil with its strict hedges and solid shapes of ownership. But here comes the paradox of Shaw; the greatest of all his paradoxes and the one of which he is unconscious. These one or two plain truths which quite stupid people learn at the beginning are exactly the one or two truths which Bernard Shaw may not learn even at the end. He is a daring pilgrim who has set out from the grave to find the cradle. He started from points of view which no one else was clever enough to discover, and he is at last discovering points of view which no one else was ever stupid enough to ignore. This absence of the red-hot truisms of boyhood; this sense that he is not rooted in the ancient sagacities of infancy, has, I think, a great deal to do with his position as a member of an alien minority in Ireland. He who has no real country can have no real home. The average autochthonous Irishman is close to patriotism because he is close to the earth; he is close to domesticity because he is close to the earth; he is close to doctrinal theology and elaborate ritual because he is close to the earth. In short, he is close to the heavens because he is close to the earth. But we must not expect any of these elemental and collective virtues in the man of the garrison. He cannot be expected to exhibit the virtues of a people, but only (as Ibsen would say) of an enemy of the people. Mr. Shaw has no living traditions, no schoolboy tricks, no college customs, to link him with other men. Nothing about him can be supposed to refer to a family feud or to a family joke. He does not drink toasts; he does not keep anniversaries; musical as he is I doubt if he would consent to sing. All this has something in it of a tree with its roots in the air. The best way to shorten winter is to prolong Christmas; and the only way to enjoy the sun of April is to be an April Fool. When people asked Bernard Shaw to attend the Stratford Tercentenary, he wrote back with characteristic contempt: "I do not keep my own birthday, and I cannot see why I should keep Shakespeare's." I think that if Mr. Shaw had always kept his own birthday he would be better able to understand Shakespeare's birthday — and Shakespeare's poetry.

In conjecturally referring this negative side of the man, his lack of the smaller charities of our common childhood, to his birth in the dominant Irish sect, I do not write without historic memory or reference to other cases. That minority of Protestant exiles which mainly represented Ireland to England during the eighteenth century did contain some specimens of the Irish lounger and even of the Irish blackguard; Sheridan and even Goldsmith suggest the type. Even in their irresponsibility these figures had a touch of Irish tartness and realism; but the type has been too much insisted on to the exclusion of others equally national and interesting. To one of these it is worth while to draw attention. At intervals during the eighteenth and nineteenth centuries there has appeared a peculiar kind of Irishman. He is so unlike the English image of Ireland that the English have actually fallen back on the pretence that he was not Irish at all. The type is commonly Protestant; and sometimes seems to be almost antinational in its acrid instinct for judging itself. Its nationalism only appears when it flings itself with even bitterer pleasure into judging the foreigner or the invader. The first and greatest of such figures was Swift. Thackeray simply denied that Swift was an Irishman, because he was not a stage Irishman. He was not (in the English novelist's opinion) winning and agreeable enough to be Irish. The truth is that Swift was much too harsh and disagreeable to be English. There is a great deal of Jonathan Swift in Bernard Shaw. Shaw is like Swift, for instance, in combining extravagant fancy with a curious sort of coldness. But he is most like Swift in that very quality which Thackeray said was impossible in an Irishman, benevolent bullying, a pity touched with contempt, and a habit of knocking men down for their own good. Characters in novels are often described as so amiable that they hate to be thanked. It is not an amiable quality, and it is an extremely rare one; but Swift possessed it. When Swift was buried the Dublin poor came in crowds and wept by the grave of the broadest and most freehanded of their benefactors. Swift deserved the public tribute; but he might have writhed and kicked in his grave at the thought of receiving it. There is in G. B. S. something of the same inhuman humanity. Irish history has offered a third instance of this particular type of educated and Protestant Irishman, sincere, unsympathetic, aggressive, alone. I mean Parnell; and with him also a bewildered England tried the desperate dodge of saying that he was not Irish at all. As if any thinkable sensible snobbish law-abiding Englishman would ever have defied all the drawingrooms by disdaining the House of Commons! Despite the difference between taciturnity and a torrent of fluency there is much in common also between Shaw and Parnell; something in common even in the figures of the two men, in the bony bearded faces with their almost Satanic self-possession. It will not do to pretend that none of these three men belong to their own nation; but it is true that they belonged to one special, though recurring, type of that nation. And they all three have this peculiar mark, that while Nationalists in their various ways they all give to the more genial English one common impression; I mean the impression that they do not so much love Ireland as hate England.

I will not dogmatise upon the difficult question as to whether there is any religious significance in the fact that these three rather ruthless Irishmen were Protestant Irishmen. I incline to think myself that the Catholic Church has added charity and gentleness to the virtues of a people which would otherwise have been too keen and contemptuous, too aristocratic. But however this may be, there can surely be no question that Bernard Shaw's Protestant education in a Catholic country has made a great deal of difference to his mind. It has affected it in two ways, the first negative and the second positive. It has affected him by cutting him off (as we have said) from the fields and fountains of his real home and history; by making him an Orangeman. And it has affected him by the particular colour of the particular religion which he received; by making him a Puritan.

In one of his numerous prefaces he says, "I have always been on the side of the Puritans in the matter of Art"; and a closer study will, I think, reveal that he is on the side of the Puritans in almost everything. Puritanism was not a mere code of cruel regulations, though some of its regulations were more cruel than any that have disgraced Europe. Nor was Puritanism a mere nightmare, an evil shadow of eastern gloom and fatalism, though this element did enter it, and was as it were the symptom and punishment of its essential error. Something much nobler (even if almost equally mistaken) was the original energy in the Puritan creed. And it must be defined with a little more delicacy if we are really to understand the attitude of G. B. S., who is the greatest of the modern Puritans and perhaps the last.

I should roughly define the first spirit in Puritanism thus. It was a refusal to contemplate God or goodness with anything lighter or milder than the most fierce concentration of the intellect. A Puritan meant originally a man whose mind had no holidays. To use his own favourite phrase, he would let no living thing come between him and his God; an attitude which involved eternal torture for him and a cruel contempt for all the living things. It was better to worship in a barn than in a cathedral for the specific and specified reason that the cathedral was beautiful. Physical beauty was a false and sensual symbol coming in between the intellect and the object of its intellectual worship. The human brain ought to be at every instant a consuming fire which burns through all conventional images until they were as transparent as glass.

This is the essential Puritan idea, that God can only be praised by direct contemplation of Him. You must praise God only with your brain; it is wicked to praise Him with your passions or your physical habits or your gesture or instinct of beauty. Therefore it is wicked to worship by singing or dancing or drinking sacramental wines or building beautiful churches or saying prayers when you are half asleep. We must not worship by dancing, drinking, building or singing; we can only worship by thinking. Our heads can praise God, but never our hands and feet. That is the true and original impulse of the Puritans. There is a great deal to be said for it, and a great deal was said for it in Great Britain steadily for two hundred years. It has gradually decayed in England and Scotland, not because of the advance of modern thought (which means nothing), but because of the slow revival of the mediæval energy and character in the two peoples. The English were always hearty and humane, and they have made up their minds to be hearty and humane in spite of the Puritans. The result is that Dickens and W. W. Jacobs have picked up the tradition of Chaucer and Robin Hood. The Scotch were always romantic, and they have made up their minds to be romantic in spite of the Puritans. The result is that Scott and Stevenson have picked up the tradition of Bruce, Blind Harry and the vagabond Scottish kings. England has become English again; Scotland has become Scottish again, in spite of the splendid incubus, the noble nightmare of Calvin. There is only one place in the British Islands where one may naturally expect to find still surviving in its fulness the fierce detachment of the true Puritan. That place is the Protestant part of Ireland. The Orange Calvinists can be disturbed by no national resurrection, for they have no nation. In them, if in any people, will be found the rectangular consistency of the Calvinist. The Irish Protestant rioters are at least immeasurably finer fellows than any of their brethren in England. They have the two enormous superiorities: first, that the Irish Protestant rioters really believe in Protestant theology; and second, that the Irish Protestant rioters do really riot. Among these people, if anywhere, should be found the cult of theological clarity combined with barbarous external simplicity. Among these people Bernard Shaw was born.

There is at least one outstanding fact about the man we are studying; Bernard Shaw is never frivolous. He never gives his opinions a holiday; he is never irresponsible even for an instant. He has no nonsensical second self which he can get into as one gets into a dressing-gown; that ridiculous disguise which is yet more real than the real person. That collapse and humorous confession of futility was much of the force in Charles Lamb and in Stevenson. There is nothing of this in Shaw; his wit is never a weakness; therefore it is never a sense of humour. For wit is always connected with the idea that truth is close and clear. Humour, on the other hand, is always connected with the idea that truth is tricky and mystical and easily mistaken. What Charles Lamb said of the Scotchman is far truer of this type of Puritan Irishman; he does not see things suddenly in a new light; all his brilliancy is a blindingly rapid calculation and deduction. Bernard Shaw never said an indefensible thing; that is, he never said a thing that he was not prepared brilliantly to defend. He never breaks out into that cry beyond reason and conviction, that cry of Lamb when he cried, "We would indict our dreams!" or of Stevenson, "Shall we never shed blood?" In short he is not a humorist, but a great wit, almost as great as Voltaire. Humour is akin to agnosticism, which is only the negative side of mysticism. But pure wit is akin to Puritanism; to the perfect and painful consciousness of the final fact in the universe. Very briefly, the man who sees the consistency in things is a wit — and a Calvinist. The man who sees the inconsistency in things is a humorist — and a Catholic. However this may be, Bernard Shaw exhibits all that is purest in the Puritan; the desire to see truth face to face even if it slay us, the high impatience with irrelevant sentiment or obstructive symbol; the constant effort to keep the soul at its highest pressure and speed. His instincts upon all social customs and questions are Puritan. His favourite author is Bunyan.

But along with what was inspiring and direct in Puritanism Bernard Shaw has inherited also some of the things that were cumbersome and traditional. If ever Shaw exhibits a prejudice it is always a Puritan prejudice. For Puritanism has not been able to sustain through three centuries that native ecstacy of the direct contemplation of truth; indeed it was the whole mistake of Puritanism to imagine for a moment that it could. One cannot be serious for three hundred years. In institutions built so as to endure for ages you must have relaxation, symbolic relativity and healthy routine. In eternal temples you must have frivolity. You must "be at ease in Zion" unless you are only paying it a flying visit.

By the middle of the nineteenth century this old austerity and actuality in the Puritan vision had fallen away into two principal lower forms. The first is a sort of idealistic garrulity upon which Bernard Shaw has made fierce and on the whole fruitful war. Perpetual talk about righteousness and unselfishness, about things that should elevate and things which cannot but degrade, about social purity and true Christian manhood, all poured out with fatal fluency and with very little reference to the real facts of anybody's soul or salary — into this weak and lukewarm torrent has melted down much of that mountainous ice which sparkled in the seventeenth century, bleak indeed, but blazing. The hardest thing of the seventeenth century bids fair to be the softest thing of the twentieth.

Of all this sentimental and deliquescent Puritanism Bernard Shaw has always been the antagonist; and the only respect in which it has soiled him was that he believed for only too long that such sloppy idealism was the whole idealism of Christendom and so used "idealist" itself as a term of reproach. But there were other and negative effects of Puritanism which he did not escape so completely. I cannot think that he has wholly escaped that element in Puritanism which may fairly bear the title of the taboo. For it is a singular fact that although extreme Protestantism is dying in elaborate and over-refined civilisation, yet it is the barbaric patches of it that live longest and die last. Of the creed of John Knox the modern Protestant has abandoned the civilised part and retained only the savage part. He has given up that great and systematic philosophy of Calvinism which had much in common with modern science and strongly resembles ordinary and recurrent determinism. But he has retained the accidental veto upon cards or comic plays, which Knox only valued as mere proof of his people's concentration on their theology. All the awful but sublime affirmations of Puritan theology are gone. Only savage negations remain; such as that by which in Scotland on every seventh day the creed of fear lays his finger on all hearts and makes an evil silence in the streets.

By the middle of the nineteenth century when Shaw was born this dim and barbaric element in Puritanism, being all that remained of it, had added another taboo to its philosophy of taboos; there had grown up a mystical horror of those fermented drinks which are part of the food of civilised mankind. Doubtless many persons take an extreme line on this matter solely because of some calculation of social harm; many, but not all and not even most. Many people think that paper money is a mistake and does much harm. But they do not shudder or snigger when they see a cheque-book. They do not whisper with unsavoury slyness that such and such a man was "seen" going into a bank. I am quite convinced that the English aristocracy is the curse of England, but I have not noticed either in myself or others any disposition to ostracise a man simply for accepting a peerage, as the modern Puritans would certainly ostracise him (from any of their positions of trust) for accepting a drink. The sentiment is certainly very largely a mystical one, like the sentiment about the seventh day. Like the Sabbath, it is defended with sociological reasons; but those reasons can be simply and sharply tested. If a Puritan tells you that all humanity should rest once a week, you have only to propose that they should rest on Wednesday. And if a Puritan tells you that he does not object to beer but to the tragedies of excess in beer, simply propose to him that in prisons and workhouses (where the amount can be absolutely regulated) the inmates should have three glasses of beer a day. The Puritan cannot call that excess; but he will find something to call it. For it is not the excess he objects to, but the beer. It is a transcendental taboo, and it is one of the two or three positive and painful prejudices with which Bernard Shaw began. A similar severity of outlook ran through all his earlier attitude towards the drama; especially towards the lighter or looser drama. His Puritan teachers could not prevent him from taking up theatricals, but they made him take theatricals seriously. All his plays were indeed "plays for Puritans." All his criticisms quiver with a refined and almost tortured contempt for the indulgencies of ballet and burlesque, for the tights and the *double entente*. He can endure lawlessness but not levity. He is not repelled by the divorces and the adulteries as he is by the "splits." And he has always been foremost among the fierce modern critics who ask indignantly, "Why do you object to a thing full of sincere philosophy like *The Wild Duck* while you tolerate a mere dirty joke like *The Spring Chicken* ?" I do not think he has ever understood what seems to me the very sensible answer of the man in the street, "I laugh at the dirty joke of *The Spring Chicken* because it is a joke. I criticise the philosophy of *The Wild Duck* because it is a philosophy."

Shaw does not do justice to the democratic ease and sanity on this subject; but indeed, whatever else he is, he is not democratic. As an Irishman he is an aristocrat, as a Calvinist he is a soul apart; he drew the breath of his nostrils from a land of fallen principalities and proud gentility, and the breath of his spirit from a creed which made a wall of crystal around the elect. The two forces between them produced this potent and slender figure, swift, scornful, dainty and full of dry magnanimity; and it only needed the last touch of oligarchic mastery to be given by the overwhelming oligarchic atmosphere of our present age. Such was the Puritan Irishman who stepped out into the world. Into what kind of world did he step?

The Progressive

It is now partly possible to justify the Shavian method of putting the explanations before the events. I can now give a fact or two with a partial certainty at least that the reader will give to the affairs of Bernard Shaw something of the same kind of significance which they have for Bernard Shaw himself. Thus, if I had simply said that Shaw was born in Dublin the average reader might exclaim, "Ah yes — a wild Irishman, gay, emotional and untrustworthy." The wrong note would be struck at the start. I have attempted to give some idea of what being born in Ireland meant to the man who was really born there. Now therefore for the first time I may be permitted to confess that Bernard Shaw was, like other men, born. He was born in Dublin on the 26th of July, 1856.

Just as his birth can only be appreciated through some vision of Ireland, so his family can only be appreciated by some realisation of the Puritan. He was the youngest son of one George Carr Shaw, who had been a civil servant and was afterwards a somewhat unsuccessful business man. If I had merely said that his family was Protestant (which in Ireland means Puritan) it might have been passed over as a quite colourless detail. But if the reader will keep in mind what has been said about the degeneration of Calvinism into a few clumsy vetoes, he will see in its full and frightful significance such a sentence as this which comes from Shaw himself: "My father was in theory a vehement teetotaler, but in practice often a furtive drinker." The two things of course rest upon exactly the same philosophy; the philosophy of the taboo. There is a mystical substance, and it can give monstrous pleasures or call down monstrous punishments. The dipsomaniac and the abstainer are not only both mistaken, but they both make the same mistake. They both regard wine as a drug and not as a drink. But if I had mentioned that fragment of family information without any ethical preface, people would have begun at once to talk nonsense about artistic heredity and Celtic weakness, and would have gained the general impression that Bernard Shaw was an Irish wastrel and the child of Irish wastrels. Whereas it is the whole point of the matter that Bernard Shaw comes of a Puritan middle-class family of the most solid respectability; and the only admission of error arises from the fact that one member of that Puritan family took a particularly Puritan view of strong drink. That is, he regarded it generally as a poison and sometimes as a medicine, if only a mental medicine. But a poison and a medicine are very closely akin, as the nearest chemist knows; and they are chiefly akin in this; that no one will drink either of them for fun. Moreover, medicine and a poison are also alike in this; that no one will by preference drink either of them in public. And this medical or poisonous view of alcohol is not confined to the one Puritan to whose failure I have referred, it is spread all over the whole of our dying Puritan civilisation. For instance, social reformers have fired a hundred shots against the public-house; but never one against its really shameful feature. The sign of decay is not in the public-house, but in the private bar; or rather the row of five or six private bars, into each of which a respectable dipsomaniac can go in solitude, and by indulging his own half-witted sin violate his own half-witted morality. Nearly all these places are equipped with an atrocious apparatus of ground-glass windows which can be so closed that they practically conceal the face of the buyer from the seller. Words cannot express the abysses of human infamy and hateful shame expressed by that elaborate piece of furniture. Whenever I go into a public-house, which happens fairly often, I always carefully open all these apertures and then leave the place, in every way refreshed.

In other ways also it is necessary to insist not only on the fact of an extreme Protestantism, but on that of the Protestantism of a garrison; a world where that religious force both grew and festered all the more for being at once isolated and protected. All the influences surrounding Bernard Shaw in boyhood were not only Puritan, but such that no non-Puritan force could possibly pierce or counteract. He belonged to that Irish group which, according to Catholicism, has hardened its heart, which, according to Protestantism has hardened its head, but which, as I fancy, has chiefly hardened its hide, lost its sensibility to the contact of the things around it. In reading about his youth, one forgets that it was passed in the island which is still one flame before the altar of St. Peter and St. Patrick. The whole thing might be happening in Wimbledon. He went to the Wesleyan Connexional School. He went to hear Moody and Sankey. "I was," he writes, "wholly unmoved by their eloquence; and felt bound to inform the public that I was, on the whole, an atheist. My letter was solemnly printed in *Public Opinion*, to the extreme horror of my numerous aunts and uncles." That is the philosophical atmosphere; those are the religious postulates. It could never cross the mind of a man of the Garrison that before becoming an atheist he might stroll into one of the churches of his own country, and learn something of the philosophy that had satisfied Dante and Bossuet, Pascal and Descartes.

In the same way I have to appeal to my theoretic preface at this third point of the drama of Shaw's career. On leaving school he stepped into a secure business position which he held steadily for four years and which he flung away almost in one day. He rushed even recklessly to London; where he was quite unsuccessful and practically starved for six years. If I had mentioned this act on the first page of this book it would have seemed to have either the simplicity of a mere fanatic or else to cover some ugly escapade of youth or some quite criminal looseness of temperament. But Bernard Shaw did not act thus because he was careless, but because he was ferociously careful, careful especially of the one thing needful. What was he thinking about when he threw away his last halfpence and went to a strange place; what was he thinking about when he endured hunger and smallpox in London almost without hope? He was thinking of what he has ever since thought of, the slow but sure surge of the social revolution; you must read into all those bald sentences and empty years what I shall attempt to sketch in the third section. You must read the revolutionary movement of the later nineteenth century, darkened indeed by materialism and made mutable by fear and free thought, but full of awful vistas of an escape from the curse of Adam.

Bernard Shaw happened to be born in an epoch, or rather at the end of an epoch, which was in its way unique in the ages of history. The nineteenth century was not unique in the success or rapidity of its reforms or in their ultimate cessation; but it was unique in the peculiar character of the failure which followed the success. The French Revolution was an enormous act of human realisation; it has altered the terms of every law and the shape of every town in Europe; but it was by no means the only example of a strong and swift period of reform. What was really peculiar about the Republican energy was this, that it left behind it, not an ordinary reaction but a kind of dreary, drawn out and utterly unmeaning hope. The strong and evident idea of reform sank lower and lower until it became the timid and feeble idea of progress. Towards the end of the nineteenth century there appeared its two incredible figures; they were the pure Conservative and the pure Progressive; two figures which would have been overwhelmed with laughter by any other intellectual commonwealth of history. There was hardly a human generation which could not have seen the folly of merely going forward or merely standing still; of mere progressing or mere conserving. In the coarsest Greek Comedy we might have a joke about a man who wanted to keep what he had, whether it was yellow gold or yellow fever. In the dullest mediæval morality we might have a joke about a progressive gentleman who, having passed heaven and come to purgatory, decided to go further and fare worse. The twelfth and thirteenth centuries were an age of quite impetuous progress; men made in one rush, roads, trades, synthetic philosophies, parliaments, university settlements, a law that could cover the world and such spires as had never struck the sky. But they would not have said that they wanted progress, but that they wanted the road, the parliaments, and the spires. In the same way the time from Richelieu to the Revolution was upon the whole a time of conservation, often of harsh and hideous conservation; it preserved tortures, legal quibbles, and despotism. But if you had asked the rulers they would not have said that they wanted conservation; but that they wanted the torture and the despotism. The old reformers and the old despots alike desired definite *things*, powers, licenses, payments, vetoes, and permissions. Only the modern progressive and the modern conservative have been content with two words.

Other periods of active improvement have died by stiffening at last into some routine. Thus the Gothic gaiety of the thirteenth century stiffening into the mere Gothic ugliness of the fifteenth. Thus the mighty wave of the Renaissance, whose crest was lifted to heaven, was touched by a wintry witchery of classicism and frozen for ever before it fell. Alone of all such movements the democratic movement of the last two centuries has not frozen, but loosened and liquefied. Instead of becoming more pedantic in its old age, it has grown more bewildered. By the analogy of healthy history we ought to have gone on worshipping the republic and calling each other citizen with increasing seriousness until some other part of the truth broke into our republican temple. But in fact we have turned the freedom of democracy into a mere scepticism, destructive of everything, including democracy itself. It is none the less destructive because it is, so to speak, an optimistic scepticism — or, as I have said, a dreary hope. It was none the better because the destroyers were always talking about the new vistas and enlightenments which their new negations opened to us. The republican temple, like any other strong building, rested on certain definite limits and supports. But the modern man inside it went on indefinitely knocking holes in his own house and saying that they were windows. The result is not hard to calculate: the moral world was pretty well all windows and no house by the time that Bernard Shaw arrived on the scene.

Then there entered into full swing that great game of which he soon became the greatest master. A progressive or advanced person was now to mean not a man who wanted democracy, but a man who wanted something newer than democracy. A reformer was to be, not a man who wanted a parliament or a republic, but a man who wanted anything that he hadn't got. The emancipated man must cast a weird and suspicious eye round him at all the institutions of the world, wondering which of them was destined to die in the next few centuries. Each one of them was whispering to himself, "What can I alter?"

This quite vague and varied discontent probably did lead to the revelation of many incidental wrongs and to much humane hard work in certain holes and corners. It also gave birth to a great deal of quite futile and frantic speculation, which seemed destined to take away babies from women, or to give votes to tomcats. But it had an evil in it much deeper and more psychologically poisonous than any superficial absurdities. There was in this thirst to be "progressive" a subtle sort of double-mindedness and falsity. A man was so eager to be in advance of his age that he pretended to be in advance of himself. Institutions that his wholesome nature and habit fully accepted he had to sneer at as oldfashioned, out of a servile and snobbish fear of the future. Out of the primal forests, through all the real progress of history, man had picked his way obeying his human instinct, or (in the excellent phrase) following his nose. But now he was trying, by violent athletic exertions, to get in front of his nose.

Into this riot of all imaginary innovations Shaw brought the sharp edge of the Irishman and the concentration of the Puritan, and thoroughly thrashed all competitors in the difficult art of being at once modern and intelligent. In twenty twopenny controversies he took the revolutionary side, I fear in most cases because it was called revolutionary. But the other revolutionists were abruptly startled by the presentation of quite rational and ingenious arguments on their own side. The dreary thing about most new causes is that they are praised in such very old terms. Every new religion bores us with the same stale rhetoric about closer fellowship and the higher life. No one ever approximately equalled Bernard Shaw in the power of finding really fresh and personal arguments for these recent schemes and creeds. No one ever came within a mile of him in the knack of actually producing a new argument for a new philosophy. I give two instances to cover the kind of thing I mean. Bernard Shaw (being honestly eager to put himself on the modern side in everything) put himself on the side of what is called the feminist movement; the proposal to give the two sexes not merely equal social privileges, but identical. To this it is often answered that women cannot be soldiers; and to this again the sensible feminists answer that women run their own kind of physical risk, while the silly feminists answer that war is an outworn barbaric thing which women would abolish. But Bernard Shaw took the line of saying that women had been soldiers, in all occasions of natural and unofficial war, as in the French Revolution. That has the great fighting value of being an unexpected argument; it takes the other pugilist's breath away for one important instant. To take the other case, Mr. Shaw has found himself, led by the same mad imp of modernity, on the side of the people who want to have phonetic spelling. The people who want phonetic spelling generally depress the world with tireless and tasteless explanations of how much easier it would be for children or foreign bagmen if "height" were spelt "hite." Now children would curse spelling whatever it was, and we are not going to permit foreign bagmen to improve Shakespeare. Bernard Shaw charged along quite a different line; he urged that Shakespeare himself believed in phonetic spelling, since he spelt his own name in six different ways. According to Shaw, phonetic spelling is merely a return to the freedom and flexibility of Elizabethan literature. That, again, is exactly the kind of blow the old speller does not expect. As a matter of fact there is an answer to both the ingenuities I have quoted. When women have fought in revolutions they have generally shown that it was not natural to them, by their hysterical cruelty and insolence; it was the men who fought in the Revolution; it was the women who tortured the prisoners and mutilated the dead. And because Shakespeare could sing better than he could spell, it does not follow that his spelling and ours ought to be abruptly altered by a race that has lost all instinct for singing. But I do not wish to discuss these points; I only quote them as examples of the startling ability which really brought Shaw to the front; the ability to brighten even our modern movements with original and suggestive thoughts.

But while Bernard Shaw pleasantly surprised innumerable cranks and revolutionists by finding quite rational arguments for them, he surprised them unpleasantly also by discovering something else. He discovered a turn of argument or trick of thought which has ever since been the plague of their lives, and given him in all assemblies of their kind, in the Fabian Society or in the whole Socialist movement, a fantastic but most formidable domination. This method may be approximately defined as that of revolutionising the revolutionists by turning their rationalism against their remaining sentimentalism. But definition leaves the matter dark unless we give one or two examples. Thus Bernard Shaw threw himself as thoroughly as any New Woman into the cause of the emancipation of women. But while the New Woman praised woman as a prophetess, the new man took the opportunity to curse her and kick her as a comrade. For the others sex equality meant the emancipation of women, which allowed them to be equal to men. For Shaw it mainly meant the emancipation of men, which allowed them to be rude to women. Indeed, almost every one of Bernard Shaw's earlier plays might be called an argument between a man and a woman, in which the woman is thumped and thrashed and outwitted until she admits that she is the equal of her conqueror. This is the first case of the Shavian trick of turning on the romantic rationalists with their own rationalism. He said in substance, "If we are democrats, let us have votes for women; but if we are democrats, why on earth should we have respect for women?" I take one other example out of many. Bernard Shaw was thrown early into what may be called the cosmopolitan club of revolution. The Socialists of the S.D.F. call it "L'Internationale," but the club covers more than Socialists. It covers many who consider themselves the champions of oppressed nationalities — Poland, Finland, and even Ireland; and thus a strong nationalist tendency exists in the revolutionary movement. Against this nationalist tendency Shaw set himself with sudden violence. If the flag of England was a piece of piratical humbug, was not the flag of Poland a piece of piratical humbug too? If we hated the jingoism of the existing armies and frontiers, why should we bring into existence new jingo armies and new jingo frontiers? All the other revolutionists fell in instinctively with Home Rule for Ireland. Shaw urged, in effect, that Home Rule was as bad as Home Influences and Home Cooking, and all the other degrading domesticities that began with the word "Home." His ultimate support of the South African war was largely created by his irritation against the other revolutionists for favouring a nationalist resistance. The ordinary Imperialists objected to

Pro-Boers because they were anti-patriots. Bernard Shaw objected to Pro-Boers because they were pro-patriots.

But among these surprise attacks of G. B. S., these turnings of scepticism against the sceptics, there was one which has figured largely in his life; the most amusing and perhaps the most salutary of all these reactions. The "progressive" world being in revolt against religion had naturally felt itself allied to science; and against the authority of priests it would perpetually hurl the authority of scientific men. Shaw gazed for a few moments at this new authority, the veiled god of Huxley and Tyndall, and then with the greatest placidity and precision kicked it in the stomach. He declared to the astounded progressives around him that physical science was a mystical fake like sacerdotalism; that scientists, like priests, spoke with authority because they could not speak with proof or reason; that the very wonders of science were mostly lies, like the wonders of religion. "When astronomers tell me," he says somewhere, "that a star is so far off that its light takes a thousand years to reach us, the magnitude of the lie seems to me inartistic." The paralysing impudence of such remarks left everyone quite breathless; and even to this day this particular part of Shaw's satiric war has been far less followed up than it deserves. For there was present in it an element very marked in Shaw's controversies; I mean that his apparent exaggerations are generally much better backed up by knowledge than would appear from their nature. He can lure his enemy on with fantasies and then overwhelm him with facts. Thus the man of science, when he read some wild passage in which Shaw compared Huxley to a tribal soothsayer grubbing in the entrails of animals, supposed the writer to be a mere fantastic whom science could crush with one finger. He would therefore engage in a controversy with Shaw about (let us say) vivisection, and discover to his horror that Shaw really knew a great deal about the subject, and could pelt him with expert witnesses and hospital reports. Among the many singular contradictions in a singular character, there is none more interesting than this combination of exactitude and industry in the detail of opinions with audacity and a certain wildness in their outline.

This great game of catching revolutionists napping, of catching the unconventional people in conventional poses, of outmarching and outmanœuvring progressives till they felt like conservatives, of undermining the mines of Nihilists till they felt like the House of Lords, this great game of dishing the anarchists continued for some time to be his most effective business. It would be untrue to say that he was a cynic; he was never a cynic, for that implies a certain corrupt fatigue about human affairs, whereas he was vibrating with virtue and energy. Nor would it be fair to call him even a sceptic, for that implies a dogma of hopelessness and definite belief in unbelief. But it would be strictly just to describe him at this time, at any rate, as a merely destructive person. He was one whose main business was, in his own view, the pricking of illusions, the stripping away of disguises, and even the destruction of ideals. He was a sort of anti-confectioner whose whole business it was to take the gilt off the gingerbread.

Now I have no particular objection to people who take the gilt off the gingerbread; if only for this excellent reason, that I am much fonder of gingerbread than I am of gilt. But there are some objections to this task when it becomes a crusade or an obsession. One of them is this: that people who have really scraped the gilt off gingerbread generally waste the rest of their lives in attempting to scrape the gilt off gigantic lumps of gold. Such has too often been the case of Shaw. He can, if he likes, scrape the romance off the armaments of Europe or the party system of Great Britain. But he cannot scrape the romance off love or military valour, because it is all romance, and three thousand miles thick. It cannot, I think, be denied that much of Bernard Shaw's splendid mental energy has been wasted in this weary business of gnawing at the necessary pillars of all possible society. But it would be grossly unfair to indicate that even in his first and most destructive stage he uttered nothing except these accidental, if arresting, negations. He threw his whole genius heavily into the scale in favour of two positive projects or causes of the period. When we have stated these we have really stated the full intellectual equipment with which he started his literary life.

I have said that Shaw was on the insurgent side in everything; but in the case of these two important convictions he exercised a solid power of choice. When he first went to London he mixed with every kind of revolutionary society, and met every kind of person except the ordinary person. He knew everybody, so to speak, except everybody. He was more than once a momentary apparition among the respectable atheists. He knew Bradlaugh and spoke on the platforms of that Hall of Science in which very simple and sincere masses of men used to hail with shouts of joy the assurance that they were not immortal. He retains to this day something of the noise and narrowness of that room; as, for instance, when he says that it is contemptible to have a craving for eternal life. This prejudice remains in direct opposition to all his present opinions, which are all to the effect that it is glorious to desire power, consciousness, and vitality even for one's self. But this old secularist tag, that it is selfish to save one's soul, remains with him long after he has practically glorified selfishness. It is a relic of those chaotic early days. And just as he mingled with the atheists he mingled with the anarchists, who were in the eighties a much more formidable body than now, disputing with the Socialists on almost equal terms the claim to be the true heirs of the Revolution. Shaw still talks entertainingly about this group. As far as I can make out, it was almost entirely female. When a book came out called *A Girl among the Anarchists*, G. B. S. was provoked to a sort of explosive reminiscence. "A girl among the anarchists!" he exclaimed to his present biographer; "if they had said 'A man among the anarchists' it would have been more of an adventure." He is ready to tell other tales of this eccentric environment, most of which does not convey an impression of a very bracing atmosphere. That revolutionary society must have contained many high public ideals, but also a fair number of low private desires. And when people blame Bernard Shaw for his pitiless and prosaic coldness, his cutting refusal to reverence or admire, I think they should remember this riffraff of lawless sentimentalism against which his commonsense had to strive, all the grandiloquent "comrades" and all the gushing "affinities," all the sweetstuff sensuality and senseless sulking against law. If Bernard Shaw became a little too fond of throwing cold water upon prophecies or ideals, remember that he must have passed much of his youth among cosmopolitan idealists who wanted a little cold water in every sense of the word.

Upon two of these modern crusades he concentrated, and, as I have said, he chose them well. The first was broadly what was called the Humanitarian cause. It did not mean the cause of humanity, but rather, if anything, the cause of everything else. At its noblest it meant a sort of mystical identification of our life with the whole life of nature. So a man might wince when a snail was crushed as if his toe were trodden on; so a man might shrink when a moth shrivelled as if his own hair had caught fire. Man might be a network of exquisite nerves running over the whole universe, a subtle spider's web of pity. This was a fine conception; though perhaps a somewhat severe enforcement of the theological conception of the special divinity of man. For the humanitarians certainly asked of humanity what can be asked of no other creature; no man ever required a dog to understand a cat or expected the cow to cry for the sorrows of the nightingale.

Hence this sense has been strongest in saints of a very mystical sort; such as St. Francis who spoke of Sister Sparrow and Brother Wolf. Shaw adopted this crusade of cosmic pity but adopted it very much in his own style, severe, explanatory, and even unsympathetic. He had no affectionate impulse to say "Brother Wolf"; at the best he would have said "Citizen Wolf," like a sound republican. In fact, he was full of healthy human compassion for the sufferings of animals; but in phraseology he loved to put the matter unemotionally and even harshly. I was once at a debating club at which Bernard Shaw said that he was not a humanitarian at all, but only an economist, that he merely hated to see life wasted by carelessness or cruelty. I felt inclined to get up and address to him the following lucid question: "If when you spare a herring you are only being oikonomikal, for what oikos are you being nomikal?" But in an average debating club I thought this question might not be quite clear; so I abandoned the idea. But certainly it is not plain for whom Bernard Shaw is economising if he rescues a rhinoceros from an early grave. But the truth is that Shaw only took this economic pose from his hatred of appearing sentimental. If Bernard Shaw killed a dragon and rescued a princess of romance, he would try to say "I have saved a princess" with exactly the same intonation as "I have saved a shilling." He tries to turn his own heroism into a sort of superhuman thrift. He would thoroughly sympathise with that passage in his favourite dramatic author in which the Button Moulder tells Peer Gynt that there is a sort of cosmic housekeeping; that God Himself is very economical, "and that is why He is so well to do."

This combination of the widest kindness and consideration with a consistent ungraciousness of tone runs through all Shaw's ethical utterance, and is nowhere more evident than in his attitude towards animals. He would waste himself to a whitehaired shadow to save a shark in an aquarium from inconvenience or to add any little comforts to the life of a carrion-crow. He would defy any laws or lose any friends to show mercy to the humblest beast or the most hidden bird. Yet I cannot recall in the whole of his works or in the whole of his conversation a single word of any tenderness or intimacy with any bird or beast. It was under the influence of this high and almost superhuman sense of duty that he became a vegetarian; and I seem to remember that when he was lying sick and near to death at the end of his *Saturday Review* career he wrote a fine fantastic article, declaring that his hearse ought to be drawn by all the animals that he had not eaten. Whenever that evil day comes there will be no need to fall back on the ranks of the brute creation; there will be no lack of men and women who owe him so much as to be glad to take the place of the animals; and the present writer for one will be glad to express his gratitude as an elephant. There is no doubt about the essential manhood and decency of Bernard Shaw's instincts in such matters. And quite apart from the vegetarian controversy, I do not doubt that the beasts also owe him much. But when we come to positive things (and passions are the only truly positive things) that obstinate doubt remains which remains after all eulogies of Shaw. That fixed fancy sticks to the mind; that Bernard Shaw is a vegetarian more because he dislikes dead beasts than because he likes live ones.

It was the same with the other great cause to which Shaw more politically though not more publicly committed himself. The actual English people, without representation in Press or Parliament, but faintly expressed in public-houses and music-halls, would connect Shaw (so far as they have heard of him) with two ideas; they would say first that he was a vegetarian, and second that he was a Socialist. Like most of the impressions of the ignorant, these impressions would be on the whole very just. My only purpose here is to urge that Shaw's Socialism exemplifies the same trait of temperament as his vegetarianism. This book is not concerned with Bernard Shaw as a politician or a sociologist, but as a critic and creator of drama. I will therefore end in this chapter all that I have to say about Bernard Shaw as a politician or a political philosopher. I propose here to dismiss this aspect of Shaw: only let it be remembered, once and for all, that I am here dismissing the most important aspect of Shaw. It is as if one dismissed the sculpture of Michael Angelo and went on to his sonnets. Perhaps the highest and purest thing in him is simply that he cares more for politics than for anything else; more than for art or for philosophy. Socialism is the noblest thing for Bernard Shaw; and it is the noblest thing in him. He really desires less to win fame than to bear fruit. He is an absolute follower of that early sage who wished only to make two blades of grass grow instead of one. He is a loyal subject of Henri Quatre, who said that he only wanted every Frenchman to have a chicken in his pot on Sunday; except, of course, that he would call the repast cannibalism. But *cæteris paribus* he thinks more of that chicken than of the eagle of the universal empire; and he is always ready to support the grass against the laurel.

Yet by the nature of this book the account of the most important Shaw, who is the Socialist, must be also the most brief. Socialism (which I am not here concerned either to attack or defend) is, as everyone knows, the proposal that all property should be nationally owned that it may be more decently distributed. It is a proposal resting upon two principles, unimpeachable as far as they go: first, that frightful human calamities call for immediate human aid; second, that such aid must almost always be collectively organised. If a ship is being wrecked, we organise a lifeboat; if a house is on fire, we organise a blanket; if half a nation is starving, we must organise work and food. That is the primary and powerful argument of the Socialist, and everything that he adds to it weakens it. The only possible line of protest is to suggest that it is rather shocking that we have to treat a normal nation as something exceptional, like a house on fire or a shipwreck. But of such things it may be necessary to speak later. The point here is that Shaw behaved towards Socialism just as he behaved towards vegetarianism; he offered every reason except the emotional reason, which was the real one. When taxed in a *Daily News* discussion with being a Socialist for the obvious reason that poverty was cruel, he said this was quite wrong; it was only because poverty was wasteful. He practically professed that modern society annoyed him, not so much like an unrighteous kingdom, but rather like an untidy room. Everyone who knew him knew, of course, that he was full of a proper brotherly bitterness about the oppression of the poor. But here again he would not admit that he was anything but an Economist.

In thus setting his face like flint against sentimental methods of argument he undoubtedly did one great service to the causes for which he stood. Every vulgar anti-humanitarian, every snob who wants monkeys vivisected or beggars flogged has always fallen back upon stereotyped phrases like "maudlin" and "sentimental," which indicated the humanitarian as a man in a weak condition of tears. The mere personality of Shaw has shattered those foolish phrases for ever. Shaw the humanitarian was like Voltaire the humanitarian, a man whose satire was like steel, the hardest and coolest of fighters, upon whose piercing point the wretched defenders of a masculine brutality wriggled like worms.

In this quarrel one cannot wish Shaw even an inch less contemptuous, for the people who call compassion "sentimentalism" deserve nothing but contempt. In this one does not even regret his coldness; it is an honourable contrast to the blundering emotionalism of the jingoes and flagellomaniacs. The truth is that the ordinary anti-humanitarian only manages to harden his heart by having already softened his head. It is the reverse of sentimental to insist that a nigger is being burned alive; for sentimentalism must be the clinging to pleasant thoughts. And no one, not even a Higher Evolutionist, can think a nigger burned alive a pleasant thought. The sentimental thing is to warm your hands at the fire while denying the existence of the nigger, and that is the ruling habit in England, as it has been the chief business of Bernard Shaw to show. And in this the brutalitarians hate him not because he is soft, but because he is hard, because he is not to be softened by conventional excuses; because he looks hard at a thing — and hits harder. Some foolish fellow of the Henley-Whibley reaction wrote that if we were to be conquerors we must be less tender and more ruthless. Shaw answered with really avenging irony, "What a light this principle throws on the defeat of the tender Dervish, the compassionate Zulu, and the morbidly humane Boxer at the hands of the hardy savages of England, France, and Germany." In that sentence an idiot is obliterated and the whole story of Europe told; but it is immensely stiffened by its ironic form. In the same way Shaw washed away for ever the idea that Socialists were weak dreamers, who said that things might be only because they wished them to be. G. B. S. in argument with an individualist showed himself, as a rule, much the better economist and much the worse rhetorician. In this atmosphere arose a celebrated Fabian Society, of which he is still the leading spirit — a society which answered all charges of impracticable idealism by pushing both its theoretic statements and its practical negotiations to the verge of cynicism. Bernard Shaw was the literary expert who wrote most of its pamphlets. In one of them, among such sections as *Fabian Temperance Reform*, *Fabian Education* and so on, there was an entry gravely headed "Fabian Natural Science," which stated that in the Socialist cause light was needed more than heat.

Thus the Irish detachment and the Puritan austerity did much good to the country and to the causes for which they were embattled. But there was one thing they did not do; they did nothing for Shaw himself in the matter of his primary mistakes and his real limitation. His great defect was and is the lack of democratic sentiment. And there was nothing democratic either in his humanitarianism or his Socialism. These new and refined faiths tended rather to make the Irishman yet more aristocratic, the Puritan yet more exclusive. To be a Socialist was to look down on all the peasant owners of the earth, especially on the peasant owners of his own island.

To be a Vegetarian was to be a man with a strange and mysterious morality, a man who thought the good lord who roasted oxen for his vassals only less bad than the bad lord who roasted the vassals. None of these advanced views could the common people hear gladly; nor indeed was Shaw specially anxious to please the common people. It was his glory that he pitied animals like men; it was his defect that he pitied men only too much like animals. Foulon said of the democracy, "Let them eat grass." Shaw said, "Let them eat greens." He had more benevolence, but almost as much disdain. "I have never had any feelings about the English working classes," he said elsewhere, "except a desire to abolish them and replace them by sensible people." This is the unsympathetic side of the thing; but it had another and much nobler side, which must at least be seriously recognised before we pass on to much lighter things.

Bernard Shaw is not a democrat; but he is a splendid republican. The nuance of difference between those terms precisely depicts him. And there is after all a good deal of dim democracy in England, in the sense that there is much of a blind sense of brotherhood, and nowhere more than among oldfashioned and even reactionary people. But a republican is a rare bird, and a noble one. Shaw is a republican in the literal and Latin sense; he cares more for the Public Thing than for any private thing. The interest of the State is with him a sincere thirst of the soul, as it was in the little pagan cities. Now this public passion, this clean appetite for order and equity, had fallen to a lower ebb, had more nearly disappeared altogether, during Shaw's earlier epoch than at any other time. Individualism of the worst type was on the top of the wave; I mean artistic individualism, which is so much crueller, so much blinder and so much more irrational even than commercial individualism. The decay of society was praised by artists as the decay of a corpse is praised by worms. The æsthete was all receptiveness, like the flea. His only affair in this world was to feed on its facts and colours, like a parasite upon blood. The ego was the all; and the praise of it was enunciated in madder and madder rhythms by poets whose Helicon was absinthe and whose Pegasus was the nightmare. This diseased pride was not even conscious of a public interest, and would have found all political terms utterly tasteless and insignificant. It was no longer a question of one man one vote, but of one man one universe.

I have in my time had my fling at the Fabian Society, at the pedantry of schemes, the arrogance of experts; nor do I regret it now. But when I remember that other world against which it reared its bourgeois banner of cleanliness and common sense, I will not end this chapter without doing it decent honour. Give me the drain pipes of the Fabians rather than the panpipes of the later poets; the drain pipes have a nicer smell. Give me even that businesslike benevolence that herded men like beasts rather than that exquisite art which isolated them like devils; give me even the suppression of "Zæo" rather than the triumph of "Salome." And if I feel such a confession to be due to those Fabians who could hardly have been anything but experts in any society, such as Mr. Sidney Webb or Mr. Edward Pease, it is due yet more strongly to the greatest of the Fabians. Here was a man who could have enjoyed art among the artists, who could have been the wittiest of all the *flâneurs* ; who could have made epigrams like diamonds and drunk music like wine. He has instead laboured in a mill of statistics and crammed his mind with all the most dreary and the most filthy details, so that he can argue on the spur of the moment about sewing-machines or sewage, about typhus fever or twopenny tubes. The usual mean theory of motives will not cover the case; it is not ambition, for he could have been twenty times more prominent as a plausible and popular humorist. It is the real and ancient emotion of the *salus populi*, almost extinct in our oligarchical chaos; nor will I for one, as I pass on to many matters of argument or quarrel, neglect to salute a passion so implacable and so pure.

The Critic

It appears a point of some mystery to the present writer that Bernard Shaw should have been so long unrecognised and almost in beggary. I should have thought his talent was of the ringing and arresting sort; such as even editors and publishers would have sense enough to seize. Yet it is quite certain that he almost starved in London for many years, writing occasional columns for an advertisement or words for a picture. And it is equally certain (it is proved by twenty anecdotes, but no one who knows Shaw needs any anecdotes to prove it) that in those days of desperation he again and again threw up chances and flung back good bargains which did not suit his unique and erratic sense of honour. The fame of having first offered Shaw to the public upon a platform worthy of him belongs, like many other public services, to Mr. William Archer.

I say it seems odd that such a writer should not be appreciated in a flash; but upon this point there is evidently a real difference of opinion, and it constitutes for me the strangest difficulty of the subject. I hear many people complain that Bernard Shaw deliberately mystifies them. I cannot imagine what they mean; it seems to me that he deliberately insults them. His language, especially on moral questions, is generally as straight and solid as that of a bargee and far less ornate and symbolic than that of a hansom-cabman. The prosperous English Philistine complains that Mr. Shaw is making a fool of him. Whereas Mr. Shaw is not in the least making a fool of him; Mr. Shaw is, with laborious lucidity, calling him a fool. G. B. S. calls a landlord a thief; and the landlord, instead of denying or resenting it, says, "Ah, that fellow hides his meaning so cleverly that one can never make out what he means, it is all so fine spun and fantastical." G. B. S. calls a statesman a liar to his face, and the statesman cries in a kind of ecstasy, "Ah, what quaint, intricate and half-tangled trains of thought! Ah, what elusive and many-coloured mysteries of half-meaning!" I think it is always quite plain what Mr. Shaw means, even when he is joking, and it generally means that the people he is talking to ought to howl aloud for their sins. But the average representative of them undoubtedly treats the Shavian meaning as tricky and complex, when it is really direct and offensive. He always accuses Shaw of pulling his leg, at the exact moment when Shaw is pulling his nose.

This prompt and pungent style he learnt in the open, upon political tubs and platforms; and he is very legitimately proud of it. He boasts of being a demagogue; "The cart and the trumpet for me," he says, with admirable good sense. Everyone will remember the effective appearance of Cyrano de Bergerac in the first act of the fine play of that name; when instead of leaping in by any hackneyed door or window, he suddenly springs upon a chair above the crowd that has so far kept him invisible; "les bras croisés, le feutre en bataille, la moustache hérissée, le nez terrible." I will not go so far as to say that when Bernard Shaw sprang upon a chair or tub in Trafalgar Square he had the hat in battle, or even that he had the nose terrible. But just as we see Cyrano best when he thus leaps above the crowd, I think we may take this moment of Shaw stepping on his little platform to see him clearly as he then was, and even as he has largely not ceased to be. I, at least, have only known him in his middle age; yet I think I can see him, younger yet only a little more alert, with hair more red but with face yet paler, as he first stood up upon some cart or barrow in the tossing glare of the gas.

The first fact that one realises about Shaw (independent of all one has read and often contradicting it) is his voice. Primarily it is the voice of an Irishman, and then something of the voice of a musician. It possibly explains much of his career; a man may be permitted to say so many impudent things with so pleasant an intonation. But the voice is not only Irish and agreeable, it is also frank and as it were inviting conference. This goes with a style and gesture which can only be described as at once very casual and very emphatic. He assumes that bodily supremacy which goes with oratory, but he assumes it with almost ostentatious carelessness; he throws back the head, but loosely and laughingly. He is at once swaggering and yet shrugging his shoulders, as if to drop from them the mantle of the orator which he has confidently assumed. Lastly, no man ever used voice or gesture better for the purpose of expressing certainty; no man can say "I tell Mr. Jones he is totally wrong" with more air of unforced and even casual conviction.

This particular play of feature or pitch of voice, at once didactic and yet not uncomrade-like, must be counted a very important fact, especially in connection with the period when that voice was first heard. It must be remembered that Shaw emerged as a wit in a sort of secondary age of wits; one of those stale interludes of prematurely old young men, which separate the serious epochs of history. Oscar Wilde was its god; but he was somewhat more mystical, not to say monstrous, than the average of its dried and decorous impudence. The *two survivals* of that time, as far as I know, are Mr. Max Beerbohm and Mr. Graham Robertson; two most charming people; but the air they had to live in was the devil. One of its notes was an artificial reticence of speech, which waited till it could plant the perfect epigram. Its typical products were far too conceited to lay down the law. Now when people heard that Bernard Shaw was witty, as he most certainly was, when they heard his *mots* repeated like those of Whistler or Wilde, when they heard things like "the Seven deadly Virtues" or "Who *was* Hall Caine?" they expected another of these silent sarcastic dandies who went about with one epigram, patient and poisonous, like a bee with his one sting. And when they saw and heard the new humorist they found no fixed sneer, no frock coat, no green carnation, no silent Savoy Restaurant good manners, no fear of looking a fool, no particular notion of looking a gentleman. They found a talkative Irishman with a kind voice and a brown coat; open gestures and an evident desire to make people really agree with him. He had his own kind of affectations no doubt, and his own kind of tricks of debate; but he broke, and, thank God, forever the spell of the little man with the single eye glass who had frozen both faith and fun at so many tea-tables. Shaw's humane voice and hearty manner were so obviously more the things of a great man than the hard, gem-like brilliancy of Wilde or the careful ill-temper of Whistler. He brought in a breezier sort of insolence; the single eyeglass fled before the single eye.

Added to the effect of the amiable dogmatic voice and lean, loose swaggering figure, is that of the face with which so many caricaturists have fantastically delighted themselves, the Mephistophelean face with the fierce tufted eyebrows and forked red beard. Yet those caricaturists in their natural delight in coming upon so striking a face, have somewhat misrepresented it, making it merely Satanic; whereas its actual expression has quite as much benevolence as mockery. By this time his costume has become a part of his personality; one has come to think of the reddish brown Jaeger suit as if it were a sort of reddish brown fur, and were, like the hair and eyebrows, a part of the animal; yet there are those who claim to remember a Bernard Shaw of yet more awful aspect before Jaeger came to his assistance; a Bernard Shaw in a dilapidated frock-coat and some sort of straw hat. I can hardly believe it; the man is so much of a piece, and must always have dressed appropriately. In any case his brown woollen clothes, at once artistic and hygienic, completed the appeal for which he stood; which might be defined as an eccentric healthy-mindedness. But something of the vagueness and equivocation of his first fame is probably due to the different functions which he performed in the contemporary world of art.

He began by writing novels. They are not much read, and indeed not imperatively worth reading, with the one exception of the crude and magnificent *Cashel Byron's Profession* . Mr. William Archer, in the course of his kindly efforts on behalf of his young Irish friend, sent this book to Samoa, for the opinion of the most elvish and yet efficient of modern critics. Stevenson summed up much of Shaw even from that fragment when he spoke of a romantic griffin roaring with laughter at the nature of his own quest. He also added the not wholly unjustified postscript: "I say, Archer, — my God, what women!"

The fiction was largely dropped; but when he began work he felt his way by the avenues of three arts. He was an art critic, a dramatic critic, and a musical critic; and in all three, it need hardly be said, he fought for the newest style and the most revolutionary school. He wrote on all these as he would have written on anything; but it was, I fancy, about the music that he cared most.

It may often be remarked that mathematicians love and understand music more than they love or understand poetry. Bernard Shaw is in much the same condition; indeed, in attempting to do justice to Shakespeare's poetry, he always calls it "word music." It is not difficult to explain this special attachment of the mere logician to music. The logician, like every other man on earth, must have sentiment and romance in his existence; in every man's life, indeed, which can be called a life at all, sentiment is the most solid thing. But if the extreme logician turns for his emotions to poetry, he is exasperated and bewildered by discovering that the words of his own trade are used in an entirely different meaning. He conceives that he understands the word "visible," and then finds Milton applying it to darkness, in which nothing is visible. He supposes that he understands the word "hide," and then finds Shelley talking of a poet hidden in the light. He has reason to believe that he understands the common word "hung"; and then William Shakespeare, Esquire, of Stratford-on-Avon, gravely assures him that the tops of the tall sea waves were hung with deafening clamours on the slippery clouds. That is why the common arithmetician prefers music to poetry. Words are his scientific instruments. It irritates him that they should be anyone else's musical instruments. He is willing to see men juggling, but not men juggling with his own private tools and possessions — his terms. It is then that he turns with an utter relief to music. Here are all the same fascination and inspiration, all the same purity and plunging force as in poetry; but not requiring any verbal confession that light conceals things or that darkness can be seen in the dark. Music is mere beauty; it is beauty in the abstract, beauty in solution. It is a shapeless and liquid element of beauty, in which a man may really float, not indeed affirming the truth, but not denying it. Bernard Shaw, as I have already said, is infinitely far above all such mere mathematicians and pedantic reasoners; still his feeling is partly the same. He adores music because it cannot deal with romantic terms either in their right or their wrong sense. Music can be romantic without reminding him of Shakespeare and Walter Scott, with whom he has had personal quarrels. Music can be Catholic without reminding him verbally of the Catholic Church, which he has never seen, and is sure he does not like. Bernard Shaw can agree with Wagner, the musician, because he speaks without words; if it had been Wagner the man he would certainly have had words with him. Therefore I would suggest that Shaw's love of music (which is so fundamental that it must be mentioned early, if not first, in his story) may itself be considered in the first case as the imaginative safety-valve of the rationalistic Irishman.

This much may be said conjecturally over the present signature; but more must not be said. Bernard Shaw understands music so much better than I do that it is just possible that he is, in that tongue and atmosphere, all that he is not elsewhere. While he is writing with a pen I know his limitations as much as I admire his genius; and I know it is true to say that he does not appreciate romance. But while he is playing on the piano he may be cocking a feather, drawing a sword or draining a flagon for all I know. While he is speaking I am sure that there are some things he does not understand. But while he is listening (at the Queen's Hall) he may understand everything, including God and me. Upon this part of him I am a reverent agnostic; it is well to have some such dark continent in the character of a man of whom one writes. It preserves two very important things — modesty in the biographer and mystery in the biography.

For the purpose of our present generalisation it is only necessary to say that Shaw, as a musical critic, summed himself up as "The Perfect Wagnerite"; he threw himself into subtle and yet trenchant eulogy of that revolutionary voice in music. It was the same with the other arts. As he was a Perfect Wagnerite in music, so he was a Perfect Whistlerite in painting; so above all he was a Perfect Ibsenite in drama. And with this we enter that part of his career with which this book is more specially concerned. When Mr. William Archer got him established as dramatic critic of the *Saturday Review*, he became for the first time "a star of the stage"; a shooting star and sometimes a destroying comet.

On the day of that appointment opened one of the very few exhilarating and honest battles that broke the silence of the slow and cynical collapse of the nineteenth century. Bernard Shaw the demagogue had got his cart and his trumpet; and was resolved to make them like the car of destiny and the trumpet of judgment. He had not the servility of the ordinary rebel, who is content to go on rebelling against kings and priests, because such rebellion is as old and as established as any priests or kings. He cast about him for something to attack which was not merely powerful or placid, but was unattacked. After a little quite sincere reflection, he found it. He would not be content to be a common atheist; he wished to blaspheme something in which even atheists believed. He was not satisfied with being revolutionary; there were so many revolutionists. He wanted to pick out some prominent institution which had been irrationally and instinctively accepted by the most violent and profane; something of which Mr. Foote would speak as respectfully on the front page of the *Freethinker* as Mr. St. Loe Strachey on the front page of the *Spectator*. He found the thing; he found the great unassailed English institution — Shakespeare.

But Shaw's attack on Shakespeare, though exaggerated for the fun of the thing, was not by any means the mere folly or firework paradox that has been supposed. He meant what he said; what was called his levity was merely the laughter of a man who enjoyed saying what he meant — an occupation which is indeed one of the greatest larks in life. Moreover, it can honestly be said that Shaw did good by shaking the mere idolatry of Him of Avon. That idolatry was bad for England; it buttressed our perilous self-complacency by making us think that we alone had, not merely a great poet, but the one poet above criticism. It was bad for literature; it made a minute model out of work that was really a hasty and faulty masterpiece. And it was bad for religion and morals that there should be so huge a terrestrial idol, that we should put such utter and unreasoning trust in any child of man. It is true that it was largely through Shaw's own defects that he beheld the defects of Shakespeare. But it needed someone equally prosaic to resist what was perilous in the charm of such poetry; it may not be altogether a mistake to send a deaf man to destroy the rock of the sirens.

This attitude of Shaw illustrates of course all three of the divisions or aspects to which the reader's attention has been drawn. It was partly the attitude of the Irishman objecting to the Englishman turning his mere artistic taste into a religion; especially when it was a taste merely taught him by his aunts and uncles. In Shaw's opinion (one might say) the English do not really enjoy Shakespeare or even admire Shakespeare; one can only say, in the strong colloquialism, that they swear by Shakespeare. He is a mere god; a thing to be invoked. And Shaw's whole business was to set up the things which were to be sworn by as things to be sworn at. It was partly again the revolutionist in pursuit of pure novelty, hating primarily the oppression of the past, almost hating history itself. For Bernard Shaw the prophets were to be stoned after, and not before, men had built their sepulchres. There was a Yankee smartness in the man which was irritated at the idea of being dominated by a person dead for three hundred years; like Mark Twain, he wanted a fresher corpse.

These two motives there were, but they were small compared with the other. It was the third part of him, the Puritan, that was really at war with Shakespeare. He denounced that playwright almost exactly as any contemporary Puritan coming out of a conventicle in a steeple-crowned hat and stiff bands might have denounced the playwright coming out of the stage door of the old Globe Theatre. This is not a mere fancy; it is philosophically true. A legend has run round the newspapers that Bernard Shaw offered himself as a better writer than Shakespeare. This is false and quite unjust; Bernard Shaw never said anything of the kind. The writer whom he did say was better than Shakespeare was not himself, but Bunyan. And he justified it by attributing to Bunyan a virile acceptance of life as a high and harsh adventure, while in Shakespeare he saw nothing but profligate pessimism, the *vanitas vanitatum* of a disappointed voluptuary. According to this view Shakespeare was always saying, "Out, out, brief candle," because his was only a ballroom candle; while Bunyan was seeking to light such a candle as by God's grace should never be put out.

It is odd that Bernard Shaw's chief error or insensibility should have been the instrument of his noblest affirmation. The denunciation of Shakespeare was a mere misunderstanding. But the denunciation of Shakespeare's pessimism was the most splendidly understanding of all his utterances. This is the greatest thing in Shaw, a serious optimism — even a tragic optimism. Life is a thing too glorious to be enjoyed. To be is an exacting and exhausting business; the trumpet though inspiring is terrible. Nothing that he ever wrote is so noble as his simple reference to the sturdy man who stepped up to the Keeper of the Book of Life and said, "Put down my name, Sir." It is true that Shaw called this heroic philosophy by wrong names and buttressed it with false metaphysics; that was the weakness of the age. The temporary decline of theology had involved the neglect of philosophy and all fine thinking; and Bernard Shaw had to find shaky justifications in Schopenhauer for the sons of God shouting for joy. He called it the Will to Live — a phrase invented by Prussian professors who would like to exist, but can't. Afterwards he asked people to worship the Life-Force; as if one could worship a hyphen. But though he covered it with crude new names (which are now fortunately crumbling everywhere like bad mortar) he was on the side of the good old cause; the oldest and the best of all causes, the cause of creation against destruction, the cause of yes against no, the cause of the seed against the stony earth and the star against the abyss.

His misunderstanding of Shakespeare arose largely from the fact that he is a Puritan, while Shakespeare was spiritually a Catholic. The former is always screwing himself up to see truth; the latter is often content that truth is there. The Puritan is only strong enough to stiffen; the Catholic is strong enough to relax. Shaw, I think, has entirely misunderstood the pessimistic passages of Shakespeare. They are flying moods which a man with a fixed faith can afford to entertain. That all is vanity, that life is dust and love is ashes, these are frivolities, these are jokes that a Catholic can afford to utter. He knows well enough that there is a life that is not dust and a love that is not ashes. But just as he may let himself go more than the Puritan in the matter of enjoyment, so he may let himself go more than the Puritan in the matter of melancholy. The sad exuberances of Hamlet are merely like the glad exuberances of Falstaff. This is not conjecture; it is the text of Shakespeare. In the very act of uttering his pessimism, Hamlet admits that it is a mood and not the truth. Heaven *is* a heavenly thing, only to him it seems a foul congregation of vapours. Man *is* the paragon of animals, only to him he seems a quintessence of dust. Hamlet is quite the reverse of a sceptic. He is a man whose strong intellect believes much more than his weak temperament can make vivid to him. But this power of knowing a thing without feeling it, this power of believing a thing without experiencing it, this is an old Catholic complexity, and the Puritan has never understood it. Shakespeare confesses his moods (mostly by the mouths of villains and failures), but he never sets up his moods against his mind. His cry of *vanitas vanitatum* is itself only a harmless vanity. Readers may not agree with my calling him Catholic with a big C; but they will hardly complain of my calling him catholic with a small one. And that is here the principal point. Shakespeare was not in any sense a pessimist; he was, if anything, an optimist so universal as to be able to enjoy even pessimism. And this is exactly where he differs from the Puritan. The true Puritan is not squeamish: the true Puritan is free to say "Damn it!" But the Catholic Elizabethan was free (on passing provocation) to say "Damn it all!"

It need hardly be explained that Bernard Shaw added to his negative case of a dramatist to be depreciated a corresponding affirmative case of a dramatist to be exalted and advanced. He was not content with so remote a comparison as that between Shakespeare and Bunyan. In his vivacious weekly articles in the *Saturday Review*, the real comparison upon which everything turned was the comparison between Shakespeare and Ibsen. He early threw himself with all possible eagerness into the public disputes about the great Scandinavian; and though there was no doubt whatever about which side he supported, there was much that was individual in the line he took. It is not our business here to explore that extinct volcano. You may say that anti-Ibsenism is dead, or you may say that Ibsen is dead; in any case, that controversy is dead, and death, as the Roman poet says, can alone confess of what small atoms we are made. The opponents of Ibsen largely exhibited the permanent qualities of the populace; that is, their instincts were right and their reasons wrong. They made the complete controversial mistake of calling Ibsen a pessimist; whereas, indeed, his chief weakness is a rather childish confidence in mere nature and freedom, and a blindness (either of experience or of culture) in the matter of original sin. In this sense Ibsen is not so much a pessimist as a highly crude kind of optimist. Nevertheless the man in the street was right in his fundamental instinct, as he always is. Ibsen, in his pale northern style, is an optimist; but for all that he is a depressing person. The optimism of Ibsen is less comforting than the pessimism of Dante; just as a Norwegian sunrise, however splendid, is colder than a southern night.

But on the side of those who fought for Ibsen there was also a disagreement, and perhaps also a mistake. The vague army of "the advanced" (an army which advances in all directions) were united in feeling that they ought to be the friends of Ibsen because he also was advancing somewhere somehow. But they were also seriously impressed by Flaubert, by Oscar Wilde and all the rest who told them that a work of art was in another universe from ethics and social good. Therefore many, I think most, of the Ibsenites praised the Ibsen plays merely as *choses vues*, æsthetic affirmations of what can be without any reference to what ought to be. Mr. William Archer himself inclined to this view, though his strong sagacity kept him in a haze of healthy doubt on the subject. Mr. Walkley certainly took this view. But this view Mr. George Bernard Shaw abruptly and violently refused to take.

With the full Puritan combination of passion and precision he informed everybody that Ibsen was not artistic, but moral; that his dramas were didactic, that all great art was didactic, that Ibsen was strongly on the side of some of his characters and strongly against others, that there was preaching and public spirit in the work of good dramatists; and that if this were not so, dramatists and all other artists would be mere panders of intellectual debauchery, to be locked up as the Puritans locked up the stage players. No one can understand Bernard Shaw who does not give full value to this early revolt of his on behalf of ethics against the ruling school of *l'art pour l'art*. It is interesting because it is connected with other ambitions in the man, especially with that which has made him somewhat vainer of being a Parish Councillor than of being one of the most popular dramatists in Europe. But its chief interest is again to be referred to our stratification of the psychology; it is the lover of true things rebelling for once against merely new things; it is the Puritan suddenly refusing to be the mere Progressive.

But this attitude obviously laid on the ethical lover of Ibsen a not inconsiderable obligation. If the new drama had an ethical purpose, what was it? and if Ibsen was a moral teacher, what the deuce was he teaching? Answers to this question, answers of manifold brilliancy and promise, were scattered through all the dramatic criticisms of those years on the *Saturday Review*. But even Bernard Shaw grew tired after a time of discussing Ibsen only in connection with the current pantomime or the latest musical comedy. It was felt that so much sincerity and fertility of explanation justified a concentrated attack; and in 1891 appeared the brilliant book called *The Quintessence of Ibsenism*, which some have declared to be merely the quintessence of Shaw. However this may be, it was in fact and profession the quintessence of Shaw's theory of the morality or propaganda of Ibsen.

The book itself is much longer than the book that I am writing; and as is only right in so spirited an apologist, every paragraph is provocative. I could write an essay on every sentence which I accept and three essays on every sentence which I deny. Bernard Shaw himself is a master of compression; he can put a conception more compactly than any other man alive. It is therefore rather difficult to compress his compression; one feels as if one were trying to extract a beef essence from Bovril. But the shortest form in which I can state the idea of *The Quintessence of Ibsenism* is that it is the idea of distrusting ideals, which are universal, in comparison with facts, which are miscellaneous. The man whom he attacks throughout he calls "The Idealist"; that is the man who permits himself to be mainly moved by a moral generalisation. "Actions," he says, "are to be judged by their effect on happiness, and not by their conformity to any ideal." As we have already seen, there is a certain inconsistency here; for while Shaw had always chucked all ideals overboard the one he had chucked first was the ideal of happiness. Passing this however for the present, we may mark the above as the most satisfying summary. If I tell a lie I am not to blame myself for having violated the ideal of truth, but only for having perhaps got myself into a mess and made things worse than they were before. If I have broken my word I need not feel (as my fathers did) that I have broken something inside of me, as one who breaks a blood vessel. It all depends on whether I have broken up something outside me; as one who breaks up an evening party. If I shoot my father the only question is whether I have made him happy. I must not admit the idealistic conception that the mere shooting of my father might possibly make me unhappy. We are to judge of every individual case as it arises, apparently without any social summary or moral ready-reckoner at all. "The Golden Rule is that there is no Golden Rule." We must not say that it is right to keep promises, but that it may be right to keep this promise. Essentially it is anarchy; nor is it very easy to see how a state could be very comfortable which was Socialist in all its public morality and Anarchist in all its private. But if it is anarchy, it is anarchy without any of the abandon and exuberance of anarchy. It is a worried and conscientious anarchy; an anarchy of painful delicacy and even caution. For it refuses to trust in traditional experiments or plainly trodden tracks; every case must be considered anew from the beginning, and yet considered with the most wide-eyed care for human welfare; every man must act as if he were the first man made. Briefly, we must always be worrying about what is best for our children, and we must not take one hint or rule of thumb from our fathers. Some think that this anarchism would make a man tread down mighty cities in his madness. I think it would make a man walk down the street as if he were walking on eggshells. I do not think this experiment in opportunism would end in frantic license; I think it would end in frozen timidity. If a man was forbidden to solve moral problems by moral science or the help of mankind, his course would be quite easy — he would not solve the problems. The world instead of being a knot so tangled as to need unravelling, would simply become a piece of clockwork too complicated to be touched. I cannot think that this untutored worry was what Ibsen meant; I have my doubts as to whether it was what Shaw meant; but I do not think that it can be substantially doubted that it was what he said.

In any case it can be asserted that the general aim of the work was to exalt the immediate conclusions of practice against the general conclusions of theory. Shaw objected to the solution of every problem in a play being by its nature a general solution, applicable to all other such problems. He disliked the entrance of a universal justice at the end of the last act; treading down all the personal ultimatums and all the varied certainties of men. He disliked the god from the machine — because he was from a machine. But even without the machine he tended to dislike the god; because a god is more general than a man. His enemies have accused Shaw of being anti-domestic, a shaker of the rooftree. But in this sense Shaw may be called almost madly domestic. He wishes each private problem to be settled in private, without reference to sociological ethics. And the only objection to this kind of gigantic casuistry is that the theatre is really too small to discuss it. It would not be fair to play David and Goliath on a stage too small to admit Goliath. And it is not fair to discuss private morality on a stage too small to admit the enormous presence of public morality; that character which has not appeared in a play since the Middle Ages; whose name is Everyman and whose honour we have all in our keeping.

The Dramatist

No one who was alive at the time and interested in such matters will ever forget the first acting of *Arms and the Man*. It was applauded by that indescribable element in all of us which rejoices to see the genuine thing prevail against the plausible; that element which rejoices that even its enemies are alive. Apart from the problems raised in the play, the very form of it was an attractive and forcible innovation. Classic plays which were wholly heroic, comic plays which were wholly and even heartlessly ironical, were common enough. Commonest of all in this particular time was the play that began playfully, with plenty of comic business, and was gradually sobered by sentiment until it ended on a note of romance or even of pathos. A commonplace little officer, the butt of the mess, becomes by the last act as high and hopeless a lover as Dante. Or a vulgar and violent pork-butcher remembers his own youth before the curtain goes down. The first thing that Bernard Shaw did when he stepped before the footlights was to reverse this process. He resolved to build a play not on pathos, but on bathos. The officer should be heroic first and then everyone should laugh at him; the curtain should go up on a man remembering his youth, and he should only reveal himself as a violent pork-butcher when someone interrupted him with an order for pork. This merely technical originality is indicated in the very title of the play. The *Arma Virumque* of Virgil is a mounting and ascending phrase, the man is more than his weapons. The Latin line suggests a superb procession which should bring on to the stage the brazen and resounding armour, the shield and shattering axe, but end with the hero himself, taller and more terrible because unarmed. The technical effect of Shaw's scheme is like the same scene, in which a crowd should carry even more gigantic shapes of shield and helmet, but when the horns and howls were at their highest, should end with the figure of Little Tich. The name itself is meant to be a bathos; arms — and the man.

It is well to begin with the superficial; and this is the superficial effectiveness of Shaw; the brilliancy of bathos. But of course the vitality and value of his plays does not lie merely in this; any more than the value of Swinburne lies in alliteration or the value of Hood in puns. This is not his message; but it is his method; it is his style. The first taste we had of it was in this play of *Arms and the Man*; but even at the very first it was evident that there was much more in the play than that. Among other things there was one thing not unimportant; there was savage sincerity. Indeed, only a ferociously sincere person can produce such effective flippancies on a matter like war; just as only a strong man could juggle with cannon balls. It is all very well to use the word "fool" as synonymous with "jester"; but daily experience shows that it is generally the solemn and silent man who is the fool. It is all very well to accuse Mr. Shaw of standing on his head; but if you stand on your head you must have a hard and solid head to stand on. In *Arms and the Man* the bathos of form was strictly the incarnation of a strong satire in the idea. The play opens in an atmosphere of military melodrama; the dashing officer of cavalry going off to death in an attitude, the lovely heroine left in tearful rapture; the brass band, the noise of guns and the red fire. Into all this enters Bluntschli, the little sturdy crop-haired Swiss professional soldier, a man without a country but with a trade. He tells the army-adoring heroine frankly that she is a humbug; and she, after a moment's reflection, appears to agree with him. The play is like nearly all Shaw's plays, the dialogue of a conversion. By the end of it the young lady has lost all her military illusions and admires this mercenary soldier not because he faces guns, but because he faces facts.

This was a fitting entrance for Shaw to his didactic drama; because the commonplace courage which he respects in Bluntschli was the one virtue which he was destined to praise throughout. We can best see how the play symbolises and summarises Bernard Shaw if we compare it with some other attack by modern humanitarians upon war. Shaw has many of the actual opinions of Tolstoy. Like Tolstoy he tells men, with coarse innocence, that romantic war is only butchery and that romantic love is only lust. But Tolstoy objects to these things because they are real; he really wishes to abolish them. Shaw only objects to them in so far as they are ideal; that is in so far as they are idealised. Shaw objects not so much to war as to the attractiveness of war. He does not so much dislike love as the love of love. Before the temple of Mars, Tolstoy stands and thunders, "There shall be no wars"; Bernard Shaw merely murmurs, "Wars if you must; but for God's sake, not war songs." Before the temple of Venus, Tolstoy cries terribly, "Come out of it!"; Shaw is quite content to say, "Do not be taken in by it." Tolstoy seems really to propose that high passion and patriotic valour should be destroyed. Shaw is more moderate; and only asks that they should be desecrated. Upon this note, both about sex and conflict, he was destined to dwell through much of his work with the most wonderful variations of witty adventure and intellectual surprise. It may be doubted perhaps whether this realism in love and war is quite so sensible as it looks. *Securus judicat orbis terrarum*; the world is wiser than the moderns. The world has kept sentimentalities simply because they are the most practical things in the world. They alone make men do things. The world does not encourage a quite rational lover, simply because a perfectly rational lover would never get married. The world does not encourage a perfectly rational army, because a perfectly rational army would run away.

The brain of Bernard Shaw was like a wedge in the literal sense. Its sharpest end was always in front; and it split our society from end to end the moment it had entrance at all. As I have said he was long unheard of; but he had not the tragedy of many authors, who were heard of long before they were heard. When you had read any Shaw you read all Shaw. When you had seen one of his plays you waited for more. And when he brought them out in volume form, you did what is repugnant to any literary man — you bought a book.

The dramatic volume with which Shaw dazzled the public was called, *Plays, Pleasant and Unpleasant*. I think the most striking and typical thing about it was that he did not know very clearly which plays were unpleasant and which were pleasant. "Pleasant" is a word which is almost unmeaning to Bernard Shaw. Except, as I suppose, in music (where I cannot follow him), relish and receptivity are things that simply do not appear. He has the best of tongues and the worst of palates. With the possible exception of *Mrs. Warren's Profession* (which was at least unpleasant in the sense of being forbidden) I can see no particular reason why any of the seven plays should be held specially to please or displease. First in fame and contemporary importance came the reprint of *Arms and the Man*, of which I have already spoken. Over all the rest towered unquestionably the two figures of Mrs. Warren and of Candida. They were neither of them pleasant, except as all good art is pleasant. They were neither of them really unpleasant except as all truth is unpleasant. But they did represent the author's normal preference and his principal fear; and those two sculptured giantesses largely upheld his fame.

I fancy that the author rather dislikes *Candida* because it is so generally liked. I give my own feeling for what it is worth (a foolish phrase), but I think that there were only two moments when this powerful writer was truly, in the ancient and popular sense, inspired; that is, breathing from a bigger self and telling more truth than he knew. One is that scene in a later play where after the secrets and revenges of Egypt have rioted and rotted all round him, the colossal sanity of Cæsar is suddenly acclaimed with swords. The other is that great last scene in *Candida* where the wife, stung into final speech, declared her purpose of remaining with the strong man because he is the weak man. The wife is asked to decide between two men, one a strenuous self-confident popular preacher, her husband, the other a wild and weak young poet, logically futile and physically timid, her lover; and she chooses the former because he has more weakness and more need of her. Even among the plain and ringing paradoxes of the Shaw play this is one of the best reversals or turnovers ever effected. A paradoxical writer like Bernard Shaw is perpetually and tiresomely told that he stands on his head. But all romance and all religion consist in making the whole universe stand on its head. That reversal is the whole idea of virtue; that the last shall be first and the first last. Considered as a pure piece of Shaw therefore, the thing is of the best. But it is also something much better than Shaw. The writer touches certain realities commonly outside his scope; especially the reality of the normal wife's attitude to the normal husband, an attitude which is not romantic but which is yet quite quixotic; which is insanely unselfish and yet quite cynically clearsighted. It involves human sacrifice without in the least involving idolatry.

The truth is that in this place Bernard Shaw comes within an inch of expressing something that is not properly expressed anywhere else; the idea of marriage. Marriage is not a mere chain upon love as the anarchists say; nor is it a mere crown upon love as the sentimentalists say. Marriage is a fact, an actual human relation like that of motherhood which has certain human habits and loyalties, except in a few monstrous cases where it is turned to torture by special insanity and sin. A marriage is neither an ecstasy nor a slavery; it is a commonwealth; it is a separate working and fighting thing like a nation. Kings and diplomatists talk of "forming alliances" when they make weddings; but indeed every wedding is primarily an alliance. The family is a fact even when it is not an agreeable fact, and a man is part of his wife even when he wishes he wasn't. The twain are one flesh — yes, even when they are not one spirit. Man is duplex. Man is a quadruped.

Of this ancient and essential relation there are certain emotional results, which are subtle, like all the growths of nature. And one of them is the attitude of the wife to the husband, whom she regards at once as the strongest and most helpless of human figures. She regards him in some strange fashion at once as a warrior who must make his way and as an infant who is sure to lose his way. The man has emotions which exactly correspond; sometimes looking down at his wife and sometimes up at her; for marriage is like a splendid game of see-saw. Whatever else it is, it is not comradeship. This living, ancestral bond (not of love or fear, but strictly of marriage) has been twice expressed splendidly in literature. The man's incurable sense of the mother in his lawful wife was uttered by Browning in one of his two or three truly shattering lines of genius, when he makes the execrable Guido fall back finally upon the fact of marriage and the wife whom he has trodden like mire:

"Christ! Maria! God,
Pompilia, will you let them murder me?"

And the woman's witness to the same fact has been best expressed by Bernard Shaw in this great scene where she remains with the great stalwart successful public man because he is really too little to run alone.

There are one or two errors in the play; and they are all due to the primary error of despising the mental attitude of romance, which is the only key to real human conduct. For instance, the love making of the young poet is all wrong. He is supposed to be a romantic and amorous boy; and therefore the dramatist tries to make him talk turgidly, about seeking for "an archangel with purple wings" who shall be worthy of his lady. But a lad in love would never talk in this mock heroic style; there is no period at which the young male is more sensitive and serious and afraid of looking a fool. This is a blunder; but there is another much bigger and blacker. It is completely and disastrously false to the whole nature of falling in love to make the young Eugene complain of the cruelty which makes Candida defile her fair hands with domestic duties. No boy in love with a beautiful woman would ever feel disgusted when she peeled potatoes or trimmed lamps. He would like her to be domestic. He would simply feel that the potatoes had become poetical and the lamps gained an extra light. This may be irrational; but we are not talking of rationality, but of the psychology of first love. It may be very unfair to women that the toil and triviality of potato peeling should be seen through a glamour of romance; but the glamour is quite as certain a fact as the potatoes. It may be a bad thing in sociology that men should deify domesticity in girls as something dainty and magical; but all men do. Personally I do not think it a bad thing at all; but that is another argument. The argument here is that Bernard Shaw, in aiming at mere realism, makes a big mistake in reality. Misled by his great heresy of looking at emotions from the outside, he makes Eugene a coldblooded prig at the very moment when he is trying, for his own dramatic purposes, to make him a hot-blooded lover. He makes the young lover an idealistic theoriser about the very things about which he really would have been a sort of mystical materialist. Here the romantic Irishman is much more right than the very rational one; and there is far more truth to life as it is in Lover's couplet —

"And envied the chicken
That Peggy was pickin'."

than in Eugene's solemn, æsthetic protest against the potato-skins and the lamp-oil. For dramatic purposes, G. B. S., even if he despises romance, ought to comprehend it. But then, if once he comprehended romance, he would not despise it.

The series contained, besides its more substantial work, tragic and comic, a comparative frivolity called *The Man of Destiny*. It is a little comedy about Napoleon, and is chiefly interesting as a foreshadowing of his after sketches of heroes and strong men; it is a kind of parody of *Cæsar and Cleopatra* before it was written. In this connection the mere title of this Napoleonic play is of interest. All Shaw's generation and school of thought remembered Napoleon only by his late and corrupt title of "The Man of Destiny," a title only given to him when he was already fat and tired and destined to exile. They forgot that through all the really thrilling and creative part of his career he was not the man of destiny, but the man who defied destiny. Shaw's sketch is extraordinarily clever; but it is tinged with this unmilitary notion of an inevitable conquest; and this we must remember when we come to those larger canvases on which he painted his more serious heroes. As for the play, it is packed with good things, of which the last is perhaps the best. The long duologue between Bonaparte and the Irish lady ends with the General declaring that he will only be beaten when he meets an English army under an Irish general. It has always been one of Shaw's paradoxes that the English mind has the force to fulfil orders, while the Irish mind has the intelligence to give them, and it is among those of his paradoxes which contain a certain truth.

A far more important play is *The Philanderer*, an ironic comedy which is full of fine strokes and real satire; it is more especially the vehicle of some of Shaw's best satire upon physical science. Nothing could be cleverer than the picture of the young, strenuous doctor, in the utter innocence of his professional ambition, who has discovered a new disease, and is delighted when he finds people suffering from it and cast down to despair when he finds that it does not exist. The point is worth a pause, because it is a good, short way of stating Shaw's attitude, right or wrong, upon the whole of formal morality. What he dislikes in young Doctor Paramore is that he has interposed a secondary and false conscience between himself and the facts. When his disease is disproved, instead of seeing the escape of a human being who thought he was going to die of it, Paramore sees the downfall of a kind of flag or cause. This is the whole contention of *The Quintessence of Ibsenism*, put better than the book puts it; it is a really sharp exposition of the dangers of "idealism," the sacrifice of people to principles, and Shaw is even wiser in his suggestion that this excessive idealism exists nowhere so strongly as in the world of physical science. He shows that the scientist tends to be more concerned about the sickness than about the sick man; but it was certainly in his mind to suggest here also that the idealist is more concerned about the sin than about the sinner.

This business of Dr. Paramore's disease while it is the most farcical thing in the play is also the most philosophic and important. The rest of the figures, including the Philanderer himself, are in the full sense of those blasting and obliterating words "funny without being vulgar," that is, funny without being of any importance to the masses of men. It is a play about a dashing and advanced "Ibsen Club," and the squabble between the young Ibsenites and the old people who are not yet up to Ibsen. It would be hard to find a stronger example of Shaw's only essential error, modernity — which means the seeking for truth in terms of time. Only a few years have passed and already almost half the wit of that wonderful play is wasted, because it all turns on the newness of a fashion that is no longer new. Doubtless many people still think the Ibsen drama a great thing, like the French classical drama. But going to "The Philanderer" is like going among periwigs and rapiers and hearing that the young men are now all for Racine. What makes such work sound unreal is not the praise of Ibsen, but the praise of the novelty of Ibsen. Any advantage that Bernard Shaw had over Colonel Craven I have over Bernard Shaw; we who happen to be born last have the meaningless and paltry triumph in that meaningless and paltry war. We are the superiors by that silliest and most snobbish of all superiorities, the mere aristocracy of time. All works must become thus old and insipid which have ever tried to be "modern," which have consented to smell of time rather than of eternity. Only those who have stooped to be in advance of their time will ever find themselves behind it.

But it is irritating to think what diamonds, what dazzling silver of Shavian wit has been sunk in such an out-of-date warship. In *The Philanderer* there are five hundred excellent and about five magnificent things. The rattle of repartees between the doctor and the soldier about the humanity of their two trades is admirable. Or again, when the colonel tells Chartaris that "in his young days" he would have no more behaved like Chartaris than he would have cheated at cards. After a pause Chartaris says, "You're getting old, Craven, and you make a virtue of it as usual." And there is an altitude of aerial tragedy in the words of Grace, who has refused the man she loves, to Julia, who is marrying the man she doesn't, "This is what they call a happy ending — these men."

There is an acrid taste in *The Philanderer*; and certainly he might be considered a super-sensitive person who should find anything acrid in *You Never Can Tell*. This play is the nearest approach to frank and objectless exuberance in the whole of Shaw's work. *Punch*, with wisdom as well as wit, said that it might well be called not "You Never Can Tell" but "You Never Can be Shaw." And yet if anyone will read this blazing farce and then after it any of the romantic farces, such as *Pickwick* or even *The Wrong Box*, I do not think he will be disposed to erase or even to modify what I said at the beginning about the ingrained grimness and even inhumanity of Shaw's art. To take but one test: love, in an "extravaganza," may be light love or love in idleness, but it should be hearty and happy love if it is to add to the general hilarity. Such are the ludicrous but lucky love affairs of the sportsman Winkle and the Maestro Jimson. In Gloria's collapse before her bullying lover there is something at once cold and unclean; it calls up all the modern supermen with their cruel and fishy eyes. Such farces should begin in a friendly air, in a tavern. There is something very symbolic of Shaw in the fact that his farce begins in a dentist's.

20The only one out of this brilliant batch of plays in which I think that the method adopted really fails, is the one called *Widower's Houses*. The best touch of Shaw is simply in the title. The simple substitution of widowers for widows contains almost the whole bitter and yet boisterous protest of Shaw; all his preference for undignified fact over dignified phrase; all his dislike of those subtle trends of sex or mystery which swing the logician off the straight line. We can imagine him crying, "Why in the name of death and conscience should it be tragic to be a widow but comic to be a widower?" But the rationalistic method is here applied quite wrong as regards the production of a drama. The most dramatic point in the affair is when the open and indecent rack-renter turns on the decent young man of means and proves to him that he is equally guilty, that he also can only grind his corn by grinding the faces of the poor. But even here the point is undramatic because it is indirect; it is indirect because it is merely sociological. It may be the truth that a young man living on an unexamined income which ultimately covers a great deal of house-property is as dangerous as any despot or thief. But it is a truth that you can no more put into a play than into a triolet. You can make a play out of one man robbing another man, but not out of one man robbing a million men; still less out of his robbing them unconsciously.

Of the plays collected in this book I have kept *Mrs. Warren's Profession* to the last, because, fine as it is, it is even finer and more important because of its fate, which was to rouse a long and serious storm and to be vetoed by the Censor of Plays. I say that this drama is most important because of the quarrel that came out of it. If I were speaking of some mere artist this might be an insult. But there are high and heroic things in Bernard Shaw; and one of the highest and most heroic is this, that he certainly cares much more for a quarrel than for a play. And this quarrel about the censorship is one on which he feels so strongly that in a book embodying any sort of sympathy it would be much better to leave out Mrs. Warren than to leave out Mr. Redford. The veto was the pivot of so very personal a movement by the dramatist, of so very positive an assertion of his own attitude towards things, that it is only just and necessary to state what were the two essential parties to the dispute; the play and the official who prevented the play.

The play of *Mrs. Warren's Profession* is concerned with a coarse mother and a cold daughter; the mother drives the ordinary and dirty trade of harlotry; the daughter does not know until the end the atrocious origin of all her own comfort and refinement. The daughter, when the discovery is made, freezes up into an iceberg of contempt; which is indeed a very womanly thing to do. The mother explodes into pulverising cynicism and practicality; which is also very womanly. The dialogue is drastic and sweeping; the daughter says the trade is loathsome; the mother answers that she loathes it herself; that every healthy person does loathe the trade by which she lives. And beyond question the general effect of the play is that the trade is loathsome; supposing anyone to be so insensible as to require to be told of the fact. Undoubtedly the upshot is that a brothel is a miserable business, and a brothel-keeper a miserable woman. The whole dramatic art of Shaw is in the literal sense of the word, tragi-comic; I mean that the comic part comes after the tragedy. But just as *You Never Can Tell* represents the nearest approach of Shaw to the purely comic, so *Mrs. Warren's Profession* represents his only complete, or nearly complete, tragedy. There is no twopenny modernism in it, as in *The Philanderer*. Mrs. Warren is as old as the Old Testament; "for she hath cast down many wounded, yea, many strong men have been slain by her; her house is in the gates of hell, going down into the chamber of death." Here is no subtle ethics, as in *Widowers' Houses*; for even those moderns who think it noble that a woman should throw away her honour, surely cannot think it especially noble that she should sell it. Here is no lighting up by laughter, astonishment, and happy coincidence, as in *You Never Can Tell*. The play is a pure tragedy about a permanent and quite plain human problem; the problem is as plain and permanent, the tragedy is as proud and pure, as in *Œdipus* or *Macbeth*. This play was presented in the ordinary way for public performance and was suddenly stopped by the Censor of Plays.

The Censor of Plays is a small and accidental eighteenth-century official. Like nearly all the powers which Englishmen now respect as ancient and rooted, he is very recent. Novels and newspapers still talk of the English aristocracy that came over with William the Conqueror. Little of our effective oligarchy is as old as the Reformation; and none of it came over with William the Conqueror. Some of the older English landlords came over with William of Orange; the rest have come by ordinary alien immigration. In the same way we always talk of the Victorian woman (with her smelling salts and sentiment) as the oldfashioned woman. But she really was a quite new-fashioned woman; she considered herself, and was, an advance in delicacy and civilisation upon the coarse and candid Elizabethan woman to whom we are now returning. We are never oppressed by old things; it is recent things that can really oppress. And in accordance with this principle modern England has accepted, as if it were a part of perennial morality, a tenth-rate job of Walpole's worst days called the Censorship of the Drama. Just as they have supposed the eighteenth-century parvenus to date from Hastings, just as they have supposed the eighteenth-century ladies to date from Eve, so they have supposed the eighteenth-century Censorship to date from Sinai. The origin of the thing was in truth purely political. Its first and principal achievement was to prevent Fielding from writing plays; not at all because the plays were coarse, but because they criticised the Government. Fielding was a free writer; but they did not resent his sexual freedom; the Censor would not have objected if he had torn away the most intimate curtains of decency or rent the last rag from private life. What the Censor disliked was his rending the curtain from public life. There is still much of that spirit in our country; there are no affairs which men seek so much to cover up as public affairs. But the thing was done somewhat more boldly and baldly in Walpole's day; and the Censorship of plays has its origin, not merely in tyranny, but in a quite trifling and temporary and partisan piece of tyranny; a thing in its nature far more ephemeral, far less essential, than Ship Money. Perhaps its brightest moment was when the office of censor was held by that filthy writer, Colman the younger; and when he gravely refused to license a work by the author of *Our Village*. Few funnier notions can ever have actually been facts than this notion that the restraint and chastity of George Colman saved the English public from the eroticism and obscenity of Miss Mitford.

Such was the play; and such was the power that stopped the play. A private man wrote it; another private man forbade it; nor was there any difference between Mr. Shaw's authority and Mr. Redford's, except that Mr. Shaw did defend his action on public grounds and Mr. Redford did not. The dramatist had simply been suppressed by a despot; and what was worse (because it was modern) by a silent and evasive despot; a despot in hiding. People talk about the pride of tyrants; but we at the present day suffer from the modesty of tyrants; from the shyness and the shrinking secrecy of the strong. Shaw's preface to *Mrs. Warren's Profession* was far more fit to be called a public document than the slovenly refusal of the individual official; it had more exactness, more universal application, more authority. Shaw on Redford was far more national and responsible than Redford on Shaw.

The dramatist found in the quarrel one of the important occasions of his life, because the crisis called out something in him which is in many ways his highest quality — righteous indignation. As a mere matter of the art of controversy of course he carried the war into the enemy's camp at once. He did not linger over loose excuses for licence; he declared at once that the Censor was licentious, while he, Bernard Shaw, was clean. He did not discuss whether a Censorship ought to make the drama moral. He declared that it made the drama immoral. With a fine strategic audacity he attacked the Censor quite as much for what he permitted as for what he prevented. He charged him with encouraging all plays that attracted men to vice and only stopping those which discouraged them from it. Nor was this attitude by any means an idle paradox. Many plays appear (as Shaw pointed out) in which the prostitute and the procuress are practically obvious, and in which they are represented as revelling in beautiful surroundings and basking in brilliant popularity. The crime of Shaw was not that he introduced the Gaiety Girl; that had been done, with little enough decorum, in a hundred musical comedies. The crime of Shaw was that he introduced the Gaiety Girl, but did not represent her life as all gaiety. The pleasures of vice were already flaunted before the playgoers. It was the perils of vice that were carefully concealed from them. The gay adventures, the gorgeous dresses, the champagne and oysters, the diamonds and motor-cars, dramatists were allowed to drag all these dazzling temptations before any silly housemaid in the gallery who was grumbling at her wages. But they were not allowed to warn her of the vulgarity and the nausea, the dreary deceptions and the blasting diseases of that life. *Mrs. Warren's Profession* was not up to a sufficient standard of immorality; it was not spicy enough to pass the Censor. The acceptable and the accepted plays were those which made the fall of a woman fashionable and fascinating; for all the world as if the Censor's profession were the same as Mrs. Warren's profession.

Such was the angle of Shaw's energetic attack; and it is not to be denied that there was exaggeration in it, and what is so much worse, omission. The argument might easily be carried too far; it might end with a scene of screaming torture in the Inquisition as a corrective to the too amiable view of a clergyman in *The Private Secretary* . But the controversy is definitely worth recording, if only as an excellent example of the author's aggressive attitude and his love of turning the tables in debate. Moreover, though this point of view involves a potential overstatement, it also involves an important truth. One of the best points urged in the course of it was this, that though vice is punished in conventional drama, the punishment is not really impressive, because it is not inevitable or even probable. It does not arise out of the evil act. Years afterwards Bernard Shaw urged this argument again in connection with his friend Mr. Granville Barker's play of *Waste* , in which the woman dies from an illegal operation. Bernard Shaw said, truly enough, that if she had died from poison or a pistol shot it would have left everyone unmoved, for pistols do not in their nature follow female unchastity. Illegal operations very often do. The punishment was one which might follow the crime, not only in that case, but in many cases. Here, I think, the whole argument might be sufficiently cleared up by saying that the objection to such things on the stage is a purely artistic objection. There is nothing wrong in talking about an illegal operation; there are plenty of occasions when it would be very wrong not to talk about it. But it may easily be just a shade too ugly for the shape of any work of art. There is nothing wrong about being sick; but if Bernard Shaw wrote a play in which all the characters expressed their dislike of animal food by vomiting on the stage, I think we should be justified in saying that the thing was outside, not the laws of morality, but the framework of civilised literature. The instinctive movement of repulsion which everyone has when hearing of the operation in *Waste* is not an ethical repulsion at all. But it is an æsthetic repulsion, and a right one.

But I have only dwelt on this particular fighting phase because it leaves us facing the ultimate characteristics which I mentioned first. Bernard Shaw cares nothing for art; in comparison with morals, literally nothing. Bernard Shaw is a Puritan and his work is Puritan work. He has all the essentials of the old, virile and extinct Protestant type. In his work he is as ugly as a Puritan. He is as indecent as a Puritan. He is as full of gross words and sensual facts as a sermon of the seventeenth century. Up to this point of his life indeed hardly anyone would have dreamed of calling him a Puritan; he was called sometimes an anarchist, sometimes a buffoon, sometimes (by the more discerning stupid people) a prig. His attitude towards current problems was felt to be arresting and even indecent; I do not think that anyone thought of connecting it with the old Calvinistic morality. But Shaw, who knew better than the Shavians, was at this moment on the very eve of confessing his moral origin. The next book of plays he produced (including The *Devil's Disciple* , *Captain Brassbound's Conversion* , and *Cæsar and Cleopatra*), actually bore the title of *Plays for Puritans* .

The play called *The Devil's Disciple* has great merits, but the merits are incidental. Some of its jokes are serious and important, but its general plan can only be called a joke. Almost alone among Bernard Shaw's plays (except of course such things as *How he Lied to her Husband* and *The Admirable Bashville*) this drama does not turn on any very plain pivot of ethical or philosophical conviction. The artistic idea seems to be the notion of a melodrama in which all the conventional melodramatic situations shall suddenly take unconventional turns. Just where the melodramatic clergyman would show courage he appears to show cowardice; just where the melodramatic sinner would confess his love he confesses his indifference. This is a little too like the Shaw of the newspaper critics rather than the Shaw of reality. There are indeed present in the play two of the writer's principal moral conceptions. The first is the idea of a great heroic action coming in a sense from nowhere; that is, not coming from any commonplace motive; being born in the soul in naked beauty, coming with its own authority and testifying only to itself. Shaw's agent does not act towards something, but from something. The hero dies, not because he desires heroism, but because he has it. So in this particular play the Devil's Disciple finds that his own nature will not permit him to put the rope around another man's neck; he has no reasons of desire, affection, or even equity; his death is a sort of divine whim. And in connection with this the dramatist introduces another favourite moral; the objection to perpetual playing upon the motive of sex. He deliberately lures the onlooker into the net of Cupid in order to tell him with salutary decision that Cupid is not there at all. Millions of melodramatic dramatists have made a man face death for the woman he loves; Shaw makes him face death for the woman he does not love — merely in order to put woman in her place. He objects to that idolatry of sexualism which makes it the fountain of all forcible enthusiasms; he dislikes the amorous drama which makes the female the only key to the male. He is Feminist in politics, but Anti-feminist in emotion. His key to most problems is, "Ne cherchez pas la femme."

As has been observed, the incidental felicities of the play are frequent and memorable, especially those connected with the character of General Burgoyne, the real full-blooded, freethinking eighteenth century gentleman, who was much too much of an aristocrat not to be a liberal. One of the best thrusts in all the Shavian fencing matches is that which occurs when Richard Dudgeon, condemned to be hanged, asks rhetorically why he cannot be shot like a soldier. "Now there you speak like a civilian," replies General Burgoyne. "Have you formed any conception of the condition of marksmanship in the British Army?" Excellent, too, is the passage in which his subordinate speaks of crushing the enemy in America, and Burgoyne asks him who will crush their enemies in England, snobbery and jobbery and incurable carelessness and sloth. And in one sentence towards the end, Shaw reaches a wider and more genial comprehension of mankind than he shows anywhere else; "it takes all sorts to make a world, saints as well as soldiers." If Shaw had remembered that sentence on other occasions he would have avoided his mistake about Cæsar and Brutus. It is not only true that it takes all sorts to make a world; but the world cannot succeed without its failures. Perhaps the most doubtful point of all in the play is why it is a play for Puritans; except the hideous picture of a Calvinistic home is meant to destroy Puritanism. And indeed in this connection it is constantly necessary to fall back upon the facts of which I have spoken at the beginning of this brief study; it is necessary especially to remember that Shaw could in all probability speak of Puritanism from the inside. In that domestic circle which took him to hear Moody and Sankey, in that domestic circle which was teetotal even when it was intoxicated, in that atmosphere and society Shaw might even have met the monstrous mother in *The Devil's Disciple* , the horrible old woman who declares that she has hardened her heart to hate her children, because the heart of man is desperately wicked, the old ghoul who has made one of her children an imbecile and the other an outcast. Such types do occur in small societies drunk with the dismal wine of Puritan determinism. It is possible that there were among Irish Calvinists people who denied that charity was a Christian virtue. It is possible that among Puritans there were people who thought a heart was a kind of heart disease. But it is enough to make one tear one's hair to think that a man of genius received his first impressions in so small a corner of Europe that he could for a long time suppose that this Puritanism was current among Christian men. The question, however, need not detain us, for the batch of plays contained two others about which it is easier to speak.

The third play in order in the series called *Plays for Puritans* is a very charming one; *Captain Brassbound's Conversion*. This also turns, as does so much of the Cæsar drama, on the idea of vanity of revenge — the idea that it is too slight and silly a thing for a man to allow to occupy and corrupt his consciousness. It is not, of course, the morality that is new here, but the touch of cold laughter in the core of the morality. Many saints and sages have denounced vengeance. But they treated vengeance as something too great for man. "Vengeance is Mine, saith the Lord; I will repay." Shaw treats vengeance as something too small for man — a monkey trick he ought to have outlived, a childish storm of tears which he ought to be able to control. In the story in question Captain Brassbound has nourished through his whole erratic existence, racketting about all the unsavoury parts of Africa — a mission of private punishment which appears to him as a mission of holy justice. His mother has died in consequence of a judge's decision, and Brassbound roams and schemes until the judge falls into his hands. Then a pleasant society lady, Lady Cicely Waynefleet tells him in an easy conversational undertone — a rivulet of speech which ripples while she is mending his coat — that he is making a fool of himself, that his wrong is irrelevant, that his vengeance is objectless, that he would be much better if he flung his morbid fancy away for ever; in short, she tells him he is ruining himself for the sake of ruining a total stranger. Here again we have the note of the economist, the hatred of mere loss. Shaw (one might almost say) dislikes murder, not so much because it wastes the life of the corpse as because it wastes the time of the murderer. If he were endeavouring to persuade one of his moonlighting fellow-countrymen not to shoot his landlord, I can imagine him explaining with benevolent emphasis that it was not so much a question of losing a life as of throwing away a bullet. But indeed the Irish comparison alone suggests a doubt which wriggles in the recesses of my mind about the complete reliability of the philosophy of Lady Cicely Waynefleet, the complete finality of the moral of *Captain Brassbound's Conversion*. Of course, it was very natural in an aristocrat like Lady Cicely Waynefleet to wish to let sleeping dogs lie, especially those whom Mr. Blatchford calls under-dogs. Of course it was natural for her to wish everything to be smooth and sweet-tempered. But I have the obstinate question in the corner of my brain, whether if a few Captain Brassbounds did revenge themselves on judges, the quality of our judges might not materially improve.

When this doubt is once off one's conscience one can lose oneself in the bottomless beatitude of Lady Cicely Waynefleet, one of the most living and laughing things that her maker has made. I do not know any stronger way of stating the beauty of the character than by saying that it was written specially for Ellen Terry, and that it is, with Beatrice, one of the very few characters in which the dramatist can claim some part of her triumph.

We may now pass to the more important of the plays. For some time Bernard Shaw would seem to have been brooding upon the soul of Julius Cæsar. There must always be a strong human curiosity about the soul of Julius Cæsar; and, among other things, about whether he had a soul. The conjunction of Shaw and Cæsar has about it something smooth and inevitable; for this decisive reason, that Cæsar is really the only great man of history to whom the Shaw theories apply. Cæsar *was* a Shaw hero. Cæsar was merciful without being in the least pitiful; his mercy was colder than justice. Cæsar was a conqueror without being in any hearty sense a soldier; his courage was lonelier than fear. Cæsar was a demagogue without being a democrat. In the same way Bernard Shaw is a demagogue without being a democrat. If he had tried to prove his principle from any of the other heroes or sages of mankind he would have found it much more difficult. Napoleon achieved more miraculous conquest; but during his most conquering epoch he was a burning boy suicidally in love with a woman far beyond his age. Joan of Arc achieved far more instant and incredible worldly success; but Joan of Arc achieved worldly success because she believed in another world. Nelson was a figure fully as fascinating and dramatically decisive; but Nelson was "romantic"; Nelson was a devoted patriot and a devoted lover. Alexander was passionate; Cromwell could shed tears; Bismarck had some suburban religion; Frederick was a poet; Charlemagne was fond of children. But Julius Cæsar attracted Shaw not less by his positive than by his negative enormousness. Nobody can say with certainty that Cæsar cared for anything. It is unjust to call Cæsar an egoist; for there is no proof that he cared even for Cæsar. He may not have been either an atheist or a pessimist. But he may have been; that is exactly the rub. He may have been an ordinary decently good man slightly deficient in spiritual expansiveness. On the other hand, he may have been the incarnation of paganism in the sense that Christ was the incarnation of Christianity. As Christ expressed how great a man can be humble and humane, Cæsar may have expressed how great a man can be frigid and flippant. According to most legends Antichrist was to come soon after Christ. One has only to suppose that Antichrist came shortly before Christ; and Antichrist might very well be Cæsar.

It is, I think, no injustice to Bernard Shaw to say that he does not attempt to make his Cæsar superior except in this naked and negative sense. There is no suggestion, as there is in the Jehovah of the Old Testament, that the very cruelty of the higher being conceals some tremendous and even tortured love. Cæsar is superior to other men not because he loves more, but because he hates less. Cæsar is magnanimous not because he is warmhearted enough to pardon, but because he is not warmhearted enough to avenge. There is no suggestion anywhere in the play that he is hiding any great genial purpose or powerful tenderness towards men. In order to put this point beyond a doubt the dramatist has introduced a soliloquy of Cæsar alone with the Sphinx. There if anywhere he would have broken out into ultimate brotherhood or burning pity for the people. But in that scene between the Sphinx and Cæsar, Cæsar is as cold and as lonely and as dead as the Sphinx.

But whether the Shavian Cæsar is a sound ideal or no, there can be little doubt that he is a very fine reality. Shaw has done nothing greater as a piece of artistic creation. If the man is a little like a statue, it is a statue by a great sculptor; a statue of the best period. If his nobility is a little negative in its character, it is the negative darkness of the great dome of night; not as in some "new moralities" the mere mystery of the coal-hole. Indeed, this somewhat austere method of work is very suitable to Shaw when he is serious. There is nothing Gothic about his real genius; he could not build a mediæval cathedral in which laughter and terror are twisted together in stone, molten by mystical passion. He can build, by way of amusement, a Chinese pagoda; but when he is in earnest, only a Roman temple. He has a keen eye for truth; but he is one of those people who like, as the saying goes, to put down the truth in black and white. He is always girding and jeering at romantics and idealists because they will not put down the truth in black and white. But black and white are not the only two colours in the world. The modern man of science who writes down a fact in black and white is not more but less accurate than the mediæval monk who wrote it down in gold and scarlet, sea-green and turquoise. Nevertheless, it is a good thing that the more austere method should exist separately, and that some men should be specially good at it. Bernard Shaw is specially good at it; he is preeminently a black and white artist.

And as a study in black and white nothing could be better than this sketch of Julius Cæsar. He is not so much represented as "bestriding the earth like a Colossus" (which is indeed a rather comic attitude for a hero to stand in), but rather walking the earth with a sort of stern levity, lightly touching the planet and yet spurning it away like a stone. He walks like a winged man who has chosen to fold his wings. There is something creepy even about his kindness; it makes the men in front of him feel as if they were made of glass. The nature of the Cæsarian mercy is massively suggested. Cæsar dislikes a massacre, not because it is a great sin, but because it is a small sin. It is felt that he classes it with a flirtation or a fit of the sulks; a senseless temporary subjugation of man's permanent purpose by his passing and trivial feelings. He will plunge into slaughter for a great purpose, just as he plunges into the sea. But to be stung into such action he deems as undignified as to be tipped off the pier. In a singularly fine passage Cleopatra, having hired assassins to stab an enemy, appeals to her wrongs as justifying her revenge, and says, "If you can find one man in all Africa who says that I did wrong, I will be crucified by my own slaves." "If you can find one man in all the world," replies Cæsar, "who can see that you did wrong, he will either conquer the world as I have done or be crucified by it." That is the high water mark of this heathen sublimity; and we do not feel it inappropriate, or unlike Shaw, when a few minutes afterwards the hero is saluted with a blaze of swords.

As usually happens in the author's works, there is even more about Julius Cæsar in the preface than there is in the play. But in the preface I think the portrait is less imaginative and more fanciful. He attempts to connect his somewhat chilly type of superman with the heroes of the old fairy tales. But Shaw should not talk about the fairy tales; for he does not feel them from the inside. As I have said, on all this side of historic and domestic traditions Bernard Shaw is weak and deficient. He does not approach them as fairy tales, as if he were four, but as "folklore" as if he were forty. And he makes a big mistake about them which he would never have made if he had kept his birthday and hung up his stocking, and generally kept alive inside him the firelight of a home. The point is so peculiarly characteristic of Bernard Shaw, and is indeed so much of a summary of his most interesting assertion and his most interesting error, that it deserves a word by itself, though it is a word which must be remembered in connection with nearly all the other plays.

His primary and defiant proposition is the Calvinistic proposition: that the elect do not earn virtue, but possess it. The goodness of a man does not consist in trying to be good, but in being good. Julius Cæsar prevails over other people by possessing more *virtus* than they; not by having striven or suffered or bought his virtue; not because he has struggled heroically, but because he is a hero. So far Bernard Shaw is only what I have called him at the beginning; he is simply a seventeenth-century Calvinist. Cæsar is not saved by works, or even by faith; he is saved because he is one of the elect. Unfortunately for himself, however, Bernard Shaw went back further than the seventeenth century; and professing his opinion to be yet more antiquated, invoked the original legends of mankind. He argued that when the fairy tales gave Jack the Giant Killer a coat of darkness or a magic sword it removed all credit from Jack in the "common moral" sense; he won as Cæsar won only because he was superior. I will confess, in passing, to the conviction that Bernard Shaw in the course of his whole simple and strenuous life was never quite so near to hell as at the moment when he wrote down those words. But in this question of fairy tales my immediate point is, not how near he was to hell, but how very far off he was from fairyland. That notion about the hero with a magic sword being the superman with a magic superiority is the caprice of a pedant; no child, boy, or man ever felt it in the story of Jack the Giant Killer. Obviously the moral is all the other way. Jack's fairy sword and invisible coat are clumsy expedients for enabling him to fight at all with something which is by nature stronger. They are a rough, savage substitute for psychological descriptions of special valour or unwearied patience. But no one in his five wits can doubt that the idea of "Jack the Giant Killer" is exactly the opposite to Shaw's idea. If it were not a tale of effort and triumph hardly earned it would not be called "Jack the Giant Killer." If it were a tale of the victory of natural advantages it would be called "Giant the Jack Killer." If the teller of fairy tales had merely wanted to urge that some beings are born stronger than others he would not have fallen back on elaborate tricks of weapon and costume for conquering an ogre. He would simply have let the ogre conquer. I will not speak of my own emotions in connection with this incredibly caddish doctrine that the strength of the strong is admirable, but not the valour of the weak. It is enough to say that I have to summon up the physical presence of Shaw, his frank gestures, kind eyes, and exquisite Irish voice, to cure me of a mere sensation of contempt. But I do not dwell upon the point for any such purpose; but merely to show how we must be always casting back to those concrete foundations with which we began. Bernard Shaw, as I have said, was never national enough to be domestic; he was never a part of his past; hence when he tries to interpret tradition he comes a terrible cropper, as in this case. Bernard Shaw (I strongly suspect) began to disbelieve in Santa Claus at a discreditably early age. And by this time Santa Claus has avenged himself by taking away the key of all the prehistoric scriptures; so that a noble and honourable artist flounders about like any German professor. Here is a whole fairy literature which is almost exclusively devoted to the unexpected victory of the weak over the strong; and Bernard Shaw manages to make it mean the inevitable victory of the strong over the weak — which, among other things, would not make a story at all. It all comes of that mistake about not keeping his birthday. A man should be always tied to his mother's apron strings; he should always have a hold on his childhood, and be ready at intervals to start anew from a childish standpoint. Theologically the thing is best expressed by saying, "You must be born again." Secularly it is best expressed by saying, "You must keep your birthday." Even if you will not be born again, at least remind yourself occasionally that you were born once.

Some of the incidental wit in the Cæsarian drama is excellent although it is upon the whole less spontaneous and perfect than in the previous plays. One of its jests may be mentioned in passing, not merely to draw attention to its failure (though Shaw is brilliant enough to afford many failures) but because it is the best opportunity for mentioning one of the writer's minor notions to which he obstinately adheres. He describes the Ancient Briton in Cæsar's train as being exactly like a modern respectable Englishman. As a joke for a Christmas pantomime this would be all very well; but one expects the jokes of Bernard Shaw to have some intellectual root, however fantastic the flower. And obviously all historic common sense is against the idea that that dim Druid people, whoever they were, who dwelt in our land before it was lit up by Rome or loaded with varied invasions, were a precise facsimile of the commercial society of Birmingham or Brighton. But it is a part of the Puritan in Bernard Shaw, a part of the taut and high-strung quality of his mind, that he will never admit of any of his jokes that it was only a joke. When he has been most witty he will passionately deny his own wit; he will say something which Voltaire might envy and then declare that he has got it all out of a Blue book. And in connection with this eccentric type of self-denial, we may notice this mere detail about the Ancient Briton. Someone faintly hinted that a blue Briton when first found by Cæsar might not be quite like Mr. Broadbent; at the touch Shaw poured forth a torrent of theory, explaining that climate was the only thing that affected nationality; and that whatever races came into the English or Irish climate would become like the English or Irish. Now the modern theory of race is certainly a piece of stupid materialism; it is an attempt to explain the things we are sure of, France, Scotland, Rome, Japan, by means of the things we are not sure of at all, prehistoric conjectures, Celts, Mongols, and Iberians. Of course there is a reality in race; but there is no reality in the theories of race offered by some ethnological professors. Blood, perhaps, is thicker than water; but brains are sometimes thicker than anything. But if there is one thing yet more thick and obscure and senseless than this theory of the omnipotence of race it is, I think, that to which Shaw has fled for refuge from it; this doctrine of the omnipotence of climate. Climate again is something; but if climate were everything, Anglo-Indians would grow more and more to look like Hindoos, which is far from being the case. Something in the evil spirit of our time forces people always to pretend to have found some material and mechanical explanation. Bernard Shaw has filled all his last days with affirmations about the divinity of the non-mechanical part of man, the sacred quality in creation and choice. Yet it never seems to have occurred to him that the true key to national differentiations is the key of the will and not of the environment. It never crosses the modern mind to fancy that perhaps a people is chiefly influenced by how that people has chosen to behave. If I have to choose between race and weather I prefer race; I would rather be imprisoned and compelled by ancestors who were once alive than by mud and mists which never were. But I do not propose to be controlled by either; to me my national history is a chain of multitudinous choices. It is neither blood nor rain that has made England, but hope, the thing that all those dead men have desired. France was not France because she was made to be by the skulls of the Celts or by the sun of Gaul. France was France because she chose.

I have stepped on one side from the immediate subject because this is as good an instance as any we are likely to come across of a certain almost extraneous fault which does deface the work of Bernard Shaw. It is a fault only to be mentioned when we have made the solidity of the merits quite clear. To say that Shaw is merely making game of people is demonstrably ridiculous; at least a fairly systematic philosophy can be traced through all his jokes, and one would not insist on such a unity in all the songs of Mr. Dan Leno. I have already pointed out that the genius of Shaw is really too harsh and earnest rather than too merry and irresponsible. I shall have occasion to point out later that Shaw is, in one very serious sense, the very opposite of paradoxical. In any case if any real student of Shaw says that Shaw is only making a fool of him, we can only say that of that student it is very superfluous for anyone to make a fool. But though the dramatist's jests are always serious and generally obvious, he is really affected from time to time by a certain spirit of which that climate theory is a case — a spirit that can only be called one of senseless ingenuity. I suppose it is a sort of nemesis of wit; the skidding of a wheel in the height of its speed. Perhaps it is connected with the nomadic nature of his mind. That lack of roots, this remoteness from ancient instincts and traditions is responsible for a certain bleak and heartless extravagance of statement on certain subjects which makes the author really unconvincing as well as exaggerative; satires that are *saugrenu*, jokes that are rather silly than wild, statements which even considered as lies have no symbolic relation to truth. They are exaggerations of something that does not exist. For instance, if a man called Christmas Day a mere hypocritical excuse for drunkenness and gluttony that would be false, but it would have a fact hidden in it somewhere. But when Bernard Shaw says that Christmas Day is only a conspiracy kept up by poulterers and wine merchants from strictly business motives, then he says something which is not so much false as startlingly and arrestingly foolish. He might as well say that the two sexes were invented by jewellers who wanted to sell wedding rings. Or again, take the case of nationality and the unit of patriotism. If a man said that all boundaries between clans, kingdoms, or empires were nonsensical or non-existent, that would be a fallacy, but a consistent and philosophical fallacy. But when Mr. Bernard Shaw says that England matters so little that the British Empire might very well give up these islands to Germany, he has not only got hold of the sow by the wrong ear but the wrong sow by the wrong ear; a mythical sow, a sow that is not there at all. If Britain is unreal, the British Empire must be a thousand times more unreal. It is as if one said, "I do not believe that Michael Scott ever had any existence; but I am convinced, in spite of the absurd legend, that he had a shadow."

As has been said already, there must be some truth in every popular impression. And the impression that Shaw, the most savagely serious man of his time, is a mere music-hall artist must have reference to such rare outbreaks as these. As a rule his speeches are full, not only of substance, but of substances, materials like pork, mahogany, lead, and leather. There is no man whose arguments cover a more Napoleonic map of detail. It is true that he jokes; but wherever he is he has topical jokes, one might almost say family jokes. If he talks to tailors he can allude to the last absurdity about buttons. If he talks to the soldiers he can see the exquisite and exact humour of the last gun-carriage. But when all his powerful practicality is allowed, there does run through him this erratic levity, an explosion of ineptitude. It is a queer quality in literature. It is a sort of cold extravagance; and it has made him all his enemies.

The Philosopher

I should suppose that *Cæsar and Cleopatra* marks about the turning tide of Bernard Shaw's fortune and fame. Up to this time he had known glory, but never success. He had been wondered at as something brilliant and barren, like a meteor; but no one would accept him as a sun, for the test of a sun is that it can make something grow. Practically speaking the two qualities of a modern drama are, that it should play and that it should pay. It had been proved over and over again in weighty dramatic criticisms, in careful readers' reports, that the plays of Shaw could never play or pay; that the public did not want wit and the wars of intellect. And just about the time that this had been finally proved, the plays of Bernard Shaw promised to play like *Charley's Aunt* and to pay like Colman's Mustard. It is a fact in which we can all rejoice, not only because it redeems the reputation of Bernard Shaw, but because it redeems the character of the English people. All that is bravest in human nature, open challenge and unexpected wit and angry conviction, are not so very unpopular as the publishers and managers in their motor-cars have been in the habit of telling us. But exactly because we have come to a turning point in the man's career I propose to interrupt the mere catalogue of his plays and to treat his latest series rather as the proclamations of an acknowledged prophet. For the last plays, especially *Man and Superman*, are such that his whole position must be restated before attacking them seriously.

For two reasons I have called this concluding series of plays not again by the name of "The Dramatist," but by the general name of "The Philosopher." The first reason is that given above, that we have come to the time of his triumph and may therefore treat him as having gained complete possession of a pulpit of his own. But there is a second reason: that it was just about this time that he began to create not only a pulpit of his own, but a church and creed of his own. It is a very vast and universal religion; and it is not his fault that he is the only member of it. The plainer way of putting it is this: that here, in the hour of his earthly victory, there dies in him the old mere denier, the mere dynamiter of criticism. In the warmth of popularity he begins to wish to put his faith positively; to offer some solid key to all creation. Perhaps the irony in the situation is this: that all the crowds are acclaiming him as the blasting and hypercritical buffoon, while he himself is seriously rallying his synthetic power, and with a grave face telling himself that it is time he had a faith to preach. His final success as a sort of charlatan coincides with his first grand failures as a theologian.

For this reason I have deliberately called a halt in his dramatic career, in order to consider these two essential points: What did the mass of Englishmen, who had now learnt to admire him, imagine his point of view to be? and second, What did he imagine it to be? or, if the phrase be premature, What did he imagine it was going to be? In his latest work, especially in *Man and Superman*, Shaw has become a complete and colossal mystic. That mysticism does grow quite rationally out of his older arguments; but very few people ever troubled to trace the connection. In order to do so it is necessary to say what was, at the time of his first success, the public impression of Shaw's philosophy.

Now it is an irritating and pathetic thing that the three most popular phrases about Shaw are false. Modern criticism, like all weak things, is overloaded with words. In a healthy condition of language a man finds it very difficult to say the right thing, but at last says it. In this empire of journalese a man finds it so very easy to say the wrong thing that he never thinks of saying anything else. False or meaningless phrases lie so ready to his hand that it is easier to use them than not to use them. These wrong terms picked up through idleness are retained through habit, and so the man has begun to think wrong almost before he has begun to think at all. Such lumbering logomachy is always injurious and oppressive to men of spirit, imagination or intellectual honour, and it has dealt very recklessly and wrongly with Bernard Shaw. He has contrived to get about three newspaper phrases tied to his tail; and those newspaper phrases are all and separately wrong. The three superstitions about him, it will be conceded, are generally these: first that he desires "problem plays," second that he is "paradoxical," and third that in his dramas as elsewhere he is specially "a Socialist." And the interesting thing is that when we come to his philosophy, all these three phrases are quite peculiarly inapplicable.

To take the plays first, there is a general disposition to describe that type of intimate or defiant drama which he approves as "the problem play." Now the serious modern play is, as a rule, the very reverse of a problem play; for there can be no problem unless both points of view are equally and urgently presented. *Hamlet* really is a problem play because at the end of it one is really in doubt as to whether upon the author's showing Hamlet is something more than a man or something less. *Henry IV* and *Henry V* are really problem plays; in this sense, that the reader or spectator is really doubtful whether the high but harsh efficiency, valour, and ambition of Henry V are an improvement on his old blackguard camaraderie; and whether he was not a better man when he was a thief. This hearty and healthy doubt is very common in Shakespeare; I mean a doubt that exists in the writer as well as in the reader. But Bernard Shaw is far too much of a Puritan to tolerate such doubts about points which he counts essential. There is no sort of doubt that the young lady in *Arms and the Man* is improved by losing her ideals. There is no sort of doubt that Captain Brassbound is improved by giving up the object of his life. But a better case can be found in something that both dramatists have been concerned with; Shaw wrote *Cæsar and Cleopatra* ; Shakespeare wrote *Antony and Cleopatra* and also *Julius Cæsar*. And exactly what annoys Bernard Shaw about Shakespeare's version is this: that Shakespeare has an open mind or, in other words, that Shakespeare has really written a problem play. Shakespeare sees quite as clearly as Shaw that Brutus is unpractical and ineffectual; but he also sees, what is quite as plain and practical a fact, that these ineffectual men do capture the hearts and influence the policies of mankind. Shaw would have nothing said in favour of Brutus; because Brutus is on the wrong side in politics. Of the actual problem of public and private morality, as it was presented to Brutus, he takes actually no notice at all. He can write the most energetic and outspoken of propaganda plays; but he cannot rise to a problem play. He cannot really divide his mind and let the two parts speak independently to each other. He has never, so to speak, actually split his head in two; though I daresay there are many other people who are willing to do it for him.

Sometimes, especially in his later plays, he allows his clear conviction to spoil even his admirable dialogue, making one side entirely weak, as in an Evangelical tract. I do not know whether in *Major Barbara* the young Greek professor was supposed to be a fool. As popular tradition (which I trust more than anything else) declared that he is drawn from a real Professor of my acquaintance, who is anything but a fool, I should imagine not. But in that case I am all the more mystified by the incredibly weak fight which he makes in the play in answer to the elephantine sophistries of Undershaft. It is really a disgraceful case, and almost the only case in Shaw of there being no fair fight between the two sides. For instance, the Professor mentions pity. Mr. Undershaft says with melodramatic scorn, "Pity! the scavenger of the Universe!" Now if any gentleman had said this to me, I should have replied, "If I permit you to escape from the point by means of metaphors, will you tell me whether you disapprove of scavengers?" Instead of this obvious retort, the miserable Greek professor only says, "Well then, love," to which Undershaft replies with unnecessary violence that he won't have the Greek professor's love, to which the obvious answer of course would be, "How the deuce can you prevent my loving you if I choose to do so?" Instead of this, as far as I remember, that abject Hellenist says nothing at all. I only mention this unfair dialogue, because it marks, I think, the recent hardening, for good or evil, of Shaw out of a dramatist into a mere philosopher, and whoever hardens into a philosopher may be hardening into a fanatic.

And just as there is nothing really problematic in Shaw's mind, so there is nothing really paradoxical. The meaning of the word paradoxical may indeed be made the subject of argument. In Greek, of course, it simply means something which is against the received opinion; in that sense a missionary remonstrating with South Sea cannibals is paradoxical. But in the much more important world, where words are used and altered in the using, paradox does not mean merely this: it means at least something of which the antinomy or apparent inconsistency is sufficiently plain in the words used, and most commonly of all it means an idea expressed in a form which is verbally contradictory. Thus, for instance, the great saying, "He that shall lose his life, the same shall save it," is an example of what modern people mean by a paradox. If any learned person should read this book (which seems immeasurably improbable) he can content himself with putting it this way, that the moderns mistakenly say paradox when they should say oxymoron. Ultimately, in any case, it may be agreed that we commonly mean by a paradox some kind of collision between what is seemingly and what is really true.

Now if by paradox we mean truth inherent in a contradiction, as in the saying of Christ that I have quoted, it is a very curious fact that Bernard Shaw is almost entirely without paradox. Moreover, he cannot even understand a paradox. And more than this, paradox is about the only thing in the world that he does not understand. All his splendid vistas and startling suggestions arise from carrying some one clear principle further than it has yet been carried. His madness is all consistency, not inconsistency. As the point can hardly be made clear without examples, let us take one example, the subject of education. Shaw has been all his life preaching to grownup people the profound truth that liberty and responsibility go together; that the reason why freedom is so often easily withheld, is simply that it is a terrible nuisance. This is true, though not the whole truth, of citizens; and so when Shaw comes to children he can only apply to them the same principle that he has already applied to citizens. He begins to play with the Herbert Spencer idea of teaching children by experience; perhaps the most fatuously silly idea that was ever gravely put down in print. On that there is no need to dwell; one has only to ask how the experimental method is to be applied to a precipice; and the theory no longer exists. But Shaw effected a further development, if possible more fantastic. He said that one should never tell a child anything without letting him hear the opposite opinion. That is to say, when you tell Tommy not to hit his sick sister on the temple, you must make sure of the presence of some Nietzscheite professor, who will explain to him that such a course might possibly serve to eliminate the unfit. When you are in the act of telling Susan not to drink out of the bottle labelled "poison," you must telegraph for a Christian Scientist, who will be ready to maintain that without her own consent it cannot do her any harm. What would happen to a child brought up on Shaw's principle I cannot conceive; I should think he would commit suicide in his bath. But that is not here the question. The point is that this proposition seems quite sufficiently wild and startling to ensure that its author, if he escapes Hanwell, would reach the front rank of journalists, demagogues, or public entertainers. It is a perfect paradox, if a paradox only means something that makes one jump. But it is not a paradox at all in the sense of a contradiction. It is not a contradiction, but an enormous and outrageous consistency, the one principle of free thought carried to a point to which no other sane man would consent to carry it. Exactly what Shaw does not understand is the paradox; the unavoidable paradox of childhood. Although this child is much better than I, yet I must teach it. Although this being has much purer passions than I, yet I must control it. Although Tommy is quite right to rush towards a precipice, yet he must be stood in the corner for doing it. This contradiction is the only possible condition of having to do with children at all; anyone who talks about a child without feeling this paradox might just as well be talking about a merman. He has never even seen the animal. But this paradox Shaw in his intellectual simplicity cannot see; he cannot see it because it is a paradox. His only intellectual excitement is to carry one idea further and further across the world. It never occurs to him that it might meet another idea, and like the three winds in *Martin Chuzzlewit*, they might make a night of it. His only paradox is to pull out one thread or cord of truth longer and longer into waste and fantastic places. He does not allow for that deeper sort of paradox by which two opposite cords of truth become entangled in an inextricable knot. Still less can he be made to realise that it is often this knot which ties safely together the whole bundle of human life.

This blindness to paradox everywhere perplexes his outlook. He cannot understand marriage because he will not understand the paradox of marriage; that the woman is all the more the house for not being the head of it. He cannot understand patriotism, because he will not understand the paradox of patriotism; that one is all the more human for not merely loving humanity. He does not understand Christianity because he will not understand the paradox of Christianity; that we can only really understand all myths when we know that one of them is true. I do not underrate him for this anti-paradoxical temper; I concede that much of his finest and keenest work in the way of intellectual purification would have been difficult or impossible without it. But I say that here lies the limitation of that lucid and compelling mind; he cannot quite understand life, because he will not accept its contradictions.

Nor is it by any means descriptive of Shaw to call him a Socialist; in so far as that word can be extended to cover an ethical attitude. He is the least social of all Socialists; and I pity the Socialist state that tries to manage him. This anarchism of his is not a question of thinking for himself; every decent man thinks for himself; it would be highly immodest to think for anybody else. Nor is it any instinctive licence or egoism; as I have said before, he is a man of peculiarly acute public conscience. The unmanageable part of him, the fact that he cannot be conceived as part of a crowd or as really and invisibly helping a movement, has reference to another thing in him, or rather to another thing not in him.

The great defect of that fine intelligence is a failure to grasp and enjoy the things commonly called convention and tradition; which are foods upon which all human creatures must feed frequently if they are to live. Very few modern people of course have any idea of what they are. "Convention" is very nearly the same word as "democracy." It has again and again in history been used as an alternative word to Parliament. So far from suggesting anything stale or sober, the word convention rather conveys a hubbub; it is the coming together of men; every mob is a convention. In its secondary sense it means the common soul of such a crowd, its instinctive anger at the traitor or its instinctive salutation of the flag. Conventions may be cruel, they may be unsuitable, they may even be grossly superstitious or obscene; but there is one thing that they never are. Conventions are never dead. They are always full of accumulated emotions, the piled-up and passionate experiences of many generations asserting what they could not explain. To be inside any true convention, as the Chinese respect for parents or the European respect for children, is to be surrounded by something which whatever else it is is not leaden, lifeless or automatic, something which is taut and tingling with vitality at a hundred points, which is sensitive almost to madness and which is so much alive that it can kill. Now Bernard Shaw has always made this one immense mistake (arising out of that bad progressive education of his), the mistake of treating convention as a dead thing; treating it as if it were a mere physical environment like the pavement or the rain. Whereas it is a result of will; a rain of blessings and a pavement of good intentions. Let it be remembered that I am not discussing in what degree one should allow for tradition; I am saying that men like Shaw do not allow for it at all. If Shaw had found in early life that he was contradicted by *Bradshaw's Railway Guide* or even by the *Encyclopædia Britannica* , he would have felt at least that he might be wrong. But if he had found himself contradicted by his father and mother, he would have thought it all the more probable that he was right. If the issue of the last evening paper contradicted him he might be troubled to investigate or explain. That the human tradition of two thousand years contradicted him did not trouble him for an instant. That Marx was not with him was important. That Man was not with him was an irrelevant prehistoric joke. People have talked far too much about the paradoxes of Bernard Shaw. Perhaps his only pure paradox is this almost unconscious one; that he has tended to think that because something has satisfied generations of men it must be untrue.

Shaw is wrong about nearly all the things one learns early in life and while one is still simple. Most human beings start with certain facts of psychology to which the rest of life must be somewhat related. For instance, every man falls in love; and no man falls into free love. When he falls into that he calls it lust, and is always ashamed of it even when he boasts of it. That there is some connection between a love and a vow nearly every human being knows before he is eighteen. That there is a solid and instinctive connection between the idea of sexual ecstasy and the idea of some sort of almost suicidal constancy, this I say is simply the first fact in one's own psychology; boys and girls know it almost before they know their own language. How far it can be trusted, how it can best be dealt with, all that is another matter. But lovers lust after constancy more than after happiness; if you are in any sense prepared to give them what they ask, then what they ask, beyond all question, is an oath of final fidelity. Lovers may be lunatics; lovers may be children; lovers may be unfit for citizenship and outside human argument; you can take up that position if you will. But lovers do not only desire love; they desire marriage. The root of legal monogamy does not lie (as Shaw and his friends are for ever drearily asserting) in the fact that the man is a mere tyrant and the woman a mere slave. It lies in the fact that *if* their love for each other is the noblest and freest love conceivable, it can only find its heroic expression in both becoming slaves. I only mention this matter here as a matter which most of us do not need to be taught; for it was the first lesson of life. In after years we may make up what code or compromise about sex we like; but we all know that constancy, jealousy, and the personal pledge are natural and inevitable in sex; we do not feel any surprise when we see them either in a murder or in a valentine. We may or may not see wisdom in early marriages; but we know quite well that wherever the thing is genuine at all, early loves will mean early marriages. But Shaw had not learnt about this tragedy of the sexes, what the rustic ballads of any country on earth would have taught him. He had not learnt, what universal common sense has put into all the folklore of the earth, that love cannot be thought of clearly for an instant except as monogamous. The old English ballads never sing the praises of "lovers." They always sing the praises of "true lovers," and that is the final philosophy of the question.

The same is true of Mr. Shaw's refusal to understand the love of the land either in the form of patriotism or of private ownership. It is the attitude of an Irishman cut off from the soil of Ireland, retaining the audacity and even cynicism of the national type, but no longer fed from the roots with its pathos or its experience.

This broader and more brotherly rendering of convention must be applied particularly to the conventions of the drama; since that is necessarily the most democratic of all the arts. And it will be found generally that most of the theatrical conventions rest on a real artistic basis. The Greek Unities, for instance, were not proper objects of the meticulous and trivial imitation of Seneca or Gabriel Harvey. But still less were they the right objects for the equally trivial and far more vulgar impatience of men like Macaulay. That a tale should, if possible, be told of one place or one day or a manageable number of characters is an ideal plainly rooted in an æsthetic instinct. But if this be so with the classical drama, it is yet more certainly so with romantic drama, against the somewhat decayed dignity of which Bernard Shaw was largely in rebellion. There was one point in particular upon which the Ibsenites claimed to have reformed the romantic convention which is worthy of special allusion.

Shaw and all the other Ibsenites were fond of insisting that a defect in the romantic drama was its tendency to end with wedding-bells. Against this they set the modern drama of middleage, the drama which described marriage itself instead of its poetic preliminaries. Now if Bernard Shaw had been more patient with popular tradition, more prone to think that there might be some sense in its survival, he might have seen this particular problem much more clearly. The old playwrights have left us plenty of plays of marriage and middleage. *Othello* is as much about what follows the wedding-bells as *The Doll's House*. *Macbeth* is about a middleaged couple as much as *Little Eyolf*. But if we ask ourselves what is the real difference, we shall, I think, find that it can fairly be stated thus. The old tragedies of marriage, though not love stories, are like love stories in this, that they work up to some act or stroke which is irrevocable as marriage is irrevocable; to the fact of death or of adultery.

Now the reason why our fathers did not make marriage, in the middleaged and static sense, the subject of their plays was a very simple one; it was that a play is a very bad place for discussing that topic. You cannot easily make a good drama out of the success or failure of a marriage, just as you could not make a good drama out of the growth of an oak tree or the decay of an empire. As Polonius very reasonably observed, it is too long. A happy love-affair will make a drama simply because it is dramatic; it depends on an ultimate yes or no. But a happy marriage is not dramatic; perhaps it would be less happy if it were. The essence of a romantic heroine is that she asks herself an intense question; but the essence of a sensible wife is that she is much too sensible to ask herself any questions at all. All the things that make monogamy a success are in their nature undramatic things, the silent growth of an instinctive confidence, the common wounds and victories, the accumulation of customs, the rich maturing of old jokes. Sane marriage is an untheatrical thing; it is therefore not surprising that most modern dramatists have devoted themselves to insane marriage.

To summarise; before touching the philosophy which Shaw has ultimately adopted, we must quit the notion that we know it already and that it is hit off in such journalistic terms as these three. Shaw does not wish to multiply problem plays or even problems. He has such scepticism as is the misfortune of his age; but he has this dignified and courageous quality, that he does not come to ask questions but to answer them. He is not a paradox-monger; he is a wild logician, far too simple even to be called a sophist. He understands everything in life except its paradoxes, especially that ultimate paradox that the very things that we cannot comprehend are the things that we have to take for granted. Lastly, he is not especially social or collectivist. On the contrary, he rather dislikes men in the mass, though he can appreciate them individually. He has no respect for collective humanity in its two great forms; either in that momentary form which we call a mob, or in that enduring form which we call a convention.

The general cosmic theory which can so far be traced through the earlier essays and plays of Bernard Shaw may be expressed in the image of Schopenhauer standing on his head. I cheerfully concede that Schopenhauer looks much nicer in that posture than in his original one, but I can hardly suppose that he feels more comfortable. The substance of the change is this. Roughly speaking, Schopenhauer maintained that life is unreasonable. The intellect, if it could be impartial, would tell us to cease; but a blind partiality, an instinct quite distinct from thought, drives us on to take desperate chances in an essentially bankrupt lottery. Shaw seems to accept this dingy estimate of the rational outlook, but adds a somewhat arresting comment. Schopenhauer had said, "Life is unreasonable; so much the worse for all living things." Shaw said, "Life is unreasonable; so much the worse for reason." Life is the higher call, life we must follow. It may be that there is some undetected fallacy in reason itself. Perhaps the whole man cannot get inside his own head any more than he can jump down his own throat. But there is about the need to live, to suffer, and to create that imperative quality which can truly be called supernatural, of whose voice it can indeed be said that it speaks with authority, and not as the scribes.

This is the first and finest item of the original Bernard Shaw creed: that if reason says that life is irrational, life must be content to reply that reason is lifeless; life is the primary thing, and if reason impedes it, then reason must be trodden down into the mire amid the most abject superstitions. In the ordinary sense it would be specially absurd to suggest that Shaw desires man to be a mere animal. For that is always associated with lust or incontinence; and Shaw's ideals are strict, hygienic, and even, one might say, old-maidish. But there is a mystical sense in which one may say literally that Shaw desires man to be an animal. That is, he desires him to cling first and last to life, to the spirit of animation, to the thing which is common to him and the birds and plants. Man should have the blind faith of a beast: he should be as mystically immutable as a cow, and as deaf to sophistries as a fish. Shaw does not wish him to be a philosopher or an artist; he does not even wish him to be a man, so much as he wishes him to be, in this holy sense, an animal. He must follow the flag of life as fiercely from conviction as all other creatures follow it from instinct.

But this Shavian worship of life is by no means lively. It has nothing in common either with the braver or the baser forms of what we commonly call optimism. It has none of the omnivorous exultation of Walt Whitman or the fiery pantheism of Shelley. Bernard Shaw wishes to show himself not so much as an optimist, but rather as a sort of faithful and contented pessimist. This contradiction is the key to nearly all his early and more obvious contradictions and to many which remain to the end. Whitman and many modern idealists have talked of taking even duty as a pleasure; it seems to me that Shaw takes even pleasure as a duty. In a queer way he seems to see existence as an illusion and yet as an obligation. To every man and woman, bird, beast, and flower, life is a love-call to be eagerly followed. To Bernard Shaw it is merely a military bugle to be obeyed. In short, he fails to feel that the command of Nature (if one must use the anthropomorphic fable of Nature instead of the philosophic term God) can be enjoyed as well as obeyed. He paints life at its darkest and then tells the babe unborn to take the leap in the dark. That is heroic; and to my instinct at least Schopenhauer looks like a pigmy beside his pupil. But it is the heroism of a morbid and almost asphyxiated age. It is awful to think that this world which so many poets have praised has even for a time been depicted as a mantrap into which we may just have the manhood to jump. Think of all those ages through which men have talked of having the courage to die. And then remember that we have actually fallen to talking about having the courage to live.

It is exactly this oddity or dilemma which may be said to culminate in the crowning work of his later and more constructive period, the work in which he certainly attempted, whether with success or not, to state his ultimate and cosmic vision; I mean the play called *Man and Superman*. In approaching this play we must keep well in mind the distinction recently drawn: that Shaw follows the banner of life, but austerely, not joyously. For him nature has authority, but hardly charm. But before we approach it it is necessary to deal with three things that lead up to it. First it is necessary to speak of what remained of his old critical and realistic method; and then it is necessary to speak of the two important influences which led up to his last and most important change of outlook.

First, since all our spiritual epochs overlap, and a man is often doing the old work while he is thinking of the new, we may deal first with what may be fairly called his last two plays of pure worldly criticism. These are *Major Barbara* and *John Bull's Other Island*. *Major Barbara* indeed contains a strong religious element; but, when all is said, the whole point of the play is that the religious element is defeated. Moreover, the actual expressions of religion in the play are somewhat unsatisfactory as expressions of religion — or even of reason. I must frankly say that Bernard Shaw always seems to me to use the word God not only without any idea of what it means, but without one moment's thought about what it could possibly mean. He said to some atheist, "Never believe in a God that you cannot improve on." The atheist (being a sound theologian) naturally replied that one should not believe in a God whom one could improve on; as that would show that he was not God. In the same style in *Major Barbara* the heroine ends by suggesting that she will serve God without personal hope, so that she may owe nothing to God and He owe everything to her. It does not seem to strike her that if God owes everything to her He is not God. These things affect me merely as tedious perversions of a phrase. It is as if you said, "I will never have a father unless I have begotten him."

But the real sting and substance of *Major Barbara* is much more practical and to the point. It expresses not the new spirituality but the old materialism of Bernard Shaw. Almost every one of Shaw's plays is an expanded epigram. But the epigram is not expanded (as with most people) into a hundred commonplaces. Rather the epigram is expanded into a hundred other epigrams; the work is at least as brilliant in detail as it is in design. But it is generally possible to discover the original and pivotal epigram which is the centre and purpose of the play. It is generally possible, even amid that blinding jewellery of a million jokes, to discover the grave, solemn and sacred joke for which the play itself was written.

The ultimate epigram of *Major Barbara* can be put thus. People say that poverty is no crime; Shaw says that poverty is a crime; that it is a crime to endure it, a crime to be content with it, that it is the mother of all crimes of brutality, corruption, and fear. If a man says to Shaw that he is born of poor but honest parents, Shaw tells him that the very word "but" shows that his parents were probably dishonest. In short, he maintains here what he had maintained elsewhere: that what the people at this moment require is not more patriotism or more art or more religion or more morality or more sociology, but simply more money. The evil is not ignorance or decadence or sin or pessimism; the evil is poverty. The point of this particular drama is that even the noblest enthusiasm of the girl who becomes a Salvation Army officer fails under the brute money power of her father who is a modern capitalist. When I have said this it will be clear why this play, fine and full of bitter sincerity as it is, must in a manner be cleared out of the way before we come to talk of Shaw's final and serious faith. For his serious faith is in the sanctity of human will, in the divine capacity for creation and choice rising higher than environment and doom; and so far as that goes, *Major Barbara* is not only apart from his faith but against his faith. *Major Barbara* is an account of environment victorious over heroic will. There are a thousand answers to the ethic in *Major Barbara* which I should be inclined to offer. I might point out that the rich do not so much buy honesty as curtains to cover dishonesty: that they do not so much buy health as cushions to comfort disease. And I might suggest that the doctrine that poverty degrades the poor is much more likely to be used as an argument for keeping them powerless than as an argument for making them rich. But there is no need to find such answers to the materialistic pessimism of *Major Barbara*. The best answer to it is in Shaw's own best and crowning philosophy, with which we shall shortly be concerned.

John Bull's Other Island represents a realism somewhat more tinged with the later transcendentalism of its author. In one sense, of course, it is a satire on the conventional Englishman, who is never so silly or sentimental as when he sees silliness and sentiment in the Irishman. Broadbent, whose mind is all fog and his morals all gush, is firmly persuaded that he is bringing reason and order among the Irish, whereas in truth they are all smiling at his illusions with the critical detachment of so many devils. There have been many plays depicting the absurd Paddy in a ring of Anglo-Saxons; the first purpose of this play is to depict the absurd Anglo-Saxon in a ring of ironical Paddies. But it has a second and more subtle purpose, which is very finely contrived. It is suggested that when all is said and done there is in this preposterous Englishman a certain creative power which comes from his simplicity and optimism, from his profound resolution rather to live life than to criticise it. I know no finer dialogue of philosophical cross-purposes than that in which Broadbent boasts of his commonsense, and his subtler Irish friend mystifies him by telling him that he, Broadbent, has no commonsense, but only inspiration. The Irishman admits in Broadbent a certain unconscious spiritual force even in his very stupidity. Lord Rosebery coined the very clever phrase "a practical mystic." Shaw is here maintaining that all practical men are practical mystics. And he is really maintaining also that the most practical of all the practical mystics is the one who is a fool.

There is something unexpected and fascinating about this reversal of the usual argument touching enterprise and the business man; this theory that success is created not by intelligence, but by a certain half-witted and yet magical instinct. For Bernard Shaw, apparently, the forests of factories and the mountains of money are not the creations of human wisdom or even of human cunning; they are rather manifestations of the sacred maxim which declares that God has chosen the foolish things of the earth to confound the wise. It is simplicity and even innocence that has made Manchester. As a philosophical fancy this is interesting or even suggestive; but it must be confessed that as a criticism of the relations of England to Ireland it is open to a strong historical objection. The one weak point in *John Bull's Other Island* is that it turns on the fact that Broadbent succeeds in Ireland. But as a matter of fact Broadbent has not succeeded in Ireland. If getting what one wants is the test and fruit of this mysterious strength, then the Irish peasants are certainly much stronger than the English merchants; for in spite of all the efforts of the merchants, the land has remained a land of peasants. No glorification of the English practicality as if it were a universal thing can ever get over the fact that we have failed in dealing with the one white people in our power who were markedly unlike ourselves. And the kindness of Broadbent has failed just as much as his commonsense; because he was dealing with a people whose desire and ideal were different from his own. He did not share the Irish passion for small possession in land or for the more pathetic virtues of Christianity. In fact the kindness of Broadbent has failed for the same reason that the gigantic kindness of Shaw has failed. The roots are different; it is like tying the tops of two trees together. Briefly, the philosophy of *John Bull's Other Island* is quite effective and satisfactory except for this incurable fault: the fact that John Bull's other island is not John Bull's.

This clearing off of his last critical plays we may classify as the first of the three facts which lead up to *Man and Superman*. The second of the three facts may be found, I think, in Shaw's discovery of Nietzsche. This eloquent sophist has an influence upon Shaw and his school which it would require a separate book adequately to study. By descent Nietzsche was a Pole, and probably a Polish noble; and to say that he was a Polish noble is to say that he was a frail, fastidious, and entirely useless anarchist. He had a wonderful poetic wit; and is one of the best rhetoricians of the modern world. He had a remarkable power of saying things that master the reason for a moment by their gigantic unreasonableness; as, for instance, "Your life is intolerable without immortality; but why should not your life be intolerable?" His whole work is shot through with the pangs and fevers of his physical life, which was one of extreme bad health; and in early middle age his brilliant brain broke down into impotence and darkness. All that was true in his teaching was this: that if a man looks fine on a horse it is so far irrelevant to tell him that he would be more economical on a donkey or more humane on a tricycle. In other words, the mere achievement of dignity, beauty, or triumph is strictly to be called a good thing. I do not know if Nietzsche ever used the illustration; but it seems to me that all that is creditable or sound in Nietzsche could be stated in the derivation of one word, the word "valour." Valour means *valeur* ; it means a value; courage is itself a solid good; it is an ultimate virtue; valour is in itself *valid* . In so far as he maintained this Nietzsche was only taking part in that great Protestant game of see-saw which has been the amusement of northern Europe since the sixteenth century. Nietzsche imagined he was rebelling against ancient morality; as a matter of fact he was only rebelling against recent morality, against the half-baked impudence of the utilitarians and the materialists. He thought he was rebelling against Christianity; curiously enough he was rebelling solely against the special enemies of Christianity, against Herbert Spencer and Mr. Edward Clodd. Historic Christianity has always believed in the valour of St. Michael riding in front of the Church Militant; and in an ultimate and absolute pleasure, not indirect or utilitarian, the intoxication of the spirit, the wine of the blood of God.

There are indeed doctrines of Nietzsche that are not Christian, but then, by an entertaining coincidence, they are also not true. His hatred of pity is not Christian, but that was not his doctrine but his disease. Invalids are often hard on invalids. And there is another doctrine of his that is not Christianity, and also (by the same laughable accident) not commonsense; and it is a most pathetic circumstance that this was the one doctrine which caught the eye of Shaw and captured him. He was not influenced at all by the morbid attack on mercy. It would require more than ten thousand mad Polish professors to make Bernard Shaw anything but a generous and compassionate man. But it is certainly a nuisance that the one Nietzsche doctrine which attracted him was not the one Nietzsche doctrine that is human and rectifying. Nietzsche might really have done some good if he had taught Bernard Shaw to draw the sword, to drink wine, or even to dance. But he only succeeded in putting into his head a new superstition, which bids fair to be the chief superstition of the dark ages which are possibly in front of us — I mean the superstition of what is called the Superman.

In one of his least convincing phrases, Nietzsche had said that just as the ape ultimately produced the man, so should we ultimately produce something higher than the man. The immediate answer, of course, is sufficiently obvious: the ape did not worry about the man, so why should we worry about the Superman? If the Superman will come by natural selection, may we leave it to natural selection? If the Superman will come by human selection, what sort of Superman are we to select? If he is simply to be more just, more brave, or more merciful, then Zarathustra sinks into a Sunday-school teacher; the only way we can work for it is to be more just, more brave, and more merciful; sensible advice, but hardly startling. If he is to be anything else than this, why should we desire him, or what else are we to desire? These questions have been many times asked of the Nietzscheites, and none of the Nietzscheites have even attempted to answer them.

The keen intellect of Bernard Shaw would, I think, certainly have seen through this fallacy and verbiage had it not been that another important event about this time came to the help of Nietzsche and established the Superman on his pedestal. It is the third of the things which I have called stepping-stones to *Man and Superman* , and it is very important. It is nothing less than the breakdown of one of the three intellectual supports upon which Bernard Shaw had reposed through all his confident career. At the beginning of this book I have described the three ultimate supports of Shaw as the Irishman, the Puritan, and the Progressive. They are the three legs of the tripod upon which the prophet sat to give the oracle; and one of them broke. Just about this time suddenly, by a mere shaft of illumination, Bernard Shaw ceased to believe in progress altogether.

It is generally implied that it was reading Plato that did it. That philosopher was very well qualified to convey the first shock of the ancient civilisation to Shaw, who had always thought instinctively of civilisation as modern. This is not due merely to the daring splendour of the speculations and the vivid picture of Athenian life, it is due also to something analogous in the personalities of that particular ancient Greek and this particular modern Irishman. Bernard Shaw has much affinity to Plato — in his instinctive elevation of temper, his courageous pursuit of ideas as far as they will go, his civic idealism; and also, it must be confessed, in his dislike of poets and a touch of delicate inhumanity. But whatever influence produced the change, the change had all the dramatic suddenness and completeness which belongs to the conversions of great men. It had been perpetually implied through all the earlier works not only that mankind is constantly improving, but that almost everything must be considered in the light of this fact. More than once he seemed to argue, in comparing the dramatists of the sixteenth with those of the nineteenth century, that the latter had a definite advantage merely because they were of the nineteenth century and not of the sixteenth. When accused of impertinence towards the greatest of the Elizabethans, Bernard Shaw had said, "Shakespeare is a much taller man than I, but I stand on his shoulders" — an epigram which sums up this doctrine with characteristic neatness. But Shaw fell off Shakespeare's shoulders with a crash. This chronological theory that Shaw stood on Shakespeare's shoulders logically involved the supposition that Shakespeare stood on Plato's shoulders. And Bernard Shaw found Plato from his point of view so much more advanced than Shakespeare that he decided in desperation that all three were equal.

Such failure as has partially attended the idea of human equality is very largely due to the fact that no party in the modern state has heartily believed in it. Tories and Radicals have both assumed that one set of men were in essentials superior to mankind. The only difference was that the Tory superiority was a superiority of place; while the Radical superiority is a superiority of time. The great objection to Shaw being on Shakespeare's shoulders is a consideration for the sensations and personal dignity of Shakespeare. It is a democratic objection to anyone being on anyone else's shoulders. Eternal human nature refuses to submit to a man who rules merely by right of birth. To rule by right of century is to rule by right of birth. Shaw found his nearest kinsman in remote Athens, his remotest enemies in the closest historical proximity; and he began to see the enormous average and the vast level of mankind. If progress swung constantly between such extremes it could not be progress at all. The paradox was sharp but undeniable; if life had such continual ups and downs, it was upon the whole flat. With characteristic sincerity and love of sensation he had no sooner seen this than he hastened to declare it. In the teeth of all his previous pronouncements he emphasised and re-emphasised in print that man had not progressed at all; that ninety-nine hundredths of a man in a cave were the same as ninety-nine hundredths of a man in a suburban villa.

It is characteristic of him to say that he rushed into print with a frank confession of the failure of his old theory. But it is also characteristic of him that he rushed into print also with a new alternative theory, quite as definite, quite as confident, and, if one may put it so, quite as infallible as the old one. Progress had never happened hitherto, because it had been sought solely through education. Education was rubbish. "Fancy," said he, "trying to produce a greyhound or a racehorse by education!" The man of the future must not be taught; he must be bred. This notion of producing superior human beings by the methods of the stud-farm had often been urged, though its difficulties had never been cleared up. I mean its practical difficulties; its moral difficulties, or rather impossibilities, for any animal fit to be called a man need scarcely be discussed. But even as a scheme it had never been made clear. The first and most obvious objection to it of course is this: that if you are to breed men as pigs, you require some overseer who is as much more subtle than a man as a man is more subtle than a pig. Such an individual is not easy to find.

It was, however, in the heat of these three things, the decline of his merely destructive realism, the discovery of Nietzsche, and the abandonment of the idea of a progressive education of mankind, that he attempted what is not necessarily his best, but certainly his most important work. The two things are by no means necessarily the same. The most important work of Milton is *Paradise Lost*; his best work is *Lycidas*. There are other places in which Shaw's argument is more fascinating or his wit more startling than in *Man and Superman*; there are other plays that he has made more brilliant. But I am sure that there is no other play that he wished to make more brilliant. I will not say that he is in this case more serious than elsewhere; for the word serious is a double-meaning and double-dealing word, a traitor in the dictionary. It sometimes means solemn, and it sometimes means sincere. A very short experience of private and public life will be enough to prove that the most solemn people are generally the most insincere. A somewhat more delicate and detailed consideration will show also that the most sincere men are generally not solemn; and of these is Bernard Shaw. But if we use the word serious in the old and Latin sense of the word "grave," which means weighty or valid, full of substance, then we may say without any hesitation that this is the most serious play of the most serious man alive.

The outline of the play is, I suppose, by this time sufficiently well known. It has two main philosophic motives. The first is that what he calls the life-force (the old infidels called it Nature, which seems a neater word, and nobody knows the meaning of either of them) desires above all things to make suitable marriages, to produce a purer and prouder race, or eventually to produce a Superman. The second is that in this effecting of racial marriages the woman is a more conscious agent than the man. In short, that woman disposes a long time before man proposes. In this play, therefore, woman is made the pursuer and man the pursued. It cannot be denied, I think, that in this matter Shaw is handicapped by his habitual hardness of touch, by his lack of sympathy with the romance of which he writes, and to a certain extent even by his own integrity and right conscience. Whether the man hunts the woman or the woman the man, at least it should be a splendid pagan hunt; but Shaw is not a sporting man. Nor is he a pagan, but a Puritan. He cannot recover the impartiality of paganism which allowed Diana to propose to Endymion without thinking any the worse of her. The result is that while he makes Anne, the woman who marries his hero, a really powerful and convincing woman, he can only do it by making her a highly objectionable woman. She is a liar and a bully, not from sudden fear or excruciating dilemma; she is a liar and a bully in grain; she has no truth or magnanimity in her. The more we know that she is real, the more we know that she is vile. In short, Bernard Shaw is still haunted with his old impotence of the unromantic writer; he cannot imagine the main motives of human life from the inside. We are convinced successfully that Anne wishes to marry Tanner, but in the very process we lose all power of conceiving why Tanner should ever consent to marry Anne. A writer with a more romantic strain in him might have imagined a woman choosing her lover without shamelessness and magnetising him without fraud. Even if the first movement were feminine, it need hardly be a movement like this. In truth, of course, the two sexes have their two methods of attraction, and in some of the happiest cases they are almost simultaneous. But even on the most cynical showing they need not be mixed up. It is one thing to say that the mousetrap is not there by accident. It is another to say (in the face of ocular experience) that the mousetrap runs after the mouse.

But whenever Shaw shows the Puritan hardness or even the Puritan cheapness, he shows something also of the Puritan nobility, of the idea that sacrifice is really a frivolity in the face of a great purpose. The reasonableness of Calvin and his followers will by the mercy of heaven be at last washed away; but their unreasonableness will remain an eternal splendour. Long after we have let drop the fancy that Protestantism was rational it will be its glory that it was fanatical. So it is with Shaw. To make Anne a real woman, even a dangerous woman, he would need to be something stranger and softer than Bernard Shaw. But though I always argue with him whenever he argues, I confess that he always conquers me in the one or two moments when he is emotional.

There is one really noble moment when Anne offers for all her cynical husband-hunting the only defence that is really great enough to cover it. "It will not be all happiness for me. Perhaps death." And the man rises also at that real crisis, saying, "Oh, that clutch holds and hurts. What have you grasped in me? Is there a father's heart as well as a mother's?" That seems to me actually great; I do not like either of the characters an atom more than formerly;

but I can see shining and shaking through them at that instant the splendour of the God that made them and of the image of God who wrote their story.

A logician is like a liar in many respects, but chiefly in the fact that he should have a good memory. That cutting and inquisitive style which Bernard Shaw has always adopted carries with it an inevitable criticism. And it cannot be denied that this new theory of the supreme importance of sound sexual union, wrought by any means, is hard logically to reconcile with Shaw's old diatribes against sentimentalism and operatic romance. If Nature wishes primarily to entrap us into sexual union, then all the means of sexual attraction, even the most maudlin or theatrical, are justified at one stroke. The guitar of the troubadour is as practical as the ploughshare of the husbandman. The waltz in the ballroom is as serious as the debate in the parish council. The justification of Anne, as the potential mother of Superman, is really the justification of all the humbugs and sentimentalists whom Shaw had been denouncing as a dramatic critic and as a dramatist since the beginning of his career. It was to no purpose that the earlier Bernard Shaw said that romance was all moonshine. The moonshine that ripens love is now as practical as the sunshine that ripens corn. It was vain to say that sexual chivalry was all rot; it might be as rotten as manure — and also as fertile. It is vain to call first love a fiction; it may be as fictitious as the ink of the cuttle or the doubling of the hare; as fictitious, as efficient, and as indispensable. It is vain to call it a self-deception; Schopenhauer said that all existence was a self-deception; and Shaw's only further comment seems to be that it is right to be deceived. To *Man and Superman*, as to all his plays, the author attaches a most fascinating preface at the beginning. But I really think that he ought also to attach a hearty apology at the end; an apology to all the minor dramatists or preposterous actors whom he had cursed for romanticism in his youth. Whenever he objected to an actress for ogling she might reasonably reply, "But this is how I support my friend Anne in her sublime evolutionary effort." Whenever he laughed at an oldfashioned actor for ranting, the actor might answer, "My exaggeration is not more absurd than the tail of a peacock or the swagger of a cock; it is the way I preach the great fruitful lie of the life-force that I am a very fine fellow." We have remarked the end of Shaw's campaign in favour of progress. This ought really to have been the end of his campaign against romance. All the tricks of love that he called artificial become natural; because they become Nature. All the lies of love become truths; indeed they become the Truth.

The minor things of the play contain some thunderbolts of good thinking. Throughout this brief study I have deliberately not dwelt upon mere wit, because in anything of Shaw's that may be taken for granted. It is enough to say that this play which is full of his most serious quality is as full as any of his minor sort of success. In a more solid sense two important facts stand out: the first is the character of the young American; the other is the character of Straker, the chauffeur. In these Shaw has realised and made vivid two most important facts. First, that America is not intellectually a go-ahead country, but both for good and evil an oldfashioned one. It is full of stale culture and ancestral simplicity, just as Shaw's young millionaire quotes Macaulay and piously worships his wife. Second, he has pointed out in the character of Straker that there has arisen in our midst a new class that has education without breeding. Straker is the man who has ousted the hansom-cabman, having neither his coarseness nor his kindliness. Great sociological credit is due to the man who has first clearly observed that Straker has appeared. How anybody can profess for a moment to be glad that he has appeared, I do not attempt to conjecture.

Appended to the play is an entertaining though somewhat mysterious document called "The Revolutionist's Handbook." It contains many very sound remarks; this, for example, which I cannot too much applaud: "If you hit your child, be sure that you hit him in anger." If that principle had been properly understood, we should have had less of Shaw's sociological friends and their meddling with the habits and instincts of the poor. But among the fragments of advice also occurs the following suggestive and even alluring remark: "Every man over forty is a scoundrel." On the first personal opportunity I asked the author of this remarkable axiom what it meant. I gathered that what it really meant was something like this: that every man over forty had been all the essential use that he was likely to be, and was therefore in a manner a parasite. It is gratifying to reflect that Bernard Shaw has sufficiently answered his own epigram by continuing to pour out treasures both of truth and folly long after this allotted time. But if the epigram might be interpreted in a rather looser style as meaning that past a certain point a man's work takes on its final character and does not greatly change the nature of its merits, it may certainly be said that with *Man and Superman*, Shaw reaches that stage. The two plays that have followed it, though of very great interest in themselves, do not require any revaluation of, or indeed any addition to, our summary of his genius and success. They are both in a sense casts back to his primary energies; the first in a controversial and the second in a technical sense. Neither need prevent our saying that the moment when John Tanner and Anne agree that it is doom for him and death for her and life only for the thing unborn, is the peak of his utterance as a prophet.

The two important plays that he has since given us are *The Doctor's Dilemma* and *Getting Married*. The first is as regards its most amusing and effective elements a throw-back to his old game of guying the men of science. It was a very good game, and he was an admirable player. The actual story of the *Doctor's Dilemma* itself seems to me less poignant and important than the things with which Shaw had lately been dealing. First of all, as has been said, Shaw has neither the kind of justice nor the kind of weakness that goes to make a true problem. We cannot feel the Doctor's Dilemma, because we cannot really fancy Bernard Shaw being in a dilemma. His mind is both fond of abruptness and fond of finality; he always makes up his mind when he knows the facts and sometimes before. Moreover, this particular problem (though Shaw is certainly, as we shall see, nearer to pure doubt about it than about anything else) does not strike the critic as being such an exasperating problem after all. An artist of vast power and promise, who is also a scamp of vast profligacy and treachery, has a chance of life if specially treated for a special disease. The modern doctors (and even the modern dramatist) are in doubt whether he should be specially favoured because he is æsthetically important or specially disregarded because he is ethically anti-social. They see-saw between the two despicable modern doctrines, one that geniuses should be worshipped like idols and the other that criminals should be merely wiped out like germs. That both clever men and bad men ought to be treated like men does not seem to occur to them. As a matter of fact, in these affairs of life and death one never does think of such distinctions. Nobody does shout out at sea, "Bad citizen overboard!" I should recommend the doctor in his dilemma to do exactly what I am sure any decent doctor would do without any dilemma at all: to treat the man simply as a man, and give him no more and no less favour than he would to anybody else. In short, I am sure a practical physician would drop all these visionary, unworkable modern dreams about type and criminology and go back to the plain businesslike facts of the French Revolution and the Rights of Man.

The other play, *Getting Married*, is a point in Shaw's career, but only as a play, not, as usual, as a heresy. It is nothing but a conversation about marriage; and one cannot agree or disagree with the view of marriage, because all views are given which are held by anybody, and some (I should think) which are held by nobody. But its technical quality is of some importance in the life of its author. It is worth consideration as a play, because it is not a play at all. It marks the culmination and completeness of that victory of Bernard Shaw over the British public, or rather over their official representatives, of which I have spoken. Shaw had fought a long fight with business men, those incredible people, who assured him that it was useless to have wit without murders, and that a good joke, which is the most popular thing everywhere else, was quite unsalable in the theatrical world. In spite of this he had conquered by his wit and his good dialogue; and by the time of which we now speak he was victorious and secure. All his plays were being produced as a matter of course in England and as a matter of the fiercest fashion and enthusiasm in America and Germany. No one who knows the nature of the man will doubt that under such circumstances his first act would be to produce his wit naked and unashamed. He had been told that he could not support a slight play by mere dialogue. He therefore promptly produced mere dialogue without the slightest play for it to support. *Getting Married* is no more a play than Cicero's dialogue *De Amicitiâ*, and not half so much a play as Wilson's *Noctes Ambrosianæ*. But though it is not a play, it was played, and played successfully. Everyone who went into the theatre felt that he was only eavesdropping at an accidental conversation. But the conversation was so sparkling and sensible that he went on eavesdropping. This, I think, as it is the final play of Shaw, is also, and fitly, his final triumph. He is a good dramatist and sometimes even a great dramatist. But the occasions when we get glimpses of him as really a great man are on these occasions when he is utterly undramatic.

From first to last Bernard Shaw has been nothing but a conversationalist. It is not a slur to say so; Socrates was one, and even Christ Himself. He differs from that divine and that human prototype in the fact that, like most modern people, he does to some extent talk in order to find out what he thinks; whereas they knew it beforehand. But he has the virtues that go with the talkative man; one of which is humility. You will hardly ever find a really proud man talkative; he is afraid of talking too much. Bernard Shaw offered himself to the world with only one great qualification, that he could talk honestly and well. He did not speak; he talked to a crowd. He did not write; he talked to a typewriter. He did not really construct a play; he talked through ten mouths or masks instead of through one. His literary power and progress began in casual conversations — and it seems to me supremely right that it should end in one great and casual conversation. His last play is nothing but garrulous talking, that great thing called gossip. And I am happy to say that the play has been as efficient and successful as talk and gossip have always been among the children of men.

Of his life in these later years I have made no pretence of telling even the little that there is to tell. Those who regard him as a mere self-advertising egotist may be surprised to hear that there is perhaps no man of whose private life less could be positively said by an outsider. Even those who know him can make little but a conjecture of what has lain behind this splendid stretch of intellectual self-expression; I only make my conjecture like the rest. I think that the first great turning-point in Shaw's life (after the early things of which I have spoken, the taint of drink in the teetotal home, or the first fight with poverty) was the deadly illness which fell upon him, at the end of his first flashing career as a Saturday Reviewer. I know it would goad Shaw to madness to suggest that sickness could have softened him. That is why I suggest it. But I say for his comfort that I think it hardened him also; if that can be called hardening which is only the strengthening of our souls to meet some dreadful reality. At least it is certain that the larger spiritual ambitions, the desire to find a faith and found a church, come after that time. I also mention it because there is hardly anything else to mention; his life is singularly free from landmarks, while his literature is so oddly full of surprises. His marriage to Miss Payne-Townsend, which occurred not long after his illness, was one of those quite successful things which are utterly silent. The placidity of his married life may be sufficiently indicated by saying that (as far as I can make out) the most important events in it were rows about the Executive of the Fabian Society. If such ripples do not express a still and lake-like life, I do not know what would. Honestly, the only thing in his later career that can be called an event is the stand made by Shaw at the Fabians against the sudden assault of Mr. H. G. Wells, which, after scenes of splendid exasperations, ended in Wells' resignation. There was another slight ruffling of the calm when Bernard Shaw said some quite sensible things about Sir Henry Irving. But on the whole we confront the composure of one who has come into his own.

The method of his life has remained mostly unchanged. And there is a great deal of method in his life; I can hear some people murmuring something about method in his madness. He is not only neat and businesslike; but, unlike some literary men I know, does not conceal the fact. Having all the talents proper to an author, he delights to prove that he has also all the talents proper to a publisher; or even to a publisher's clerk. Though many looking at his light brown clothes would call him a Bohemian, he really hates and despises Bohemianism; in the sense that he hates and despises disorder and uncleanness and irresponsibility. All that part of him is peculiarly normal and efficient. He gives good advice; he always answers letters, and answers them in a decisive and very legible hand. He has said himself that the only educational art that he thinks important is that of being able to jump off tram-cars at the proper moment. Though a rigid vegetarian, he is quite regular and rational in his meals; and though he detests sport, he takes quite sufficient exercise. While he has always made a mock of science in theory, he is by nature prone to meddle with it in practice. He is fond of photographing, and even more fond of being photographed. He maintained (in one of his moments of mad modernity) that photography was a finer thing than portrait-painting, more exquisite and more imaginative; he urged the characteristic argument that none of his own photographs were like each other or like him. But he would certainly wash the chemicals off his hands the instant after an experiment; just as he would wash the blood off his hands the instant after a Socialist massacre. He cannot endure stains or accretions; he is of that temperament which feels tradition itself to be a coat of dust; whose temptation it is to feel nothing but a sort of foul accumulation or living disease even in the creeper upon the cottage or the moss upon the grave. So thoroughly are his tastes those of the civilised modern man that if it had not been for the fire in him of justice and anger he might have been the most trim and modern among the millions whom he shocks: and his bicycle and brown hat have been no menace in Brixton. But God sent among those suburbans one who was a prophet as well as a sanitary inspector. He had every qualification for living in a villa — except the necessary indifference to his brethren living in pigstyes. But for the small fact that he hates with a sickening hatred the hypocrisy and class cruelty, he would really accept and admire the bathroom and the bicycle and asbestos-stove, having no memory of rivers or of roaring fires. In these things, like Mr. Straker, he is the New Man. But for his great soul he might have accepted modern civilisation; it was a wonderful escape. This man whom men so foolishly call crazy and anarchic has really a dangerous affinity to the fourth-rate perfections of our provincial and Protestant civilisation. He might even have been respectable if he had had less selfrespect.

His fulfilled fame and this tone of repose and reason in his life, together with the large circle of his private kindness and the regard of his fellow-artists, should permit us to end the record in a tone of almost patriarchal quiet. If I wished to complete such a picture I could add many touches: that he has consented to wear evening dress; that he has supported the *Times* Book Club; and that his beard has turned grey; the last to his regret, as he wanted it to remain red till they had completed colour-photography. He can mix with the most conservative statesmen; his tone grows continuously more gentle in the matter of religion. It would be easy to end with the lion lying down with the lamb, the wild Irishman tamed or taming everybody, Shaw reconciled to the British public as the British public is certainly largely reconciled to Shaw.

But as I put these last papers together, having finished this rude study, I hear a piece of news. His latest play, *The Showing Up of Blanco Posnet*, has been forbidden by the Censor. As far as I can discover, it has been forbidden because one of the characters professes a belief in God and states his conviction that God has got him. This is wholesome; this is like one crack of thunder in a clear sky. Not so easily does the prince of this world forgive. Shaw's religious training and instinct is not mine, but in all honest religion there is something that is hateful to the prosperous compromise of our time. You are free in our time to say that God does not exist; you are free to say that He exists and is evil; you are free to say (like poor old Renan) that He would like to exist if He could. You may talk of God as a metaphor or a mystification; you may water Him down with gallons of long words, or boil Him to the rags of metaphysics; and it is not merely that nobody punishes, but nobody protests. But if you speak of God as a fact, as a thing like a tiger, as a reason for changing one's conduct, then the modern world will stop you somehow if it can. We are long past talking about whether an unbeliever should be punished for being irreverent. It is now thought irreverent to be a believer. I end where I began: it is the old Puritan in Shaw that jars the modern world like an electric shock. That vision with which I meant to end, that vision of culture and commonsense, of red brick and brown flannel, of the modern clerk broadened enough to embrace Shaw and Shaw softened enough to embrace the clerk, all that vision of a new London begins to fade and alter. The red brick begins to burn red-hot; and the smoke from all the chimneys has a strange smell. I find myself back in the fumes in which I started.... Perhaps I have been misled by small modernities. Perhaps what I have called fastidiousness is a divine fear. Perhaps what I have called coldness is a predestinate and ancient endurance. The vision of the Fabian villas grows fainter and fainter, until I see only a void place across which runs Bunyan's Pilgrim with his fingers in his ears.

Bernard Shaw has occupied much of his life in trying to elude his followers. The fox has enthusiastic followers, and Shaw seems to regard his in much the same way. This man whom men accuse of bidding for applause seems to me to shrink even from assent. If you agree with Shaw he is very likely to contradict you; I have contradicted Shaw throughout, that is why I come at last almost to agree with him. His critics have accused him of vulgar self-advertisement; in his relation to his followers he seems to me rather marked with a sort of mad modesty. He seems to wish to fly from agreement, to have as few followers as possible. All this reaches back, I think, to the three roots from which this meditation grew. It is partly the mere impatience and irony of the Irishman. It is partly the thought of the Calvinist that the host of God should be thinned rather than thronged; that Gideon must reject soldiers rather than recruit them. And it is partly, alas, the unhappy Progressive trying to be in front of his own religion, trying to destroy his own idol and even to desecrate his own tomb. But from whatever causes, this furious escape from popularity has involved Shaw in some perversities and refinements which are almost mere insincerities, and which make it necessary to disentangle the good he has done from the evil in this dazzling course. I will attempt some summary by stating the three things in which his influence seems to me thoroughly good and the three in which it seems bad. But for the pleasure of ending on the finer note I will speak first of those that seem bad.

The primary respect in which Shaw has been a bad influence is that he has encouraged fastidiousness. He has made men dainty about their moral meals. This is indeed the root of his whole objection to romance. Many people have objected to romance for being too airy and exquisite. Shaw objects to romance for being too rank and coarse. Many have despised romance because it is unreal; Shaw really hates it because it is a great deal too real. Shaw dislikes romance as he dislikes beef and beer, raw brandy or raw beefsteaks. Romance is too masculine for his taste. You will find throughout his criticisms, amid all their truth, their wild justice or pungent impartiality, a curious undercurrent of prejudice upon one point: the preference for the refined rather than the rude or ugly. Thus he will dislike a joke because it is coarse without asking if it is really immoral. He objects to a man sitting down on his hat, whereas the austere moralist should only object to his sitting down on someone else's hat. This sensibility is barren because it is universal. It is useless to object to man being made ridiculous. Man is born ridiculous, as can easily be seen if you look at him soon after he is born. It is grotesque to drink beer, but it is equally grotesque to drink soda-water; the grotesqueness lies in the act of filling yourself like a bottle through a hole. It is undignified to walk with a drunken stagger; but it is fairly undignified to walk at all, for all walking is a sort of balancing, and there is always in the human being something of a quadruped on its hind legs. I do not say he would be more dignified if he went on all fours; I do not know that he ever is dignified except when he is dead. We shall not be refined till we are refined into dust. Of course it is only because he is not wholly an animal that man sees he is a rum animal; and if man on his hind legs is in an artificial attitude, it is only because, like a dog, he is begging or saying thank you.

Everything important is in that sense absurd from the grave baby to the grinning skull; everything practical is a practical joke. But throughout Shaw's comedies, curiously enough, there is a certain kicking against this great doom of laughter. For instance, it is the first duty of a man who is in love to make a fool of himself; but Shaw's heroes always seem to flinch from this, and attempt, in airy, philosophic revenge, to make a fool of the woman first. The attempts of Valentine and Charteris to divide their perceptions from their desires, and tell the woman she is worthless even while trying to win her, are sometimes almost torturing to watch; it is like seeing a man trying to play a different tune with each hand. I fancy this agony is not only in the spectator, but in the dramatist as well. It is Bernard Shaw struggling with his reluctance to do anything so ridiculous as make a proposal. For there are two types of great humorist:

those who love to see a man absurd and those who hate to see him absurd. Of the first kind are Rabelais and Dickens; of the second kind are Swift and Bernard Shaw.

So far as Shaw has spread or helped a certain modern reluctance or *mauvaise honte* in these grand and grotesque functions of man I think he has definitely done harm. He has much influence among the young men; but it is not an influence in the direction of keeping them young. One cannot imagine him inspiring any of his followers to write a war-song or a drinking-song or a love-song, the three forms of human utterance which come next in nobility to a prayer. It may seem odd to say that the net effect of a man so apparently impudent will be to make men shy. But it is certainly the truth. Shyness is always the sign of a divided soul; a man is shy because he somehow thinks his position at once despicable and important. If he were without humility he would not care; and if he were without pride he would not care. Now the main purpose of Shaw's theoretic teaching is to declare that we ought to fulfil these great functions of life, that we ought to eat and drink and love. But the main tendency of his habitual criticism is to suggest that all the sentiments, professions, and postures of these things are not only comic but even contemptibly comic, follies and almost frauds. The result would seem to be that a race of young men may arise who do all these things, but do them awkwardly. That which was of old a free and hilarious function becomes an important and embarrassing necessity. Let us endure all the pagan pleasures with a Christian patience. Let us eat, drink, and be serious.

The second of the two points on which I think Shaw has done definite harm is this: that he has (not always or even as a rule intentionally) increased that anarchy of thought which is always the destruction of thought. Much of his early writing has encouraged among the modern youth that most pestilent of all popular tricks and fallacies; what is called the argument of progress. I mean this kind of thing. Previous ages were often, alas, aristocratic in politics or clericalist in religion; but they were always democratic in philosophy; they appealed to man, not to particular men. And if most men were against an idea, that was so far against it. But nowadays that most men are against a thing is thought to be in its favour; it is vaguely supposed to show that some day most men will be for it. If a man says that cows are reptiles, or that Bacon wrote Shakespeare, he can always quote the contempt of his contemporaries as in some mysterious way proving the complete conversion of posterity. The objections to this theory scarcely need any elaborate indication. The final objection to it is that it amounts to this: say anything, however idiotic, and you are in advance of your age. This kind of stuff must be stopped. The sort of democrat who appeals to the babe unborn must be classed with the sort of aristocrat who appeals to his deceased great-grandfather. Both should be sharply reminded that they are appealing to individuals whom they well know to be at a disadvantage in the matter of prompt and witty reply. Now although Bernard Shaw has survived this simple confusion, he has in his time greatly contributed to it. If there is, for instance, one thing that is really rare in Shaw it is hesitation. He makes up his mind quicker than a calculating boy or a county magistrate. Yet on this subject of the next change in ethics he has felt hesitation, and being a strictly honest man has expressed it.

"I know no harder practical question than how much selfishness one ought to stand from a gifted person for the sake of his gifts or on the chance of his being right in the long run. The Superman will certainly come like a thief in the night, and be shot at accordingly; but we cannot leave our property wholly undefended on that account. On the other hand, we cannot ask the Superman simply to add a higher set of virtues to current respectable morals; for he is undoubtedly going to empty a good deal of respectable morality out like so much dirty water, and replace it by new and strange customs, shedding old obligations and accepting new and heavier ones. Every step of his progress must horrify conventional people; and if it were possible for even the most superior man to march ahead all the time, every pioneer of the march towards the Superman would be crucified."

When the most emphatic man alive, a man unmatched in violent precision of statement, speaks with such avowed vagueness and doubt as this, it is no wonder if all his more weak-minded followers are in a mere whirlpool of uncritical and unmeaning innovation. If the superior person will be apparently criminal, the most probable result is simply that the criminal person will think himself superior. A very slight knowledge of human nature is required in the matter. If the Superman may possibly be a thief, you may bet your boots that the next thief will be a Superman. But indeed the Supermen (of whom I have met many) have generally been more weak in the head than in the moral conduct; they have simply offered the first fancy which occupied their minds as the new morality. I fear that Shaw had a way of encouraging these follies. It is obvious from the passage I have quoted that he has no way of restraining them.

The truth is that all feeble spirits naturally live in the future, because it is featureless; it is a soft job; you can make it what you like. The next age is blank, and I can paint it freely with my favourite colour. It requires real courage to face the past, because the past is full of facts which cannot be got over; of men certainly wiser than we and of things done which we could not do. I know I cannot write a poem as good as *Lycidas*. But it is always easy to say that the particular sort of poetry I can write will be the poetry of the future.

This I call the second evil influence of Shaw: that he has encouraged many to throw themselves for justification upon the shapeless and the unknown. In this, though courageous himself, he has encouraged cowards, and though sincere himself, has helped a mean escape. The third evil in his influence can, I think, be much more shortly dealt with. He has to a very slight extent, but still perceptibly, encouraged a kind of charlatanism of utterance among those who possess his Irish impudence without his Irish virtue. For instance, his amusing trick of self-praise is perfectly hearty and humorous in him; nay, it is even humble; for to confess vanity is itself humble. All that is the matter with the proud is that they will not admit that they are vain. Therefore when Shaw says that he alone is able to write such and such admirable work, or that he has just utterly wiped out some celebrated opponent, I for one never feel anything offensive in the tone, but, indeed, only the unmistakable intonation of a friend's voice. But I have noticed among younger, harder, and much shallower men a certain disposition to ape this insolent ease and certitude, and that without any fundamental frankness or mirth. So far the influence is bad. Egoism can be learnt as a lesson like any other "ism." It is not so easy to learn an Irish accent or a good temper. In its lower forms the thing becomes a most unmilitary trick of announcing the victory before one has gained it.

When one has said those three things, one has said, I think, all that can be said by way of blaming Bernard Shaw. It is significant that he was never blamed for any of these things by the Censor. Such censures as the attitude of that official involves may be dismissed with a very light sort of disdain. To represent Shaw as profane or provocatively indecent is not a matter for discussion at all; it is a disgusting criminal libel upon a particularly respectable gentleman of the middle classes, of refined tastes and somewhat Puritanical views. But while the negative defence of Shaw is easy, the just praise of him is almost as complex as it is necessary; and I shall devote the last few pages of this book to a triad corresponding to the last one — to the three important elements in which the work of Shaw has been good as well as great.

In the first place, and quite apart from all particular theories, the world owes thanks to Bernard Shaw for having combined being intelligent with being intelligible. He has popularised philosophy, or rather he has repopularised it, for philosophy is always popular, except in peculiarly corrupt and oligarchic ages like our own. We have passed the age of the demagogue, the man who has little to say and says it loud. We have come to the age of the mystagogue or don, the man who has nothing to say, but says it softly and impressively in an indistinct whisper. After all, short words must mean something, even if they mean filth or lies; but long words may sometimes mean literally nothing, especially if they are used (as they mostly are in modern books and magazine articles) to balance and modify each other. A plain figure 4, scrawled in chalk anywhere, must always mean something; it must always mean $2 + 2$. But the most enormous and mysterious algebraic equation, full of letters, brackets, and fractions, may all cancel out at last and be equal to nothing. When a demagogue says to a mob, "There is the Bank of England, why shouldn't you have some of that money?" he says something which is at least as honest and intelligible as the figure 4. When a writer in the *Times* remarks, "We must raise the economic efficiency of the masses without diverting anything from those classes which represent the national prosperity and refinement," then his equation cancels out; in a literal and logical sense his remark amounts to nothing.

There are two kinds of charlatans or people called quacks to-day. The power of the first is that he advertises — and cures. The power of the second is that though he is not learned enough to cure he is much too learned to advertise. The former give away their dignity with a pound of tea; the latter are paid a pound of tea merely for being dignified. I think them the worse quacks of the two. Shaw is certainly of the other sort. Dickens, another man who was great enough to be a demagogue (and greater than Shaw because more heartily a demagogue), puts for ever the true difference between the demagogue and the mystagogue in *Dr. Marigold* : "Except that we're cheap-jacks and they're dear-jacks, I don't see any difference between us." Bernard Shaw is a great cheap-jack, with plenty of patter and I dare say plenty of nonsense, but with this also (which is not wholly unimportant), with goods to sell. People accuse such a man of self-advertisement. But at least the cheap-jack does advertise his wares, whereas the don or dear-jack advertises nothing except himself. His very silence, nay his very sterility, are supposed to be marks of the richness of his erudition. He is too learned to teach, and sometimes too wise even to talk. St. Thomas Aquinas said: "In auctore auctoritas." But there is more than one man at Oxford or Cambridge who is considered an authority because he has never been an author.

Against all this mystification both of silence and verbosity Shaw has been a splendid and smashing protest. He has stood up for the fact that philosophy is not the concern of those who pass through Divinity and Greats, but of those who pass through birth and death. Nearly all the most awful and abstruse statements can be put in words of one syllable, from "A child is born" to "A soul is damned." If the ordinary man may not discuss existence, why should he be asked to conduct it? About concrete matters indeed one naturally appeals to an oligarchy or select class. For information about Lapland I go to an aristocracy of Laplanders; for the ways of rabbits to an aristocracy of naturalists or, preferably, an aristocracy of poachers. But only mankind itself can bear witness to the abstract first principles of mankind, and in matters of theory I would always consult the mob. Only the mass of men, for instance, have authority to say whether life is good. Whether life is good is an especially mystical and delicate question, and, like all such questions, is asked in words of one syllable. It is also answered in words of one syllable, and Bernard Shaw (as also mankind) answers "yes."

This plain, pugnacious style of Shaw has greatly clarified all controversies. He has slain the polysyllable, that huge and slimy centipede which has sprawled over all the valleys of England like the "loathly worm" who was slain by the ancient knight. He does not think that difficult questions will be made simpler by using difficult words about them. He has achieved the admirable work, never to be mentioned without gratitude, of discussing Evolution without mentioning it. The good work is of course more evident in the case of philosophy than any other region; because the case of philosophy was a crying one. It was really preposterous that the things most carefully reserved for the study of two or three men should actually be the things common to all men. It was absurd that certain men should be experts on the special subject of everything. But he stood for much the same spirit and style in other matters; in economics, for example. There never has been a better popular economist; one more lucid, entertaining, consistent, and essentially exact. The very comicality of his examples makes them and their argument stick in the mind; as in the case I remember in which he said that the big shops had now to please everybody, and were not entirely dependent on the lady who sails in "to order four governesses and five grand pianos." He is always preaching collectivism; yet he does not very often name it. He does not talk about collectivism, but about cash; of which the populace feel a much more definite need. He talks about cheese, boots, perambulators, and how people are really to live. For him economics really means housekeeping, as it does in Greek. His difference from the orthodox economists, like most of his differences, is very different from the attacks made by the main body of Socialists. The old Manchester economists are generally attacked for being too gross and material. Shaw really attacks them for not being gross or material enough. He thinks that they hide themselves behind long words, remote hypotheses or unreal generalisations. When the orthodox economist begins with his correct and primary formula, "Suppose there is a Man on an Island — —" Shaw is apt to interrupt him sharply, saying, "There is a Man in the Street."

The second phase of the man's really fruitful efficacy is in a sense the converse of this. He has improved philosophic discussions by making them more popular. But he has also improved popular amusements by making them more philosophic. And by more philosophic I do not mean duller, but funnier; that is more varied. All real fun is in cosmic contrasts, which involve a view of the cosmos. But I know that this second strength in Shaw is really difficult to state and must be approached by explanations and even by eliminations. Let me say at once that I think nothing of Shaw or anybody else merely for playing the daring sceptic. I do not think he has done any good or even achieved any effect simply by asking startling questions. It is possible that there have been ages so sluggish or automatic that anything that woke them up at all was a good thing. It is sufficient to be certain that ours is not such an age. We do not need waking up; rather we suffer from insomnia, with all its results of fear and exaggeration and frightful waking dreams. The modern mind is not a donkey which wants kicking to make it go on. The modern mind is more like a motor-car on a lonely road which two amateur motorists have been just clever enough to take to pieces, but are not quite clever enough to put together again. Under these circumstances kicking the car has never been found by the best experts to be effective. No one, therefore, does any good to our age merely by asking questions — unless he can answer the questions. Asking questions is already the fashionable and aristocratic sport which has brought most of us into the bankruptcy court. The note of our age is a note of interrogation. And the final point is so plain; no sceptical philosopher can ask any questions that may not equally be asked by a tired child on a hot afternoon. "Am I a boy? — Why am I a boy? — Why aren't I a chair? — What is a chair?" A child will sometimes ask questions of this sort for two hours. And the philosophers of Protestant Europe have asked them for two hundred years.

If that were all that I meant by Shaw making men more philosophic, I should put it not among his good influences but his bad. He did do that to some extent; and so far he is bad. But there is a much bigger and better sense in which he has been a philosopher. He has brought back into English drama all the streams of fact or tendency which are commonly called undramatic. They were there in Shakespeare's time; but they have scarcely been there since until Shaw. I mean that Shakespeare, being interested in everything, put everything into a play. If he had lately been thinking about the irony and even contradiction confronting us in self-preservation and suicide, he put it all into *Hamlet*. If he was annoyed by some passing boom in theatrical babies he put that into *Hamlet* too. He would put anything into *Hamlet* which he really thought was true, from his favourite nursery ballads to his personal (and perhaps unfashionable) conviction of the Catholic purgatory. There is no fact that strikes one, I think, about Shakespeare, except the fact of how dramatic he could be, so much as the fact of how undramatic he could be.

In this great sense Shaw has brought philosophy back into drama — philosophy in the sense of a certain freedom of the mind. This is not a freedom to think what one likes (which is absurd, for one can only think what one thinks); it is a freedom to think about what one likes, which is quite a different thing and the spring of all thought. Shakespeare (in a weak moment, I think) said that all the world is a stage. But Shakespeare acted on the much finer principle that a stage is all the world. So there are in all Bernard Shaw's plays patches of what people would call essentially undramatic stuff, which the dramatist puts in because he is honest and would rather prove his case than succeed with his play. Shaw has brought back into English drama that Shakespearian universality which, if you like, you can call Shakespearian irrelevance. Perhaps a better definition than either is a habit of thinking the truth worth telling even when you meet it by accident. In Shaw's plays one meets an incredible number of truths by accident.

To be up to date is a paltry ambition except in an almanac, and Shaw has sometimes talked this almanac philosophy. Nevertheless there is a real sense in which the phrase may be wisely used, and that is in cases where some stereotyped version of what is happening hides what is really happening from our eyes. Thus, for instance, newspapers are never up to date. The men who write leading articles are always behind the times, because they are in a hurry. They are forced to fall back on their oldfashioned view of things; they have no time to fashion a new one. Everything that is done in a hurry is certain to be antiquated; that is why modern industrial civilisation bears so curious a resemblance to barbarism. Thus when newspapers say that the *Times* is a solemn old Tory paper, they are out of date; their talk is behind the talk in Fleet Street. Thus when newspapers say that Christian dogmas are crumbling, they are out of date; their talk is behind the talk in public-houses. Now in this sense Shaw has kept in a really stirring sense up to date. He has introduced into the theatre the things that no one else had introduced into a theatre — the things in the street outside. The theatre is a sort of thing which proudly sends a hansom-cab across the stage as Realism, while everybody outside is whistling for motor-cabs.

Consider in this respect how many and fine have been Shaw's intrusions into the theatre with the things that were really going on. Daily papers and daily matinées were still gravely explaining how much modern war depended on gunpowder. *Arms and the Man* explained how much modern war depends on chocolate. Every play and paper described the Vicar who was a mild Conservative. *Candida* caught hold of the modern Vicar who is an advanced Socialist. Numberless magazine articles and society comedies describe the emancipated woman as new and wild. Only *You Never Can Tell* was young enough to see that the emancipated woman is already old and respectable. Every comic paper has caricatured the uneducated upstart. Only the author of *Man and Superman* knew enough about the modern world to caricature the educated upstart — the man Straker who can quote Beaumarchais, though he cannot pronounce him. This is the second real and great work of Shaw — the letting in of the world on to the stage, as the rivers were let in upon the Augean Stable. He has let a little of the Haymarket into the Haymarket Theatre. He has permitted some whispers of the Strand to enter the Strand Theatre. A variety of solutions in philosophy is as silly as it is in arithmetic, but one may be justly proud of a variety of materials for a solution. After Shaw, one may say, there is nothing that cannot be introduced into a play if one can make it decent, amusing, and relevant. The state of a man's health, the religion of his childhood, his ear for music, or his ignorance of cookery can all be made vivid if they have anything to do with the subject. A soldier may mention the commissariat as well as the cavalry; and, better still, a priest may mention theology as well as religion. That is being a philosopher; that is bringing the universe on the stage.

Lastly, he has obliterated the mere cynic. He has been so much more cynical than anyone else for the public good that no one has dared since to be really cynical for anything smaller. The Chinese crackers of the frivolous cynics fail to excite us after the dynamite of the serious and aspiring cynic. Bernard Shaw and I (who are growing grey together) can remember an epoch which many of his followers do not know: an epoch of real pessimism. The years from 1885 to 1898 were like the hours of afternoon in a rich house with large rooms; the hours before teatime. They believed in nothing except good manners; and the essence of good manners is to conceal a yawn. A yawn may be defined as a silent yell. The power which the young pessimist of that time showed in this direction would have astonished anyone but him. He yawned so wide as to swallow the world. He swallowed the world like an unpleasant pill before retiring to an eternal rest. Now the last and best glory of Shaw is that in the circles where this creature was found, he is not. He has not been killed (I don't know exactly why), but he has actually turned into a Shaw idealist. This is no exaggeration. I meet men who, when I knew them in 1898, were just a little too lazy to destroy the universe. They are now conscious of not being quite worthy to abolish some prison regulations. This destruction and conversion seem to me the mark of something actually great. It is always great to destroy a type without destroying a man. The followers of Shaw are optimists; some of them are so simple as even to use the word. They are sometimes rather pallid optimists, frequently very worried optimists, occasionally, to tell the truth, rather cross optimists: but they not pessimists; they can exult though they cannot laugh. He has at least withered up among them the mere pose of impossibility. Like every great teacher, he has cursed the barren fig-tree. For nothing except that impossibility is really impossible.

I know it is all very strange. From the height of eight hundred years ago, or of eight hundred years hence, our age must look incredibly odd. We call the twelfth century ascetic. We call our own time hedonist and full of praise and pleasure. But in the ascetic age the love of life was evident and enormous, so that it had to be restrained. In an hedonist age pleasure has always sunk low, so that it has to be encouraged. How high the sea of human happiness rose in the Middle Ages, we now only know by the colossal walls that they built to keep it in bounds. How low human happiness sank in the twentieth century our children will only know by these extraordinary modern books, which tell people that it is a duty to be cheerful and that life is not so bad after all. Humanity never produces optimists till it has ceased to produce happy men. It is strange to be obliged to impose a holiday like a fast, and to drive men to a banquet with spears. But this shall be written of our time: that when the spirit who denies besieged the last citadel, blaspheming life itself, there were some, there was one especially, whose voice was heard and whose spear was never broken.

THE END

Shaw wrote many of his works in this summer house in his garden.
Shaw's ashes were scattered in his garden in Hertfordshire

Love Among The Artists

The Author to the Reader

Dear Sir or Madam:

Will you allow me a word of personal explanation now that I am, for the second time, offering you a novel which is not the outcome of my maturer experience and better sense? If you have read my *Irrational Knot* to the bitter end, you will not accuse me of mock modesty when I admit that it was very long; that it did not introduce you to a single person you could conceivably have been glad to know; and that your knowledge of the world must have forewarned you that no satisfactory ending was possible. You may, it is true, think that a story teller should not let a question of mere possibility stand between his audience and the satisfaction of a happy ending. Yet somehow my conscience stuck at it; for I am not a professional liar: I am even ashamed of the extent to which in my human infirmity I have been an amateur one. No: my stories were meant to be true *ex hypothesi* : the persons were fictitious; but had they been real, they must (or so I thought at the time) have acted as I said. For, if you can believe such a prodigy, I was but an infant of twenty-four when, being at that time, one of the unemployed, I sat down to mend my straitened fortunes by writing *The Irrational Knot* . I had done the same thing once before; and next year, still unemployed, I did it again. That third attempt of mine is about to see the light in this volume. And now a few words of warning to you before you begin it.

(1)Though the wisdom of the book is the fruit of a quarter century's experience, yet the earlier years of that period were much preoccupied with questions of bodily growth and nutrition; so that it may be as well to bear in mind that even the youngest of us may be wrong sometimes. (2)*Love among the Artists* is what is called a novel with a purpose; I will not undertake to say at this distant me what the main purpose was; but I remember that I had a notion of illustrating the difference between that enthusiasm for the fine arts which people gather from reading about them, and the genuine artistic faculty which cannot help creating, interpreting, and unaffectedly enjoying music and pictures. (3)This book has no winding-up at the end. Mind: it is not, as in *The Irrational Knot* , a case of the upshot being unsatisfactory! There is absolutely no upshot at all. The parties are married in the middle of the book; and they do not elope with or divorce one another, or do anything unusual or improper. When as much is told concerning them as seemed to me at the time germane to my purpose, the novel breaks off. But, if you prefer something more conclusive, pray do not scruple to add a final chapter of your own invention. (4)If you find yourself displeased with my story, remember that it is not I, but the generous and appreciative publisher of the book, who puts it forward as worth reading. I shall polish it up for you the best way I can, and here and there remove some absurdity out of which I have grown since I wrote it, but I cannot substantially improve it, much less make it what a novel ought to be; for I have given up novel writing these many years, during which I have lost the impudence of the apprentice without gaining the skill of the master.

There is an end to all things, even to stocks of unpublished manuscript. It may be a relief to you to know that when this "Love among the Artists" shall have run its course, you need apprehend no more furbished-up early attempts at fiction from me. I have written but five novels in my life; and of these there will remain then unpublished only the first — a very remarkable work, I assure you, but hardly one which I should be well advised in letting loose whilst my livelihood depends on my credit as a literary workman.

I can recall a certain difficulty, experienced even whilst I was writing the book, in remembering what it was about. Twice I clean forgot the beginning, and had to read back, as I might have read any other man's novel, to learn the story. If I could not remember then, how can I presume on my knowledge of the book now so far as to make promises about it? But I suspect you will find yourself in less sordid company than that into which *The Irrational Knot* plunged you. And I can guarantee you against any plot. You will be candidly dealt with. None of the characters will turn out to be somebody else in the last chapter: no violent accidents or strokes of pure luck will divert events from their normal course: no forger, long lost heir, detective, nor any commonplace of the police court or of the realm of romance shall insult your understanding, or tempt you to read on when you might better be in bed or attending to your business. By this time you should be eager to be at the story. Meanwhile I must not forget that it is only by your exceptional indulgence that I have been suffered to detain you so long about a personal matter; and so I thank you and proceed to business.

29, Fitzroy Square, London, W.

BOOK I

CHAPTER I

One fine afternoon during the Easter holidays, Kensington Gardens were in their freshest spring green, and the steps of the Albert Memorial dotted with country visitors, who alternately conned their guidebooks and stared up at the golden gentleman under the shrine, trying to reconcile the reality with the description, whilst their Cockney friends, indifferent to shrine and statue, gazed idly at the fashionable drive below. One group in particular was composed of an old gentleman intent upon the Memorial, a young lady intent upon her guidebook, and a young gentleman intent upon the young lady. She looked a woman of force and intelligence; and her boldly curved nose and chin, elastic step, upright carriage, resolute bearing, and thick black hair, secured at the base of the neck by a broad crimson ribbon, made those whom her appearance pleased think her strikingly handsome. The rest thought her strikingly ugly; but she would perhaps have forgiven them for the sake of the implied admission that she was at least not commonplace ; for her costume, consisting of an ample black cloak lined with white fur, and a broad hat with red feather and underbrim of sea green silk, was of the sort affected by women who strenuously cultivate themselves, and insist upon their individuality. She was not at all like her father, the grey-haired gentleman who, scanning the Memorial with eager watery eyes, was uttering occasional ejaculations of wonder at the sum it must have cost. The younger man, who might have been thirty or thereabout, was slight and of moderate stature. His fine hair, of a pale golden color, already turning to a silvery brown, curled delicately over his temples, where it was beginning to wear away. A short beard set off his features, which were those of a man of exceptional sensitiveness and refinement. He was the Londoner of the party; and he waited with devoted patience whilst his companions satisfied their curiosity. It was pleasant to watch them, for he was not gloating over her, nor she too conscious that she was making the sunshine brighter for him; and yet they were quite evidently young lovers, and as happy as people at their age know how to be.

At last the old gentleman's appetite for the Memorial yielded to the fatigue of standing on the stone steps and looking upwards. He proposed that they should find a seat and examine the edifice from a little distance.

"I think I see a bench down there with only one person on it, Mary," he said, as they descended the steps at the west side. "Can you see whether he is respectable?"

The young lady, who was shortsighted, placed a pair of glasses on her salient nose, lifted her chin, and deliberately examined the person on the bench. He was a short, thick-chested young man, in an old creased frock coat, with a worn-out hat and no linen visible. His skin, pitted by smallpox, seemed grained with black, as though he had been lately in a coal mine, and had not yet succeeded in toweling the coal-dust from his pores. He sat with his arms folded, staring at the ground before him. One hand was concealed under his arm: the other displayed itself, thick in the palm, with short fingers, and nails bitten to the quick. He was clean shaven, and had a rugged, resolute mouth, a short nose, marked nostrils, dark eyes, and black hair, which curled over his low, broad forehead.

"He is certainly not a handsome man," said the lady; "but he will do us no harm, I suppose?"

"Of course not," said the younger gentleman seriously. "But I can get some chairs, if you prefer them."

"Nonsense! I was only joking." As she spoke, the man on the bench looked up at her; and the moment she saw his eyes, she began to stand in some awe of him. His vague stare changed to a keen scrutiny, which she returned hardily. Then he looked for a moment at her dress; glanced at her companions; and relapsed into his former attitude.

The bench accommodated four persons easily. The old gentleman sat at the unoccupied end, next his daughter. Their friend placed himself between her and the man, at whom she presently stole another look. His attention was again aroused: this time he was looking at a child who was eating an apple near him. His expression gave the lady an uncomfortable sensation. The child, too, caught sight of him, and stopped eating to regard him mistrustfully. He smiled with grim good humor, and turned his eyes to the gravel once more.

"It is certainly a magnificent piece of work, Herbert," said the old gentleman. "To you, as an artist, it must be a treat indeed. I don't know enough about art to appreciate it properly. Bless us! And are all those knobs made of precious stones?"

"More or less precious: yes, I believe so, Mr. Sutherland," said Herbert, smiling.

"I must come and look at it again," said Mr. Sutherland, turning from the memorial, and putting his spectacles on the bench beside him. "It is quite a study. I wish I had this business of Charlie's off my mind."

"You will find a tutor for him without any difficulty," said Herbert. "There are hundreds to choose from in London."

"Yes; but if there were a thousand, Charlie would find a new objection to every one of them. You see the difficulty is the music."

Herbert, incommoded by a sudden movement of the strange man, got a little nearer to Mary, and replied, "I do not think the music ought to present much difficulty. Many young men qualifying for holy orders are very glad to obtain private tutorships; and nowadays a clergyman is expected to have some knowledge of music."

"Yes." said the lady; "but what is the use of that when Charlie expressly objects to clergymen? I sympathize with him there, for once. Divinity students are too narrow and dogmatic to be comfortable to live with."

"There!" exclaimed Mr. Sutherland, suddenly indignant: "you are beginning to make objections. Do you expect to get an angel from heaven to teach Charlie?"

"No, papa; but I doubt if anything less will satisfy him."

"I will speak to some of my friends about it," said Herbert. "There is no hurry for a week or two, I suppose?"

"Oh, no, none whatever," said Mr. Sutherland, ostentatiously serene after his outburst: "there is no hurry certainly. But Charlie must not be allowed to contract habits of idleness; and if the matter cannot be settled to his liking, I shall exert my authority, and select a tutor myself. I cannot understand his objection to the man we saw at Archdeacon Downes's. Can you, Mary?"

"I can understand that Charlie is too lazy to work," said Mary. Then, as if tired of the subject, she turned to Herbert, and said, "You have not yet told us when we may come to your studio and see *The Lady of Shalott*. I am very anxious to see it. I shall not mind its being unfinished."

"But I shall," said Herbert, suddenly becoming self-conscious and nervous. "I fear the picture will disappoint you in any case; but at least I wish it to be as good as I can make it, before you see it. I must ask you to wait until Thursday."

"Certainly, if you like," said Mary earnestly. She was about to add something, when Mr. Sutherland, who had become somewhat restive when the conversation turned upon pictures, declared that he had sat long enough. So they rose to go; and Mary turned to get a last glimpse of the man. He was looking at them with a troubled expression; and his lips were white. She thought he was about to speak, and involuntarily retreated a step. But he said nothing: only she was struck, as he composed himself in his old attitude, by his extreme dejection.

"Did you notice that man sitting next you?" she whispered to Herbert, when they had gone a little distance.

"Not particularly."

Do you think he is very poor?"

"He certainly does not appear to be very rich," said Herbert, looking back.

"I saw a very odd look in his eyes. I hope he is not hungry."

They stopped. Then Herbert walked slowly on. "I should think not so bad as that," he said. "I don't think his appearance would justify me in offering him —"

"Oh, dear, dear me!" said Mr Sutherland. "I am very stupid."

"What is the matter now, papa?"

"I have lost my glasses. I must have left them on that seat. Just wait one moment whilst I go back for them. No, no, Herbert: I will go back myself. I recollect exactly where I laid them down. I shall be back in a moment."

"Papa always takes the most exact notes of the places in which he puts things; and he always leaves them behind him after all," said Mary. "There is that man in precisely the same position as when we first saw him."

"No. He is saying something to your father, begging, I am afraid, or he would not stand up and lift his hat"

"How dreadful!"

Herbert laughed. "If, as you suspected, he is hungry, there is nothing very dreadful in it, poor fellow. It is natural enough."

"I did not mean that. I meant that it was dreadful to think of his being forced to beg. Papa has not given him anything — I wish he would. He evidently wants to get rid of him, and, of course, does not know how to do it. Let us go back."

"If you wish," said Herbert, reluctantly. "But I warn you that London is full of begging impostors."

Meanwhile Mr Sutherland, finding his spectacles where he had left them, took them up; wiped them with his handkerchief; and was turning away, when he found himself confronted by the strange man, who had risen.

"Sir," said the man, raising his shabby hat, and speaking in a subdued voice of remarkable power: "I have been a tutor; and I am a musician. I can convince you that I am an honest and respectable man. I am in need of employment. Something I overheard just now leads me to hope that you can assist me. I will —" Here the man, though apparently self-possessed, stopped as if his breath had failed him.

Mr. Sutherland's first impulse was to tell the stranger stiffly that he had no occasion for his services. But as there were no bystanders, and the man's gaze was impressive, he became nervous, and said hastily, "Oh, thank you: I have not decided what I shall do as yet." And he attempted to pass on.

The man immediately stepped aside, saying, "If you will favor me with your address, sir, I can send you testimonials which will prove that I have a right to seek such a place as you describe. If they do not satisfy you, I shall trouble you no further. Or if you will be so good as to accept my card, you can consider at your leisure whether to communicate with me or not."

"Certainly, I will take your card," said Mr. Sutherland, flurried and conciliatory. "Thank you. I can write to you, you, know, if I —"

"I am much obliged to you." Here he produced an ordinary visiting card, with the name "Mr. Owen Jack" engraved, and an address at Church Street, Kensington, written in a crabbed but distinct hand in the corner. Whilst Mr. Sutherland was pretending to read it, his daughter came up, purse in hand, hurrying before Herbert, whose charity she wished to forestall. Mr. Owen Jack looked at her; and she hid her purse quickly. "I am sorry to have delayed you, sir," he said. "Good morning." He raised his hat again, and walked away.

"Good morning, sir," said Mr Sutherland. "Lord bless me! that's a cool fellow," he added, recovering himself, and beginning to feel ashamed of having been so courteous to a poorly dressed stranger.

"What did he want, papa?"

"Indeed, my dear, he has shown me that we cannot be too careful of how we talk before strangers in London. By the purest accident —, the merest chance, I happened, whilst we were sitting here five minutes ago, to mention that we wanted a tutor for Charlie. This man was listening to us; and now he has offered himself for the place. Just fancy the quickness of that. Here is his card."

"Owen Jack!" said Mary. "What a name!"

"Did he overhear anything about the musical difficulty?" said Herbert. "Nature does not seem to have formed Mr Jack for the pursuit of a fine art."

"Yes: he caught up even that. According to his own account, he understands music — , in fact he can do everything."

Mary looked thoughtful. "After all," she said slowly, "he might suit us. He is certainly not handsome; but he does not seem stupid; and he would probably not want a large salary. I think Archdeacon Downes's man's terms are perfectly ridiculous."

"I am afraid it would be rather a dangerous experiment to give a responsible post to an individual whom we have chanced upon in a public park." said Herbert.

"Oh! out of the question," said Mr Sutherland. "I only took his card as the shortest way of getting rid of him. Perhaps I was wrong to do even that."

"Of course we should have to make inquiries," said Mary. "Somehow, I cannot get it out of my head that he is in very bad circumstances. He might be a gentleman. He does not look common."

"I agree with you so far," said Herbert. "And I am not sorry that such models are scarce. But of course you are quite right in desiring to assist this man, if he is unfortunate."

"Engaging a tutor is a very commonplace affair," said Mary; "but we may as well do some good by it if we can. Archdeacon Downes's man is in no immediate want of a situation: he has dozens of offers to choose from. Why not give the place to whoever is in the greatest need of it?"

"Very well," cried Mr. Sutherland. "Send after him and bring him home at once in a carriage and pair, since you have made up your mind not to hear to reason on the subject."

"After all," interposed Herbert, "it will do no harm to make a few inquiries. If you will allow me, I will take the matter in hand, so as to prevent all possibility of his calling on or disturbing you. Give me his card. I will write to him for his testimonials and references, and so forth; and if anything comes of it, I can then hand him over to you."

Mary locked gratefully at him, and said, "Do, papa. Let Mr Herbert write. It cannot possibly do any harm; and it will be no trouble to you."

"I do not object to the trouble" said Mr Sutherland. "I have taken the trouble of coming up to London, all the way from Windsor, solely for Charlie's sake. However, Herbert, perhaps you could manage the affair better than I. In fact, I should prefer to remain in the background. But then your time is valuable —"

"It will cost me only a few minutes to write the necessary letters — minutes that would be no better spent in any case. I assure you it will be practically no trouble to me."

"There, papa. Now we have settled that point, let us go on to the National Gallery. I wish we were going to your studio instead."

"You must not ask for that yet," said Herbert earnestly. "I promise you a special private view of *The Lady of Shalott* on Thursday next at latest."

CHAPTER II

Sir — In answer to your letter of the 12th instant, I am instructed by Miss Wilson to inform you that Mr. Jack was engaged here for ten months as professor of music and elocution. At the end of that period he refused to impart any further musical instruction, to three young ladies who desired a set of finishing lessons. He therefore considered himself bound to vacate his post, though Miss Wilson desires me to state expressly that she did not insist on that course. She has much pleasure in testifying to the satisfactory manner in which Mr. Jack maintained his authority in the school. He is an exacting teacher, but a patient and thoroughly capable one. During his stay at Alton College, his general conduct was irreproachable, and his marked personal influence gained for him the respect and good wishes of his pupils. —

I am, sir, your obedient servant,
Phillis Ward, F.C.P., *etc.*

14 West Precinct, Lipport Cathedral, South Wales.
Sir — Mr. Owen Jack is a native of this town, and was, in his boyhood, a member of the Cathedral Choir. He is respectably connected, and is personally known to me as a strictly honorable young man. He has musical talent of a certain kind, and is undoubtedly qualified to teach the rudiments of music, though he never, whilst under our guidance, gave any serious consideration to the higher forms of composition — more, I should add, from natural ineptitude than from want of energy and perseverance. I should be glad to hear of his obtaining a good position. —

Yours truly,
John Burton, Mus. Doc,

(*These were the replies to the inquiries about Mr Jack.*)

On Thursday afternoon Herbert stood before his easel, watching the light changing on his picture as the clouds shifted in the wind. At moments when the effect on the color pleased him, he wished that Mary would enter and see it so at her first glance. But as the afternoon wore it became duller; and when she at last arrived, he felt sorry he had not appointed one o'clock instead of three. She was accompanied by a tall lad of sixteen, with light blue eyes, fair hair, and an expression of irreverent good humor.
"How do you do" said Herbert. "Take care of those sketches, Charlie, old fellow. They are wet."
"Papa felt very tired: he thought it best to lie down for a little," said Mary, throwing off her cloak and appearing in a handsome dress of marmalade-colored silk. "He left the arrangements with Mr Jack to you. I suspect the dread of having to confront that mysterious stranger again had something to do with his fatigue. Is the Lady of Shalott ready to be seen?"
"The light is bad, I am sorry to say," said Herbert, lingering whilst Mary made a movement towards the easel.
"Don't push into the room like that, Mary," said Charlie. "Artists always have models in their studios. Give the young lady time to dress herself."
"There is a gleam of sunshine now," said Herbert, gravely, ignoring the lad. "Better have your first look at it while it lasts."
Mary placed herself before the easel, and gazed earnestly at it, finding that expression the easiest mask for a pang of disappointment which followed her first glance at the canvas. Herbert did not interrupt her for some moments. Then he said in a low voice: "You understand her action, do you not?"

"Yes. She has just seen the reflexion of Lancelot's figure in the mirror; and she is turning round to look at the reality."

"She has a deuce of a scraggy collar-bone," said Charlie.

"Oh, hush, Charlie," cried Mary, dreading that her brother might roughly express her own thoughts. "It seems quite right to me."

"The action of turning to look over her shoulder brings out the clavicle," said Herbert, smiling. "It is less prominent in the picture than it would be in nature: I had to soften it a little."

"Why didn't you paint her in some other attitude?" said Charlie.

"Because I happened to be aiming at the seizure of a poetic moment, and not at the representation of a pretty bust, my critical young friend," said Herbert quietly. "I think you are a little too close to the canvas, Miss Sutherland. Remember: the picture is not quite finished."

"She can't see anything unless she is close to it," said Charlie. "In fact, she never can get close enough, because her nose is longer than her sight. I don't understand that window up there above the woman's head. In reality there would be nothing to see through it except the sky. But there is a river, and flowers, and a man from the Lord Mayor's show. Are they up on a mountain?"

"Charlie, please stop. How can you be so rude?"

"Oh, I am accustomed to criticism," said Herbert. "You are a born critic, Charlie, since you cannot distinguish a mirror from a window. Have you never read your Tennyson?"

"Read Tennyson! I should think not. What sensible man would wade through the adventures of King Arthur and his knights? I one would think that Don Quixote had put a stop to that style of nonsense. Who was the Lady of Shalott? One of Sir Lancelot's, or Sir Galahad's, or Sir Somebody else's young women, I suppose."

"Do not mind him, Mr Herbert. It is pure affectation, He knows perfectly well."

"I don't," said Charlie; "and what's more, I don't believe you know either."

"The Lady of Shalott," said Herbert, "had a task to perform; and whilst she was at work upon it, she was, on pain of a curse, only to see the outer world as it was reflected by a mirror which hung above her head. One day, Sir Lancelot rode by; and when she saw his image she forgot the curse and turned to look at him."

"Very interesting and sensible," said Charlie.

"Why mightn't she as well have looked at the world Straight off out of the window, as seen it left handed in a mirror? The notion of a woman spending her life making a Turkey carpet is considered poetic, I suppose. What happened when she looked round?"

"Ah, I see you are interested. Nothing happened, except that the mirror broke and the lady died."

"Yes, and then got into a boat; rowed herself down to Hampton Court into the middle of a water party; and arranged her corpse in an attitude for the benefit of Lancelot. I've seen a picture of that.

"I see you do know something about Tennyson. Now, Miss Sutherland, what is your honest opinion?"

"I think it is beautiful. The coloring seemed rather dull to me at first, because I had been thinking of the river bank, the golden grain, the dazzling sun, the gorgeous loom, the armor of Sir Lancelot, instead of the Lady herself. But now that I have grasped your idea, there is a certain sadness and weakness about her that is very pathetic."

"Do you think the figure is weak?" said Herbert dubiously.

"Not really weak," replied Mary hastily. "I mean that the weakness proper to her story is very touchingly expressed."

"She means that it is too sober and respectable for her," said Charlie. "She likes screaming colors. If you had dressed the lady in red and gold; painted the Turkey carpet in full bloom; and made Lancelot like a sugar stick, she would have liked it better. That armor, by the bye, would be the better for a rub of emery paper."

"Armor is hard to manage, particularly in distance," said Herbert. "Here I had to contend with the additional difficulty of not making the reflexion in the mirror seem too real."

"You seem to have got over that pretty successfully," said Charlie.

"Yes," said Mary. "There is a certain unreality about the landscape and the figure in armor that I hardly understood at first. The more I strive to exercise my judgment upon art, the more I feel my ignorance. I wish you would always tell me when make foolish comments. There is someone knocking, I think."

"It is only the housekeeper," said Herbert, opening the door.

"Mr Jack, sir," said the housekeeper.

"Dear me! we must have been very late," said Mary. "It is four o'clock. Now Charlie, pray behave like a gentleman."

"I suppose he had better come in here," said Herbert. "Or would you rather not meet him?"

"Oh, I must meet him. Papa told me particularly to speak to him myself."

Mr Jack was accordingly shewn in by the housekeeper. this time, he displayed linen — a clean collar; and he carried a new hat. He made a formal bow, and looked at the artist and his guests, who became a little nervous.

"Good evening, Mr Jack," said Herbert. "I see you got my letter."

"You are Mr Herbert?" said Jack, in his resonant voice which, in the lofty studio, had a bright, close quality like the middle notes of a trumpet. Herbert nodded. "You are not the gentleman to whom I spoke on Saturday?"

"No. Mr Sutherland is not well; and I am acting for him. This is the young gentleman whom I mentioned to you."

Charlie blushed, and grinned. Then, seeing a humorous wrinkling in the stranger's face, he stepped forward and offered him his hand. Jack shook it heartily. "I shall get on very well with you," he said, "if you think you will like me as a tutor."

"Charlie never works," said Mary: "that is his great failing, Mr Jack."

"You have no right to say that," said Charlie, reddening. "How do you know whether I work or not? I can make a start with Mr Jack without being handicapped by your amiable recommendations."

"This is Miss Sutherland," said Herbert, interposing quickly. "She is the mistress of Mr Sutherland's household; and she will explain to you how you will be circumstanced as regards your residence with the family."

Jack bowed again. "I should like to know, first, at what studies this young gentleman requires my assistance."

"I want to learn something about music — about the theory of music, you know," said Charlie; "and I can grind at anything else you like."

"His general education must not be sacrificed to the music," said Mary anxiously.

"Oh! don't you be afraid of my getting off too easily," said Charlie. "I dare say Mr Jack knows his business without being told it by you."

"Pray don't interrupt me, Charlie. I wish you would go into the next room and look at the sketches. I shall have to arrange matters with Mr Jack which do not concern you."

"Very well," said Charlie, sulkily. "I don't want to interfere with your arrangements; but don't you interfere with mine. Let Mr Jack form his own opinion of me; and keep yours to yourself." Then he left the studio.

"If there is to be any serious study of music — I understood from Mr. Herbert that your young brother desires to make it his profession — other matters must give place to it," said Jack bluntly. "A little experience will shew us the best course to take with him."

"Yes," said Mary. After hesitating a moment she added timidly, "Then you are willing to undertake his instruction?"

"I am willing, so far," said Jack.

Mary looked nervously at Herbert, who smiled, and said, "Since we are satisfied on that point, the only remaining question, I presume, is one of terms."

"Sir," said Jack abruptly, "I hate business and know nothing about it. Therefore excuse me if I put my terms in my own way. If I am to live with Mr Sutherland at Windsor, I shall want, besides food and lodging, a reasonable time to myself every day, with permission to use Miss Sutherland's piano when I can do so without disturbing anybody, and money enough to keep me decently clothed, and not absolutely penniless. I will say thirty-five pounds a year."

"Thirty-five pounds a year" repeated Herbert. "To confess the truth, I am not a man of business myself; but that seems quite reasonable."

"Oh, quite," said Mary. "I think papa would not mind giving more."

"It is enough for me," said Jack, with something like a suppressed chuckle at Mary's simplicity. "Or, I will take a church organ in the neighborhood, if you can procure it for me, in lieu of salary."

"I think we had better adhere to the usual arrangement," said Herbert. Jack nodded, and said, "I have no further conditions to make."

"Do you wish to say anything?" said Herbert, looking inquiringly at Mary.

"No, I — I think not. I thought Mr. Jack would like to know something of our domestic arrangements."

"Thank you," said Jack curtly, "I need not trouble you. If your house does not suit me, I can complain, or leave it." He paused, and then added more courteously, "You may reassure yourself as to my personal comfort, Miss Sutherland. I am well used to greater privation than I am likely to suffer with you."

Mary had nothing more to say. Herbert coughed and turned his ring round a few times upon his finger. Jack stood motionless, and looked very ugly.

"Although Mr. Sutherland has left this matter altogether in my hands," said Herbert at last, "I hardly like to conclude it myself. He is staying close by, in Onslow Gardens. Would you mind calling on him now? If you will allow me, I will give you a note to the effect that our interview has been a satisfactory one." Jack bowed. "Excuse me for one moment. My writing materials are in the next room. I will say a word or two to Charlie, and send him in to you."

There was a mirror in the room, which Herbert had used as a model. It was so placed that Mary could see the image of the new tutor's face, as, being now alone with her, he looked for the first time at the picture. A sudden setting of his mouth and derisive twinkle in his eye shewed that he found something half ludicrous, half contemptible, in the work; and she, observing this, felt hurt, and began to repent having engaged him. Then the expression softened to one of compassion; he sighed as he turned away from the easel. Before she could speak Charlie entered, saying:

"I am to go back with you to Onslow Gardens, Mr Jack, if you don't mind."

"Oh, no, Charlie: you must stay with me," said Mary.

"Don't be alarmed: Adrian is going on to the Museum with you directly; and the housekeeper is here to do propriety. I have no particular fancy for lounging about that South Kensington crockery shop with you; and, besides, Mr Jack does not know his way to Jermyn's. Here is Adrian."

Herbert came in, and handed a note to the tutor, who took it; nodded briefly to them; and went out with Charlie.

"That is certainly the ugliest man I ever saw," said Herbert. "I think he has got the better of us, too. We are a pretty pair to transact business."

"Yes," said Mary, laughing. "He said he was not a man of business; but I wonder what he thinks of us."

"As of two young children whom fate has delivered into his hand, doubtless, shall we start now for South Kensington?"

"Yes. But I don't want to disturb my impression of the Lady of Shalott by any more art to-day. It is so fine this afternoon that I think it would be more sensible for us to take a walk in the Park than to shut ourselves up in the Museum."

Herbert agreeing, they walked together to Hyde Park. "Now that we are here," said he, "where shall we go to? The Row?"

"Certainly not. It is the most vulgar place in London. If we could find a pleasant seat, I should like to rest."

"We had better try Kensington Gardens, then."

"No," said Mary, remembering Mr Jack. "I do not like Kensington Gardens."

"I have just thought of the very thing," exclaimed Herbert. "Let us take a boat. The Serpentine is not so pretty as the Thames at Windsor; but it will have the charm of novelty for you. Will you come?"

"I should like it of all things. But I rely upon you as to the propriety of my going with you."

Herbert hesitated. "I do not think there can be any harm."

"There: I was only joking. Do you think I allow myself to be influenced by such nonsense as that? Let us go."

So they went to the boat-house and embarked. Herbert sculled aimlessly about, enjoying the spring sunshine, until they found themselves in an unfrequented corner of the Serpentine, when he half shipped his sculls, and said, "Let us talk for a while now. I have worked enough, I think."

"By all means," said Mary. "May I begin?"

Herbert looked quickly at her, and seemed a little disconcerted. "Of course." said he.

"I want to make a confession," she said. "it concerns the Lady of Shalott, of which I have been busily thinking since we started."

"Have you reconsidered your good opinion of it?"

"No. Better and yet worse than that. I have reconsidered my bad impression of it — at least, I do not mean that — I never had a bad impression of it, but my vacant, stupid first idea. My confession is that I was disappointed at the first sight of it. Wait: let me finish. It was different from what I imagined, as it ought to have been; for I am not an artist, and therefore do not imagine things properly. But it has grown upon me since; and now I like it better than if it had dazzled my ignorant eyes at first. I have been thinking that if it had the gaudy qualities I missed in it, I should not have respected you so much for painting it, nor should I have been forced to dwell on the poetry of the conception as I have been. I remember being secretly disappointed the first time we went to the National Gallery; and, as to my first opera, I suffered agonies of disenchantment. It is a comfort to me — a mean one, I fear — to know that Sir Joshua Reynolds was disappointed at his first glimpse of Raphael's frescoes in the Vatican, and that some of the great composers thought Beethoven's music hideous before they became familiar with it."

"You find that my picture improves on acquaintance?"

"Oh. yes! Very much. Or rather I improve."

"But are you sure youre not coaxing yourself into a false admiration of it for my — to avoid hurting me?"

"No, indeed," said Mary vehemently, trying by force of assertion to stifle this suspicion, which had come into her own mind before Herbert mentioned it.

"And do you still feel able to sympathize with my aims, and willing to encourage me, and to keep the highest aspects of my art before me, as you have done hitherto?"

"I feel willing, but not able. How often must I remind you that I owe all my feeling for art to you, and that I am only the faint reflexion of you in all matters concerning it?"

"Nevertheless without your help I should long ago have despaired. Are you quite sure — I beg you to answer me faithfully — that you do not despise me?"

"Mr. Herbert! How can you think such a thing of me? How can you think it of yourself?"

"I am afraid my constant self-mistrust is only too convincing a proof of my weakness. I sometimes despise myself."

"It is a proof of your artistic sensibility. You do not need to learn from me that all the great artists have left passages behind them proving that they have felt sometimes as you feel now. Take the oars again; and let us spin down to the bridge. The exercise will cure your fancies."

"Not yet. I have something else to say. Has it occurred to you that if by any accident — by the forming of a new tie, for instance — your sympathies came to be diverted from me, I should lose the only person whose belief in me has helped me to believe in myself? How utterly desolate I should be!"

"Desolate! Nonsense. Some day you will exhaust the variety of the sympathy you compliment me so highly upon. You will find it growing shallow and monotonous; and then you will not be sorry to be rid of it."

"I am quite serious. Mary: I have felt for some time past that it is neither honest nor wise in me to trifle any longer with my only chance of happiness. Will you become engaged to me? You may meet many better and stronger men than I, but none who will value you more highly — perhaps none to whose life you can be so indispensable."

There was a pause, Mary being too full of the responsibility she felt placed upon her to reply at once. Of the ordinary maidenly embarrassment she shewed not a trace.

"Why cannot we go on as we have been doing so happily?" she said, thoughtfully.

"Of course, if you wish it, we can. That is, if you do not know your own mind on the subject. But such happiness as there may be in our present indefinite relations will be all on your side."

"It seems so ungrateful to hesitate. It is doubt of myself that makes me do so. You have always immensely overrated me; and I should not like you to feel at some future day that you had made a mistake. When you are famous, you will be able to choose whom you please, and where you please."

"If that is the only consideration that hinders you, I claim your consent. Do you not think that I, too, do not feel how little worthy of your acceptance my offer is? But if we can love one another, what does all that matter? It is not as though we were strangers: we have proved one another. It is absurd that we two should say 'Mr Herbert' and 'Miss Sutherland, as if our friendship were an acquaintance of ceremony."

"I have often wished that you would call me Mary. At home we always speak of you as Adrian. But I could hardly have asked you to, could I?"

"I am sorry you did not. And now, will you give me a definite answer? Perhaps I have hardly made you a definite offer; but you know my position. I am too poor with my wretched £300 a year to give you a proper home at present. For that I must depend on my brush. You can fancy how I shall work when every exertion will bring my wedding day nearer; though, even at the most hopeful estimate, I fear I am condemning you to a long engagement. Are you afraid to venture on it?"

"Yes, I am afraid; but only lest you should find out the true worth of what you are waiting for. If you will risk that, I consent."

CHAPTER III

On one of the last days of July, Mary Sutherland was in her father's house at Windsor, copying a sketch signed A. H. The room had a French window opening on a little pleasure ground and shrubbery, far beyond which, through the swimming summer atmosphere, was the river threading the distant valley. But Mary did not look that way. With her attention concentrated on a stained scrap of paper, she might have passed for an æsthetic daughter of the Man with the Muck Rake. At last a shadow fell upon the drawing board. Then she turned, and saw a tall, handsome lady, a little past middle age, standing at the window.

"Mrs Herbert!" she exclaimed, throwing down her brush, and running to embrace the new-comer. "I thought you were in Scotland."

"So I was, until last week. The first person I saw in London was your Aunt Jane; and she has persuaded me to stay at Windsor with her for a fortnight How well you are looking! I saw your portrait in Adrian's studio; and it is not the least bit like you."

"I hope you did not tell him so. Besides, it must be like me. All Adrian's artistic friends admire it."

"Yes; and he admires their works in return. It is a well understood bargain. Poor Adrian! He did not know that I was coming back from Scotland; and I gave him a very disagreeable surprise by walking into his studio on Monday afternoon."

"Disagreeable! I am sure he was delighted."

"He did not even pretend to be pleased. His manners are really getting worse and worse. Who is the curious person that opened the shrubbery gate for me? — a sort of Cyclop with a voice of bronze."

"It is only Mr Jack, Charlie's tutor. He has nothing to do at present, as Charlie is spending a fortnight at Cambridge."

"Oh, indeed! Your Aunt Jane has a great deal to say about him. She does not like him; and his appearance rather confirms her, I must say, though he has good eyes. Whose whim was Mr Jack, pray?"

"Mine, they say; though I had no more to do with his being engaged than papa or Charlie had."

"I am glad Adrian had nothing to do with it. Well, Mary, have you any news for me? Has anything wonderful happened since I went to Scotland?"

"No. At least, I think not. You heard of papa's aunt Dorcas's death."

"That was in April, just before I went away. I heard that you left London early in the season. It is childish to bury yourself down here. You must get married, dear."

Mary blushed. "Did Adrian tell you of his new plans?" she said.

"Adrian never tells me anything. And indeed I do not care to hear of any plans of his until he has, once for all, given up his absurd notion of becoming a painter. Of course he will not hear of that: he has never forgiven me for suggesting it. All that his fine art has done for him as yet is to make him dislike his mother; and I hope it may never do worse."

"But, Mrs Herbert, you are mistaken: I assure you you are quite mistaken. He is a little sore, perhaps, because you do not appreciate his genius; but he loves you very dearly."

"Do not trouble yourself about my not appreciating his genius, as you call it, my dear. I am not one bit prejudiced against art; and if Adrian had the smallest chance of becoming a good painter, I would share my jointure with him and send him abroad to study. But he will never paint. I am not what is called an &ligae;sthete; and pictures that are generally understood to be the perfection of modern art invariably bore me, because I do not understand them. But I do understand Adrian's daubs; and I know that they are invariably weak and bad. All the Royal Academy could not persuade me to the contrary — though, indeed, they are not likely to try. I wish I could make you understand that anyone who dissuades Adrian from pursuing art will be his best friend. Don't you feel that yourself when you look at his pictures, Mary?"

"No," said Mary, fixing her glasses and looking boldly at her visitor, "I feel just the contrary."

"Then you must be blind or infatuated. Take his portrait of you as an example! No one could recognize it. Even Adrian told me that he would have destroyed it, had you not forbidden him; though he was bursting with suppressed resentment because I did not pretend to admire it."

"I believe that Adrian will be a great man yet, and that you will acknowledge that you were mistaken in him."

"Well, my dear, you are young, and not very wise, for all your cleverness. Besides, you did not know Adrian's father."

"No; but I know Adrian — very well, I think. I have faith in the entire worthiness of his conceptions; and he has proved that he does not grudge the hard work which is all that is requisite to secure the power of executing what he conceives. You cannot expect him to be a great painter without long practice and study."

"I do not understand metaphysics, Mary. Conceptions and executions are Greek to me. But I know very well that Adrian will never be happy until he is married to some sensible woman. And married he never can be whilst he remains an artist."

"Why?"

"What a question! How can he marry with only three hundred a year? He would not accept an allowance from me, even if I could afford to make him one; for since we disagreed about this wretched art, he has withdrawn himself from me in every possible way, and with an ostentation, too, which — natural feeling apart — is in very bad taste. He will never add a penny to his income by painting: of that I am certain; and he has not enterprise enough to marry a woman with money. If he persists in his infatuation, you will find that he will drag out his life waiting for a success that will never come. And he has no social talents. If he were a genius, like Raphael, his crotchets would not matter. If he were a humbug, like his uncle John he would flourish as all humbugs do in this wicked world. But Adrian is neither: he is only a duffer, poor fellow."

Mary reddened, and said nothing.

"Have you any influence over him?" said Mrs. Herbert, watching her.

"If I had," replied Mary "I would not use it to discourage him."

"I am sorry for that. I had some hope that you would help me to save him from wasting his opportunities. Your Aunt Jane has been telling me that you are engaged to him; but that is such an old story now that I never pay any attention to it."

"Has Adrian not told you?"

"My dear, I have already said a dozen times that Adrian never tells me anything. The more important his affairs are, the more openly and purposely he excludes me from them. I hope you have not been so silly as to rely on his visions of fame for your future support."

"The truth is that we have been engaged since last April. I wanted Adrian to write to you; but he said he preferred to speak to you about it. I thought he would have done so the moment you returned. However, I am sure he had good reasons for leaving me to tell you; and I am quite content to wait until he reaps the reward of his labor. We must agree to differ about his genius. I have perfect faith in him."

"Well, Mary, I am very sorry for your sake. I am afraid, if you do not lose patience and desert him in time, you will live to see all your own money spent, and to try bringing up a family on three hundred a year. If you would only be advised, and turn him from his artistic conceit, you would be the best wife in England for him. You have such force of character — just what he wants."

Mary laughed. "You are so mistaken in everything concerning Adrian!" she said. "It is he who has all the force of character: I am only his pupil. He has imposed all his ideas on me, more, perhaps, by dint of their purity and truth than of his own assertiveness; for he is no dogmatist. I am always the follower: he the leader."

"All very fine, Mary; but my oldfashioned common sense is better than your clever modern nonsense. However, since Adrian has turned your head, there is nothing for it but to wait until you both come to your senses. That must be your Aunt Jane at the door. She promised to follow me within half an hour."

Mary frowned, and recovered her serenity with an effort as she rose to greet her aunt, Mrs. Beatty, an elderly lady, with features like Mr. Sutherland's but fat and imperious. She exclaimed, "I hope I've not come too soon, Mary. How surprised you must have been to see Mrs Herbert!"

"Yes. Mr Jack let her into the shrubbery; and she appeared to me at the window without a word of warning."

"Mr Jack is a nice person to have in a respectable house," said Mrs. Beatty scornfully. "Do you know where I saw him last?"

"No," said Mary impatiently; "and I do not want to know. I am tired of Mr Jack's misdemeanors."

"Misdemeanors! I call it scandal, Mary. A perfect disgrace!"

"Dear me! What has he done now?"

"You may well ask. He is at present shewing himself in the streets of Windsor in company with common soldiers, openly entering the taverns with them."

"O Aunt Jane! Are you sure?"

Perhaps you will allow me to believe my senses. I drove through the town on my way here — you know what a small town is, Mrs Herbert, and how everybody knows everybody else by sight in it, let alone such a remarkable looking person as this Mr Jack; and the very first person I saw was Private Charles, the worst character in my husband's regiment, conversing with my nephew's tutor at the door of the 'Green Man.' They went into the bar together before my eyes. Now, what do you think of your Mr Jack?"

"He may have had some special reason"

"Special reason! Fiddlestick! What right has any servant of my brother's to speak to a profligate soldier in broad daylight in the streets?* There can be no excuse for it. If Mr Jack, had a particle of selfrespect he would maintain a proper distance between himself and even a full sergeant. But this Charles is such a drunkard that he spends half his time in cells. He would have been dismissed from the regiment long since, only he is a bandsman; and the bandmaster begs Colonel Beatty not to get rid of him, as he cannot be replaced."

"If he is a bandsman," said Mary, "that explains it. Mr Jack wanted musical information from him, I suppose."

"I declare, Mary, it is perfectly wicked to hear you defend such conduct. Is a public house the proper place for learning music? Why could not Mr Jack apply to your uncle? If he had addressed himself properly to me, Colonel Beatty could have ordered the man to give him whatever information was required of him."

"I must say, aunt, that you are the last person I should expect Mr Jack to ask a favor from, judging by your usual manner towards him."

"There!" said Mrs Beatty, turning indignantly to Mrs Herbert. "That is the way I am treated in this house to gratify Mr Jack. Last week I was told that I was in the habit of gossiping with servants, because Mrs Williams housemaid met him in the Park on Sunday — on Sunday, mind — whistling and singing and behaving like a madman. And now, when Mary's favorite is convicted in the very act of carousing with the lowest of the low, she turns it off by saying that I do not know how to behave myself before a tutor."

"I did not say so, aunt; and you know that very well."

"Oh, well, of course if you are going to fly out at me —"

"I am not flying at you, aunt; but you are taking offence without the least reason; and you are making Mrs Herbert believe that I am Mr Jack's special champion — you called him my favorite. The truth is, Mrs Herbert, that nobody likes this Mr Jack; and we only keep him because Charlie makes some progress with him, and respects him. Aunt Jane took a violent dislike to him"

"I, Mary! What is Mr Jack to me that I should like or dislike him, pray?"

" — and she is always bringing me stories of his misdoings, as if they were my fault. Then, when I try to defend him from obvious injustice, I am accused of encouraging and shielding him."

"So you do," said Mrs Beatty.

"I say whatever I can for him," said Mary sharply, "because I dislike him too much to condescend to join in attacks made on him behind his back. And I am not afraid of him, though you are, and so is Papa."

"Oh, really you are too ridiculous," said Mrs Beatty. "Afraid!"

"I see," said Mrs Herbert smoothly, "that my acquaintance the Cyclop has made himself a bone of contention here. Since you all dislike him, why not dismiss him and get a more popular character in his place? He is really not an ornament to your establishment. Where is your father, Mary?"

"He has gone out to dine at Eton; and he will not be back until midnight. He will be so sorry to have missed you. But he will see you tomorrow, of course."

"And you are alone here?"

"Yes. Alone with my work."

"Then what about our plan of taking you back with us and keeping you for the evening'"

"I think I would rather stay and finish my work."

"Nonsense, child," said Mrs Beatty. "You cannot be working always. Come out and enjoy yourself."

Mary yielded with a sigh, and went for her hat.

"I am sure that all this painting and poetry reading is not good for a young girl," said Mrs Beatty, whilst Mary was away. "It is very good of your Adrian to take such trouble to cultivate Mary's mind; but so much study cannot but hurt her brain. She is very self-willed and full of outlandish ideas. She is not under proper control. Poor Charles has no more resolution than a baby. And she will not listen to me, alth —"

"I am ready," said Mary, returning.

"You make me nervous — you do everything so quickly," said Mrs. Beatty, querulously. "I wish you would take shorter steps," she added, looking disparagingly at her niece's skirts as they went out through the shrubbery. "It is not nice to see a girl striding like a man. It gives you quite a bold appearance when you swing along, peering at people through your glasses."

"That is an old crime of mine, Mrs Herbert," said Mary. "I never go out with Aunt Jane without being lectured for not walking as if I had high heeled boots. Even the Colonel took me too task one evening here. He said a man should walk like a horse, and a woman like a cow. His complaint was that I walked like a horse; and he said that you, aunt, walked properly, like a cow. It is not worth any woman's while to gain such a compliment as that. It made Mr Jack laugh for the first and only time in our house."

Mrs Beatty reddened, and seemed about to make an angry reply, when the tutor came in at the shrubbery gate, and held it open for them to pass. Mrs Herbert thanked him. Mrs Beatty, following her, tried to look haughtily at him, but quailed, and made him a slight bow, in response to which he took off his hat.

"Mr Jack," said Mary, stopping: "if papa comes back before I am in, will you please tell him that I am at Colonel Beatty's."

"At what hour do you expect him?"

"Not until eleven, at soonest. I am almost sure to be back first; but if by any chance I should not be —"

"I will tell him," said Jack. Mary passed on; and he watched them until Mrs Beatty's carriage disappeared. Then he hurried indoors, and brought a heap of manuscript music into the room the ladies had just left. He opened the pianoforte and sat down before it; but instead of playing he began to write, occasionally touching the keys to try the effect of a progression, or rising to walk up and down the room with puckered brows.

He labored in this fashion until seven o'clock, when, hearing someone whistling in the road, he went out into the shrubbery, and presently came back with a soldier, not perfectly sober, who carried a roll of music paper and a case containing three clarionets.

"Now let us hear what you can make of it," said Jack, seating himself at the piano.

"It's cruel quick, that allagrow part is," said the soldier, trying to make his sheet of music stand properly on Mary's table easel. "Just give us your B fat, will you. Mister." Jack struck the note; and the soldier blew. "'Them ladies' singin' pianos is always so damn low," he grumbled. "I've drorn the slide as far as it'll come. Just wait while I stick a washer in the bloomin' thing."

"It seems to me that you have been drinking instead of practising, since I saw you," said Jack.

"S' help me, governor, I've been practising all the afternoon. I only took a glass on my way here to set me to rights. Now, Mister, I'm ready." Jack immediately attacked Mary's piano with all the vigor of an orchestra; and the clarinet soon after made its entry with a brilliant cadenza. The soldier was a rapid expectant; his tone was fine; and the only varieties of expression he was capable of, the spirited and the pathetic, satisfied even Jack, who, on other points, soon began to worry the soldier by his fastidiousness.

"Stop," he cried, "That is not the effect I want at all. It is not bright enough. Take the other clarinet. Try it in C."

"Wot! Play all them flats on a clarinet in C! It can't be done. Least ways I'm damned if I can — Hello! 'Eire's a gent for you, sir."

Jack turned. Adrian Herbert was standing on the threshold, astonished, holding the handle of the open door. "I have been listening outside for some time," he said politely. "I hope I do not disturb you."

"No," replied Jack. "Friend Charles here is worth listening to. Eh, Mr Herbert?"

Private Charles looked down modestly; jingled his spurs; coughed; and spat through the open window. Adrian did not appreciate his tone or his execution; but he did appreciate his sodden features, his weak and husky voice, and his barrack accent. Seeing a clarinet and a red handkerchief lying on a satin cushion which he had purchased for Mary at a bazaar, the looked at the soldier with disgust, and at Jack with growing indignation.

"I presume there is no one at home," he said coldly.

"Miss Sutherland is at Mrs Beatty's, and will not return until eleven," said Jack, looking at Adrian with his most rugged expression, and not subduing his powerful voice, the sound of which always afflicted the artist with a sensation of insignificance. "Mrs Beatty and a lady who is visiting her called and brought her out with them. Mr Sutherland is at Eton, and will not be back till midnight. My pupil is still at Cambridge."

"H'm" said Adrian. "I shall go on to Mrs Beatty's. I should probably disturb you by remaining."

Jack nodded and turned to the piano without further ceremony. Private Charles had taken one of Mary's paint-brushes and fixed it upon the desk against his sheet of music, which was rolling itself up. This was the last thing Herbert saw before he left. As he walked away he heard the clarinet begin the slow movement of the concerto, a melody which, in spite of his annoyance, struck him as quite heavenly. He nevertheless hastened out of earshot, despising the whole art of music because a half-drunken soldier could so affect him by it.

Half a mile from the Sutherlands' house was a gate, though which he passed into a flower-garden, in which a tall gentleman with sandy hair was smoking a cigar. This was Colonel Beatty, from whom he learnt that the ladies were in the drawing room. There he found his mother and Mrs Beatty working in colored wools, whilst Mary, at a distance from them, was reading a volume of Browning. She gave a sigh of relief as he entered.

"Is this your usual hour for making calls?" said Mrs Herbert, in response to her son's cool "Good evening, mother."

"Yes," said he. "I cannot work at night." He passed on and sat down beside Mary at the other end of the room. Mrs Beatty smiled significantly at Mrs Herbert, who shrugged her shoulders and went on with her work

"What is the matter, Adrian?" said Mary, in a low voice.

"Why?"

"You look annoyed."

"I am not annoyed. But I am not quite satisfied with the way in which your household is managed in your absence by Mr Jack."

"Good heavens!" exclaimed Mary, "you too! Am I never to hear the last of Mr Jack? It is bad enough to have to meet him every day, without having his misdeeds dinned into my ears from morning till night."

"I think an end should be put to such a state of things, Mary. I have often reproached myself for having allowed you to engage this man with so little consideration. I thought his mere presence in the house could not affect you — that his business would be with Charlie only. My experience of the injury that can be done by the mere silent contact of coarse natures with fine ones should have taught me better. Mr Jack is not fit to live with you, Mary."

"But perhaps it is our fault. He has no idea of the region of thought from which I wish I never had to descend; but, after all, we have no fault to find with him. We cannot send him away because he does not appreciate pictures."

"No. But I have reason to believe that he is not quite so well-behaved in your absence as he is when you are at home. When I arrived tonight, for instance, I, of course, went straight to your house. There I heard a musical entertainment going forward. When I went in I was greeted with a volley of oaths which a drunken soldier was addressing to Jack. The two were in the drawingroom and did not perceive me at first, Jack being seated at your pianoforte, accompanying the soldier, who was playing a flageolet. The fellow was using your table easel for a desk, and your palette knife as a paper weight to keep his music flat. Has Jack your permission to introduce his military friends whenever you are out?"

"Certainly not," said Mary, reddening. "I never heard of such a thing. I think Mr Jack is excessively impertinent."

"What is the matter?" said Mrs. Beatty, perceiving that her niece was vexed.

"Nothing, aunt," said Mary hastily. "Please do not tell Aunt Jane," she added in an undertone to Adrian.

"Why not?"

"Oh, she will only worry about it. Pray do not mention it. What ought we to do about it, Adrian?"

"Simply dismiss Mr Jack forthwith?"

"But — Yes, I suppose we should. The only difficulty is —" Mary hesitated, and at last added, "I am afraid he will think that it is out of revenge for his telling Charlie not to take his ideas of music from my way of playing it, and because he despises my painting."

"Despises your painting! Do you mean to say that he has been insolent to you? You should dismiss him at once. Surely such fears as you expressed just now have no weight with you, Mary?"

Mary reddened again, and said, a little angrily, "It is very easy for you to talk of dismissing people, Adrian; but if you had to do it yourself, you would feel how unpleasant it is."

Adrian looked grave and did not reply. After a short silence Mary rose; crossed the room carelessly; and began to play the piano. Herbert, instead of sitting by her and listening, as his habit was, went out and joined the Colonel in the garden.

"What have you quarreled about, dear?" said Mrs Herbert.

"We have not quarreled," said Mary. "What made you think that?"

"Adrian is offended."

"Oh, no. At least I cannot imagine why he should be."

"He is. I know what Adrian's slightest shrug signifies."

Mary shook her head and went on playing. Adrian did not return until they went into another room to sup. Then Mary said she must go home; and Herbert rose to accompany her.

"Goodnight, mother," he said. "I shall see you tomorrow. I have a bed in the town, and will go there directly when I have left Mary safely at home." He nodded; shook hands with Mrs Beatty and the Colonel; and went out with Mary. They walked a hundred yards in silence. Then Mary said:

"Are you offended, Adrian? Mrs Herbert said you were."

He started as if he had been stung. "I do not believe I could make a movement," he replied indignantly, "for which my mother would not find some unworthy motive. She never loses an opportunity to disparage me and to make mischief."

"She does not mean it, Adrian. It is only that she does not quite understand you. You sometimes say hard things of her, although I know you do not mean to speak unkindly."

"Pardon me, Mary, I do. I hate hypocrisy of all kinds; and you annoy me when you assume any tenderness on my part towards my mother. I dislike her. I believe I should do so even it she had treated me well, and shewed me the ordinary respect which I have much right to from a parent as from any other person. Our natures are antagonistic, our views of life and duty incompatible: we have nothing in common. That is the plain truth; and however much it may shock you, unless you are willing to accept it as unalterable, I had rather you would drop the subject."

"Oh, Adrian, I do not think it is right to —"

"I do not think, Mary, that you can tell me anything concerning what is called filial duty that I am not already familiar with. I cannot help my likes and dislikes: I have to entertain them when they come to me, without regard to their propriety. You may be quite tranquil as far as my mother's feelings are concerned. My undutiful sentiments afford her her chief delight a pretext for complaining of me."

Mary looked wistfully at him, and walked on, down-east. He stopped; turned towards her gravely; and resumed: "Mary: I suspect from one or two things you have said, that you cherish a project for reconciling me to my mother. You must relinquish that idea. I myself exhausted every effort to that end long ago. I disguised the real nature of my feeling towards her until even self-deception, the most persistent of all forms of illusion, was no longer possible. In those days should have hailed your good offices with pleasure. Now I have not the least desire to be reconciled to her. As I have said, we have nothing in common: her affection would be a burden to me. Therefore think no more of it. Whenever you wish to see me in my least amiable mood, re-open the subject, and you will be gratified."

"I shall avoid it since you wish me to. I only wished to say that you left me in an awkward position today by not telling her of our engagement."

"True. That was inconsiderate of me. I intended to tell her; but I got no opportunity. It matters little; she would only have called me a fool. Did you tell her?"

"Yes, when I found that Aunt Jane had told her already."

"And what did she say?"

'Oh, nothing. She reminded me that you were not rich enough to marry."

"And proclaimed her belief that I should never become so unless I gave up painting?"

"She was quite kind to me about it. But she is a little prejudiced —"

"Yes, I know. For heaven's sake let us think and talk about something else. Look at the stars. What a splendid dome they make of the sky now that there is no moon to distract attention from them. And yet a great artist, with a miserable yard of canvas, can move us as much as that vast expanse of air and fire."

"Yes. — I am very uncomfortable about Mr Jack, Adrian. If he is to be sent away, it must be done before Charlie returns, or else there will be a quarrel about it. But then, who is to speak to him? He is a very hard person to find fault with; and very likely papa will make excuses for him sooner than face him with a dismissal. Or, worse again, he might give him some false reason for sending him away, in order to avoid an explosion; and somehow I would rather do anything than condescend to tell Mr Jack a story. If he were anyone else I should not mind so much."

"There is no occasion to resort to untruth, which is equally odious, no matter to whom it is addressed. It was agreed that his employment should be terminable by a month's notice on either side. Let Mr. Sutherland write him a letter giving that notice. No reason need be mentioned; and the letter can be courteously worded, thanking him for his past services, and simply saying that Charlie is to be placed in other hands."

"But it will be so unpleasant to have him with us for a month under a sentence of dismissal."

"Well, it cannot be helped. There is no alternative but to turn him out of the house for misconduct."

"That is impossible. A letter will be the best. I wish we had never Been him, or that he were gone already. Hush. Listen a moment."

They stopped. The sound of a pianoforte came to their ears.

"He is playing still," said Mary. "Let us go back for Colonel Beatty. He will know how to deal with the soldier."

"The soldier must have left long ago," said Adrian. "I can hear nothing but the piano. Let us go in. He is within his bargain as far as his own playing goes. He stipulated for that when we engaged him."

They went on. As they neared the house, grotesque noises mingled with the notes of the pianoforte. Mary hesitated, and would have stopped again ; but Adrian, with a stern face, walked quickly ahead. Mary had a key of the shrubbery; and they went round that way, the noise becoming deafening as they approached. The player was not only pounding the keyboard so that the window rattled in its frame, but was making an extraordinary variety of sounds with his own larynx. Mary caught Adrian's arm as they advanced to the window and looked in. Jack was alone, seated at the pianoforte, his brows knitted, his eyes glistening under them, his wrists bounding and rebounding upon the keys, his rugged countenance transfigured by an expression of extreme energy and exaltation. He was playing from a manuscript score, and was making up for the absence of an orchestra by imitations of the instruments. He was grunting and buzzing the bassoon parts, humming when the violoncello had the melody, whistling for the flutes, singing hoarsely for the horns, barking for the trumpets, squealing for the oboes, making indescribable sounds in imitation of clarionets and drums, and marking each *sforzando* by a toss of his head and a gnash of his teeth. At last, abandoning this eccentric orchestration, he chanted with the full strength of his formidable voice until he came to the final chord, which he struck violently, and repeated in every possible inversion from one end of the keyboard to the other. Then he sprang up, and strode excitedly to and fro in the room. At the second turn he saw Herbert and Mary, who had just entered, staring at him. He started, and stared back at them, quite disconcerted.

"I fear I have had the misfortune to disturb you a second time," said Herbert, with suppressed anger.

"No," said Jack, in a voice strained by his recent abuse of it, "I was playing by myself. The soldier whom you saw here has gone to his quarters." As he mentioned the soldier, he looked at Mary.

"It was hardly necessary to mention that you were playing," said Adriaa. "We heard you at a considerable distance."

Jack's cheek glowed like a sooty copper kettle, and he looked darkly at Herbert for a moment. Then, with some humor in his eye, he said, "Did you hear much of my performance?"

"We heard quite enough, Mr. Jack." said Mary, approaching the piano to place her hat on it. Jack quickly took his manuscript away as she did so. "I am afraid you have not improved my poor spinet," she added, looking ruefully at the keys.

"That is what a pianoforte is for," said Jack gravely. "It may have suffered; but when next you touch it you will feel that the hands of a musician have been on it, and that its heart has beaten at last." He looked hard at her for a moment after saying this, and then turned to Herbert, and continued, "Miss Sutherland was complaining some time ago that she had never heard me play. Neither had she, because she usually sits here when she is at home; and I do not care to disturb her then. I am glad she has been gratified at last by a performance which is, I assure you, very characteristic of me. Perhaps you thought it rather odd'"

"I did think so," said Herbert, severely.

"Then," said Jack, with a perceptible surge of his subsiding excitement, "I am fortunate in having escaped all observation except that of a gentleman who understands so well what an artist is. If I cannot compose as you paint, believe that it is because the art which I profess lies nearer to a strong man's soul than one which nature has endowed you with the power of appreciating. Goodnight." He looked for a moment at the two; turned on his heel; and left the room. They stared after him in silence, and heard him laugh subduedly as he ascended the stairs.

"I will make papa write to him tomorrow," said Mary, when she recovered herself. "No one shall have a second chance of addressing a sarcasm to you, Adrian, in my father's house, whilst I am mistress of it."

"Do not let that influence you, Mary. I am not disposed to complain of the man's conceited ignorance. But he was impertinent to you."

"I do not mind that."

"But I do. Nothing could be more grossly insolent than what he said about your piano. Many of his former remarks have passed with us as the effect of a natural brusquerie, which he could not help. I believe now that he is simply ill-mannered and ill-conditioned. That sort of thing is not to be tolerated for one moment."

"I have always tried to put the best construction on his actions, and to defend him from Aunt Jane," said Mary. "I am very sorry now that I did so. The idea of his calling himself an artist!"

"Musicians often arrogate that title to themselves," said Herbert; "and he does not seem overburdened with modesty. I think I hear Mr Sutherland letting himself in at the hall door. If so, I need not stay any longer, unless you wish me to speak to him about what has occurred."

"Oh no, not tonight: it would only spoil his rest. I will tell him in the morning."

Herbert waited only to bid Mr. Sutherland good night Then he kissed his betrothed, and went to his lodging.

CHAPTER IV

Two days later, Mary was finishing the sketch which Mrs Herbert had interrupted. Something was wrong with her: at every sound in the house she changed color and stopped to listen. Suddenly the door was opened; and a housemaid entered, rigid with indignation.

"Oh Clara, you frightened me. What is it?"

"If you please, Miss, is it my place to be called names and swore at by the chootor?"

"Why? What has happened?"

"Master gave me a note after breakfast to give Mr Jack, Miss. He was not in his room then; so I left it on the table. As soon as I heard him moving about, I went and asked him had he got it. The answer I got — begging your pardon, Miss — was, 'Go to the devil, you jade.' If I am expected to put up with that from the likes of him, I should wish to give warning."

"I am very sorry, Clara. Why did he behave so? Did you say anything rude to him?"

"Not likely, Miss. I hope I respect myself more than to stop and bandy words. His door was wide open; and he had his portmanteau in the middle of the floor, and was heaping his things into it as fast as he could. He was grinding his teeth, too, and looked reg'lar wicked."

"Well, Clara, as Mr Jack will be leaving very soon, I think you had better pass it over."

"Indeed, Miss? Is Mr Jack going?"

"Yes," said Mary, turning to her easel.

"Oh!" said the housemaid slowly. After lingering a moment in vain for further information, she hastened to the kitchen to tell the news. She had closed the door; but it did not fasten, and presently a draught from an open window in the hall blew it softly open. Though Mary wanted it shut, so that Jack should not see her if he passed on his way out, she was afraid to stir. She had never been so unreasonably nervous in her life before; and she sat there helpless pretending to draw until she heard the dreaded footstep on the stairs. Her heart beat in a terrible crescendo as the steps approached, passed, stopped, returned, and entered the room. When she forced herself to look up, he was standing there eying her, with her father's letter in his hand.

"What does this mean?" he said.

Mary glanced round as it to escape from his eyes but had to look at him as she replied faintly, "You had better ask Mr Sutherland."

"Mr Sutherland has nothing to do with it. You are mistress here."

He waited long enough for an answer to shew that she had none to make. Then, shaking his head, he deliberately tore the letter into fragments. That stung her into saying:

"I do not wish to pursue the subject with you."

"I have not asked your leave," he replied. "I give you a lesson for the benefit cf the next wretch that will hold my position at the mercy of your ignorant caprice. You have spoiled the labor of the past three months for me; upset my plans; ruined me, for aught I know. Tell your father, who wants to discharge me at the end of the month, that I discharge myself now. I am not a dog, to sit at his table after the injustice he has done me."

"He has done you no injustice, Mr Jack. He has a perfect right to choose who shall remain in his household. And I think he has acted rightly. So does Mr Herbert."

Jack laughed gruffly. "Poor devil!" he said, "he fancies he can give ideas to the world because a few great men have given some to him. I am sorry I let his stiff manners put me out of temper with him the other night. He hates me instinctively because he feels in me what he misses in himself. But you ought to know better. Why, he hated that drunken rascal I had here, because he could handle his clarinet like a man with stuff in him. I have no more time for talking now. I have been your friend and have worked hard with your brother for your sake, because I thought you helped me to this place when I was desperately circumstanced. But now I shall not easily forgive you." He shook his head again at her, and walked out, shutting the door behind him. The housemaid was in the hall. "My portmanteau and a couple of other things are on the landing outside my door," he said, stopping as he passed her. "You will please give them to the man I send."

"And by whose orders am I to trouble myself about your luggage, pray?"

Jack turned and slowly advanced upon her until she, retreating, stood against the wall. "By my orders, Mrs. Boldface," he said. "Do as you are bid — and paid for, you hussy."

"Well, certainly," began the housemaid, as he turned away, "that's —"

Jack halted and looked round wickedly at her. She retired quickly, grumbling. As he left the house, Herbert, coming in at the gate, was surprised to see him laughing heartily; for he had never seen him in good humor before.

"Good morning, Mr Jack," said Adrian as they passed.

"Goodbye," said Jack, derisively. And he went on. Before Adrian reached the doorstep, he heard the other roaring with laughter in the road.

Jack, when he had had his laugh out, walked quickly away, chuckling, and occasionally shaking his fist at the sky. When he came to Colonel Beatty's house, he danced fantastically past the gate, snapping his fingers. He laughed boisterously at this performance at intervals until he came into the streets. Here, under the eye of the town, he was constrained to behave himself less remarkably; and the constraint made him so impatient that he suddenly gave up an intention he had formed of taking a lodging there, and struck off to the railway station at Slough.

"When is there a train to London?" he said, presenting himself at the booking-office.

"There's one going now," replied the clerk coolly.

"Now!" exclaimed Jack. "Give me a ticket — third class — single."

"Go to the other window. First class only here."

"First class, then," cried Jack, exasperated. "Quick." And he pushed in a half sovereign.

The clerk, startled by Jack's voice, hastily gave him a ticket and an installment of the change. Jack left the rest, and ran to the platform just in time to hear the engine whistle.

"Late, sir. You're late," said a man in the act of slamming the barrier. By way of reply, Jack dragged it violently back and rushed after the departing train. There was a shout and a rush of officials to stop him; and one of them seized him, but, failing to hold him, was sent reeling by the collision. The next moment Jack opened the door of a first-class carriage, and plunged in in great disorder. The door was shut after him by an official, who stood on the footboard to cry out, "You will be summonsed for this, sir, so you shall. You shall be sum —"

"Go to the deuce," retorted Jack, in a thundering voice. As the man jumped off, he turned from the door, and found himself confronted by a tall thin old gentleman, sprucely dressed, who cried in a high voice:

"Sir, this is a private compartment. I have engaged this compartment. You have no business here."

"You should have had the door locked then," said Jack, with surly humor, seating himself, and folding his arms with an air of concentrated doggedness.

"I — I consider your intrusion most unwarrantable — most unjustifiable," continued the the gentleman.

Jack chuckled too obviously, at the old gentleman's curious high voice and at his discomfiture. Then, deferring a little to white hairs, he said, "Well, well: I can get into another carriage at the next station."

"You can do nothing of the sort, sir," cried the gentleman, more angrily than before. "This is an express train. It does not stop."

"Then *I* do, — where I am," aid Jack curtly, with a new and more serious expression of indignation; for he had just remarked that there was one other person in the carriage — a young lady.

"I will not submit to this, sir. I will stop the train."

"Stop it then," said Jack, scowling at him. "But let me alone."

The gentleman, with flushes of color coming and going on his withered cheek, turned to the alarum and began to read the printed instructions as to its use. "You had better not stop the train, father," said the lady. "You will only get fined. The half-crown you gave the guard does not —"

"Hold your tongue," said the gentleman. "I desire you not to speak to me, Magdalen, on any pretext whatsoever." Jack, who had relented a little on learning the innocent relationship between his fellow travellers glanced at the daughter. She was a tall lady with chestnut hair, burnished by the rays which came aslant through the carriage window. Her eyes were bright hazel; her mouth small, but with full lips, the upper one, like her nose, tending to curl upward. She was no more than twenty; but in spite of her youth and trivial style of beauty, her manner was self-reliant and haughty. She did not seem to enjoy her journey, and took no pains to conceal her illhumor, which was greatly increased by the rebuke which her father had addressed to her. Her costume of maize color and pale blue was very elegant, and harmonized admirably with her fine complexion. Jack repeated his glance at short intervals until he discovered that her face was mirrored in the window next which he sat. He then turned away from her, and studied her appearance at his ease.

Meanwhile the gentleman, grumbling in an undertone, had seated himself without touching the alarum, and taken up a newspaper. Occasionally he looked over at his daughter, who, with her cheek resting on her glove, was frowning at the landscape as they passed swiftly through it. Presently he uttered an exclamation of impatience, and blew off some dust and soot which had just settled on his paper. Then he rose, and shut the window.

"Oh, pray don't close it altogether, father," said the lady. "It is too warm. I am half suffocated as it is."

"Magdalen: I forbid you to speak to me."

Magdalen pouted, and shook her shoulders angrily. Her father then went to the other door of the carriage, and closed the window there also. Jack instantly let it down with a crash, and stared truculently at him.

"Sir," said the gentleman: "if, you — if sir — had you politely requested me not to close the window, I should not have — I would have respected your objection."

"And if you, sir," returned Jack, "had politely asked my leave before meddling with my window, I should, with equal politeness, have conveyed to you my invincible determination to comply with the lady's reasonable request."

"Ha! Indeed!" said the gentleman loftily. "I shall not — ah — dispute the matter with you." And he resumed his seat, whilst his daughter, who had looked curiously at Jack for a moment, turned again to the landscape with her former chagrined expression.

For some time after this they travelled in peace: the old gentleman engaged with his paper: Jack chuckling over his recent retort. The speed of the train now increased speed; and the musician became exhilarated as the telegraph poles shot past, hardly visible.

When the train reached a part of the line at which the rails were elevated on iron chairs, the smooth grinding of the wheels changed to a rhythmic clatter. The racket became deafening; and Jack's exhilaration had risen to a reckless excitement, when he was recalled to his senses by the gentleman, whom he had forgotten, calling out:

"Sir: will you oblige me by stopping those infernal noises."

Jack, confused, suddenly ceased to grind his teeth and whistle through them. Then he laughed and said goodhumoredly, "I beg your pardon: I am a composer."

"Then have the goodness to remember that you are not now in a printing office," said the gentleman, evidently Supposing him to be a compositor. "You are annoying this lady, and driving me distracted with your hissing."

"I do not mind it in the least" said the lady stubbornly.

"Magdalen: I have already desired you twice to be silent."

"I shall speak if I please," she muttered. Her father pretended not to hear her, and sat still for the next ten minutes, during which he glanced at Jack several times, with an odd twinkle in his eye. Then he said:

"What did you say you were, sir, may I ask?"

"A composer."

"You are a discomposer, sir," cried the old gentleman man promptly. "You are a discomposer." And he began a chirping laughter, which Jack, after a pause of wonder, drowned with a deeptoned roar of merriment. Even the lady, determined as she was to be sulky, could not help smiling. Her father then took up the newspaper, and hid his face with it, turning his back to Jack, who heard him occasionally laughing to himself.

"I wish I had something to read," said the young lady after some time, turning discontentedly from the window.

"A little reflexion will do you no harm," said her parent. "A little reflexion, and, I will add, Magdalen, a little repentance perhaps."

"I have nothing but disappointment and misery to reflect about, and I have no reason to be repentant. Please get me a novel at the next station — or give me some money, and I will get one myself."

"Certainly not. You are not to be trusted with money. I forbid you ever to open a novel again. It is from such pestilential nonsense that you got the ideas which led to your present disgraceful escapade. Now, I must beg of you not to answer me, Magdalen. I do not wish to enter into a discussion with you, particularly before strangers."

"Then do not make strangers believe that —"

"Hold your tongue, Magdalen. Do you disobey me intentionally? You should be ashamed to speak to me."

The young lady bit her lip and reddened. "I think —" she began.

"Be silent." cried her father, seizing his umbrella and rapping it peremptorily on the floor. Jack sprang up.

"Sir," he said: "how dare you behave so to a lady?"

"This lady is my daughter, k — k — confound your impertinence," replied the other irascibly.

"Then don't treat her as if she were your dog," retorted Jack "I am an artist, sir — an artist — a poet; and I will not permit a young and beautiful woman to be tyrannized in my presence."

"It I were a younger man —" began the gentleman, grasping his umbrella

"If you were," shouted Jack, "you would have nothing but tenderness and respect for the lady; or else, by the power of sound, I would pulverize you —" allegro martellatissimo — on the spot."

"Do not threaten me, sir," said the old gentleman spiritedly, rising and confronting his adversary. "What right have you to interfere with the affairs of strangers — perfect strangers? Are you mad, sir; or are you merely ignorant?"

"Neither. I am as well versed in the usages of the world as you; and I have sworn not to comply with them when they demand a tacit tolerance of oppression. The laws of society, sir, are designed to make the world easy for cowards and liars. And lest by the infirmity of my nature I should become either the one or the other, or perhaps both, I never permit myself to witness tyranny without rebuking it, or to hear falsehood without exposing it. If more people were of my mind, you would never have dared to take it for granted that I would witness your insolence towards your daughter without interfering to protect her."

To this speech the old gentleman could find no reply. He stared at Jack a few moments, and then, saying, "I request you to mind your own business, sir. I have nothing to say to you," went back in dudgeon to his seat. The lady then leaned forward and said haughtily, "Your interference is quite unnecessary, thank you. I can take care of myself."

"Aye," retorted Jack, frowning at her: "you are like other children. I was not such a fool as to expect gratitude from you." The girl blushed and looked away towards the landscape. Her father again stared at Jack, who resumed his seat with a bounce; folded his arms; and glowered. Five minutes later the train stopped; and the guard came for their tickets.

"I relied on you," said the gentleman to him, for an empty carriage. Instead of that, I have had a most unpleasant journey. I have been annoyed — damnably annoyed."

"Ha! ha!" roared Jack. "Ha! ha! ha!"

The guard turned sternly to him, and said, "Ticket, sir, please," as though he expected the ticket to prove a third class one. When he received it he held it between his lips, whilst he opened a memorandum and then continued, "I want your name and address, sir, please."

"What for?"

"For getting in when the train was in motion, sir, at Slough. The Company's orders are strict against it. You might have been killed, sir."

"And what the devil is it to the Company whether I am killed or not?"

"Be quick, sir, please," said the guard, uncertain whether to coax or be peremptory. "Our time is up."

Jack looked angry for a moment; then shrugged his shoulders and said, "My name is Jack; and I live nowhere."

The man let his book fall to his side, and mutely appealed to the old gentleman to witness the treatment he was enduring.

"Come, sir," be said, "what's the use in this? We'll only have to detain you; and that won't be pleasant for either of us."

"Is that a threat" said Jack fiercely.

"No, sir, There's no one threatening you. We're all gentlemen here. I only do my duty, as you understand, sir — none better. What is your name, sir?"

"My name is Jack. I tell you. Mr Owen Jack."

"Oh! I didn't take it rightly at first. Now your address, sir, please."

"I have none. Did you never hear of a man without any home? If the place where 1 slept last night, and where my property is, will do you, you can put care of Mr Charles Sutherland, Beulah, Windsor. Here's a card for you."

"I know Mr Sutherland well, sir," said the guard, putting up his book."

"And by Heaven," said Jack, vehemently, "if I hear another word of this, I will complain of you for taking half-a-crown from this gentleman and then shutting me and a lady in with him for a whole journey. I believe him to be insane."

"Guard," screamed the old gentleman, quite beside himself. But the guard, disconcerted at Jack's allusion to the half-crown, hurried away and started the train. Nevertheless the gentleman would not be silenced. "How dare you, sir, speak of me as being insane?" he said.

"How dare you, sir, grumble at a journey which has only been marred by your own peevishness? I have enjoyed myself greatly. I have enjoyed the sunshine, the scenery, the rhythm of the train, and the company of my fellow travellers — except you, sir; and even your interruptions are no worse than untimely pleasantries. I never enjoyed a journey more in my life."

"You are the most impertinent man I ever met, sir."

"Precisely my opinion of you, sir. You commenced hostilities; and if you have caught a Tartar you have only yourself to thank."

"You broke into my carriage."

"Your carriage, sir! My carriage just as much as yours — more so. You are an unsocial person, sir."

"Enough said, sir," said the gentleman. "It does not matter. Enough said, if you please."

"Well, sir," said Jack, more good humoredly, "I apologize. I have been unnaturally repressed for the last three months; and I exploded this morning like a bombshell. The force of the explosion was not quite spent when I met you; and perhaps I had less regard for your seniority than I might have shewn at another time."

"My seniority has nothing to do with the question, sir. My age is no concern of yours."

"Hush, father," whispered the lady. "Do not reply to him. It is not dignified."

The old gentleman was about to make some angry reply, when the train ran alongside the platform at Paddington, and a porter opened the door, crying, "Ensom or foa' w'eol, sir."

"Get me a hansom, porter."

"Right, sir. Luggage, sir?"

"There is a tin box," said the lady, "a brown one With the initials M. B. on it."

The porter touched his cap and went away. The gentleman got out, and stood wiih his daughter at the carriage door, awaiting the return of the porter. Jack slowly followed, and stood, irresolute, near them, the only person there without business or destination.

"I wonder what is delaying that fellow with our cab" said the old gentleman, after about fifteen seconds. "The vagabond has been picked up by someone else, and has forgotten us. Are we to stand here all day?"

"He will be here presently" said Magdalen. "He has not had time —"

"He has had time to call twenty cabs since. Remain here until I return, Madge. Do you hear?"

"Yes." said the girl. He looked severely at her, and walked away towards the luggage van. Her color rose as she looked after him. Meanwhile the porter had placed the box on a cab; and he now returned to Magdalen.

"This way, Miss, W"ere's the genlman?" She looked quickly at the porter; then towards the crowd in which her father had disappeared; then, after a moment of painful hesitation, at Jack, who was still standing near.

"Never mind the gentleman," she said to the porter: "he is not coming with me." And as he turned to lead the way to the cab, she pulled off her glove; took a ring from her finger; and addressed Jack with a burning but determined face.

"I have no money to pay for my cab. Will you give me some in exchange for this ring — a few shillings will be enough? Pray do not delay me. Yes or no?"

Jack lost only a second in staring amazedly at her before he thrust his hand in his pocket, and drew out a quantity of gold, silver and bronze coin, more than she could grasp with ease. "Keep the ring," he said. "Away with you."

"You must take it," she said impatiently. "And I do not need all this money."

"Thousand thunders!" exclaimed Jack with sudden excitement, "here is your father. Be quick."

She looked round, scared; but as Jack pushed her unceremoniously towards the cab, she recovered herself and hurried into the hansom.

"Here, porter: give this ring to that gentleman," she said, giving the man a shilling and the ring. "Why doesn't he drive on?" she added, as the cab remained motionless, and the porter stood touching his cap.

"Whereto, Miss?"

"Bond Street," she cried. "As fast as possible. Do make him start at once."

"Bond Street, " shouted Jack commandingly to the driver. "Make haste. Double fare. Prestissimo!" And the cab dashed out of the station as if the horse had caught Jack's energy.

The lady gev me this for you, sir," said the porter. Yes," said Jack, "Thank you." It was an oldfashioned ring, with a diamond and three emeralds, too small for his little finger. He pocketed it, and was considering what he should do next, when the old gentleman, no longer impatient and querulous, but pale and alarmed, came by, looking anxiously about him. When he saw Jack he made a movement as though to approach him, but checked himself and resumed his search in another direction. Jack began feel compunction; for the gentleman's troubled expression was changing into one of grief and fear. The crowd and bustle were diminishing. Soon there was no difficulty in examining separately all the passengers who remained on the platform. Jack resolved to go lest he betray the young lady's destination to her father; but he had walked only a few yards, when, hearing a voice behind him say "This is him, sir," he turned and found himself face to face with the old gentleman. The porter stood by, saying, "How could I know, sir? I seen the gen'lman in the carriage with you, an' I seen the lady speakin to him arterwards. She took money off him and gev him a ring, as I told you. If youd left the luggage to me, sir, 'stead of going arter it to the wrong van, you wouldnt ha' lost her."

"Very well: that will do." The porter made a pretence of retiring but remained within hearing.

"Now, sir," continued the gentleman, addressing Jack, "I know what you are, If you dont tell me once at once, the name and address of the theatrical scoundrels to whom you are spy and kidnapper: by — by — by God! I'll give you to the nearest policeman."

"Sir," said Jack sternly: "if your daughter has run away from you. it is your own fault for not treating her kindly. The porter has told you what happened between us. I know no more of the matter than he does."

"I don't believe you. You followed her from Windsor. The porter saw you give her" (here the old gentleman choked) — "saw what passed here just now."

"Yes, sir. You leave your daughter penniless, and compel her to offer her ornaments for sale to a stranger at a railway station. By my soul, you are a nice man to have charge of a young girl."

"My daughter is incapable of speaking to a stranger. You are in the pay of one of those infernal theatrical agents with whom she has been corresponding. But I'll unmask you, sir. I'll unmask you."

"If you were not an inveterately wrongheaded old fool," said Jack hotly, "you would not mistake a man of genius for a crimp. You ought to be ashamed of your temper. You are collecting a crowd too. Do you want the whole railway staff to know that you have driven your daughter away?"

"You lie, you villain," cried the gentleman, seizing him by the collar, "you lie. How dare you, you — you — pock-marked ruffian, say that I drove away my daughter? I have been invariably kind to her — no parent more so. She was my special favorite. If you repeat that slander, I'll — I'll " He shook his fist in Jack's face, and released him. Jack, who had suffered the grasp on his collar without moving, turned away deeply offended, and buttoned his coat. Then, as the other was about to recommence, he interrupted him by walking away. The gentleman followed him promptly.

"You shall not escape by running off," he said, panting.

You have insulted me, sir," said Jack. "If you address another word to me, I'll hand you to the police. As I cannot protect myself against a man of your years, I will make the law protect me."

The gentleman hesitated. Then his eyes brightened; and he said, "Then call the police. Call them quickly. You have a ring of mine about you — an heirloom of my family. You shall account for it. Ah! I have you now, you vagabond."

"Pshaw!" said Jack, recovering from a momentary check, "she sent me the ring by the hands of that porter, although I refused it. I might as well accuse her of stealing my money."

"It shall be refunded at once," said the gentleman, reddening and pulling out his purse. "How much did you give her'"

"How should I know?" said Jack with scorn. "I do not count what I give to women who are in need. I gave her what I found in my pocket. Are you willing to give me what you find in yours?"

"By heaven, you are an incredibly impudent swindler," cried the gentleman, looking at him with inexpressible feeling.

"Come, gentlemen. " said an official, advancing between them, "couldn't you settle your little difference somewhere else?*

"I am a passenger," said Jack; "and am endeavoring to leave the station. If it is your business to keep order here, I wish you would rid me of this gentleman. He has annoyed me ever since the train started from Slough."

"I am in a most painful position," said the old gentleman, with emotion. "I have lost my child here; and this man knows her whereabouts. He will tell me nothing; and I — I don't know what to do." Then, turning to Jack with a fresh explosion of wrath, he cried, "Once for all, you villain, will you tell me who your employers are?"

"Once for all," replied Jack, "I will tell you nothing, because I have nothing to tell you. You refuse to believe me; you are infernally impertinent to me; you talk about my employers and of spying and kidnapping: I think you are mad."

"Are you not a theatrical agent? Answer that."

"No. I am not a theatrical agent. As I told you before, I am a composer and teacher of music. If you have any pupils for me, I shall be glad to teach them: if not, go your way, and let me go mine. I am tired of you."

"There, sir," said the official, "the gentleman can't answer you no fairer nor that. If you have a charge to make against him, why, charge him. If not, as he says, you had better move on. Let me call you a cab, and you can follow the young lady. That's the best thing you can do. She might run as far as Scotland while you're talking. Send down a 'ansom there, Bill, will you?"

The man laid his hand persuasively on the arm of the old gentleman, who hesitated, with his lip trembling.

"Sir," said Jack, with sudden dignity: "on my honor I am a perfect stranger to your daughter and her affairs. You know all that passed between us. If you do not wish to lose sight of me, give me your card; and I will send you my address as soon as I have one."

"I request — I — I implore you not to trifle with me in this matter," said the gentleman, slowly taking out his card case. "It would be a — a heartless thing to do. Here is my card. If you have any information, or can acquire any, it shall be liberally paid for — most liberally paid."

Jack, offended afresh, looked at him with scorn; snatched the card, and turned on his heel. The gentleman looked wistfully after him, sighed, shivered, and got into the cab.

The card was inscribed, "Mr. Sigismund Brailsford, Kensington Palace Gardens."

CHAPTER V

A fortnight later the Sutherlands, accompanied by Mrs Beatty, were again in London, on their way to the Isle of Wight. It had been settled that Herbert should go to Ventnor for a month with his mother, so that Mary and he might sketch the scenery of the island together. He had resisted this arrangement at first on the ground that Mrs Herbert's presence would interfere with his enjoyment; but Mary, who had lost her own mother when an infant, had ideas of maternal affection which made Adrian's unfilial feeling shocking to her. She entreated him to come to Ventnor; and he yielded, tempted by the prospect of working beside her, and foreseeing that he could easily avoid his mother's company whenever it became irksome to him.

One day, whilst they were still in London at the hotel in Onslow Gardens, Mr Sutherland, seeing his daughter with her hat and cloak on, asked whither she was going.

"I am going to the Brailsfords', to see Madge," she replied.

"Now what do you want to go there for?" grumbled Mr. Sutherland. "I do not like your associating with that girl."

"Why, papa? Are you afraid that she will make me run away and go on the stage?"

"I didn't say anything of the kind. But she can't be a very rightminded young woman, or she wouldn't have done so herself. However, I have no objection to your calling on the family. They are very nice people — well connected; and Mr. Brailsford is a clever man. But don't go making a companion of Madge."

"I shall not have the opportunity, I am sorry to say. Poor Madge! Nobody has a good word for her."

Mr. Sutherland muttered a string t>f uncomplimentary epithets; but Mary went out without heeding him. At Kensington Palace Gardens she found Magdalen Brailsford alone.

"They are all out," said Magdalen when Mary had done kissing her. "They are visiting, or shopping, or doing something else equally intellectual. I am supposed to be in disgrace; so I am never asked to go with them. As I would not go if they begged me on their knees, I bear the punishment with fortitude."

"But what have you done, Madge? Won't you tell me? Aunt Jane said that her conscience would not permit her to pour such a story into my young ears; and then, of course, I refused to hear it from anybody but yourself, much to Aunt Jane's disgust; for she was burning to tell me. Except that you ran away and went on the stage, I know nothing."

"There is nothing else to know; for that is all that happened."

"But how did it come about?"

"Will you promise not to tell?"

"I promise faithfully."

"You must keep your promise; for I have accomplices who are not suspected, and who will help me when I repeat the exploit, as I fully intend to do the very instant I see my way to success. Do you know where we lived before we came to this house?"

"No. You have lived here ever since I knew you."

"We had lodgings in Gower Street. Mary, did you ever ride in an omnibus?"

"No. But I should not be in the least ashamed to do so if I had occasion."

"How would you like to have to make five pounds worth of clothes last you for two years?"

"I should not like that."

"Lots of people have to do it. We had, when we lived in Gower Street. Father wrote for the papers; and we never had any money, and were always in debt. But we went to the theatres — with orders, of course — much oftener than we do now; and we either walked home or took our carriage, the omnibus. We were recklessly extravagant, and thought nothing of throwing away a shilling on flowers and paper fans to decorate the rooms. I am sure we spent a fortune on three-penny cretonne, to cover the furniture when its shabbiness became downright indecent. We were very fond of dwelling on the lavish way we would spend money if father ever came into the Brailsford property, which seemed the most unlikely thing in the world. But it happened, as unlikely things often do. All the rest of the family — I mean all of it that concerned us — were drowned in the Solent in a yacht accident; and we found ourselves suddenly very rich, and, as I suppose you have remarked — especially in Myra — very stingy. Poor father, whom we used to revile as a miser in Gower Street, is the only one of us who spends money as if he was above caring about it. But the worst of it is that we have got respectable, and taken to society — at least, society has taken to us; — and we have returned the compliment. I haven't, though. I can't stand these Kensington people with their dances and athomes. It's not what I call living really. In Grower Street we used to know a set that had some brains. We gave ourselves airs even then; hut still on Sunday evenings we used to have plenty of people with us to supper whom you are not likely to meet here. One of them was a man named Tarleton, who made money as a theatrical agent and lost it as a manager alternately."

"And you fell in love with him, of course," said Mary.

"Bosh! Fell in love with old Tommy Tarleton! This is not a romance, but a prosaic Gower Street narrative. I never thought about him after we came here until a month ago, when I saw that he was taking a company to Windsor. I always wanted to go on the stage, because nowadays a woman must be either an actress or nothing. So I wrote to him for an engagement, and sent him my photograph."

"Oh, Madge!"

"Why not? His company was playing opera bouffe; and I knew he wanted good looks as much as talent. You don't suppose I sent it as a love token. He wrote back that he had no

101

part open that I could take, but that if I wished to accustom myself to the stage and would find my own dresses, he would let me walk on every night in the chorus, and perhaps find me a small part to understudy."

"Very kind, indeed. And what did you say to his noble offer?"

"I accepted it, and was very glad to get it. It was better than sitting here quarreling with the girls, and going over the same weary argument with father about disgracing the family. I managed it easily enough, after all. There is a woman who keeps a lodging house in Church Street here, who is a sister of the landlady at Gower Street, and knows all about us. She has a second sister whose daughter is a ballet girl, and who is used to theatres. I ran away to Church Street — five minutes' walk; told Polly what I had done; and made her send for Mrs Wilkins, the other sister, whom I carried off to Windsor as chaperon that evening. But the company turned out to be a thirdrate one; and I wasn't comfortable with them: they were rather rowdy. However, I did not stay long. I was recognized on the very first night by someone — I don't know whom — who told Colonel Beatty. He wrote to my father; and I was captured on the third day. You can imagine the scene when the poor old governor walked suddenly into our lodging. He tried to be shocked and stern, and of course only succeeded in being furious. I was stubborn — I can be very mulish when I like; but I was getting tired of walking on in the chorus at night and spending the day with Mrs Wilkins; so I consented to go back with him. He took my purse, which I was foolish enough to leave within his reach whilst I was putting on my bonnet, and so left me without a farthing, helplessly dependent on him. He would not give it me back; and to revenge myself I became very uncivil to him; and then he forbade me to speak. I took him at his word, and made him still madder by taking no notice of the homilies on duty and respectability which he poured forth as we drove to the train."

"Yes: I can quite imagine that. And so you came home and returned to the ways of well conducted girls."

"Not at all. You have only heard the prologue to my real adventure. When we got to the railway station, father, who intended to preach at me during the whole journey, bribed the guard to prevent people from coming into our compartment. The train started, and I had just been requested to attend to something very that must be said to me, when there was an uproar on the platform, and a man burst headlong into the carriage, sat down, folded his arms, and stared majestically at father, who began to abuse him furiously for intruding on us. They quarreled all the way up to London. When they had exhausted the subject of our carriage being private, the man objected to the window being shut — I think because I had done so just before, though perhaps it was more from love of contradiction. Then father objected to his grinding his teeth. Then I interfered and was bidden to hold my tongue. Up jumped the man and asked father what he meant by speaking so to me. He even said — you will not repeat this, please, Mary."

"No. Why? What did he say?"

"He said — it sounded ridiculous — that he would not permit a young and beautiful woman to be tyrannized over."

"Oh! Was he very handsome?"

"N — no. He was not conventionally handsome; but there was something about him that I cannot very well describe. It was a sort of latent power. However, it does not matter, as I suppose I shall never see him again."

"I think I can understand what you mean," said Mary thoughtfully. "There are some men who are considered quite ugly, but who are more remarkable than pretty people. You often see that in artists."

"This man was not in the least like your Adrian, though, Mary. No two people could be more different."

"I know. I was thinking of a very different person."

"Father speaks of him as though he were a monster; but that is perfect nonsense."

"Well, what was the upshot of this interference?"

"Oh, I thought they would have come to blows at first. Father would fight duels every day if they were still in fashion. But the man made an admirable speech which shewed me that his opinions were exactly the same as mine; and father could say nothing in reply. Then they accused each other of being insane, and kept exchanging insults until we came to Paddington, where the guard wanted to give the man to the police for getting into the train after it had started. At last we all got out; and then I committed my capital crime — it really was a dreadful thing to do. But ever since father had taken my purse and made a prisoner of me, I had been thinking of how I could give him the slip and come home just how and when I pleased. Besides, I was quite resolved to apply to a London agent for a regular engagement in some theatre. So when father got into a passion about my box not being found instantly, and went off to look for it, leaving me by myself, the idea of escaping and going to the agent at once occurred to me. I made up my mind and unmade it twenty times in every second. I should not have hesitated a moment if I had had my purse but as it was, I had only my ring;, so that I should have had to stop the cab at the nearest pawnbrokers and I was ashamed to go into such a place — although we sometimes used to send Mrs. Wilkina there, without letting father know, in the Gower Street days. Then the porter came up and said that the cab was waiting and I knew he would expect something then and there from me if I went off by myself. What do you think I did? I went straight up the the man who had travelled with us — he was standing close by, watching me, I think — and asked him to buy my ring."

"Well. Madge: really — :"

"It was an impulse I don't know what put it into my head but the desperate necessity paying the porter hurried me into obeying it. I said I had no money and asked him for a little in exchange for the ring. The man looked at me in the most terrifying way; and just as I was expecting him to seize me and deliver me up to father, he plunged his hand into his pocket and gave me a handful of money. He would not count it, nor touch the ring. I was insisting on his taking either the ring or the money, when he suddenly shouted at me that father was coming, and bundled me me into the cab before I had collected my wits. Then he startled the driver with another shout; and away went the cab. I managed to give the ring to the porter for him. I drove to the agents in Bond Street, and on my way counted the money: two sovereigns, three half-sovereigns, thirteen and sixpence in silver, and seven pennies."

"Four pounds, four, and a penny," said Mary.

"He must have been mad. But there was something chivalrous about it, especially for a nineteenth century incident at Paddington."

"I think it was sheer natural nobility of heart, Mary. Father enrages me by saying that he was a thief, and made fifty pounds profit out of my innocence. As if his refusing the ring was not an absolute proof to the contrary. He got our address from father afterwards, and promised to send us his; but he has never done so."

"I wonder why. He certainly ought to. Your ring is worth a great deal more than four pounds."

"He might not wish to give it up to my father, as it was mine. If he wishes to keep it he is welcome. I am sure he deserves it. Mind: he refused it after giving me the money."

"If you had a nose like mine, and wore a pince-nez, I doubt whether you would have found him so generous. I believe he fell in love with you."

"Nonsense. Who ever knew a man to sacrifice all his money — all he had in the world, perhaps — for the sake of love? I know what men are too well. Besides, he was quite rude to me once in the carriage."

"Well, since he has the ring, and intends to keep it, he has the best of the bargain. Go on with your own adventures. What did the agents say?"

"They all took half-crowns from me, and put my name on their books. They are to write to me if they can procure me an engagement; but I saw enough to convince me that there is not much chance. They are all very agreeable — that is, they thought themselves so — except one grumpy old man, who asked me what I expected when I could neither walk nor speak. That, and my sensations on the stage at Windsor, convinced me that I need some instruction; and I have set Mrs Simpson, the woman in Church Street, to find somebody who can teach me. However, to finish my story, when I saw that there was nothing more to be done that day or the next either, I told the cabman to drive me home, where I found father nearly in hysterics. As soon as the family recovered from their amazement at seeing me, we began to scold and abuse one another. They were so spiteful that father at last took my part; and poor mother vainly tried to keep the peace. At last they retreated, one by one crying, and left me alone with father. I fancy we gave them as good as they brought; for no allusion has been made to my escapade since.

Mary looked at her friend for a while. Then she said, "Madge: you are quite mad. There is not a doubt of it: that episode of the ring settles the question finally. I suppose you regard this bedlamite adventure as the most simple and natural thing in the world."

"When I have my mind made up to do something, it seems the most natural thing in the world to go and do it. I hope you are not going to lecture me for adopting a profession, after all your rhapsodies about high art and so forth."

"But opera bouffe is not high art, Madge. If you had appeared in one of Shakespeare's characters, I should sympathize with you."

"Yes, make a fool of myself as a lady amateur! I have no more ambition to play Shakespeare than you have to paint Transfigurations. Now, don't begin to argue about Art. I have had enough of argument lately to last me for life."

"And you mean to persist?"

"Yes. Why not?"

"Of course, if you have talent —"

"Which you don't believe, although you can see nothing ridiculous in your own dreams of being another Claude Lorraine. You are just like Myra, with her pet formula of, 'Well, Madge, the idea of you being able to act!' Why should I not be able to act as well as anybody else? I intend to try, at any rate."

"You need not be angry with me, Madge. I don't doubt your cleverness; but an actress's life must be a very queer one. And I never said I could paint better than Claude. If you knew how wretched my own productions seem to me, you —"

"Yes, yes: I know all that stuff of Adrian's by heart. If you don't like your own pictures, you may depend upon it no one else will. I am going to be an actress because I think I can act. You are going to be a painter because you think you can't paint. So there's an end of that. Would you mind coming over to Polly's with me?"

"Who is Polly?"

"Our old landlady's sister — my accomplice — the woman who keeps the lodging house in Church Street, Mrs Simpson."

"You don't mean to run away again?"

"No. At least not yet. But she has a lodger who teaches elocution; and as he is very poor, Mrs. Wilkins — Polly's other sister and my late chaperon — thinks he would give me some cheap lessons. And I must have them very cheap, or else go without; for father will hardly trust me with a shilling now. He has never even given me back my purse I have only the remainder of the man's money, and ten pounds that I had laid up."

"And are you going toke a lesson today?"

"No, no. I only want to see the man and ask his terms. If I try to go alone, I shall be watched and suspected. With you I shall be safe: they regard you as a monument of good sense and propriety. If we meet any of the girls, and they ask where we are going, do not mention Church Street."

"But how can we evade them if they ask us?"

"We won't evade them. We will tell them a lie."

"I certainly will not, Madge.

"I certainly will. If people interfere with my liberty, and ask have no business to ask, I will meet force with fraud, and fool them to the top of their bent, as your friend Shakespeare says.

You need not look shocked. You, who are mistress of your house, and rule your father with a rod of iron, are no judge of my position. Put on your hat, and come along. We can walk there in five minutes."

"I will go with but I shall not be a party to any deception."

Madge made a face, but got her bonnet without further words. They went out together, and traversed the passage from Kensington Palace Gardens to Church Street, where Magdalen led the way to a shabby house, with a card inscribed Furnished Apartments in the window.

"Is Mrs Simpson in her room?" said Magdalen, entering unceremoniously as soon as the door was opened.

"Yes, ma'am," said the servant, whose rule it was to address women in bonnets as ma'am, and women in hats as Miss. "She 'ave moved to the second floor since you was here last. The parlors is let."

"I will go up," said Magdalen. "Come on, Mary." And she ran upstairs, followed more slowly by Mary, who thought the house close and ill kept, and gathered her cloak about her to prevent it touching the banisters. When they reached the second floor, they knocked at the door; but no one answered. Above them was a landing, accessible by a narrow uncarpeted stair. They could hear a shrill voice in conversation with a deep one on the third floor, Whilst they waited, the shrill voice rose higher and higher; and the deep voice began to growl ominously.

"A happy pair," whispered Mary. "We had better go downstairs and get the servant to find Mrs Simpson."

"No: wait a little. That is Polly's voice, I am sure. Hark!"

The door above was opened violently and a powerful voice resounded, saying, "Begone, you Jezebel."

"The man!" exclaimed Madge.

Mr Jack!" exclaimed Mary. And they looked wonderingly at one another, and listened.

"How dare you offer me sich language, sir? Do you know whose 'ouse this is?"

"I tell you once for all that I am neither able nor willing to pay you one farthing. Hold your tongue until I have finished." This command was emphasized by a stamp that shook the floor. "I have eaten nothing today; and I cannot afford to starve. Here is my shirt. Here is my waistcoat. Take them — come! take them, or I'll stuff them down your throat — and give them to your servant to pawn: she has pawned the shirt before; and let her get me something to eat with the money. Do you hear?"

"I will not have my servant go to the pawnshop for you and get my house a bad name."

"Then go and pawn them yourself. And do not come to this room again with your threats and complaints unless you wish to be strangled.*

"I'd like to see you lay a finger on me a married woman. Do you call yourself a gentleman —"

Here there was a low growl, a sound of hasty footprints, an inarticulate remonstrance, a checked scream, and then a burst of sobbing and then the words, "You're as hard as a stone, Mr Jack. My poor little Rosie. Ohoo!"

"Stop that noise, you crocodile. What is the matter with you now?"

"My Rosie."

"What is the matter with your Rosie? You are sniveling to have her back because she is happier in the country than stifling in this den with you, you ungovernable old hag."

"God forgive you for that word — ohoo! She ain't in the country."

"Then where the devil is she; and what did you mean by telling me she was there?"

"She's in the 'ospittle. For the Lord's sake don't let it get out on me, Mr Jack, or I should have my house empty. The poor little darling took the scarlet fever; and — and —"

"And you deserve to be hanged for letting her catch it. Why didn't you take proper care of her?"

"How could I help it, Mr. Jack? I'm sure if I could have took it myself instead —"

"I wish to Heaven you had, and the unfortunate child and everybody else might have been well rid of you."

"Oh, don't say that, Mr Jack. I may have spoke hasty to you; but its very hard to be owed money, and not be able to get the things for my blessed angel to be sent to the country in, and she going to be discharged on Friday. You needn't look at me like that, Mr Jack. I wouldn't deceive you of all people."

"You would deceive your guardian angel — if you had one — for a shilling. Give me back those things. Here is a ring which you can pawn instead. It is worth something considerable, I suppose. Take what money you require for the child, and bring me the rest. But mind! Not one farthing of it shall you have for yourself, nor should you if I owed you ten years' rent. I would not pawn it to save you from starvation. And get me some dinner, and some music paper — the same you used to get me, twenty-four staves to the page. Off with you. What are you gaping at?"

"Why, wherever did you get this ring, Mr. Jack?"

"That's nothing to you. Take it away; and make haste with my dinner."

"But did you buy it? Or was it —" The voice abruptly broke into a smothered remonstrance; and the landlady appeared on the landing, apparently pushed out by the shoulders. Then the lodger's door slammed.

"Polly," cried Magdalen impatiently. "Polly."

"Lor', Miss Madge!"

"Come down here. We have waited ten minutes for you."

Mrs. Simpson came down, and brought her two visitors into her sittingroom on the second floor. "Won't you sit down Miss?" she said to Mary. "Don't pull that chair from the wall, Miss Madge, its leg is broke. Oh, dear! I'm greatly worried, what with one thing and another."

"We have been listening to a battle between you and the and the lodger upstairs" said Magdalen, "and you seemed to be getting the worst of it."

"No one knows what I've gone through with that man." said Mrs. Simpson, wiping her eyes. "He walked into the room a fortnight ago when I was out, without asking leave. Knocks at the door at one o'clock in the day and asks the girl if the garret is let to anyone. 'No sir,' says she. So he goes up and plants himself as if he owned the house. To be sure, she knew him of old; but that was all the more reason for keeping him out; for he never had a halfpenny. The first thing he sent her to do was to pawn his watch. And the things I have to put up with from him! He thinks no more of calling me every name he can lay his tongue to, and putting me out of my own room than if he was a prince, and me his kitchen maid. He is as strong as a bull, and cares for nothing nor nobody but himself."

"What is he?" said Magdalen. "His name is Jack, isn't it?"

"Yes; and a fit name it is for him. He came here first, to my sorrow, last December, and took the garret for half-a-crown a week. He had a portmanteau then and some little money; and he was quiet enough for almost a month. But he kept very much to himself except for letting poor little Rosie play about his room, and teaching her little songs. You can't think what a queer child she is, Miss Sutherland. I'm sure you'd say so if you saw Mr. Jack, the only lodger she took any fancy to. At last he sent the servant to pawn his things; and I, like a fool, was loath to see him losing his clothes, and offered to let the rent run if he could pay at the end of the month. Then it came out that he was in the music profession, and akshally expected to get pupils while he was living in a garret. I did a deal for him, although he was nothing to me. I got him a stationer's daughter from High Street to teach. After six lessons, if you'll believe it, Miss, and she as pleased as anything with the way she was getting along, he told the stationer that it was waste of money to have the girl taught, because she had no qualification but vanity. So he lost her; and now she has lessons at four guineas a dozen from a lady that gets all the credit for what he taught her. Then Simpson's brother-in-law got him a place in a chapel in the Edgeware Road to play the harmonium and train the choir. But they couldn't stand him. He treated them as if they were dogs; and the three richest old ladies in the congregation, who had led the singing for forty-five years, walked out the second night, and said they wouldn't enter the chapel till he was gone. When the minister rebuked him, he up and said that if he was a God and they sang to him like that, he'd scatter 'em with lightning. That's his notion of manners. So he had to leave; but a few of the choir liked him and got him occasionally to play the piano at a glee club on the first floor of B public house. he got five shillings once a fortnight or so for that; and not another halfpenny had he to live on except pawning his clothes bit by bit. You may imagine all the rent 1 got. At last he managed someway to get took on as tutor by a gentleman at Windsor. I had to release his clothes out of my own money before he could go. I was five pound out of pocket by him, between rent and other things."

"Did he ever pay you?" said Mary.

"Oh, yes, Miss. He certainly sent me the money. I am far from saying that he is not honorable when he has the means."

"It is a funny coincidence," said Mary. "It was to us that Mr Jack came as tutor. He taught Charlie."

"To you!" said Magdalen, surprised and by no means pleased. "Then you know him?"

"Yes. He left us about a fortnight ago."

"Just so," said Mrs. Simpson, "and was glad enough to come straight back here without a penny in his pocket. And here he is like to be until some other situation drops into his lap. If I may ask, Miss, why did he leave you?"

"Oh. for no particular reason," said Mary uneasily. "That is, my brother had left Windsor; and we did not require Mr Jack anymore."

"So he was the tutor of whom Mrs Beatty told mother." said Magdalen significantly.

"Yes."

"I hope he was pleasanter in your house, Miss, than he is in mine. However, that's not my business. I have no wish to intrude. Except the letter he wrote me with the money, not a civil word have I ever had from him."

"A lady whom I know," said Mary, "employed him, whilst he was with us, to correct some songs which she wrote. Perhaps I could induce her to give him some more. I should like to get him something to do. But I am afraid she was offended by the way he altered her composition last time."

"Well, Polly," said Magdalen, "we are forgetting my business. Where is the professor that Mrs Wilkins told me of? I wish Mr Jack gave lessons in elocution. I should like to have him for a master."

"Why, Miss Madge, to tell you the honest truth, it is Mr Jack. But wait till I show you something. He's given me a ring to pawn; and it's the very moral of your own that you used to wear in Gower Street."

"It is mine, Polly. I owe Mr Jack four guineas; and I must pay him today. Don't stare: I will tell you all about it afterwards. I have to thank him too, for getting me out of a great scrape. Mary: do you wish to see him?"

"Well, I would rather not, " said Mary slowly: "at least, I think it would be better not. But after all it can do no harm; and I suppose it would not be right for you to see him alone."

"Oh, never mind that," said Magdalen suspiciously. "I can have Polly with me."

"If you had rather not have me present, I will go."

"Oh, I don't care. Only you seemed to make some difficulty about it yourself."

"There can be no real difficulty, now that I come to consider it. Yet — I hardly know what I ought to do."

"You had better make up your mind," said Magdalen impatiently.

"Well, Madge, I have made up my mind," said Mary, perching her spectacles and looking composedly at her friend. "I will stay."

"Very well." Said Madge, not with a very good grace: "I suppose we must not go to Mr. Jack, so he had better come to us. Polly go and tell him that two ladies wish to see him."

"You had better say on business." added Mary.

"And don't mention our names I want to see whether he will know me again." said Magdalen. Mary looked hard at her.

107

"D'ye really mean it, Miss Madge?"

"Good gracious, yes!" replied Magdalen angrily.

The landlady, after lingering a moment in doubt and wonder went out. Silence ensued. Magdalen's color brightened; and she moved her chair to a place whence she could see herself in the mirror. Mary closed her lips, and sat motionless and rather pale. Not a word passed between them until the door opened abruptly and Jack, with his coat buttoned up to his chin, made a short step into the room. Recognizing Mary, he stopped and frowned.

"How do you do, Mr Jack?*" she said, bowing steadily to him. He bowed slightly, and looked around the room. Seeing Magdalen, he was amazed. She bowed too, and he gave her a scared nod.

"Won't you sit down, Mr Jack?" said the landlady, assuming the manner in which she was used to receive company.

"Have you pawned that ring yet?" he said, turning suddenly to her.

"No," she retorted, scandalized.

"Then give it back to me." She did so; and he looked at Magdalen, saying, "You have come just in time."

"I came to thank you."

"You need not thank me. I was sorry afterwards for having helped a young woman to run away from her father. If I were not the most hotheaded fool in England, I should have stopped you. I hope no harm came of it."

"I am sorry to have caused you any uneasiness," said Magdalen, coloring. "The young woman drove straight home after transacting some business that she wished to conceal from her father. That was all."

"So much the better. If I had known you were at home, I should have sent you your ring."

"My father expected you to write."

"I told him I would; but I thought better of it. I had nothing to tell him."

"You must allow me to repay you the sum you so kindly lent me that day, Mr. Jack," said Magdalen in a lower voice, confusing herself by an unskilled effort to express gratitude by her tone and manner.

"It will be welcome, he replied moodily. Magdalen slowly took out a new purse. "Give it to Mrs. Simpson," he added, turning away. The movement brought him face to face with Mary, before whom his brow gathered portentously. She bore his gaze steadily, but could not trust herself to speak.

"I have some further business, Mr Jack," said Magdalen.

"I beg your pardon," said he, turning again towards her.

" Mrs. Simpson told me —"

"Ah!" said he, interrupting her, and casting a threatening look at the landlady. "It was she who told you where I was located, was it?"

"Well, I don't see the harm if I did," said Mrs. Simpson. "If you look on it as a liberty on my part to recommend you, Mr. Jack, I can easily stop doing it."

"Recommend me! What does she mean, Miss Brailsford —you are Miss Brailsford, are you not?"

"Yes, I was about to say that Mrs Simpson told me that you gave — that is —I should perhaps explain first that I intend to go on the stage."

"What do you want to go on the stage for?"

"The same as anybody else, I suppose," said Mrs Simpson indignantly.

"I wish to make it my profession," said Magdalen.

"Do you mean make your living by it?"

"I hope so."

"Humph!"

"Do you think I should have any chance of success?"

"I suppose, if you have intelligence and perseverance, and can drudge and be compliant, and make stepping stones of your friends — but there! I know nothing about success. What have I got to do with it? Do you think, as your father did, that I am a theatrical agent?"

"Well I must say, Mr. Jack," exclaimed the landlady, "that those who try to befriend you get very little encouragement. I am right sorry, so I am, that I brought Miss Madge to ask you for lessons."

"Lessons!" said Jack. "Oh! I did not understand. Lessons in what? Music?"

"No," said Magdalen. "I wanted lessons in elocution and so forth. At least, I was told the other day that I did not know how to speak."

"Neither do you. That is true enough," said Jack thoughtfully. "Well, I don't profess to prepare people for the stage; but I can teach you to speak, if you have anything to say or any feeling for what better people put into your mouth."

"You are not very sanguine as to the result, I fear."

"The result, as far as it goes, is certain, if you practice. If not, I shall give you up. After all, there is no reason why you should not do something better than be a fine lady. Your appearance is good: all the rest can be acquired — except a genius for tomfoolery, which you must take your chance of. The public want actresses, because they think all actresses bad. They don't want music or poetry because they know that both are good. So actors and actresses thrive, as I hope you will; and poets and composers starve, as I do. When do you wish to begin?"

It was soon arranged that Magdalen should take lessons in Mrs Simpson's sitting room, and in her presence, every second weekday, and that she should pay Mr Jack for them at the rate of three guineas a dozen. The first was to take place on the next day but one. Then the two ladies rose to go. But Magdalen first drew Mrs Simpson aside to pay her the money which Jack had lent her; so that he was left near the door with Mary, who had only spoken once since he entered the room.

"Mr. Jack," she said, in an undertone: "I fear I have intruded on you. But I assure you I did not know who it was that we were coming to see."

"Else you would not have come."

"Only because I should have expected to be unwelcome."

"It does not matter. I am glad to see you, though I have no reason to be. How is Mr Adrian?"

"Mr Herbert"

"I beg his pardon. Mr Herbert, of course."

"He is quite well, thank you."

Jack rubbed hands stealthily, and looked at Mary as though the recollection of Adrian tickled his sense of humor. As she tried to look coldly at him, he said, with a shade of pity in his tone, "Ah, Miss Sutherland, it one thing to be very fond of music: it is quite another to be able to compose."

"Is it?" said Mary, puzzled.

He shook his head. "You don't see the relevance of that," said he. "Well, never mind."

She looked at him uneasily, and hesitated. Then she said slowly, "Mr. Jack: some people at Windsor, friends of mine, have been asking about you. I think, if you could come down once a week, I could get a music class together for you."

"No doubt," he said. his angry look returning. "They will take lessons because you ask them to be charitable to your discarded tutor. Why did you discard him if you think him fit to teach your friends?"

"Not at all. The project was mentioned last season, before I knew you. It is simply that we wish to take lessons. If you do not get the class somebody else will. It is very difficult to avoid offending you, Mr Jack."

"Indeed! Why does the world torment me, if it expects to find me gracious to it? And who are the worthy people that are burning to soar in the realms of song?"

"Well, to begin with. I should l —"

"You! I would not give you lessons though your life depended on it. No, by Heaven! At least," he continued, more placably, as she recoiled, evidently hurt, "you shall have no lessons from me for money. I will teach you, if you wish to learn; but you shall not try to make amends for your old caprice of beggaring me, by a new caprice to patronize me."

"Then of course I cannot take any lessons."

"I thought not. You will confer favors on your poor music maker; but you will not stoop to accept them from him. Your humble dog, Miss Sutherland." He made her a bow.

"You quite mistake me," said Mary, unable to control her vexation. "Will you take the class or not?"

"Where will the class be?"

"I could arrange to have it at our house if —"

"Never. I have crossed its threshold for the last time. So long as it is not there, I do not care where it is. Not less than one journey a week, and not less than a guinea clear profit for each journey. Those are my lowest terms: I will take as much more as I can get, but nothing less. Perhaps you are thinking better of getting the class for me."

"I never break my word, Mr Jack."

"Ha! Don't you! I do. A fortnight ago I swore never to speak to you again. The same day I swore never to part with your friend's ring except to herself. Well, here I am speaking to you for no better reason than that you met me and offered to put some money in my way. And you stopped me in the act of pawning her ring, which I was going to do because I thought I would rather have a beefsteak. But you are adamant. You never change your mind. You have a soul above fate and necessity! Ha! ha!"

"Magdalen," said Mary, turning to her friend, who had waiting for the end of the conversation: "I think we had better go." Mary was crimson with suppressed resentment; and Magdalen, not displeased to see it, advanced to bid Jack farewell in her most attractive manner. He immediately put off his bantering air, and ceremoniously accompanied them downstairs to the door, where Magdalen, going out first, gave him her hand. Mary hesitated; and he wrinkled his brow as he looked at her.

"I will tell Miss Cairns to write to you about the class," she said. He listened to her with an attention which she thought derisive. Flushing with displeasure, she added, "And as Miss Cairns has done nothing to incur your anger, I beg, Mr Jack that you will remember that she is a lady, and will expect to be treated with common civility."

"Oho!" said Jack, delighted. "Have I been rude? Have I?"

"You have been excessively rude, Mr. Jack." She went out quickly, sending the words with an angry glance over her shoulder. He shut the door, and went upstairs to Mrs Simpson's room, braying like a donkey.

"Well, Jezebel," he cried. "Well, Polly. Well, Mrs. Quickly. How are you?"

"I never was so ashamed in my life, Mr Jack. There were those young ladies only too anxious to do what they could for you, and you like a bear. No wonder you can't get on, when you won't control yourself and have behavior."

"I am a bear, am I? You had better recollect that I am a hungry bear, and that if my dinner does not come up, you will get a hug that will break every bone in your stays. Don't forget the music paper. You have plenty of money now. Four pounds four and a penny, eh?"

"You've no call to fear: none of it will be stolen. Miss Madge thought you hadn't counted it. Little did she know you."

"She knew me better than you, you sordid hag. I counted my money that morning — four pounds nine and sevenpence. I gave the railway clerk ten shillings; he gave me five back — that left four pounds four and sevenpence. I arrived here with sixpence in my pocket; and from that I knew that I gave her four, four, and a penny. That reminds me that you sat there and let Miss Sutherland go away without making me ask her to send on my portmanteau, now that I have money to pay the carriage. You're very stupid."

"How could I tell whether you wanted me to mention it or not? I was thinking of it all the time; but —"

"You were thinking of it all the time!" cried Jack, in a frenzy. "And you never mentioned it! Here go for my dinner. You would drive the most patient man living out of his senses."

CHAPTER VI

When Mrs Beatty had been a fortnight in the Isle of Wight with her brother's family, her husband came down from Windsor to see her. On the morning after his arrival, they were in the garden, he smoking, and she in a rocking chair near him, with a newspaper in her hand.

"My dear," he said, after a preliminary cough.

"Yes, Richard," she said amiably, putting down the paper.

"I was saying last night that Clifton is leaving us."

"Oh, the bandmaster! Yes" Mrs Beatty was not interested, and she took up the paper again.

"Mary was speaking to me about it this morning."

Mrs Beatty put down the paper decisively, and looked at her husband.

"She wants me to get that fellow — Charlie's tutor — into Clinton's place. I don't know whether he is fit for it?"

"You don't know whether he is fit for it! Pray, Richard, did you allow Mary to think that we will countenance any further transactions between her and that man."

"I thought I would speak to you about it."

"She ought to ashamed of herself. Don't listen to her on any account, Richard."

"Well, will you speak to her? It is not exactly a subject that I can take her to task about; and I really don't exactly know what to say to her when she comes at me. She always argues; and I hate argument."

"Then I suppose I must face her arguments — I will make short work of them too. Whenever there is anything pleasant to be said in the family, you are willing enough to take it out of my mouth. The unpleasant things are left to me. Then people say, 'Poor Colonel Beatty: he has such a disagreeable wife."

"Who says so?"

"It is not your fault if they do not say so."

"If the fellow comes into the regiment, he will soon be taught how to behave himself. Though for all I have seen to the contrary, he can behave himself well enough. That is my difficulty in talking to Mary. If she has no fault to find with him, I am sure I have none."

"You are going to take his part against me, Colonel Beatty. It does not matter that he repeatedly insulted me — everybody does that. But I thought you might have had some little fault to find with a person who debauched your men and held drunken orgies in my brother's house."

"Well, Jane, if you come to that, you know very well that Charles was an incorrigible scamp long enough before Jack ever met him. As to bringing him to play at Beulah, Charles got five shillings for his trouble, and went as he might have gone to one of your dances. He spoke to me of Jack as a gentleman who had employed him, not as a comrade."

"To you, no doubt he did. Adrian Herbert heard how he spoke to Jack."

"Besides, Mary expressly says that she does not complain of that at all."

"And what does she complain of?"

Colonel Beatty considered for a moment, and then answered, "She does not complain of anything, as far as I can make out."

"Indeed! She dismissed him. You will at least not deny that."

"My dear, I am not denying anyth —"

"Then let nothing induce you to bring them together again. You ought to understand that much without any hint from me, knowing. as you do, what a strange girl she is."

"Why? Do you think there is anything between them?"

"I never said so. I know very well what I think."

Colonel Beatty smoked a while in silence. Then, seeing Mary come from the house, carrying a box of colors, he busied himself with his pipe, and strolled away.

"What is the matter?" said Mary.

"Nothing that I am aware of," said Mrs. Beatty. "Why?"

"You do not look happy. And Uncle Richard's shoulders have a resigned set, as if he had been blown up lately."

"Ha! Oh! You are a wonderful observer, Mary. Are you going out?"

"I am waiting for Adrian."

Mary went round the garden in search of a flower. She was adorning her bosom with one, when Mrs. Beatty, who had been pretending to read, could contain herself no longer, and exclaimed:

"Now, Mary, it is of no use your asking Richard to get that man as bandmaster. He shall not do it."

"So that is what was the matter," said Mary coolly.

"I mean what I say, Mary. He shall never show his face in Windsor again with my consent."

"He shows his face there once a week already, aunt. Miss Cairns writes to say that he has a singing class at their house, and three pianoforte pupils in the neighborhood."

"If I had known that," said Mrs Beatty, angrily, "I should not have left Windsor. It is of a piece with the rest of his conduct. However, no matter. We shall see how long he will keep his pupils after I go back."

"Why, aunt? Would you take away his livelihood because you do not happen to like him personally?"

"I have nothing to do with his livelihood. I do not consider it proper for him to be at Windsor, after being dismissed by Richard. There are plenty of other places for him to go to. I have quite made up my mind on the subject. If you attempt to dispute me, I shall be offended."

"I have made up my mind too. Whatever mischief you may do to Mr Jack at Windsor will be imputed to me, aunt."

"I never said that I would do him any mischief."

"You said you would drive him out of Windsor. As he lives by his teaching, I think that would be as great a mischief as it is in your power to do him."

"Well, I cannot help it. It is your fault."

"If I have helped to get him the pupils, and am begging you not to interfere with him, how is it my fault?"

"Ah! I thought you had something to do with it. And now let me tell you, Mary, that it is perfectly disgraceful, the open way in which you hanker after —"

"Aunt!"

" — that common man. I wonder at a girl of your tastes and understanding having so little selfrespect as to to let everybody see that your head has been turned by a creature without polish or appearance — not even a gentleman. And all this too while you are engaged to Adrian Herbert, his very opposite in every respect. I tell you, Mary, it's not proper: it's not decent. A tutor! If it were anybody else it would not matter so much — but Oh for shame, Mary, for shame."

"Aunt Jane —"

"Hush, for goodness sake. Here he is."

"Who?" cried Mary, turning quickly. But it was only Adrian, equipped for sketching.

"Good morning," he said gaily, but with a thoughtful, polite gaiety. "This is the very sky we want for that bit of the undercliff."

"We were just saying how late you were," said Mrs Beatty graciously. He shook her hand, and looked in some surprise at Mary, whose expression, as she stood motionless, puzzled him.

"Do you know what we were really saying when you interrupted us, Adrian?"

"Mary," exclaimed Mrs. Beatty.

"Aunt Jane was telling me," continued Mary, not heeding her, "that I was hankering after Mr Jack, and that my conduct was not decent. Have you ever remarked anything indecent about my conduct, Adrian?"

Herbert looked helplessly from her to her aunt in silence. Mrs. Beatty's confusion, culminating in a burst of tears, relieved him from answering.

"Do not listen to her," she said presently, striving to control herself. "She is an ungrateful girl."

"I have quoted her exact words," said Mary, unmoved; "and I am certainly not grateful for them. Come, Adrian. We had better lose no more time if we are to finish our sketches before luncheon?"

"But we cannot leave Mrs. Beatty in this —"

"Never mind me: I am ashamed of myself for giving way, Mr Herbert. It was not your fault. I had rather not detain you."

Adrian hesitated. But seeing that he had better go, he took up his bundle of easels and stools, and went out with Mary, who did not even look at her aunt. They had gone some distance before either spoke. Then he said, "I hope Mrs Beatty has not been worrying you, Mary?"

"If she has, I do not think she will do it again without serious reflexion. I have found that the way to deal with worldly people is to frighten them by repeating their scandalous whisperings aloud. Oh, I was very angry that time, Adrian."

"But what brought Jack on the carpet again? I thought we were rid of him and done with him?"

"I heard that he was very badly off in London; and I asked Colonel Beatty to get him made bandmaster of the regiment in place of John Sebastian Clifton — the man you used to laugh at — who is going to America. Then Aunt Jane interfered, and imputed motives to my intercession — such motives as she could appreciate herself."

"But bow did you find out Jack's position in London."

"From Madge Brailsford, who is taking lessons from him. Why? Are you jealous?"

"If you really mean that question, it will spoil my day's work, or rather my day's pleasure; for my work is all pleasure, nowadays."

"No, of course I do not mean it. I beg your pardon."

"Will you make a new contract with me, Mary'"

"What is it?"

"Never to allude to that execrable musician again. I have remarked that his name alone suffices to breed discord everywhere."

"It is true," said Mary, laughing. "I have quarreled a little with Madge, a great deal with Aunt Jane, almost with you, and quite with Charlie about him."

Then let us consider him, from henceforth, in the *Index expurgatorius*. I swear never to mention him on a sketching excursion — never at all, in fact, unless on very urgent occasion, which is not likely to arise. Will you swear also?"

"I swear," said Mary, raising her hand." *Lo giuro* as they say in the Opera. But without prejudice to his bandmastership."

"As to that, I am afraid you have spoiled his chance with Colonel Aunt Jane?"

"Yes," said Mary slowly: "I forgot that. I was thinking only of my own outraged feelings when I took my revenge. And I had intended to coax her into seconding me in the matter."

Herbert laughed.

"It is not at all a thing to be laughed at, Adrian, when you come to think of it. I used to fancy that I had set myself aside from the ordinary world to live a higher life than most of those about me. But I am beginning to find out that when I have to act, I do very much as they do. As I suppose they judge me by my actions and not by my inner life, no doubt they see me much as I see them. Perhaps they have an inner life too. If so, the only difference between us is that I have trained my eye to see more material for pictures in a landscape than they. They may even enjoy the landscape as much, without knowing why."

"Do you know why?"

"I suppose not. I mean that I can point out those aspects of the landscape which please me, and they cannot. But that is not a moral difference. Art cannot take us out of the world."

"Not if we are worldly, Mary."

"But how can we help being worldly? I was born into the world: I have lived all my life in it: I have never seen or known a person or thing that did not belong to it. How can I be anything else than worldly?"

"Does the sun above us belong to it, Mary? Do the stars, the dreams that poets have left us, the realms that painters have shewn us, the thoughts you and I interchange sometimes when nothing has occurred to disturb your faith? Do these things belong to it?"

"I don't believe they belong exclusively to us two. If they did, I think we should be locked up as lunatics for perceiving them. Do you know, Adrian, lots of people whom we consider quite foreign to us spiritually, are very romantic in their own way. Aunt Jane cries over novels which make me laugh. Your mother reads a good deal of history, and she likes pictures, I remember when she used to sing very nicely."

"Yes. She likes pictures, provided they are not too good."

"She says the same of you. And really, when she pats me on the shoulder in her wise way, and asks me when I will be tired of playing at what she calls transcendentalism, I hear, or fancy I hear, an echo of her thought in my own mind. I have been very happy in my art studies and I don't think I shall ever find a way of life more tranquil and pleasant than they led me to; but, for all that, I have a notion sometimes that it is a way of life which I am outgrowing. I am getting wickeder as I get older, very likely."

"You think so for the moment. If you leave your art, the world will beat you back to it. The world has not an ambition worth sharing, or a prize worth handling, Corrupt success, disgraceful failures, or sheeplike vegetation are all it has to offer. I prefer Art, which gives me a sixth sense of beauty, with selfrespect: perhaps also an immortal reputation in return for honest endeavor in a labor of love."

"Yes, Adrian. That used to suffice for me: indeed, it does so still when I am in the right frame of mind. But other worlds are appearing vaguely on the horizon. Perhaps woman's art is of woman's life a thing apart, 'tis man's whole existence; just as love is said to be the reverse — though it isn't."

"It does not scan that way," said Adrian, with an uneasy effort to be flippant.

No," said Mary, laughing. "This is the place."

"Yes," said Adrian, unstrapping the easels. "You must paint off the fit of depression that is seizing you. The wind has gone round to the southwest. What an exquisite day!"

"It is a little oppressive, I think. I am just in the humor for a sharp evening breeze, with the sea broken up into slate colored waves, and the yachts ripping them up in their hurry home. Thank you, I would rather have the stool that has no back: I will settle the rest myself. Adrian: do you think me ill-tempered?"

"What a question to explode on me! Why?"

"No matter why. Answer my question."

"I think you always control yourself admirably."

"You mean when I am angry?"

"Yes."

"But, putting my selfcontrol out of the question, do you think I get angry often — too often, even though I do not let my anger get the better of me?"

"Not too often, certainly."

"But often?"

"Well, no. That is, not absolutely angry. I think you are quick to perceive and repel an attack, even when it is only thoughtlessly implied. But now we must drop introspection for the present, Mary. If our sketches are to be finished before luncheon, I must work hard; and so must you. No more conversation until a quarter past one."

"So be it," said Mary, taking her seat on the campstool. They painted silently for two hours, interrupted occasionally by strollers, who stopped to look on, much to Herbert's annoyance, and somewhat to Mary's gratification. Meanwhile the day grew warmer and warmer; and the birds and insects sang and shrilled incessantly.

"Finished," said Mary at last, putting down her palette "And not in the least like nature. I ventured a little Prussian blue in that corner of the sky, with disastrous results."

"I will look presently," said Herbert, without turning from his canvas, "It will take at least another day to finish mine."

"You are too conscientious, Adrian. I feel sure your sketches have too much work in them."

"I have seen many pictures without enough work in them: never with too much. I suppose I must stop now for the present. It is time to return."

"Yes," said Mary, packing her sketching furniture. "Oh, dear!" As Faulconbridge says, 'Now, by my life, the day grows wondrous hot.' Falonbridge, by the bye, would have thought us a pair of fools. Nevertheless I like him."

"I am sorry to hear it. Most women like men who are arrogant bullies. Let me see your sketch."

"It is not a masterpiece, as you may perceive."

"No. You are impatient, Mary, and draw with a stiff, heavy hand. Look before you into the haze. There is no such thing as an outline in the landscape."

"I cannot help it. I try to soften everything as much as possible; but it only makes the colors look sodden. It is all nonsense my trying to paint. I shall give it up."

Must I pay you compliments to keep up your courage. You are unusually diffident today. You have done the cottage and the potato field better than I."

"Very likely. My touch suits potato fields. I think I had better make a specialty of them. Since I can paint neither sky nor sea nor golden grain, I shall devote myself to potato fields in wet weather."

Herbert, glancing up at her as he stooped to shoulder his easel, did not answer. A little later, when they were on their way home, he said, "Are you conscious of any change in yourself since you came down here, Mary?"

"No. What kind of change?" She had been striding along beside him, looking boldly ahead in her usual alert manner; but now she slackened her pace, and turned her eyes uneasily downward.

"I have noticed a certain falling off in the steady seriousness that used to be your chief characteristic. You are becoming a little inconsiderate and even frivolous about things that you formerly treated with unvarying sympathy and reverence. This makes me anxious. Our engagement is likely to be such a long one, that the least change in you alarms me. Mary: is it that you are getting tired of Art, or only of me?"

"Oh, absurd! nonsense, Adrian!"

"There is nothing of your old seriousness in that answer, Mary."

"It is not so much a question as a reproach that you put to me. You should have more confidence in yourself; and then you would not fear my getting tired of you. As to Art, I am not exactly getting tired of it; but I find that I cannot live on Art alone; and I am beginning to doubt whether I might not spend my time better than in painting, at which I am sure I shall never do much good. If Art were a game of pure skill, I should persevere; but it is like whist, chance and skill mixed. Nature may have given you her ace of trumps — genius; but she has not given me any trumps at all — not even court cards."

"If we all threw up our cards merely because we had not the ace of trumps in our hand, I fear there would be no more whist played in the world. But, to drop your metaphor, which I do not like, I can assure you that Nature has been kinder to you than to me. I had to paint harder and longer than you have before I could paint as well as you can."

"That sort of encouragement kept up my ardor for a long time, Adrian; but its power is exhausted now. In future I may sketch to amuse myself and to keep mementos with which I have pleasant associations, but not to elevate my tastes and perfect my morals. Perhaps it is that change of intention which makes me frivolous, as you say I have suddenly become.

"And since when," said Herbert gravely, "have you meditated this very important change?"

"I never meditated it at all. It came upon me unawares. I did not even know what it was until your question forced me to give an account of it. What an infidel I am! But let me tell you this, Adrian. If you suddenly found yourself a Turner, Titian, Michael Angelo and Holbein all rolled into one, would you be a bit happier?"

"I cannot conceive how r you can doubt it."

"I know you would paint better" (Herbert winced), "but it is not at all obvious to me that you would be happier. However, I am in a silly humor to-day; for I can see nothing in a proper way. We had better talk about something else."

"The humor has lasted for some days, already, Mary. And it must be talked about, and seriously too, if you have concluded, like my mother, that I am wasting my life in pursuit of a chimera. Has she been speaking to you about me?"

"Oh, Adrian, you are accusing me of treachery. You must not think, because I have lost faith in my own artistic destiny, that I have lost faith in yours also."

"I fear, if you have lost your respect for Art, you have lost your respect for me. If so, you know that you may consider yourself free as far as I am concerned. You must not hold yourself in bondage to a dreamer, as people consider me."

"I do not exactly understand. Are you offering me my liberty, or claiming your own?"

"I am offering you yours. I think you might have guessed that."

"I don't think I might. It is not pleasant to be invited to consider oneself free. If you really wish it, I shall consider myself so."

"The question is, do you wish it?"

"Excuse me, Adrian: the question is, do you wish it?"

"My feelings towards you are quite unchanged."

"And so are mine towards you."

After this they walked for a little time in silence. Then Mary said, "Adrian: do you remember our congratulating ourselves last June on our immunity from the lovers' quarrels which occur in the vulgar world? I think — perhaps it is due to my sudden secession from the worship of Art — I think we made a sort of first attempt at one that time."

"Ha! ha! Yes. But we failed, did we not, Mary?"

"Thanks to our inexperience, we did. But not very disgracefully. We shall do better the next time, most likely."

"Then I hope the next time will never come."

"I hope not." Here they reached the garden gate.

"You must come in and lunch with us, to save me from facing Aunt Jane after my revenge upon her this morning."

Then they went in together, and found that Mrs Herbert had called and was at table with the Colonel and Mrs Beatty.

"Are we late?" said Mary.

Mrs. Beatty closed her lips and did not reply. The Colonel hastened to say that they had only just sat down. Mrs. Herbert promptly joined in the conversation; and the meal proceeded without Mrs Beatty's determination not to speak to her niece becoming unpleasantly obvious, until Mary put on her eyeglasses and said, looking at her aunt in her searching myopic way:

"Aunt Jane: will you come with me to the two-forty train to meet papa?"

Mrs Beatty maintained her silence for a few seconds. Then she reddened, and said sulkily, "No, Mary, I will not. You can do without me very well."

"Adrian: will you come?"

"Unfortunately," said Mrs Herbert, "Adrian is bound to me for the afternoon. We are going to Portsmouth to pay a visit. It is time for us to go now," she added, looking at her watch and rising.

During the leave taking which followed, Colonel Beatty got his hat, judging that he had better go out with the Herberts than stay between his wife and Mary in their present tempers. But Mrs Beatty did not care to face her niece alone. When the guests were gone, she moved towards the door.

"Aunt," said Mary, "don't go yet. I want to speak to you."

Mrs. Beatty did not turn.

"Very well," said Mary. "But remember, aunt, if there is to be a quarrel, it will not be of my making."

Mrs. Beatty hesitated, and said, "As soon as you express your sorrow for your conduct this morning, I will speak to you."

"I am very sorry for what passed." Mary looked at her aunt as she spoke, not contritely. Mrs Beatty, dissatisfied, held the door handle for a moment longer, then slowly came back and sat down. "I am sure you ought to be." she said.

I am sure you ought to be," said Mary.

What!" cried Mrs. Beatty, about to rise again.

'You should have taken what I said as an apology, and let well alone," said Mary. "I am sorry that I resented your accusation this morning in a way that might have made mischief between me and Adrian. But you had no right to say what you did; and I had every right to be angry with you."

"You have a right to be angry with me! Do you know who I am, Miss?"

"Aunt, if you are going to call me 'Miss,' we had better stop talking altogether."

Mrs Beatty saw extreme vexation in her niece's expression, and even a tear in her eye. She resolved to assert her authority. "Mary," she said: "do you wish to provoke me into sending you to your room?"

Mary rose. "Aunt Jane," she said, "if you don't choose to treat me with due respect, as you have to treat other women, we must live apart. If you cannot understand my feelings, at least you know my age and position. This is the second time you have insulted me today." She went to the door, looking indignantly at her aunt as she passed. The look was returned by one of alarm, as though Mrs Beatty were going to cry again. Mary, seeing this, restrained her anger with an effort as she reached the threshold, stood still for a moment, and then came back to the table.

"I am a fool to lose my temper with you, aunt," she said, dropping into the rocking chair with an air of resolute good humor, which became her less than her anger; "but really you are very aggravating. Now, don't make dignified speeches to me: it makes me feel like a housemaid and I'm sure it makes you feel 1 like a cook." Mrs Beatty colored. In temper and figure she was sufficiently like the cook of caricature to make the allusion disagreeable to her. "I always feel ridiculous and remorseful after a quarrel," continued Mary, "whether I am in the right or not — if there be any right in a quarrel."

"You are a very strange girl," said Mrs Beatty, ruefully. "When I was your age, I would not have dared to speak to my elders as you speak to me."

"When you were young," responded Mary, "the world was in a state of barbarism and young people used to spoil the old people, just as you fancy the old spoil the young nowadays. Besides, you are not so very much my elder, after all. I can remember quite well when you were married."

"That may be," said Mrs. Beatty, gravely. "It is not so much my age, perhaps; but you should remember, Mary, that I am related to your father."

"So am I."

"Don't be ridiculous, child. Ah, what a pity it is that you have no mother, Mary! It is a greater loss to you than you think."

"It is time to go to meet papa," said Mary, rising. "I hope Uncle Richard will be at the station."

"Why? What do you want with your Uncle Richard?"

"Only to tell him that we are on good terms again, and that he may regard Mr Jack as his future bandmaster." She hurried away as she spoke; and Mrs Beatty's protest was wasted on the oldfashioned sideboard.

CHAPTER VII

Miss Cairns, of whom Mary Sutherland had spoken to her aunt, was an unmarried lady of thirty-four. She had read much for the purpose of remembering it at examinations ; had taken the of Bachelor of Science; had written two articles on Woman Suffrage, and one on the Higher Education of Women, for a Radical review; and was an earnest contender for the right of her sex to share in all public functions. Having in her student days resolved not to marry, she had kept her resolution, and endeavored to persuade other girls to follow her example, which a few, who could not help themselves, did. But, as she approached her fortieth year, and found herself tiring of books, lectures, university examinations of women, and secondhand ideas in general, she ceased to dissuade her friends from marrying, and even addicted herself with some zest to advising and gossiping on the subject of their love affairs. With Mary Sutherland, who had been her pupil, and was one of her most intimate friends, she frequently corresponded on the subject of Art, for which she had a vast reverence, based on extensive reading and entire practical ignorance of the subject. She knew Adrian, and had gained Mary's gratitude by pronouncing him a great artist, though she had not seen his works. In person she was a slight, plain woman, with small features, soft brown hair, and a pleasant expresion. Much sedentary plodding had accustomed her to delicate health, but had not soured her temper, or dulled her habitual cheerfulness.

Early in September, she wrote to Mary Sutherland.

Newton Villa, Windsor,
4th September.

Dearest Mary — Many thanks for your pleasant letter, which makes me long to be at the seaside. I am sorry to hear that you are losing interest in your painting. Tell Mr Herbert that I am surprised at his not keeping you up to your work better. When you come back, you shall have a good lecture from me on the subject of lukewarm endeavor and laziness generally: however, if you are really going to study music instead, I excuse you.

"You will not be pleased to hear that the singing class is broken up. Mr Jack, unstable as dynamite, exploded yesterday, and scattered our poor choir in dismay to their homes. It happened in this way. There was a garden party at Mrs. Griffith's, to which all the girls were invited; and accordingly they appeared at class in gay attire, and were rather talkative and inattentive. Mr Jack arrived punctually, looking black as thunder. He would not even acknowledge my greeting. Just before he came in, Louisa White had been strumming over a new set of quadrilles; and she unfortunately left the music on the desk of the pianoforte. Mr Jack, without saying a word to us, sat down on the music stool, and, of course, saw poor Louisa's quadrilles, which he snatched, tore across, and threw on the floor. There was a dead silence, and Louisa looked at me, expecting me to interfere, but — I confess it — I was afraid to. Even you, audacious as you are, would have hesitated to provoke him. We sat looking at him ruefully whilst he played some chords, which he did as if he hated the piano. Then he said in a weary voice, 'Go on, go on.' I asked him what we should go on with. He looked savagely at me, and said, "Anything. Don't —" He said the rest to himself; but I think he meant, 'Don't sit there sstaring like a fool.' I distributed some music in a hurry, and put a copy before him. He was considerate enough not to tear that; but he took it off the desk and put it aside. Then he began playing the acccompaniment without book. We begain again and again and again, he listening with brooding desparation, like a man suffering from neuralgia. His silence alarmed me more than anything; for he usually shouts at us, and, if we sing a wrong note, sings the right one in a tremendous Voice. This went on for about twenty-five minutes, during which, I must confess, we got worse and Worse. At last Mr Jack rose, gave one terrible look at us, and buttoned his coat. The eyes of all were upon me — as if I could do anything. "Are you going Mr Jack!" No answer. "We shall see you on Friday as usual, I suppose Mr Jack?"

"Never, never again, by Heaven!" With this reply, made in a tortured voice with intense fervor, he walked out. Then arose a Babel of invective against Mr Jack, with infinite contradiction, and some vehement defence of him. Louisa White, torn quadrille in hand, began it by declaring that his conduct was disgraceful. 'No wonder,' cried Jane Lawrence, 'with Hetty Grahame laughing openly at him from the ottoman.' 'It was at the singing I laughed,' said Hetty indignantly: 'it was enough to make anyone laugh.' After this everybody spoke at once; but at last each agreed that all the rest had behaved very badly, and that Mr Jack had been scandalously treated. I thought, and I still think, that Mr. Jack has to thank his own ill-temper for the bad singing; and I will take care that he shall not have a second chance of being rude to me (I know by experience that it is a mistake to allow professors to trample on unprotected females), but of course I did not say so to the girls, as I do not wish to spoil his very unexpected popularity with them. He is a true male tyrant, and, like all idle women, they love tyrants — for which treachery to their working sisters they ought to be whipped and sent to bed. He is now, forsooth, to be begged to shew grace to his repentant handmaids, and to come down as usual on Friday, magnanimously overlooking his own bad behavior of yesterday. Can you manage to bring this about. You know him better than any of us; and we regard you as the proprietress of the class. Your notion that Mr. Jack objects to your joining it when you return to Windsor, is a piece of your crotchety nonsense. I asked him whether he expected you to do so, and he said he hoped so. That was not yesterday, of course, but at the previous lesson, when he was in unusually good spirits. So please try and induce his royal highness to come back to us. If you do not, I shall have to write myself, and then all will be lost; for I will encourage no living man to trample on my sex, even when they deserve it; and if I must write, Seigneur Jack shall have a glimpse of my mind. Please let me know soon what you can do for us: the girls are impatient to know the issue, and they keep calling and bothering me with questions. I will send you all the local news in my next letter, as it is too near post hour to add anything to this. —

Yours, dearest Mary, most affectionately.
"Letitia Cairns."

Mary forthwith, in a glow of anger, wrote and despatched the following to Church Street, Kensington.

Bonchurch,
5th September.

"Dear Mr Jack — I have been very greatly surprised and pained by hearing from my friend Miss Cairns that you have abruptly thrown up the class she was kind enough to form for you at Windsor. I have no right to express any opinion upon your determination not to teach her friends any more; but as I introduced you to her, I cannot but feel that I have been the means of exposing her to an affront which has evidently wounded her deeply. However, Miss Cairns, far from making any complaint, is anxious that you should continue your lessons, as it is the general desire of the class that you should do so —

Yours sincerely,
Mary Sutherland.

Early next afternoon, Miss Cairns was alone In her drawing room, preparing a lecture for a mutual improvement society which she had founded in Windsor. A servant came in.

"Please, Miss Tisha, can you see Mr Jack?"

Miss Cairns laid down her pen, and gazed at the woman. "Mr Jack! It is not his usual day."

"No, Miss, but it's him. I said you was busy; and he asked whether you told me to tell him so. I think he's in a wus temper than last day."

"You had better bring him up," said Miss Cairns, touching her hair to test it, and covering up her manuscript. Jack came in hurriedly, and cut short her salutation by exclaiming in an agitated manner, "Miss Cairns I received a letter — an infamous letter. It says that you accuse me of having affronted you, and given up my I here, and other monstrous things. I have c>me to ask you whether you really said anything of the sort, and, if so, from whom you have heard these slanders."

"I certainly never told anyone that you affronted me," said Miss Cairns, turning pale. "I may have said that you gave up the class rather abruptly; but —"

"But who told you that I had given up the class? Why did you believe it before you had given me an opportunity of denying — of repudiating it. You do not know me, Miss Cairns. I have an unfortunate manner sometimes, because I am, in a worldly sense, an unfortunate man, though in my real life, heaven knows, a most happy and fortunate one. But I would cut off my right hand sooner than insult you. I am incapable of ingratitude; and I have the truest esteem and regard for you, not only because you have been kind to me but because I appreciate the noble qualities which raise you above your sex. So far from neglecting or wishing to abandon your friends, I have taken special pains with them, and shall always do so on your account, in spite of their magpie frivolity. You have seen for yourself my efforts to make them sing. But it is the accusation of rudeness to you personally that I am determined to refute. Who is the author of it?"

"I assure you," said Miss Cairns, blushing, "that you did not offend me; and whoever told you I complained of your doing so must have misunderstood me. But as to your giving up the class —"

"Aye, aye. Somebody must have told you that."

"You told me that yourself, Mr. Jack."

He looked quickly at her, taken aback. Then he frowned obstinately, and began walking to and fro. "Ridiculous!" he said, impatiently. "I never said such a thing. You have made a mistake."

"But —"

"How could I possibly have said it when the idea never entered my head?"

"All I can say is," said Miss Cairns, firmly, being somewhat roused, "that when I asked you whether you were coming-again, you answered most emphatically, 'Never'"

Jack stood still and considered a moment. "No, no." he said, recommencing his walk, "I said nothing of the kind."

She made no comment, but looked timidly at him, and drummed on the writing with her finger.

"At least," he said, stopping again, "I may have said so thoughtlessly — as a mere passing remark. I meant nothing by it. I was little put out by the infernal manner in which the class behaved. Perhaps you did not perceive my annoyance, and so took whatever I said too seriously."

"Yes, I think that must have been it," said Miss Cairns slyly. "It was all a mistake of mine, I suppose you will continue our lessons as if nothing had happened."

"Of course, certainly. Nothing has happened."

"I am so sorry that you should have had the trouble of coming all the way from London. It is too bad."

"Well, well, it is not your fault, Miss Cairns. It cannot be helped."

"May I ask, from whom did you hear of my mistake?"

"From whom! From Miss Sutherland, of course. There is no one else living under heaven who would have the heart to write such venom."

"Miss Sutherland is a dear friend of mine, Mr Jack."

"She is no friend of mine. Though I lived in her house for months, I never gave her the least cause of enmity against me. Yet she has never lost an opportunity of stabbing at me."

"You are mistaken, Mr. Jack — won't you sit down: I beg your pardon for not asking you before — Miss Sutherland has not the least enmity to you."

"Read that," said Jack, producing the letter. Miss Cairns read it, and felt ashamed of it. "I cannot imagine what made Mary write that," she said. "I am sure my letter contained nothing that could justify her remark about me."

"Sheer cruelty — want of consideration for others — natural love of inflicting pain. She has an overbearing disposition. Nothing is more hateful than an overbearing disposition."

"You do not understand her, Mr Jack. She is only hasty. You will find that she wrote on the spur of the moment, fancying that I was annoyed. Pray think no more of it."

"It does not matter, Miss Cairns. I will not meet her again; and I request you never to mention her name in my presence."

"But she is going, I hope, to join the class on her return from Bonchurch."

"The day she enters it, I leave it. I am in earnest. You may move heaven and earth more easily than me — on this point."

"Really, Mr Jack, you are a little severe. Do not be offended if I say that you might find in your own impatience some excuse for hers."

Jack recoiled. "My impatience!" he repeated slowly. "I, who have hardened myself into a stone statue of dogged patience, impatient!" He glared at her; ground his teeth; and continued vehemently, "Here am I, a master of my profession — no easy one to master — rotting, and likely to continue rotting unheard in the midst of a pack of shallow panders, who make a hotchpotch of what they can steal from better men, and share the spoil with the corrupt performers who thrust it upon the public for them. Either this or the accursed drudgery of teaching, or grinding an organ at the pleasure of some canting villain of a parson, or death by starvation, is the lot of a musician in this century. I have, in spite of this, never composed one page of music bad enough for publication or performance. I have drudged with pupils when I could get them, starved in a garret when I could not; endured to have my works returned to me unopened or declared inexecutable by shopkeepers and lazy conductors, written new ones without any hope of getting even a hearing for them; dragged myself by excess of this fruitless labor out of horrible fits of despair that come out my own nature; and throughout it all have neither complained nor prostituted myself to write shopware. I have listened to complacent assurances that publishers and concert-givers are only too anxious to get good, original work — that it is their own interest to do so. As if the dogs would know original work if they saw it: or rather as if they would not instinctively turn away from anything good and genuine! All this I have borne without suffering from it — without the humiliation of finding it able to give me one moment of disappointment or resentment; and now you tell me that I have no patience, because I have no disposition to humor the caprices of idle young ladies. I am accustomed to hear such things from fools — or I was when I had friends; but I expected more sense from you."

Miss Cairns struggled with this speech in vain. All but the bare narrative in it seemed confused and inconsequent to her. "I did not know," she said, looking perplexedly at him. "It never occurred to me that — at least —" She stopped, unable to arrange her ideas. Then she exclaimed, "And do you really love music, Mr. Jack?"

"What do you mean?" said he sternly.

"I thought you did not care for anything. I always felt that you knew your business; we all felt so; but we never thought you had any enthusiasm. Do not be angry with me for telling you so; for I am very glad to find that I was wrong."

Jack's features relaxed. He rose, and took another turn across the room, chuckling. "I am not fond of teaching," he said; "but I must live. And so you all thought that an ugly man could not be a composer. Or was it because I don't admire the drawling which you all flatter yourselves is singing, eh? I am not like the portraits of Mozart, Miss Cairns."

"I am sure we never thought of that, only somehow we agreed that you were the very last person in the world to — to —"

"Ha! ha! Just so. I do not look like a writer of serenades. However, you were right about the enthusiasm. I am no enthusiast: I leave that to the ladies. Did you ever hear of an enthusiastically honest man, or an enthusiastic shoemaker? Never, and you are not likely to hear of an enthusiastic composer — at least not until after he is dead. No. He chuckled again, but seemed suddenly to recollect himself; for he added stiffly, "I beg your pardon. I am detaining you."

"Not in the least," said Miss Cairns, so earnestly that she blushed afterwards. "If you are not engaged, I wish you would stay for B few minutes and do me at favor."

"Certainly. Most certainly," he said. Then he added suspiciously, "What is it?"

"Only to play something for me before you go — if you don't mind." Her tone expressed that intense curiosity to witness a musical performance which is so common among unmusical people whose interest in the art has been roused by reading. Jack understood it quite well; but he seemed disposed to humor her.

"You want to see the figure work," he said goodhumoredly. "Very well. What shall it be?"

Miss Cairns, ignorant of music, but unaccustomed to appear ignorant of anything, was at a loss. "Something classical then," she ventured. "Do you know Thalberg's piece called 'Moses in Egypt'? I believe that is very fine; but it is also very difficult, is it not?"

He started, and looked at her with such an extraordinary grin that she almost began to mistrust him. Then he said, apparently to himself, "Candor, Jack, candor. You once thought so, perhaps, yourself."

He twisted his fingers until their joints crackled; shook his shoulders and gnashed his teeth once or twice at the keyboard. Then he improvised a set of variations on the prayer fr<>m "Moses" which served Miss Cairns's turn quite as well as if they had been note for note Thalberg's. She listened, deeply impressed, and was rather jarred when he suddenly stopped and rose, saying, "Well, well: enough tomfoolery, Miss Cairns."

"Not at all," she said. "I have enjoyed it greatly. Thank you very much."

"By the bye," he said abruptly, "I am not to be asked to play for your acquaintances. Don't go and talk about me: the mechanical toy will not perform for anyone else."

"But is not that a pity, when you can give such pleasure?"

"Whenever I am in the humor to play, I play; sometimes without being asked. But I am not always in the humor, whereas people are always ready to pretend that they like listening to me, particularly those who are as deaf to music as they are to everything else that is good. And one word more, Miss Cairns. If your friends think me a mere schoolmaster, let them continue to think so. I live alone, and I sometimes talk more about myself than I intend. I did so today. Don't repeat what I said."

"Certainly not, since you do not wish me to."

Jack looked into his hat; considered a moment; then made her a bow — a ceremony which he always performed with solemnity — and went away. Miss Cairns sat down by herself, and forgot all about her lecture. More accustomed to store her memory than to exercise her imagination she had a sensation of novelty in reflecting on the glimpse that she had got of Jack's private life, and the possibilities which it suggested. Her mother came in presently, to inquire concerning the visitor; but Miss Cairns merely told who he was, and mentioned carelessly that the class was to go on as before. Mrs Cairns, who disapproved of Jack, said she was sorry to hear it. Her daughter, desiring to give utterance to her thoughts, and not caring to confide in her mother, recollected that she had to write to Mary. This second letter ran thus:

Newton Villa, Windsor.
6th September.

"Dearest Mary — I am going to give you a severe scolding for what you have done at Mr. Jack. He has just been here with your wicked letter, furious, and evidently not rembering a bit what he said last day. About the class, which he positively denies having given up; but he is very angry with you — not without reason, I think. Why will you be pugnacious? I tried to make your peace; but, for the present, at least, he is implacable. He is a very strange man. I think he is very clever; but I do not understamd him, though I have passed my life among professors and clever people of all sorts, and fancied I had exhausted the species. My logic and mathematics are no avail when I try to grapple with Mr Jack: he belongs, I think, to those regions of art which you have often urged me to explore, but of which, unhappily, I know hardly anything. I got him into good humor after a great deal of trouble, and actually asked him to play for me, which he did, most magnificently. You must never let him know that I told you this because he made me promise not to tell anyone and I am sure he is a terrible person to betray. His real character — so far as I can make it out — is quite different than what we all supposed — I must break off here to go to dinner. I have no doubt he will relent towards you after a time: his wrath does not endure forever. —

Ever your affectionate,
Letita Cairns

Miss Cairns had no sooner sent this to the post than she began to doubt whether it would not have been better to have burnt it.

CHAPTER VIII

The autumn passed; and the obscure days of the London winter set in. Adrian Herbert sat daily at work in his studio, painting a companion picture to the Lady of Shalott, and taking less exercise than was good either for himself or his work. His betrothed was at Windsor, studying Greek with Miss Cairns, and music with Jack. She had carried her point with Mrs. Beatty as to the bandmastership; and Jack had been invited to apply for it; but he, on learning that a large part of his duty would be to provide the officers of the regiment with agreeable music whilst they dined, had unexpectedly repudiated the offer in an intemperate letter to the adjutant, stating that he had refused as an organist to be subject to the ministers of religion, and that he should refuse, as a conductor, to be the hireling of professional homicides. Miss Cairns, when she heard of this, in the heat of her disappointment reproached him for needlessly making an enemy of the colonel; embittering the dislike of Mrs Beatty, and exposing Mary to their resentment. Jack thereupon left Newton Villa in anger; but Miss Cairns learned next day that he had written a letter of thanks to the colonel, in which he mentioned that the recent correspondence with the adjutant had unfortunately turned on the dignity of the musical profession, and begged that it might be disassociated entirely from the personal feeling to which he now sought to give expression. To Miss Cairns herself he also wrote briefly to say that it had occurred to him that Miss Sutherland might be willing to join the singing class, and that he hoped she would be asked to do so. Over this double concession Miss Cairns exulted; but Mary, humiliated by the failure of her effort to befriend him, would not join, and resisted all persuasion, until Jack, meeting her one day in the street, stopped her, inquired about Charlie, and finally asked her to come to one of the class meetings. Glad to have this excuse for relenting, she not only entered the class, but requested him to assist her in the study of harmony, which she had recently begun to teach herself from a treatise. As it proved, however, he confused rather than assisted her; for, though an adept in the use of chords, he could make no intelligible attempt to name or classify them; and her exercises, composed according to the instructions given in the treatise, exasperated him beyond measure.

Meanwhile, Magdalen Brailsford, with many impatient sighs, was learning to speak the English language with purity and distinction, and beginning to look on certain pronunciations for which she had ignorantly ridiculed famous actors, as enviable conditions of their superiority to herself. She did not enjoy her studies, for Jack was very exacting; and the romantic aspect of their first meeting at Paddington was soon forgotten in the dread he inspired as a master. She left Church Street after her first lesson in a state of exhaustion; and, long after she had come accustomed to endure his criticism for an hour without fatigue, she often could hardly restrain her tears when he emphasized her defects by angrily mimicking them, which was the most unpleasant, but not the least effective part of his system of teaching. He was particular, even in his cheerful moods, and all but violent in his angry ones; but he was indefatigable, and spared himself no trouble in forcing her to persevere in overcoming the slovenly habits of colloquial speech. The further she progressed, the less she could satisfy him. His ear was far more acute than hers; and he demanded from her beauties of tone of which she had no conception, and refinements of utterance which she could not distinguish. He repeated sounds which he declared were as distinct as day from night, and raged at her because she could hear no difference between them, He insisted that she was grinding her voice to pieces when she was hardly daring to make it audible. Often, when she was longing for the expiry of the hour to release her, he kept her until Mrs Simpson, who was always present, could bear it no longer, and interfered in spite of the frantic abuse to which a word from her during the lesson invariably provoked him. Magdalen would have given up her project altogether, for the sake of escaping the burden of his tuition, but for her fear of the contempt she knew he would feel for her if she proved recreant. So she toiled on without a word of encouragement or approval from him; and he grimly and doggedly kept her at it, until one day, near Christmas, she came to Church Street earlier than usual, and had a long conference with Mrs Simpson before he was informed of her presence. When he came down from his garret she screwed her courage up to desperation point, and informed him that she had obtained an engagement for a small part in the opening of a pantomime at Nottingham. Instead of exploding fiercely, he stared a little; rubbed his head perplexedly; and then said, "Well, well: you must begin somewhere: the sooner the better. You will have to do poor work, in poor company, for some time, perhaps, but you must believe in yourself, and not flinch a the drudgery of the first year or two. Keep the fire always alight on the altar, and every place you go into will become a temple. Don't be mean: no grabbing at money, or opportunities, or effects! You can speak better than ninety-nine out of a hundred of them: remember that. If you ever want to do as they do, then your ear will be going wrong; and that will be a sign that your soul is going wrong too. Do you believe me, eh?"

"Yes," said Madge, dutifully."

He looked at her very suspiciously, and uttered a sort of growl, adding, "If you get hissed, occasionally, it will do you good; although you are more likely to get applauded and spoilt. Dont forget what I have taught you: you will see the use of it when you have begun to understand your profession."

Magdalen protested that she mid never forget, and tried to express her gratitude for the trouble he had taken with her. She begged that he would not reveal her destination to anyone, as it was necessary for her to evade her family a second time in order to fulfill her engagement. He replied that her private arrangements were no business of his, advising her at the same time to reflect before she quitted a luxurious home for a precarious and vagabond career, and recommending Mrs Simpson to her as an old hag whose assistance would be useful in any business that required secrecy and lying. "If you want my help," he added, "you can come and ask for it."

"She can come and pay for it, and no thanks to you," said Mrs. Simpson, goaded beyond endurance.

Jack turned on her, purple and glaring. Madge threw herself between them. Then he suddenly walked out; and, as they stood there trembling and looking at one another in silence, they heard him go upstairs to his garret.

"Oh, Polly, how could you?" said Madge at last, almost in a whisper.

"I wonder what he's gone for," said Mrs. Simpson. "There's nothing upstairs that he can do any harm with. I didn't mean anything."

He came down presently, with an old washleather purse in his hand. "Here," he said to Madge. They knew perfectly well, without further explanation, that it was the money she had paid him for her lessons.

"Mr Jack," she stammered: "I cannot."

"Come, take it," he said. "She is right: the people at Windsor pay for my wants. I have no need to be supported twice over. Has she charged you anything for the room?"

"No," said Madge.

"Then the more shame for me to charge you for your lessons," said Jack. "I shall know better another time. Here: take the money, and let us think no more about it. Goodbye! I think I can work a little now, if I set about it at once." He gave her the purse, which she did not dare refuse; shook her hand with both his; and went out hurriedly, but humbly.

Three days after this, Adrian Herbert was disturbed at his easel by Mr. Brailsford, who entered the studio in an extraordinarily excited condition,

"Mr. Brailsford! I am very glad to — What is the matter?"

"Do you know anything of Magdalen? She is missing again." Herbert assumed an air of concern. "Herbert: I appeal to you, if she has confided her plans to you, not to ruin her by a misplaced respect for her foolish secrets."

"I assure you I am as much surprised as you. Why should you assume that I am in her confidence?"

"You were much in her company during your recent visits to us; and you are the sort man a young girl would confide any crazy project to. You and she have talked together a good deal."

"Well, we have had two conversations within the last six weeks, both of which came about by accident. We were speaking of my affairs only. You know Miss Sutherland is a friend of hers. She is our leading topic."

"This is very disappointing, Herbert. Confoundedly so."

"It is unfortunate; and I am sorry I know nothing."

"Yes, yes: I knew you were not likely to: it was mere clutching at a straw. Herbert, when I get that girl back, I'll lock her up, and not let her out of her room until she leaves it to be married."

"When did she go?"

"Last night. We did not miss her until this morning. She has gone to disgrace herself a second time at some blackguard country theatre or other. And yet she has always been treated with the greatest indulgence at home. She is not like other girls who do not know the value of a comfortable home. In the days when I fought the world as a man of letters, she had opportunities of learning the value of money." Mr. Brailsford, as he spoke, moved about constantly; pulled at his collar as if it were a stock which needed to be straightened; and fidgeted with his gloves. "I am powerless," he added. "I cannot obtain the slightest clue. There is nothing for it but to sit down and let my child go."

"Are you aware," said Herbert thoughtfully, "that she has been taking lessons in acting from a professor of music during the last few months?"

"No, sir, I certainly am not aware of it," said Brailsford fiercely. "I beg your pardon, my dear Herbert; but she is a damned ungrateful girl; and her loss is a great trouble to me. I did not know; and she could not have done it if her mother had looked after her properly."

"It is certainly the case. I was very much surprised myself when Miss Sutherland told me of it, especially as I happened to have some knowledge of the person whom Miss Brailsford employed."

"Perhaps he knows. Who is he and where is he to be found?"

"His name is an odd one — Jack."

"Jack? I have heard that name somewhere. Jack? My memory is a wreck. But we are losing time. You know his address, I hope."

"I believe I have it here among some old letters. Excuse me whilst I search."

Herbert went into the ante-room. Mr. Brailsford continued his nervous movements; bit his nails; and made a dab at the picture with his glove, smudging it. The discovery that he had wantonly done mischief sobered him a little; and presently Adrian returned with one of Jack's letters.

Church street, Kensington," he said. *Will you go there?"

"Instantly, Herbert, instantly. Will you come?"

"If you wish," said Adrian, hesitating.

"Certainly. You must come. This is some low villain who has pocketed the child's money, and persuaded her that she is a Mrs Siddons. I had lessons myself long ago from the great Young, who thought highly of me, though not more so than I did of him. Perhaps I am dragging you away from your work, my dear fellow."

"It is too dark to work much today. In any case the matter is too serious to be sacrificed to my routine"

Quarter of an hour later, Mrs. Simpson's maid knocked at the door of Jack's garret, and informed him that two gentlemen were waiting in the drawing room to see him.

"What are they like?" said Jack "Are you sure they want me?"

"Certain sure," said the girl "one of 'em's a nice young gentleman with a flaxy beard; and the other his father, I think. Ain't he a dapper old toff, too!"

"Give me my boots; and tell them I shall be down presently."

The maid then appeared to Mr. Brailsford and Adrian, saying, "Mr Jax'll be down in a minnit," and vanished. Soon after, Jack came in. In an instant Mr. Brailsford's eyes lit up as if he saw through the whole plot; and he rose threateningly. Jack bade good morning ceremoniously to Herbert, who was observing with alarm the movements of his companion.

"You know me, I think, sir," said Mr. Brailsford, threateningly.

"I remember you very well," replied Jack grimly. "Be pleased to sit down."

Herbert hastily offered Mr Brailsford a chair, pushing it against his calves just in time to interrupt an angry speech at the beginning. The three sat down.

We have called on you, Mr Jack," said Adrian, in the hope that you can throw some light on a matter which is a source of great anxiety to Mr Brailsford. Miss Brailsford has disappeared"

"What!" cried Jack. "Run away again. Ha! ha! I expected as much."

"Pray be calm," said Herbert, as Mr Brailsford made a frantic gesture. "Allow me to speak, Mr Jack: I believe you have lately been in communication with the young lady."

"I have been teaching her for the last four months, if that is what you mean."

"Pray understand that we attach no blame to you in the matter. We merely wish to ascertain the whereabouts of Miss Brailsford: and we thought you might be able to assist us. If so, I feel sure you will not hesitate to give this gentleman all the information in your power."

"You may reassure yourself," said Jack." She has got an engagement at some theatre and has gone to fulfill it. "She told me so a few days ago, when she came to break off her lessons."

"We particularly wish to find out where she has gone to," said Herbert slowly.

"You must find that out as best you can," said Jack, looking attentively at him. She mentioned the place to me; but she asked me not to repeat it, and it is not my business to do so."

"Herbert," cried Mr. Brailsford, "Herbert."

"Pray: remonstrated Adrian. "Just allow me one word —"

"Herbert," persisted the other: "this is the fellow of whom I told you as we came along in the cab. He is her accomplice. You know you are," he continued, turning to Jack, and raising his voice. "Do you still deny that you are her agent?"

Jack stared at him imperturbably.

"It is a conspiracy," said Mr Brailsford. "It, has been a conspiracy from the first; and you are the prime mover in it. You shall not bully me, sir. I will make you speak."

"There, there," said Jack. "Take him away, Mr Herbert."

Adrian stepped hastily between them, fearing that his companion would proceed to violence. Before another word could be spoken the door was opened by Mrs Simpson, who started and stopped short when she saw visitors in the room.

"I beg pardon — Why, it's Mr Brailsford," she added, reddening. "I hope I see you well, sir," she continued, advancing with a propitiatory air. "I am honored by having you in my house."

"Indeed!" said the old gentleman, with a look which made her tremble. "So it is you who introduced Miss Magdalen to this man. Herbert, my dear boy, the thing is transparent. This woman is an old retainer of ours. It was her sister who took Madge away before. I told you it was all a conspiracy."

" Lord bless us!" exclaimed Mrs. Simpson. "I hope nothing ain't happened to Miss Magdalen."

"If anything has, you shall be held responsible for it. Where has she gone?"

"Oh, don't go to tell me that my sweet Miss Magdalen has gone away again, sir!"

"You hear how they contradict one another, Herbert?"

Mrs Simpson looked mistrustfully at Jack, who was grinning at her with cynical admiration. "I don't know what Mr. Jack may have put into your head about me, sir," she said cautiously; "but I assure you I know nothing of poor Miss Magdalen's doings. I haven't seen her this past month."

"You understand, of course," remarked Jack, "that that is not true. Mrs. Simpson has always been present at your daughter's lessons. She knows perfectly well that Miss Brailsford has gone to play at some theatre. She heard it in —"

"I wish you'd mind your own business, Mr Jack." said the landlady, sharply.

"When lies are needed to serve Miss Brailsford, you can speak," retorted Jack. "Until then, hold your tongue. It is clear to me, Mr Herbert, that you want this unfortunate young lady's address for the purpose of attempting to drag her back from an honorable profession to a foolish and useless existence which she hates. Therefore I shall give you no information. If she is unhappy or unsuccessful in her new career, she will return of her own accord."

"I fear," said Herbert, embarrassed by the presence of Mrs Simpson, "that we can do no good by remaining here."

"You arc right," said Mr Brailsford. "I decline to address myself further to either of you. Other steps shall be taken. And you shall repent the part you have played on this occasion, Mrs. Simpson. As for you, sir, I can only say 1 trust this will prove our last meeting."

"I shan't repent nothink," said Mrs. Simpson. "Why shouldn't I assist the pretty —"

"Come!" said Jack, interrupting her, "we have said enough. Good evening, Mr Herbert." Adrian colored, and moved towards the door, "You shall be welcome whenever you wish to see me," added lack; "but at present you had better take this gentleman away." Herbert bowed slightly, and went out, annoyed by the abrupt dismissal, and even more by the attempt to soften it. Mr Brailsford walked stiffly after him, staring indignantly at Mrs Simpson and her lodger. Provoked to mirth by this demonstration, Jack, who had hitherto behaved with dignity, rubbed his nose with the palm of his hand, and grinned hideously through his fingers at his visitor.

"As I told you before," said Mr. Brailsford, turning as he reached the threshold, "you are a vile kidnapper; and I will see that your trade is exposed and put a stop to."

"As I told you before," said Jack, removing his hand from his nose, "you are an old fool; and I wish you good afternoon."

"Sh — sh," said Mrs Simpson, as Mr Brailsford, with a menacing wave of his glove, disappeared. "You didn't ought to speak like that to an old gentleman, Mr. Jack."

"His age gives him no right to be ill-tempered and abusive to me," said Jack angrily.

"Humph!" retorted the landlady. "Your own tongue and temper are none of the sweetest. If I was you, I wouldn't be so much took aback at seeing others do the same as myself."

"Indeed. And how do you think being me would feel like, Mrs. Deceit?"

"I wouldn't make out other people to be liars before their faces, at all events, Mr Jack."

"You would prefer the truth to be told of you behind your back, perhaps. I sometimes wonder what part of my music will show the influence of your society upon me. My Giulietta Guicciardi!"

"Give me no more of your names," said Mrs. Simpson, shortly, "I don't need them."

Jack left the room slowly as if he had forgotten her. Meanwhile Mr. Brailsford was denouncing him to Herbert. "From the moment I first saw him," he said, "I felt an instinctive antipathy to him. I have never seen a worse face, or met with a worse nature."

"I certainly do not like him," said Herbert. "He has taken up an art as a trade, and knows nothing of the trials of a true artist's career. No doubts of himself; no aspirations to suggest them; nothing but a stubborn narrow self-sufficiency. I half envy him."

"The puppy!" exclaimed Mr Brailsford, not attending to Adrian: "to dare insult me! He shall suffer for it. I have put a bullet into a fellow — into a gentleman of good position — for less. And Magdalen — my daughter — is intimate with him — has visited him. Girls are going to the devil of late years, Herbert, going to the very devil. She shall not give me the slip again, when I catch her."

Mr Brailsford, however, did not catch Magdalen. Her clear delivery of the doggerel allotted to her in the pantomime, gained the favor of the Nottingham playgoers. Their applause prevented her from growing weary of repeating her worthless part nightly for six weeks, and compensated her for the discomfort and humiliation of living among people whom she could not help regarding as her inferiors, and with whom she had to co-operate in entertaining vulgar people with vulgar pleasantries, fascinating them by a display of comeliness, not only of her face, but of more of her person than she had been expected I to shew at Kensington Palace Gardens. Her costume shocked her at first; but she made up her mind to accept it without demur, partly because wearing such things was plainly part of an actress's business and partly because she felt that any objection on her part would imply an immodest self-consciousness. Besides, she had no moral conviction that it was wrong, whereas she had no doubt at all that petticoats were a nuisance. She could not bring herself to accept with equal frankness the society which the pantomime company offered to her. Miss Lafitte, the chief performer, was a favorite with the public on account of her vivacity, her skill in clog-dancing, and her command of slang, which she uttered in a piercing voice with a racy Whitechapel accent. She took a fancy to Magdalen, who at first recoiled. But Miss Lafitte (in real life Mrs. Cohen) was so accustomed to live down aversion, that she only regarded it as a sort of shyness — as indeed it was. She was vigorous, loud spoken, always full of animal spirits, and too well appreciated by her audiences to be jealous. Magdalen, who had been made miserable at first by the special favor of permission to share the best dressing-room with her, soon found the advantage of having a goodnatured and powerful companion. The drunken old woman who was attached to the theatre as dresser, needed to be kept efficient by sharp abuse and systematic bullying, neither of which Magdalen could have administered effectually. Miss Lafitte bullied her to perfection. Occasionally some of the actors would stroll into the dressing room, evidently without the least suspicion that Magdalen might prefer to put on her shoes, rouge herself, and dress her hair in private. Miss Lafitte, who had never objected to their presence on her own account, now bade them begone whenever they appeared, at which they seemed astonished, but having no intention of being intrusive, retired submissively.

"You make yourself easy, deah," she said to Magdalen. "Awe-y-'ll take kee-yerr of you. Lor' bless you, awe-y know wot you are. You're a law'ydy. But you'll get used to them. They don't mean no 'arm."

Magdalen, wondering what Jack would have said to Miss Lafitte's vowels, disclaimed all pretension to be more of a lady than those with whom she worked; but Miss Lafitte, though, she patted the young novice on the back, and soothingly assented, nevertheless continued to make a difference between her own behavior in Magdalen's presence, and the coarse chaff and reckless flirtation in which she indulged freely elsewhere. On Boxing night, when Madge was nerving herself to face the riotous audience, Miss Lafittc told her that she looked beautiful; exhorted her cheerfully to keep up her pecker and never say die; and, ridiculing her fear of putting too much paint on her face, plastered her cheeks and blackened the margins of her eyes until she blushed though the mask of pigment. When the call came, she went with her to the wing; pushed her on to the stage at the right instant; and praised her enthusiastically when she returned. Madge, who hardly knew what had passed on the stage, was grateful for these compliments, and tried to return them when Miss Lafitte came to the dressing, flushed with the exertion of singing a topical song with seven encore verses and dancing a breakdown between each.

"I'm used to it," said Miss Lafitte. "It's my knowledge of music-hall business that makes me what I am. You wouldn't catch me on the stage at all, only that my husband's a bit a swell in his own way — he'll like you for that — and he thinks the theatre more respectable. It dont pay as well, I can tell you; but of course it's surer and lasts longer."

"Were you nervous at your first appearance?" said Madge.

"Oh, wawn't I though! Just a little few. I cried at havin' to go on. I wasn't cold and plucky like you; but I got over it sooner. I know your sort: you will be nervous all your life. I don't care twopence for any audience now, nor ever did after my second night."

"I may have looked cold and plucky," said Madge, surprised. "but I never felt more miserable in my life before."

"Yes. Ain't it awful? Did you hear Lefanu? — stuck up little minx! Her song will be cut out tomorrow. She's a reg'lar duffer, she is. She gives herself plenty of airs, and tells the people that she was never used to associate with us. I know who she is well enough: her father was an apothecary in Bayswater. She's only fit to be a governess. You're worth fifty of her, either on the boards or off."

Madge did not reply. She was conscious of having contemplated escape from Miss Lafitte by attaching herself to Miss Lefanu, who was a ladylike young woman.

"She looks like a print gown after five washings," continued Miss Lafitte; "and she don't know how to speak. Now you speak lovely — almost as well as me, if you'd spit it out a bit more. Who taught you?"

When the pantomime had been played for a fortnight, Madge found herself contemptuously indifferent to Miss Lefanu, and fond of Miss Lafitte. When the latter invited her to a supper at her house, she could not refuse, though she accepted with misgiving. It proved a jovial entertainment — almost an orgie. Some of the women drank much champagne; spoke at the top of their voices; and screamed when they laughed. The men paid court to them with facetious compliments, and retorted their raillery with broad sarcasms. Madge got on best with the younger and less competent actors, who were mostly unpropertied gentlemen, with a feeble amateur bent for singing and acting, who had contrived to get on the stage, not because they were fit for it, but because society had not fitted them for anything else. They talked theatrical shop and green room scandal in addition to the usual topics of young gentlemen at dances; and they shielded Magdalen efficiently from the freer spirits. Sometimes an unusually coarse sally would reach her ears, and bring upon her a sense of disgust and humiliation; but, though she resolved to attend no more suppers, she was able next day to assure her hostess with perfect sincerity that she was none the worse for her evening's experience and that she had never enjoyed herself as much at any Kensington supper party. Miss Lafitte thereupon embraced her, and told her that she had been the belle of the ball, and that Laddie (a Gentile abbreviation of Lazarus, her husband's, name) had recognized her as a real lady, and was greatly pleased with her. Then she asked her whether she did not think Laddie a handsome man. Madge replied that she had been struck by his dark hair and eyes that his manners were elegant. "There is one thing" she added, "that puzzles me a little. I always call you Miss Lafitte here, but should I not call you by your real name at your house? I don't know the etiquette, you see."

"Call me Sal," said Mrs Cohen, kissing her.

When the pantomime was over, and the company dispersed, the only member of whose departure she felt a loss was Miss Lafitte; and she never afterwards fell into the mistake of confounding incorrigible rowdyism and a Whitechapel accent with true unfitness for society. By her advice, Madge accepted an engagement as one of the stock company of the Nottingham theater at the salary — liberal for a novice — of two pounds per week. For this she did some hard work. Every night she had to act in a farce, and in a comedy which had become famous in London. In it, as in the pantomime, she had to play the same part nightly for two weeks. Then came three weeks of Shakespeare and the legitimate drama, in which she and the rest of the company had to support an eminent tragedian, a violent and exacting man, who expected them to be perfect in long parts at a day's notice. When they disappointed him, as was usually the case, he kept them rehearsing from the forenoon to the hour of performance with hardly sufficient interval to allow of their dining. The stage manager, the musicians, the scenepainters and carpenters even, muttered sulkily that it was impossible to please him. He did not require the actors to enter into the spirit of their lines — it was supposed that he was jealous of their attempts at acting, which were certainly not always helpful — but he was inflexible in his determination to have them letter-perfect and punctual in the movements and positions he dictated to them. His displeasure was vented either in sarcasms or oaths; and often Madge, though nerved by intense indignation, could hardly refrain from weeping like many other members of the company, both male and female, from fatigue and mortification. She worked hard at her parts, which were fortunately not long ones, in order to escape the humiliation of being rebuked by him. Yet once or twice he excited her fear and hatred to such a degree that she was on the point of leaving the theatre, and abandoning her profession. It was far worse than what Jack had made her endure; for her submission to him had been voluntary; whilst with the tragedian she could not help herself, being paid to assist him, and ignorant of how to do it properly.

Towards the end of the second week her business became easier by repetition. She appeared as the player queen in Hamlet, the lady-in-waiting in Macbeth, and the widow of King Edward IV, and began to feel for the first time a certain respect for the silently listening, earnest audiences that crowded the house. It was the first dim Stirring in her of a sense that her relation as an actress to the people was above all her other relations. If the tragedian had felt this between the audience and the company of which he was a part, he might have inspired them to work all together with a will to realize the plays to the people. But he was a "star," recognizing no part and no influence but his own. She and her colleagues were dwarfed and put out of countenance; their scenes were cut short and hurried through; the expert swordsman who, as Richmond and Macduff slew the star thrice a week in mortal combat was the only person who shared with him the compliment of a call before the curtain. Naturally, they all hated Shakespeare; and the audiences distinctly preferring the tragedian to the poet, never protested his palming off on them versions by Cibber or Garrick as genuine Shakespearian plays

On the second Saturday, when Madge was congratulating herself on having only six days more of the national Bard to endure, the principal actress sprained her ankle; and the arrangements for the ensuing week were thrown into confusion. The manager came to Madge's lodging on Sunday morning, and told her that she must be prepared to play Ophelia, Lady Ann, and Marion Delorme (in Lytton's "Richelieu") in the course of the following week. It was, he added, a splendid chance for her. Madge was distracted. She said again and again that it was impossible, and at last ventured to remind the manager that she was not engaged for leading parts. He disposed of this objection by promising her an extra ten shillings for the week, and urged upon her that she would look lovely as Ophelia; that the tragedian had made a point of giving the parts to her because he liked her elocution; that his fierceness was only a little way of his which meant nothing; that he had already consented to substitute "Hamlet" and "Richelieu" for "Much Ado" and "Othello" because he was too considerate to ask her to play Beatrice and Desdemona; and, finally, that he would be enraged if she made any objection. She would, said the manager, shew herself as willing as old Mrs Walker, who had undertaken to play Lady Macbeth without a moment's hesitation. Madge, ashamed to shrink from an emergency, and yet afraid of failing to please the tyrant at rehearsal, resisted the manager's importunity until she felt hysterical. Then, in desperation, she consented, stipulating only that she should be released from playing in the farces. She spent that Sunday learning the part of Ophelia, and was able to master it and to persuade herself that the other two parts would not take long to learn, before she went to bed, dazed by study and wretched from dread of the morrow. "Hamlet" had been played twice already, and only the part of Ophelia and that of the player queen needed to be rehearsed anew. On Monday morning the tragedian was thoughtful and dignified, but hard to please. He kept Madge at his scene with Ophelia for more than an hour. She had intended to try and fancy that she was really Ophelia, and he really Hamlet; but when the time came to practice this primitive theory of acting, she did not dare to forget herself for a moment. She had to count her steps and repeat her entrance four times before she succeeded in placing herself at the right moment in the exact spot towards which the tragedian looked when exclaiming "Soft you now! The fair Ophelia." For a long time she could not offer him the packet of letters in a satisfactory manner; and by the time this difficulty was mastered, she was so bewildered that when he said, "I loved you not," she, instead of replying, "I was the more deceived," said "Indeed, my lord, you made me believe so," whereupon he started; looked at her for a moment, uttered imprecations between his teeth, and abruptly walked off the stage, leaving her alone, wondering. Suddenly, she bethought herself of of what had done; and her cheeks began to tingle. She was relieved by the return of Hamlet, who, unable to find words to express his feelings, repeated his speech without making any verbal comment on her slip. This time she made the proper answer and the rehearsal proceeded. The new player queen suffered less than Madge had done a week before, the tragedian treating her with brief disdain. He was very particular about Ophelia's chair and fan in the play scene; but when these were arranged, he left the theatre without troubling himself about the act in which he did not himself appear. Madge, left comparatively to her own devices in rehearsing it, soon felt the want of his peremptory guidance, and regretted his absence almost as much as she was relieved by it. The queen, jealous, like the other actresses, of Madge's promotion, was disparaging in her manner; and the king rehearsed with ostentatious carelessness, being out of humor at having to rehearse at all. Everybody present shewed that they did not consider the scene of the least importance; and Madge sang her snatches of ballads with a disheartening sense of being unpopular and ridiculous.

The performance made amends to her for the rehearsal. The tragedian surpassed himself; and Madge was compelled to admire him, although he was in his fiftieth year and personally disagreeable to her. For her delivery of the soliloquy following her scene with him, she received, as her share of the enthusiasm he had excited, a round of applause which gratified her the more because she had no suspicion that he bad earned the best part of it. The scene of Ophelia's madness was listened to with favor by the audience, who were impressed by the intensely earnest air which nervousness gave Madge, as well as by her good looks.

Next day she had leisure to study the part of Lady Anne in Cibber's adaptation of "Richard III," which was rehearsed on the Wednesday; and this time the tragedian was so overbearing, and corrected her so frequently and savagely, that when he handed her his sword, and requested her to stab him, she felt disposed to take him at his word. In the scene from Richard's domestic life in which he informs his wife that he hates her, he not only spoke the text with a cold ferocity which chilled her, but cursed at her under his breath quite outrageously. At last she was stung to express her resentment by an indignant look, which fell immediately before his frown. When the rehearsal, which, though incomplete, lasted from eleven to four, was over, Madge was angry and very tired. As she was leaving, she passed near Richard, who was conversing graciously with the manager and one of the actors. The night before, he had threatened to leave the theatre because the one had curtailed his stage escort by two men; and he had accused the other of intentionally insulting him by appearing on the stage without spurs.

"Who is that little girl?" he said aloud, pointing to Madge.

The manager, surprised at the question, made some reply which did not reach her, his voice and utterance being less sonorous and distinct than the tragedian's.

"Unquestionably she has played with me. I am aware of that. What is she called?"

The manager told him.

"Come here" he said to Madge, in his grand manner. She reddened and stopped.

"Come here," he repeated, more emphatically. She was too inexperienced to feel sure of her right to be treated more respectfully, so she approached him slowly.

Who taught you to speak?

"A gentleman in London," she said, coldly. "A Mr Jack."

"Jack:" The tragedian paused. "Jack!" he repeated. Then, with a smile, and a graceful action of his wrists, "I never heard of him." The other men laughed. "Would you like to tour through the provinces with me — to act with me every night?"

"Oho!"said the manager, jocularly, "I shall have something to say to that. I cannot afford to lose her."

"You need not be alarmed," said Madge, all her irritation suddenly exploding in one angry splutter. "I have not the slightest intention of breaking my present engagement, particularly now, when the most unpleasant part of it is nearly over." And she walked away, pouting and scarlet. The manager told her next day that she had ruined herself, and had made a very ungrateful return for the kindness that she, a beginner, had received from the greatest actor on the stage. She replied that she was not conscious of having received anything but rudeness from the greatest actor on the stage, and that if she had offended him she was very glad. The manager shook his head and retired, muttering that a week's leading business had turned her head. The tragedian, who had been, for so terrible a person, much wounded and put out of heart by her attack, took no further notice of her, demanding no fresh rehearsal of Ophelia, and only giving her a few curt orders in the small part of Marion Delorme. At last he departed from Nottingham; and Madge, for the first time since his arrival, lay down to sleep free from care.

Her next part was that of a peasant girl in an Irish melodrama. She looked very pretty in her Connemara cloak and short skirt, but was hampered by her stage brogue, which only made her accent aggressively English. During this period, she was annoyed by the constant attendance in the stalls of a young gentleman who flung bouquets to her; followed her to her lodging; and finally wrote her a letter in which he called her a fairy Red Riding Hood, describing his position and prospects, and begging her to marry him. Madge after some hesitation as to the advisability of noticing this appeal, replied by a note declining his offer, and requesting him to discontinue his gifts of flowers, which, she said, were a source of embarrassment, and not of pleasure, to her. After this, the young gentleman instead of applauding, as before, sat in his stall with folded arms and a gloomy expression. Madge, who was by this time sufficiently accustomed to the stage to recognize faces in the audience, took care not to look at him; and so, after a week, he ceased to attend and saw him no more.

The Irish melodrama passed on to the next town; and an English opera company came in its place for a fortnight, during which Madge found the time hung heavy on her hands, as she took no part in the performances, though she went to the theatre daily from habit. She was glad when she was at work again in a modern play with which a popular actress was making the tour of the provinces. This actress was an amiable woman; and Madge enacted Celia in *As You Like It* *at her benefit without any revival of the* dread of Shakespeare which the tragedian had implanted in her. She was now beginning to tread the boards with familiar ease. At first, the necessity of falling punctually into prearranged positions on the stage and of making her exits and entrances at prescribed sides, had so preoccupied her that all freedom of attention or identification of herself with the character she represented had been impossible. To go through her set task of speeches and man oeuvres with accuracy was the most she could hope to do. Now, however, there mechanical conditions of her art not only ceased to distract her, but enabled her to form plans of acting which stood the test of rehearsal. She became used to learning parts, not from a book of the play, but from a mere list of the fragments which she had to utter; so that she committed her lines to memory first, and found out what they were about afterwards. She was what is called by actors a quick study; and in Nottingham, where, besides the principal piece, one and often two farces were performed nightly, she had no lack of practice. In four months, she was second in skill only to the low comedian and the old woman, and decidedly superior to the rest of the stock company, most of whom had neither natural talent nor even taste for the stage, and only earned their livelihood on it because, their parents having been in the profession, they had been in a manner born into it.

Madge's artistic experience thenceforth was varied, though her daily course was monotonous. Other tragedians came to Nottingham, but none nearly so terrible, nor, she reluctantly confessed, nearly so gifted as he who had taught her the scene from Hamlet. Some of them, indeed, objected to the trouble of rehearsing, and sent substitutes who imitated them in every movement and so drilled the company to act with them. Occasionally a part in a comedy of contemporary life enabled Madge to profit by her knowledge of fashionable society and her taste in modern dress. The next week, perhaps, she would have to act in a sensational melodrama, and, in a white muslin robe, to struggle in the arms of a pickpocket in corduroys, with his clothes and hands elaborately begrimed. Once she had to play with the wreck of a celebrated actress, who was never free from the effects of brandy, and who astonished Madge by walking steadily on the stage when she could hardly stand off it. Then Shakespeare, sensation drama, Irish melodrama, comic opera or pantomime, new comedy from London over again, with farce constantly. Study, rehearsal, and performance became part of her daily habits. Her old enthusiasm for the mock passions the stage left her, and was succeeded by a desire to increase her skill in speaking by acquiring as much resource in shades of meaning as Jack had given her in pure pronunciation, and to add as many effective gestures as possible to the stock she had already learnt. When she was not engaged at the theatre she was at her lodging, practicing the management of a train, trying to acquire the knack of disposing her dress prettily in the act of sitting down, or arranging her features into various expressions before a mirror. This last branch of her craft was the most troublesome to her. She had learned from Jack, much to her surprise, that she could not make her face express anger or scorn by merely feeling angry or scornful. The result of that method was a strained frown, disagreeable to behold; and it was long before she attained perfect control of her features, and artistic judgment in exercising it. Sometimes she erred on the side of exaggeration, and failed to conceal the effort which her studied acting required. Then she recoiled into tameness and conventionality. Then, waking from this, she tried a modification of her former manner, and presently became dissatisfied with that too, and re-modified it. Not until she had gone through two years of hard study and practice did she find herself mistress of a fairly complete method; and then indeed she felt herself an actress. She ridiculed the notion that emotion had anything to do with her art, and seriously began to think of taking a pupil, feeling that she could make an actress of any girl, the matter being merely one of training. When she had been some four months in this phase, she had a love affair with a young acting manager of a touring company. The immediate effect was to open her eyes to the fact that the people were tired of her complete method, and that she was tired of it too. She flung it at once to the winds for ever, and thenceforth greatly undervalued her obligations to the study it had cost her, declaring, in the teeth of her former opinion, that study and training were useless, and that the true method was to cultivate the heart and mind and let the acting take care of itself. She cultivated her mind by high reading and high thinking as far as she could. As to the cultivation of her heart, the acting manager taught her that the secret of that art was love. Now it happened that the acting manager, though pleasant-looking and goodnatured, was by no means clever, provident, or capable of resisting temptation. Madge never could make up her mind whether he had entangled her or she him. In truth love entangled them both; and Madge found that love suited her excellently. It improved her health; it enlarged her knowledge of herself and of the world; it explained her roles to her, thawed the springs of emotion that had never flowed freely before either on or off the stage, threw down a barrier that had fenced her in from her kind, and replaced her vague aspirations, tremors, doubts, and fits of low spirits with an elate enjoyment in which she felt that she was a woman at last. Nevertheless, her attachment to the unconscious instrument of this mysterious change proved transient. The acting manager had but slender intellectual resources: when his courtship grew stale, he became a bore. After a while, their professional engagements carried them asunder; and as a correspondent he soon broke down. Madge, did not feel the parting: she found a certain delight in being fancy-free; and before that was exhausted she was already dreaming of a new lover, an innocent young English-opera librettist, whom she infatuated and ensnared and who came nearer than she suspected to blowing out his brains from remorse at having, as he thought, ensnared her. His love for her was abject in its devotion; but at last she went elsewhere and, as her letters also presently ceased, his parents, with much trouble, managed to convince him at last that no she no longer cared for him.

It must not be supposed that these proceedings cost Madge her selfrespect. She stood on her honor according to her own instinct; took no gifts, tolerated no advances from men whose affections were not truly touched, absorbed all her passion in her art when there were no such deserving claimants, never sold herself or threw herself away. would content herself at any time with poetry without love rather than endure love without poetry. She rather pitied her married colleagues, knowing perfectly well that they were not free to be so fastidious, reserved, and temperate as her instinct told her a great artist should always be. Polite society pretended to respect her when it asked her to recite at bazaars or charity concerts: at other times it did not come into contact with her, nor trouble itself as to her conformity to its rules, since she, as an actress, was out of polite society from the start. The ostracism which is so terrible to women whose whole aim is to know and be known by people of admitted social standing cannot reach the woman who is busily working with a company bound together by a common co-operative occupation, and who obtains at least some word or sign of welcome from the people every night. As to the Church, it had never gained any hold on Madge: it was to her only a tedious hypocrisy out of all relation with her life. Her idea of religion was believing the Bible because God personally dictated it to Moses, and going to church because her father's respectability required her to comply with that custom. Knowing from her secular education that such belief in the Bible was as exploded as belief in witchcraft, and despising respectability as those only can who have tasted the cream of it, she was perfectly free from all pious scruples. Habit, prejudice, and inherited moral cowardice just influenced her sufficiently to induce her to keep up appearances carefully, and to offer no contradiction to the normal assumption that her clandestine interludes of passion and poetry were sins. But she never had a moment of genuine remorse after once discovering that such sins were conditions of her full efficiency as an actress. They had brought tones into her voice that no teaching of Jack's could have endowed her with; and so completely did she now judge herself by her professional powers, that this alone brought her an accession instead of a loss of self respect. She was humiliated only when she played badly. If one of the clergymen who occasionally asked her, with many compliments, to recite at their school fêtes and the like, had demanded instead what it could profit her to gain the whole world and lose her own soul, she might have replied with perfect sincerity from her point of view that she had given up the whole world of Mrs Grundy and gained her own soul, and that, whether he considered it judicious to mention it or not, the transaction had in fact profited her greatly.

But all this belonged to a later period than the novitiate of two and a half years which began at Nottingham. These thirty months did not pass without many fits of low spirits, during which she despaired of success and hated her profession. She remained at Nottingham until July, when the theatre there was closed for a time. She then joined a travelling company and went through several towns until she obtained an engagement at Leeds. Thence she went to Liverpool, where she remained for three months, at the expiration of which she accepted an offer made her by the the manager of a theatre in Edinburgh, and went thither with a salary of five pounds a week, the largest wage she had yet received for her services. There she stayed until August in second year of her professional life, when she acted in London for the first time, and was disgusted by the coldness of the metropolitan audiences which were, besides, but scanty at that period of the year. She was glad to return to the provinces, although her first task there was to support her old acquaintance the tragedian, with whom she quarrelled at the first rehearsal with spirit and success. Here, as leading lady, she attempted the parts of Beatrice, Portia, and Lady Macbeth, succeeding fairly in the first, triumphantly in the second and only escaping failure by her insignificance in the third. By that time she had come to be known by the provincial managers as a trustworthy, hardworking young woman, safe in the lighter sorts of leading business, and likely to improve with more experience. They hardly gave her credit enough, she thought, for what seemed to her the slow and painful struggle which her progress had cost her. Those were the days in which she was building up the complete method which, though it was a very necessary part of her training, proved so shortlived. She had had to exhaust the direct cultivation of her art before she could begin the higher work of cultivating herself as the source of that art.

Shortly after her flight from Kensington, her twenty-first birthday had placed her in a position to defy the interference of her family; and she had thereupon written to her father acquainting him with her whereabouts, and with her resolve to remain upon the stage at all hazards. He had replied through his solicitor, formally disowning her. She took no notice of this; and the solicitor then sent her a cheque for one hundred pounds, and informed her that this was all she had to expect from her father, with whom she was not to attempt to establish any further communication. Madge was about to return the money, but was vehemently dissuaded from doing so by Mrs Cohen, who had not at that time quitted Nottingham. It proved very useful to her afterwards for her stage wardrobe. In defiance of the solicitor's injunction, she wrote to Mr Brailsford, thanking him for the money, and reproaching him for his opposition to her plans. He replied at great length; and eventually they corresponded regularly once a month, the family resigning themselves privately to Madge's being an actress, but telling falsehoods publicly to account for her absence. The donation of one hundred pounds was repeated next year; and many an actress whose family heavily burdened instead of aiding her, envied Madge her independence.

She wrote once to Jack, telling him that all her success, and notably her early promotion from the part of the player queen to that of Ophelia was due to the method of delivering verse which he had taught her. He answered, after a long delay, with expressions of encouragement curiously mixed with inconsequent aphorisms; but his letter needed no reply and she did not venture to write again, though she felt a desire to do so.

This was the reality which took the place of Madge's visions of the life of an actress.

CHAPTER IX

The year after that in which Madge had her autumnal glimpse of the London stage began with a General Election, followed by a change in the Ministry, a revival of trade, a general fancy that things were going to mend, and a sudden access of spirit in political agitation, commercial enterprise, public amusements, and private expenditure. The wave even reached a venerable artistic institution called the Antient Orpheus Society, established nearly a century ago for the performance of orchestral music, and since regarded as the pioneer of musical art in England. It had begun by producing Beethoven's symphonies: it had ended by producing a typical collection of old fogeys, who pioneered backwards so fast and so far that they had not finished shaking their heads over the innovations in the overture to *William Tell* when the rest of the world were growing tired of the overture to *Tannhauser*. The younger critics had introduced a fashion of treating the Antient Orpheus as obsolescent; and even their elders began to forebode the extinction of the Society unless it were speedily rejuvenated by the supercession of the majority of the committee. But the warnings of the press, as usual, did not come until long after the public had begun to abstain from the Antient Orpheus concerts; and as the Society in its turn resisted the suggestions of the press until death or dotage reduced the conservative majority of the committee to a minority, the credit of the Antient Orpheus was almost past recovery when reform was at last decided on. When the new members of the rejuvenated committee — three of whom were under fifty — realized this, they became as eager to fill the concert programmes with new works as their predecessors had been determined to exclude them. But when the business of selecting the new works came to be considered, all was discord. Some urged the advisability of performing the works of English composers, a wilful neglect of which had been one of the of the practices of the old committee of which the press had most persistently complained. To this it was objected that in spite of the patriotic complaints of critics, the public had shewed their opinion of English composers by specially avoiding the few concerts to which they had been allowed to contribute. At last it was arranged that an English work should be given at the first concert of the season, and that care should be taken to neutralize its repellent effect on the public by engaging a young Polish lady, who had recently made an extraordinary success abroad as a pianist, to make her first appearance in England on the occasion. Matters being settled so far, question now arose as to what the new English work should be. Most of the Committee had manuscript scores of their own, composed posed thirty years before in the interval between leaving the academy and getting enough teaching to use up all their energy; but as works of this class had already been heard once or twice by the public with undisguised tedium, and as each composer hesitated to propose his own opus, the question was not immediately answered. Then a recently-elected member of the Committee, not a professional musician, mentioned a fantasia for pianoforte and orchestra of which he had some private knowledge. It was composed, he said, by a young man, a Mr Owen Jack. The chairman coughed, and remarked coldly that he did not recollect the name. A member asked bluntly who Mr Jack was, and whether anybody had ever heard of him. Another member protested against the suggestion of a fantasia, and declared that if this illustrious obscure did not know enough about musical form to write a concerto, the Antient Orpheus Society, which had subsisted for nearly a century without his assistance, could probably do so a little longer. When the laughter and applause which this speech evoked had subsided, a good natured member remarked that he had met a man of the name of Jack at somebody's place in Windsor, and had heard him improvise variations on a song of the hostess's in a rather striking manner. He therefore seconded the proposal that Jack's fantasia should be immediately examined with a view to its performance by the Polish lady at the next concert. Another member, not good natured, but professionally jealous of the last speaker but one, supported the proposal on the ground that the notion that the Society could get on high-and-mightily without ever doing anything new was just what had brought it to death's door. This naturally elicited a defiant statement that the Society had never been more highly esteemed than at that hour; and a debate ensued, in the course of which Jack's ability was hotly attacked and defended in turn by persons who had never heard of him before that day. Eventually the member who had introduced the subject obtained permission to invite Mr Jack to submit his fantasia to the Committee.

At the next meeting an indignant member begged leave to call the attention of his colleagues to a document which had accompanied the score forwarded in response to the invitation by which the Antient Orpheus Society had honored Mr Owen Jack. It was a letter to the Secretary, in the following terms:

"Sir — Herewith you will find the instrumental partition of a fantasia composed by me for pianoforte and orchestra. I am willing to give the use of it to the Antient Orpheus Society gratuitously for one concert, on condition that the rehearsal be superintended by me, and that, if I require it, a second rehearsal be held."

The member said he would not dwell on the propriety of this communication to the foremost musical society in Europe from a minor teacher, as he had ascertained Mr. Jack to be. It had been sufficiently rebuked by the Secretary's reply, dispatched after the partition had been duly examined, to the effect that the work, though not destitute of merit, was too eccentric in form, and crude in harmonic structure, to be suitable for public performance at the concerts of the Society. This had elicited a second letter from Mr. Jack, of which the member would say nothing, as he preferred to leave it to speak for itself and for the character of the writer.

Church Street,
Kensington, W.

Sir — Your criticism was uninvited, and is valueless except as an illustration of the invincible ignorance of the pedants whose mouthpiece you are. I am, sir,
Yours truly,
Owen Jack."

The most astute diplomatist could not have written a more effective letter in Jack's favor than this proved. The party of reform took it as an exquisite slap at their opponents, and at once determined to make the Secretary smart for rejecting the work without the authority of the whole Committee. Jack's advocate produced a note from the Polish lady acknowledging the receipt of a pianoforte fantasia, and declaring that she should be enchanted to play for the first time to an English audience a work so poetic by one of their own nation. He explained that having borrowed a copy of the pianoforte part from a young lady relative of his who was studying it, he had sent it to the Polish artist, who had just arrived in England. Her opinion of it, he contended, was sufficient to show that the letter of the secretary was the result of an error of judgment which deserved no better answer than it had elicited. The secretary retorted that he had no right to avail himself of his private acquaintance with the pianist to influence the course of the Society, and stigmatized Jack's letter as the coarse abuse natural to the vulgar mind of a self-assertive charlatan. On the other hand, it was maintained that Jack had only shewn the sensitiveness of an artist, and that to invite a composer to send in a work and then treat it as if it were an examination paper filled by a presumptuous novice, was an impertinence likely to bring ridicule as well as odium upon the Antient Orpheus. The senior member, who occupied the chair, now declared very solemnly that he had seen the fantasia, and that it was one of those lawless compositions unhappily common of late years, which were hurrying the beautiful art of Haydn and Mozart into the abyss of modern sensationalism. Hereupon someone remarked that the gentleman had frequently spoken of the works of Wagner in the same terms, although they all knew that Richard Wagner was the greatest composer of that or any other age. This assertion was vehemently repudiated by some, and loudly cheered by others In the hubbub which followed, Jack's cause became identified with that of Wagner; and a motion to set aside the unauthorized rejection of the fantasia was carried by a majority of the admirers of the Prussian composer, not one of whom knew or cared a straw about the English one.

"I am glad we have won the day," said Mr. Phipson, the proposer of this motion, to a friend, as the meeting broke up; "but we have certainly experienced the truth of Mary's remark that this Jack creates nothing but discord in real life, whatever he may do in music."

Jack at first refused to have anything further to do with the Antient Orpheus; but as it was evident that his refusal would harm nobody except himself, he yielded to the entreaties of Mary Sutherland, and consented to make use of the opportunity she had, through Mr. Phipson, procured for him. As the negotiation proceeded; and at last, one comfortless wet spring morning, Jack got out of an omnibus in Piccadilly, and walked through the mud to St. James's Hall, where, in the gloomy rooms beneath the orchestra, he found a crowd of about eighty men, chatting, hugging themselves, and stamping because of the cold, stooping over black bags and boxes containing musical instruments, or reluctantly unwinding woolen mufflers and unbuttoning great coats. He passed them into a lower room, where he found three gentlemen standing in courtly attitudes before a young lady wrapped in furs, with a small head, light brown hair, and a pale face, rather toil worn. She received them with that natural air of a princess in her own right which is so ineffectually striven for by the ordinary princess in other people's rights. As she spoke to the gentlemen in French, occasionally helping them to understand her by a few words of broken English, she smiled occasionally, apparently more from kindness than natural gaiety, for her features always relapsed into an expression of patient but not unhappy endurance. Near her sat an old foreign lady, brown skinned, tall, and very grim.

Jack advanced a few steps into the room; glanced at the gentlemen, and took a long look at the younger lady, who, like the rest, had had her attention arrested by his impressive ugliness. He scrutinized her so openly that she turned away displeased, and a little embarrassed. Two of the gentlemen stared at him stiffly. The third came forward, and said with polite severity, "What is your business here, sir?"

Jack looked at him for a moment, wrinkling his face hideously. "I am Jack," he said, in the brassiest tone of his powerful voice. "Who are you?"

"Oh!" said the gentleman, relaxing a little. "I beg your pardon. I had not the pleasure of knowing you by sight, Mr Jack. My name is Manlius, at your service." Mr Manlius was the conductor of the Antient Orpheus orchestra. He was a learned musician, generally respected because he had given instruction to members of the Royal family, and, when conducting, never allowed his orchestra to forget the restraint due to the presence of ladies and gentlemen in the sofa stalls.

Jack bowed. Mr Manlius considered whether he should introduce the composer to the young lady. Whilst he hesitated, a trampling overhead was succeeded by the sounding of a note first on the pianoforte and then on the oboe, instantly followed by the din of an indescribable discord of fifths from innumerable strings, varied by irrelevant chromatic scales from the wood wind, and a doleful timing of slides from the brass. Jack's eyes gleamed. Troubling himself no further about Mr Manlius, he went out through a door leading to the stalls, where he found a knot of old gentlemen disputing. One of them immediately whispered something to the others; and they continued their discussion a in a lower tone. Jack looked at the orchestra for a few minutes, and then returned to the room he had left, where the elder lady was insisting in French that the pianoforte fantasia should be rehearsed before anything else, as she was not going to wait in the cold all day. Mr Manlius assured her that he had anticipated her suggestion, and should act upon it as a matter of course.

"It is oll the* same thinks," said the young lady in English. Then in French. "Even if you begin with the fantasia, Monsieur, I shall assuredly wait to hear for the first time your famous band perform in this ancient hall."

Manlius bowed. When he straightened himself again, he found Jack standing at his elbow. "Allow me to present to you Monsieur Jack," he said.

"It is for Monsieur Jacques to allow," she replied. The poor artist is honored by the presence of the illustrious English composer."

Jack nodded gravely as acknowledging that the young woman expressed herself becomingly. Manlius grinned covertly, and proposed that they should go up on the orchestra, as the band was apt to get out of humor when too much time was wasted. She rose at once, and ascended the steps on the arm of the conductor. She was received with an encouraging clapping of hands and tapping of fiddle backs. Jack followed with the elder lady, who sat down on the top stair, and began to knit.

"If you wish to conduct the rehearsal," said Manlius politely to Jack, "you are, of course, quite welcome to do so."

"Thank you," said Jack. "I will." Manlius, who had hardly expected him to accept the offer, retired to the pianoforte, and prepared to turn over the leaves for the player.

"I think I can play it from memory," she said to him, "unless Monsieur Jacques puts it all out of my head. Judging by his face, it is certain that he is not very patien — Ah! Did I not say so?"

Jack had rapped the desk sharply with his stick, and was looking balefully at the men, who did not seem in any hurry to attend to him. He put down the stick, stepped from the desk, and stooped to the conductor's ear.

I mentioned," he said, "that some of the parts ought to be given to the men to study before rehearsal. Has that been done?"

Manlius smiled. "My dear sir," he said, "I need hardly tell you that players of such standing as the members of the Antient Orpheus orchestra do not care to have suggestions of that kind offered to them. You have no cause to be uneasy. They can play anything — absolutely anything, at sight."

Jack looked black, and returned to his desk without a word. He gave one more rap with his stick, and began. The players were attentive, but many of them tried not to look so.

For a few bars, Jack conducted under some restraint, apparently striving to repress a tendency to extravagant gesticulation. Then, as certain combinations and progressions sounded strange and farfetched, slight bursts Of laughter were heard. Suddenly the first clarinetist, with an exclamation of impatience, put down his instrument.

"Well?" shouted Jack. The music ceased.

"I can't play that." said the clarinetist shortly.

"Can you play it?" said Jack, with suppressed rage, to the second clarinetist.

"No," said he. "Nobody could play it."

"That passage *has* been played; and it must be played. It has been played by a common soldier."

"If a common soldier even attempted it, much less played it," said the first clarinetist, with some contemptuous indignation at what he considered an evident falsehood, "he must have been drunk." There was general titter at this.

Jack visibly wrestled with himself for a moment. Then, with a gleam of humor like a flash of sunshine through a black thundercloud, he said: "You are right. He was drunk." The whole band roared with laughter.

"Well, *I* am not drunk," said the clarinetist, folding his arms.

"But will you not just try wh —" Here Jack, choked by the effort to be persuasive and polite, burst out raging: "It can be done. It shall be done. It must be done. You are the best clarinet player in England. I know what you can do." And Jack shook his fists wildly at the man as if he were accusing him of some infamous crime. But the compliment was loudly applauded, and the man reddened, not altogether displeased. A cornist who sat near him said soothingly in an Irish accent, "Aye, do, Joe. Try it."

"You will: you can," shouted Jack reassuringly, recovering his self-command. "Back to the double bar. Now!" The music recommenced; and the clarinetist, overborne, took up his instrument, and, when the passage was reached, played it easily, greatly to his own astonishment. The brilliancy of the effect, too, raised him for a time into a prominence which rivaled that of the pianist. The orchestra positively interrupted the movement to applaud it; and Jack joined in with high good humor.

"If you are uneasy about it," said he, with an undisguised chuckle, "I can hand it over to the violins."

"Oh, no, thank you," said the clarinetist. "Now I've got it, I'll keep it."

Jack rubbed his nose until it glowed like a coal, and the movement proceeded without another stoppage, the men now seeing that Jack was in his right place. But when a theme marked andante cantabile, which formed the middle section of the fantasia, was commenced by the pianist, Jack turned to her, said quicker. *Plus vite* ;" and began to mark his beat by striking the desk. She looked at him anxiously; played a few bars in the time indicated by him; and then threw up her hands and stopped.

"I cannot," she exclaimed. "I must play it more slowly or not at all."

"Certainly, it shall be slower if you desire it," said the elder lady from the steps. Jack looked at her as he sometimes looked at Mrs Simpson. "Certainly it shall not be slower, if all the angels desired it," he said, in well pronounced but barbarously ungrammatical French. Go on and take the time from my beat.

The Polish lady shook her head; folded her hands in her lap; and looked patiently at the music before her. There was a moment of silence, during which Jack, thus mutely defied, glared at her with distorted features. Manilius rose irresolutely. Jack stepped down from the desk; handed him the stick; and said in a smothered voice, "Be good enough to conduct this lady's portion of the fantasia. When my music recommences, I will return."

Manlius took the stick and mounted the desk, the orchestra receiving him with applause. In the midst of it Jack went out, giving the pianist a terrible look as he passed her, and transferring it to her companion, who raised her eyebrows and shoulders contemptuously.

Manlius was not the man to impose his own ideas of a composition on a refractory artist; and though he was privately disposed to agree with Jack that the Polish lady was misjudging the speed of the movement, he obediently followed her playing with his beat. But he soon lost his first impression, and began to be affected by a dread lest anyone should make a noise in the room. He moved his stick as quietly as possible, and raised his left hand as if to still the band, who were, however, either watching the pianist intently or playing without a trace of the expert offhandedness which they had affected at first. The pleasure of listening made Manlius forget to follow the score. When he roused himself and found his place, he perceived that the first horn player was altering a passage completely, though very happily. Looking questioningly in that direction, he saw Jack sitting beside the man with a pencil in his hand. Manlius observed for the first time that he had an expressive face and remarkable eyes, and was not, as he had previously seemed, unmitigatedly ugly. Meanwhile the knot of old gentlemen in the stalls, who had previously chattered subduedly, became quite silent; and a few of them closed their eyes rapturously. The lady on the steps alone did not seem to care about the music. At last the flow of melody waned and broke into snatches. The pianoforte seemed to appeal to the instruments to continue the song. A melancholy strain from the violas responded hopelessly; but the effect of this was marred by a stir in the orchestra. The trombone and trumpet players, hitherto silent, were taking up their instruments and pushing up their moustaches. The drummer, after some hasty screwing round his third drum, poised his sticks; and a supernumerary near him rose, cymbals in hand; fixed his eye on Manlius, and apparently stood ready to clap the head of the trumpet player in front of him as a lady claps a moth flying from a woolen curtain. Manlius looked at the score as if he did not quite understand the sequel. Suddenly, as the violas ceased, Jack shouted in a startling voice, "Let it be an avalanche from the top to the bottom of the Himalayas;" and rushed to the conductor's desk. Manlius made way for him precipitately; and a tremendous sound followed. "Louder," roared Jack. Less noise and more tone. Out with it like fifty million devils." As he led the movement at a merciless speed. The pianist looked bewildered, like the band, most of whom lost their places after the first fifty bars; but when the turn of a player came, he found the conductor glaring at him, and was swept into his part without clearly knowing how. It was an insensate orgies of sound. Gay melodies, daintily given out by the pianoforte, or by the string instruments, were derisively brayed out immediately afterwards by cornets, harmonized in thirds with the most ingenious vulgarity. Cadenzas, agilely executed by the Poish lady, were uncouthly imitated by the double basses. Themes constructed like ballads with choruses were introduced instead of orthodox "subjects." The old gentlemen in the stalls groaned and protested. The Polish lady, incommoded by the capricious and often excessive speed required of her, held on gallantly, Jack all the time grinding his teeth, dancing, gesticulating, and by turns shshsh-shing at the orchestra, or shouting to them for more tone and less noise. Even the lady on the steps had begun to nod to the impetuous rhythm, when the movement ended as suddenly as it had begun; and all the players rose to their feet, laughing and applauding heartily. Manlius, from whose mind the fantasia had banished all prejudice as to Jack's rank as a musician, shook his hand warmly. The Polish lady, her face transfigured by musical excitement, offered her hand too. Jack took it and held it, saying abruptly, "Listen to me. You were quite right; and I am a fool. I did not know what there was in my own music, and would have spoiled it if you had not prevented me. You are a great player, because you get the most beautiful tone possible from every note you touch, and you make every phrase say all that it was meant to say, and more. You are an angel. I would rather hear you play scales than hear myself play sonatas. And —" here he lowered his voice and drew her aside — "I rely on you to make my work succeed at the concert. Manlius will conduct the band; but you must conduct Manlius. It is not enough to be a gentleman and a contrapuntist in order to conduct. You comprehend?"

"Yes, Monsieur; I understand perfectly, perfectly. I will do my best. I shall be inspired. How magnificent it is!"

"Allow me to congratulate you, sir," said one of the old gentlemen, advancing. "Myself and colleagues have been greatly struck by your work. I am empowered to say on their behalf that whatever difference of opinion there may be among us as to the discretion with which you have employed your powers, of the extraordinary nature of those powers there can no longer be a doubt; and we are thoroughly gratified at having chosen for performance a work which displays so much originality and talent as your fantasia."

"Ten years ago" said Jack, looking steadily at him, "I might have been glad to hear you say so. At present the time for compliments is past, unless you wish to congratulate me on the private interest that has gained my work a hearing. My talent and originality have been a my chief allies here."

"Are you not a little hasty?" said the gentleman, disconcerted, "Success comes late in London; and you are still, if I may say so, a comparatively young man."

"I am not old enough to harp on being comparatively young. I am thirty-four years old; and if I had adopted any other profession than that of composer of music, I should have been seeing a respectable livelihood by this time. As it is, I have never made a farthing by my compositions. I don't blame those who have Stood between me and the public: their ignorance is their misfortune, and not their fault. But now that I have come to light by a chance in spite of their teeth, I am not in the humor to exchange pretty speeches with them. Understand, sir: I do not mean to rebuff you personally. But as for your colleagues, tell them that it does not become them to pretend to pretend to acknowledge spontaneously what I have just, after many hard years, forced them to admit. Look at those friends of yours shaking their heads over my score there. They have *heard* my music, but they do not know what to say until they *see* it. Would you like me to believe that they are admiring it?"

"I am confident that they cannot help doing so."

"They are shewing one another why it ought not to have been written — hunting out my consecutive fifths and sevenths, and my false relations — looking for my first subject, my second subject, my working out, and the rest of the childishness that could be taught to a poodle. Don't they wish they may find them?"

The gentleman seemed at a loss how to continue the conversation. "I hope you are satisfied with the orchestra," he said after a pause.

"No, I am not," said Jack. "They are over civilized. They are as much afraid of showing their individuality as if they were common gentlemen. You cannot handle a musical instrument with kid gloves on. However, they did better than I hoped. They are at least not coarse. That young woman is a genius."

"Ye-es. Almost a genius. She is young, of course. She has not the — I should call it the gigantic power and energy of such a player, for instance, as —"

Pshaw!" said Jack, interrupting him. "I, or anybody else, can get excited with the swing of a Chopin's polonaise, and thrash it out of the piano until the room shakes. But she! You talk of making a pianoforte sing — a child that can sing itself can do that. But she can make it speak. She has eloquence, the first and last quality of a great player, as it is of a great man. The finale of the fantasia is too coarse for her: it does violence to her nature. It was written to be played by a savage — like me."

"Oh, undoubtedly, undoubtedly! She is a remarkable player. I did not for a moment intend to convey —" Here Manlius rapped his desk; and Jack, with a unceremonious nod to his interlocutor, left the platform. As he passed the door leading to the public part of the hall, he heard the voice of the elder lady. "My child, they seek to deceive you. This Monsieur Jacques, with whom you are to make your debut here, is he famous in England? Not at all. My God! He is an unknown man."

"Be tranquil, mother. He will not long be unknown."

Jack opened the door a little way; thrust his face through; and smiled pleasantly at the pianist. Her mother, seeing her start, turned and saw him grimacing within a yard of her.

"Ah, Lord Jesus!" she exclaimed in German, recoiling from him. He chuckled and abruptly shut himself out of her view as the opening Coriolan overture sounded from the orchestra, The old gentleman who had congratulated him had rejoined the others in the stalls.

"Well," said one of them: "is your man delighted with himself?"

"N-no, I cannot say that he is — or rather perhaps he is too much so. I am sorry to say that he appears to rather morose — soured by his early difficulties, perhaps. He is certainly not an agreeable person to speak to."

"What did you expect?" said another gentleman coldly. "A man who degrades music to be the vehicle of his own coarse humor, and shews by his method of doing it an ignorant contempt for those laws by which the great composers established order in the chaos of sounds, is not likely to display a courteous disposition and refined nature in the ordinary business of life."

"I assure you, Professor," said a third, who had the score of the fantasia open on his knees, "this chap must know a devil of a lot. He plays old Harry with the sonata form; but he must do it on purpose, you know, really."

The gentleman addressed as Professor looked severely and incredulously at the other. "I really cannot listen to such things whilst they are playing Beethoven," he said. "I have protested against Mr Jack and his like; and my protest has passed unheeded. I wash my hands of the consequences. The Antient Orpheus Society will yet acknowledge that I did well when I counseled it to renounce the devil and all his works." He turned away; sat down on a stall a little way off; and gave all his attention ostentatiously to "Coriolan."

The pianist came presently and sat near him. The others quickly surrounded her; but she did not speak to them, and shewed by her attitude that she did not wish to be spoken to. Her mother, who did not care for Coriolan, and wanted to go home, knitted and looked appealingly at her from time to time, not venturing to express her impatience before so many members of the Antient Orpheus Society. At last Manlius came down; and the whole party rose and went into the performers' room.

"How do you find our orchestra?" said Manlius to her as she took up her muff.

"It is magnificent," she replied. "So refined, so quiet, so convenable! It is like the English gentleman." Manlius smirked. Jack, who had reappeared on the outskirts of the group with his hat on — a desperately illused hat — added:

"A Lithuanian or Hungarian orchestra could not play like that, eh?"

"No, truly," said the Polish lady, with a little shrug. "I do not think they could."

"You flatter us," said Manlius bowing. Jack began to laugh. The Polish lady hastily made her adieux and went out into Piccadilly, where a cab was brought for her. Her mother got in; and she was about follow when she heard Jack's voice again, at her elbow.

"May I send you some music?"

"If you will so gracious, Monsieur."

"Good. What direction shall I give your driver?"

"F — f — you call it Feetzroysquerre?"

"Fitzroy Square," shouted Jack to the cabman. The hansom went off; and he, running recklessly through the mud to a passing Hammersmith omnibus, which was full inside, climbed to the roof, and was borne away in the rain.

CHAPTER X

It was a yearly custom of the Antient Orpheus Society to give what they called a *soiree*, to which they invited all the celebrated persons who were at all likely to come. These meetings took place at a house in Harley Street. Large gilt tickets, signed by three of the committee, were sent to any distinguished foreign composers who happened to be in London, as well as to the president of the Royal Academy, the musical Cabinet Minister (if there was one), the popular tragedian of the day, and a few other privileged persons. The rest had little cards of invitation from the members, who were each entitled to introduce a few guests.

To the one of these entertainments next following the fantasia concert came a mob of amateurs, and a select body of pianists, singers, fiddlers, painters, actors and journalists. The noble vice-president of the society, assisted by two of the committee, received the guests in a broad corridor which had been made to resemble a miniature picture gallery. The guests were announced by two Swiss waiters, who were supposed to be able to pronounce foreign names properly because they could not pronounce English ones. Over one name on a gilt ticket, that of a young lady, they broke down; and she entered unannounced with her mother. After her came a member and his party of four: Mr and Mrs Phipson, Mr Charles Sutherland, Miss Sutherland, and Mr Adrian Herbert. Then other members with their parties.

Then the last of the gilt tickets, Mr Owen Jack, who presented the novelty of a black silk handkerchief round the neck with the bow under his right ear.

The company was crowded into two large rooms. There were many more guests than seats; and those who were weak or already weary stood round the walls or by the pianoforte and got what support they could by leaning on them. Mary Sutherland was seated on the end of a settee which supported four other persons, and would have accommodated two comfortably.

"Well?" said Jack, coming behind the settee.

"Well," echoed Mary.*Why are you so late?"

"For the usual reason — because women are so meddlesome. I could not find my studs, nor anything. I will endure Mother Simpson no longer. Next week I pack."

"So you have been threatening at any time within the last two years. I wish you would really leave Church Street."

"So you have been preaching anytime these fifty years. But I I must certainly do so: the woman is unendurable. There goes Charlie. He looks quite a man, like the rest of us, in his swallow-tail coat."

"He looks and is insufferably self-conscious. How crowded the rooms are: They ought to give their *conversazione* in St James's Hall as well as their concerts."

"They never did and never will do anything as it ought to be done. Where's your guide, philosopher, and friend?"

"Whom do you mean, Mr Jack?"

"What color is your dress?"

"Sea green. Why?"

"Nothing. I was admiring it just now."

"Does my guide, philosopher, et cetera, mean Mr Herbert?"

"Yes, as you know perfectly well. You are not above giving yourself airs occasionally. Come, where is he? Why is he not by your side?"

"I do not know, I am sure. He came in with us — Charlie?"

"Well?" said Charlie, who was beginning to stand on his manhood. "What are you shouting at me for? Oh, how d'ye do, Mr Jack?"

"Where is Adrian?" said Mary.

"In the next room, of course."

"Why of course?" said Jack.

"Because Miss Spitsneezncough — or whatever her unpronounceable name may be — is there. If I were you, Mary, I should look rather closely after Master Adrian's attentions to the fair Polack."

"Hush. Pray do not talk so loud, Charlie." Charlie turned on his heel, and strolled away, buttoning on a white glove with a negligent air.

"Come into the next room," said Jack.

"Thank you. I prefer to stay where I am."

"Come, Mrs. Obstinate. I want to see the fair Polack too: I love her to distraction. You shall see Mister Herbert supplanting me in her affections."

"I shall stay with Mrs. Phipson. Do not let me detain you, if you wish to go."

"You are going to be ill-natured and spoil our evening, eh?"

Mary suppressed an exclamation of impatience, and rose. "If you insist on it, of course I will come. Mrs. Phipson: I am going to walk through the rooms with Mr Jack."

Mrs Phipson, from mere habit, looked doubtful the propriety of the arrangement; but Jack walked off with Mary before anything further passed. In the next room they found a dense crowd and a very warm atmosphere. A violinist stood tuning his instrument near the pianoforte at which the young Polish lady sat. Close by was Adrian Herbert, looking intently at her.

"Aha!" said Jack, following his companion's look, "Mister Adrian's thoughts have come to an anchor at last." As he spoke, the music began.

"What are they playing?" said Mary with affected indifference.

"The Kreutzer Sonata."

"Oh! I am so glad."

"Are you indeed? What a thing it is to be fond of music! Do you know that we shall have to stand here mumchance for the next twenty minutes listening to them?"

"Surely if I can enjoy the Kreutzer Sonata, you can. You are only pretending to be unmusical."

"I wish they had chosen something shorter. However, since we are here, we had better hold our tongues and listen."

The Sonata proceeded; and Adrian listened, rapt. He did not join in the applause between the movements: it jarred on him.

Why don't you teach yourself to play like that?" said Jack to Mary.

"I suppose because I have no genius," she replied, not pleased by the question.

"Genius! Pshaw! What are you clapping your hands for?"

"You seem to be in a humor for asking unnecessary questions tonight, Mr Jack. I applaud Herr Josefs because I admire his playing."

"And Mademoiselle. How do you like her?"

"She is very good, of course. But I really do not see that she is so much superior to other pianists as you seem to consider her. I enjoy Josefs' playing more than hers."

"Indeed," said Jack. "Ho! Ho! Do you see that hoary-headed villain looking across at us? That is the man who protested against my fantasia as a work of the devil; and now he is coming to ask me to play."

"And will you play?"

"Yes. I promised Miss Szczymplıça that I would."

"Then you had better take me back to Mrs Phipson."

"What! You will not wait and listen to me?"

"It cannot possibly matter to you whether I listen or not. I cannot stand here alone."

"Then come back to Mrs. Phipson. I will not play."

"Now pray do not be so disagreeable, Mr Jack. I wish to go back because no one wants me here."

"Either you will stay where you are, or I will not play."

"I shall do as I please, Mr Jack. You have Mademoiselle Sczymplıça to play for. I cannot stay here alone."

"Mr Herbert will take care of you."

"I do not choose to disturb Mr Herbert."

"Well, well, here is your brother. Hush! — if you call him Charlie aloud here, he will be sulky. Mr Sutherland."

"What's the matter?" said Charlie gratefully. Jack handed Mary over to him and presently went to the piano at the invitation of the old gentleman he had pointed out, who wore a gold badge on his coat as one of the stewards of the entertainment. He had composed a symphony

— his second — that year for the Antient Orpheus: a laborious, conscientious, arid symphony, full of unconscious pickings and stealings from Mendelssohn, his favorite master, scrupulously worked up into the strictest academic form. It was a theme from this symphony that Jack now sounded on the pianoforte with one finger.

"That is not very polite." said Mr Phipson, after explaining this to the Polish lady. "Poor Maclagen! He does not seem to like having his theme treated in that fashion."

"If he intends it derisively," said Adrian indignantly, "it is in execrable taste. Mr Maclagan ought to leave the room."

"You think like me, Monsieur Herbert," said Mademoiselle Szczympliça "All must be forgiven to Monsieur Jacques; but he should not insult those who are less fortunately gifted than he. Besides, it is an old man."

Jack then began improvising on the theme with a capriciousness of which the humor was lost on the majority of the guests. He treated it with an eccentricity which burlesqued his own style, and then with a pedantry which burlesqued that of the composer. At last, abandoning this ironical vein when it had culminated in an atrociously knock-kneed fugato, he exercised his musical fancy in earnest, and succeeded so well that Maclagan felt tempted to rewrite the middle section of the movement from which the subject was taken. The audience professed to be delighted, and were in truth dazzled when Jack finished by a commonplace form of variation in which he made a prodigious noise with his left hand, embroidered by showers of arpeggios with his right.

" Magnificent!" said Mr Phipson, applauding. "Splendid."

"Ah!" said Mdlle Szczympliça, sighing, "if I had but his strength, I should fear no competitor."

"Is it possible," said Herbert, "that you, who play so beautifully, can envy such a man as that. I would rather hear you play for one minute than listen to him for an hour."

She shrugged her shoulders. "Alas!" she said, "you know what I can do; and you are so good as to flatter me that I do it well. But I! I know what I cannot do."

"How are you, Mademoiselle?" said Jack, approaching them without staying to answer several persons who were congratulating him. "Good evening, Mr Herbert. Ah, Mr Phipson."

"Mademoiselle Szczympliça has been paying you a high compliment — I fully agree with Mr Herbert that it is an exaggerated one," said Phipson, "She wishes she could play like you."

"And so Mr Herbert thinks 'God forbid! does he? Well, he is right Why do you want to trample on the pianoforte as I do, Fraulein, when you can do so much better? What would you think of a skiff on the waters envying the attempts of a cavalry charger to swim?"

"I see from your playing how far I fall short in the last movement of the fantasia, Monsieur Jacqes. I am not strong enough to play it as you think it should be played. Ah yes, yes, yes; but I know — I know."

"No, Mademoiselle; nor are you strong enough to dance the wardance as an Iroquois Indian thinks it should be danced. The higher you attain, the more you leave below you. Eh, Mr Herbert?"

"I am not a musician," said Herbert, irritated by Jack's whimsical appeals to him. "My confirmation of your opinion would not add much to its value."

"Come," said Jack: "I care nothing for professional opinions. According to them, I do not know the rudiments of music. Which would you rather hear the Fraulein play or me?"

"Since you compel me to express a preference, I had rather hear Mademoiselle Sczympliça."

"I thought so," said Jack, delighted "Now I must go back to Miss Sutherland, who has been left to take care of herself whilst I was playing."

Herbert reddened. Jack nodded and walked away.

"Miss — Miss — , I cannot say it. She is the young lady who was with you at the concert, when Monsieur Feepzon introduced us. She is very dark, and wears lunettes. Is not that so?"

"Yes."

"She is not stiff, like some of the English ladies. Is she a great friend of yours?"

"She — Her elder brother, who is married to Mrs Phipson's daughter, was at school with me; and we were great friends."

"Perhaps I should not have asked you. I fear I often shock your English ideas of reserve. I beg your pardon."

"Not at all," said Herbert, annoyed at himself for having betrayed his uneasiness. "Pray do not let any fear of our national shyness — for it is not really reserve — restrain you from questioning me whenever you are interested in anything concerning me. If you knew how much I prize that interest —" She drew back a little; and he stopped, afraid to go on without encouragement, and looking wistfully at her in the hope of seeing some in her face.

"How do you call this lady who is going to sing?" she said, judging it better to ask an irrelevant question than to look down and blush. Jack's voice, speaking to Mary close by, interrupted them.

"I can listen to Josefs because he can play the fiddle," said he, "and to Szczympliça because she can play the piano; and I would listen to her" — pointing to the singer — "if she could sing. She is only about four years older than you; and already she dare attempt nothing that cannot be screamed through by main force. She has become what they call a dramatic singer, which means a singer with a worn out voice. Come, make haste: she is going to begin."

"But perhaps she will feel hurt by your leaving the room. Now that you are famous, you cannot come and go unnoticed, as I can."

"So much the worse for those who notice me. I hate singers, a miserable crew who think that music exists only in their own throats. There she goes with her *Divinités du Styx*. Come away God's sake."

"I think this room is the pleas — No, I do not — Let us go."

Mary's habitual look of resolution had gathered into a frown. They went back to the settee which was now deserted: Mrs Phipson and her neighbors having gone to hear the music.

Ä penny for your thoughts," said Jack, sitting down beside Mary. "Are you jealous?"

She started and said "What do you mean?" Then, recovering herself a little, "Jealous of whom; and why?"

"Jealous of Sczympliça because Master Herbert seems to forget that there anyone else in the whole world tonight."

"] did not notice his absorption. I am sure she is very welcome. He ought to be tired of me by this time."

"You think to hoodwink me, do you? I saw you watching him the whole time she was playing. I wish you would quarrel with him."

"Why do you wish that."

"Because I am tired of him. If you were well rid of the fellow, you would stick to your music; pitch your nasty oil paints into the Thames; and be friendly to me without accusing yourself of treason to him. He is the most uncomfortable chap I know, and the one least suited to you. Besides, he can't paint. I could do better myself, if I tried."

"Other people do not think so. I have suspected ever since I first met you in his studio you did not admire his painting."

"You had the same idea yourself, or you would never have detected it in me. I am no draughtsman; but I recognize weakness by instinct. You feel that he is a duffer. So do I."

"Do you think, if he were a duffer, that his picture of last year would have been hung on the line at the Academy; or that the Art Union would have bought it to engrave; or that the President would have spoken of it so highly to Adrian himself?"

"Pshaw! There must be nearly two hundred pictures on the line every year at the Academy; and did you, or anyone else, ever see an Academy exhibition with ten pictures in it that had twenty years of life in them? Did the President of the Academy of Music ever speak well of me; or, if he did, do you think I should fell honored by his approval? That is another superfine duffer's quality in your Mr Adrian. He is brimming over with reverence. He is humble, and speaks with bated breath of every painter that has ever had a newspaper notice written about him. He grovels before his art because he thinks that grovelling becomes him."

"I think his modesty and reverence do become him."

"Perhaps they do, because he has nothing to be bumptious about; but they are not the qualities that make a creative artist. Ha! ha!"

Mary opened her fan, and began to fan herself, with her face turned away from Jack.

Well," said he, "are you angry?"

"No. But if you must disparage Adrian, why do you do so to me? You know the relation between us."

"I disparage him because I think he is a humbug. If he spends whole days in explaining to you what a man of genius is and feels, knowing neither the one nor the other, I do not see why I should not give you my opinion on the subject, since I am in my own way — not a humble way — a man of genius myself."

"Adrian, unfortunately, has not the same faith in himself that you have."

"Perhaps he has got a good reason. A man's own self is the last person to believe in him, and is harder to to cheat than the rest of the world. I sometimes wonder whether I am not an impostor. Old Beethoven once asked a pupil whether he really considered him a good composer. Shakespeare, as far as I can make out, only succeeded about half-a-dozen times in his attempts at play writing. Do you suppose he didn't know it?"

"Then why do you blame Adrian for his diffidence?"

"Ah! that's a horse another color. He thinks himself worse than other men, mortal like himself. I think myself a fool occasionally, because there are times when composing music seems to me to be a ridiculous thing in itself. Why should a rational man spend his life in making jingle-jingle with twelve notes? But at such times, Bach seems just as great a fool as I. Ask me at any time whether I cannot compose as good or better music than any Tom, Dick, or Harry now walking upon two legs in England; and I shall not trouble you with any cant about my humbleness or unworthiness."

"Can you compose better music than Mozart's? I believe you are boasting out of sheer antipathy to poor Adrian."

"Does Mozart's music express me? If not, what does it matter to me whether it is better or worse? I must make my own music, such as it is or such as I am — and I would as soon be myself as Mozart or Beethoven or any of them. To hear your Adrian talk one would think he would rather be anybody than himself. Perhaps he is right there, too."

"Let it be agreed, Mr Jack, that you have a low opinion of Adrian; and let us say no more about him."

"Very well. But let us go back to the other room. You are in a bad humor for a quiet chat, Miss Mary."

"Then go alone; and leave me here. I do not mind being here by myself at all. I know I am not gaily disposed; and I fear I am spoiling your evening."

"You are gay enough for me. I hate women who are always grinning. Besides, Miss Mary, I am fond of you, and find attraction in all your moods."

"Yes, I am sure you are very fond of me," said Mary with listless irony, as she walked away with him. In the other room they came upon Herbert, seeking anxiously someone in the eddy near the door, formed by people going away. Mary did not attempt to disturb him; but he presently caught sight of her. Thinking that she was alone — for Jack, buttonholed by Phipson, had fallen behind for a moment — he made his way to her and said:

"Where is Mrs Phipson, Mary? Are you alone?"

"I have not seen her for some time." She had all but added that she hoped he had not disturbed himself to come to her; but she refrained, feeling that spiteful speeches were unworthy of herself and of him.

"Where did you vanish to for so long?" he said. "I have hardly seen you the whole evening."

"Were you looking for me?"

He avoided her eyes, and stepped aside to make way for a lady who was passing. "Shall I get you an ice he said, after this welcome interruption. "It is very warm in here."

"No. thank you. You know that I never eat ices."

"I thought that this furnace of a room might have prevailed over your hygienic principles. Have you enjoyed yourself?"

I have not been especially happy or the reverse. I enjoyed the music."

"Oh yes. Don't you think *Mlle.* Sczympliça plays beautifully?"

"I saw that you thought so. She is able to bring an expression into your face that I have never seen there before."

Herbert looked at her quickly: he became quite red. "Yes." he said, "she certainly plays most poetically. By the bye, I think Mr. Jack behaved very badly in publicly making game of Mr. Maclagan. Everyone in the room was disgusted."

Mary was ready to retort in defence of Jack; but before she could utter it Mrs Phipson came up, aggrieved and and speaking more loudly than was at all necessary. "Well, Mr Herbert," she was saying, "you really have behaved most charmingly to us all the evening. I think we may go now, Mary. Josefs has gone; and Szczympliça is going, so there is really nothing to stay for. Why Adrian Herbert is gone again! How excessively odd!"

"He is gone to get Mdlle Sczympliça's carriage," said Mary, quietly. "Be careful," she added, in a lower tone: "Mdlle Sczympliça is close behind us."

"Indeed! And who is to get our carriage?" said Mrs Phipson, crossly, declining to abate her voice in the least. "Oh, really, Mary, you must speak to him about this. What is the use of your being his fiancée if he never does anything for you? He has behaved very badly. Mr Phipson is with that Frenchwoman who sang. He is only happy when he is running errands for celebrities. I suppose we must either take care of ourselves, or wait until Adrian condescends to come back for us."

"We had better not wait. I see Charlie in the next room: he will look after us. Come."

The Polish lady passed them, and followed her mother down the staircase. The cloak room was crowded; but Madame Sczympliça fought her way in, and presently returned with an armful of furs. She was assisted into some of these by her daughter, who was about to wrap herself in a cloak, when it was taken from her by Herbert.

"Allow me," he said, placing the cloak on her shoulders. "I must not delay you: your servant has brought up your carriage; but —"

"Let us go quickly, my child," said Madame. "They scream like devils for us. Au revoir, Monsieur Herbert. Come, Aurélie!"

"Adieu," said Aurélie, hurrying away. He kept beside her until she stepped into the carriage. "Certainly not adieu," he said eagerly. "May I not come to see you, as we arranged?"

"No," she replied. "Your place is beside Miss Sutherland, your affianced. Adieu." The carriage sped off; and he stood, gaping, until a footman reminded him that he was in the way of the next party. He then returned to the hall, where Mrs Phipson informed him coldly that she was sorry she could not offer him a seat in her carriage, as there was no room. So he bade them goodnight, and walked home.

CHAPTER XI

Every day, from ten in the forenoon to twelve, Mademoiselle Sczympliça practiced or neglected the pianoforte, according to her mood, whilst her mother discussed household matters with the landlady, and accompanied her to market. On the second morning after the *conversazione*, Madame went out as usual. No sooner had she disappeared in the direction of Tottenham Court Road than Adrian Herbert crossed from the opposite angle of the square, and knocked at the door of the house she had just left.

Whilst he waited on the doorstep, he could hear the exercise Aurélie was playing within. It was a simple affair, such as he had often heard little girls call "five-finger" exercises; and was slowly and steadily continued as if the player never meant to stop. The door was opened by a young woman, who, not expecting visitors at that hour, and being in a slatternly condition, hid her hand in her apron when she saw Adrian.

"Will you ask Miss Szczympliça whether she can see me, if you please."

The servant hesitated, and then went into the parlor, closing the door behind her. Presently she came out, and said with some embarrassment, "Maddim Chimpleetsa is not at home, sir."

"I know that," said he. "Tell mademoiselle that I have a special reason for calling at this hour, and that I beg her to see me for a few moments." He put his hand into his pocket for half-a-crown as he spoke; but the maid was gone before he had made up his mind to give it to her. Bribing a servant jarred his sense of honor.

"If it's very particular, madamazel says will you please to walk in," said she, returning.

Adrian followed her to the parlor, a lofty, spacious apartment with old fashioned wainscoting and a fireplace framed in white marble, carved with vases and garlands. The piano stood in the middle of the room; and the carpet was rolled up in a corner, so as not to deaden the resonance of the boards. Aurélie was standing by the piano, looking at him with a curious pucker of her shrewd face.

"I hope you are not angry with me," said Herbert, with such evident delight in merely seeing her that she lowered her eyelids. "I know I have interrupted your practicing; and I have even watched to see madame go out before coming to you. But I could not endure another day like yesterday."

Aureélie hesitated; then seated herself and motioned him to a chair, which he drew close to her. "What was the the matter yesterday?" she said, coquetting in spite of herself.

"It was a day of uncertainty as to the meaning of the change in your manner towards me at Harley Street on Monday, after I had left you for a few minutes."

Aurélie made a little grimace, but did not look at him. "Why should I change?" she said.

"That is what I ask you. You did change — somebody had been telling you tales about me; and you believed them." Aurélie's eyes lightened hopefully. "Will you not charge me openly with whatever has displeased you; and so give me an opportunity to explain."

"You must have strange customs in England," she said, her eyes flashing again, this time with anger. "What right have I to charge you with anything? What interest have I in your affairs?"

"Aurélie," he exclaimed, astonished: "do you not know that I love you like a madman?"

"You never told me so," she said. "Do Englishwomen take such things for granted?" She blushed as she said so, and immediately bent her face into her hands; laughed a little and cried a little in a breath. This lasted only an instant; for, hearing Herbert's chair drawn rapidly to the side of hers, she sat erect, and checked him by a movement of her wrist.

"Monsieur Herbert: according to our ideas in my country a declaration of love is always accompanied by an offer of marriage. Do you then offer me your love, and reserve your hand for Miss Sutherland?"

"You are unjust to yourself and to me, Aurélie. I offered you only my love because I could think of nothing else. I do not expect you to love me as blindly as I love you; but will you consent to be my wife? I feel — I know by instinct that there can be no more unhappiness for me in the world if you will only call me your dearest friend." He said this in a moment of intoxication, produced by an accidental touch of her sleeve against his hand.

Aurélie became pensive. "No doubt you are our dear friend, Monsieur Herbert, We have not many friends. I do not find that there is any such thing as love"

"You do not care for me." he said, dejected.

"Indeed, you must not think so," she said quickly. "You have been so kind to us, though we are strangers. For we are strangers, are we not? You hardly know us. And you are so foreign!"

"I! I have not a drop of foreign blood in my veins. You are not accustomed to England yet. I hope you not think me too cold. Oh! I am jealous of all your countrymen!"

"You need not be, Heaven knows! We have few friends in Poland."

"Aurélie do you know that you are saving 'we,' and 'us,' as if you did not understand that I love you alone — that I am here, not as a friend of your family, but as suitor to yourself, blind to the existence of any other person in the universe. In your presence I feel as if I were alone in some gallery of great pictures, or listening in a beautiful valley to the singing of angels, yet with some indescribable rapture added to that feeling. Since I saw you, all my old dreams and enthusiasms have come to life again. You can blot them out forever, or make them everlasting with one word. Do you love me?"

She turned hesitatingly towards him, but waited to say, "And it is then wholly false what Madame Feepson said that night?"

"What did she say?" demanded Herbert, turning red with disappointment.

She drew back, and looked earnestly at him. "Madame said," she replied in a low voice, "that Miss Sutherland was your affianced."

"Let me explain," said Adrian, embarrassed. She rose at once, shocked. "Explain!" she repeated. "Oh, Monsieur, yes or no?"

"Yes, then, since you will not listen to me," he said, with some dignity. She sat down again, slowly, looking round as if for counsel.

"What shall you not think of me if I listen now?" she said, speaking for the first time in English.

"I shall think that you love me a little, perhaps. You have condemned me on a very superficial inference, Aurélie. Engagements are not irrevocable in England. May I tell you the truth about Miss Sutherland?"

Aurélie shook her head doubtfully, and said nothing. But she listened.

"I became engaged to her more than two — nearly three years ago. As I told you, her elder brother, Mr Phipson's son-in-law, is a great friend of mine; and through him I came to know her very intimately. I owe it to her to confess that her friendship sustained me through a period of loneliness and discouragement, a period in which my hand was untrained, and my acquaintances, led by my mother, were loud in their contempt for my ability as an artist and my perverseness and selfishness in throwing away opportunities of learning banking and stockbroking. Miss Sutherland is very clever and well read. She set herself to study painting with ardor when I brought it under her notice, and soon became a greater enthusiast than I. She probably exaggerated my powers as an artist: at all events I have no doubt that she gave me credit for much of the good influence upon her that was really wrought by her new acquaintance with the handiwork of great men. However that may be, we were united in our devotion to art; and I was deeply grateful to her for being my friend when I had no other. I was so lonely that, in my fear of losing her, I begged her to betroth herself to me. She consented without hesitation, though my circumstances necessitated a long engagement. That engagement has never been formally dissolved, but fulfillment of it is now impossible. Long before I saw you and found out for the first time what love really is, our relations had insensibly altered. Miss Sutherland cooled in her enthusiasm for painting as soon as she discovered that it could not be mastered like a foreign language or an era in history. She came under the influence of Mr Jack, who may be a man of genius — I am no judge of musical matters — and who is undoubtedly, in his own way, a man of honor. But he is so far from possessing the temperament of an artist, that his whole character, his way of living, and all his actions, are absolutely destructive of that atmosphere of melancholy grandeur in which great artists find their inspiration. His musical faculty, to my mind, is as extraordinary an accident as if it had occurred in a buffalo. However, Miss Sutherland turned to him for guidance in artistic matters; and doubtless he saved her the trouble of thinking for herself; for she did not question him as she had been in the habit of questioning me. Perhaps he understood her better than I. He certainly behaved towards her as I had never behaved; and, though it still seems to me that my method was the more respectful to her, he supplanted me in her regard most effectually. I do not mean to convey that he did so intentionally; for anything less suggestive of affection for any person — even for himself —

than his general conduct, I cannot imagine; but she chose not to be displeased. I was hurt by her growing preference for him: it discouraged me more than the measure of success which I had begun to achieve in my profession elated me. Yet on my honor I never knew what jealousy meant until I saw you, playing Jack's music. I did not admire you for your performance, nor for the applause you gained. There are little things that an artist sees, Aurélie, that surpass brilliant fingering of the keyboard. I cannot describe them; they came home to me as you appeared on the platform; as you slipped quietly into your place; as you replied to Manlius's inquiring gesture by a look — it was not even a nod, and yet it reassured him instantly. When the music commenced you became dumb to me, though to the audience you began to speak. I only enjoyed that lovely strain in the middle of the fantasia, which by Jack's own confession, owed all its eloquence to you alone. When Mr. Phipson brought us under the orchestra and introduced us to you, I hardly had a word to say; but I did not lose a tone or a movement of yours. You were a stranger, ignorant of my language, a privileged person in a place where I was only present on sufferance. For all I knew, you might have been married. Yet I felt that there was some tie between us that far transcended my friendship with Miss Sutherland, though she was bound to me by her relationship to my old school friend, and by every coincidence of taste, culture, and position that can exist between man and woman. I knew at once that I loved you, and had never loved her. Had I met her as I met you, do you think I would have troubled Mr Phipson to introduce me to her? My jealousy of Jack vanished: I was content that he should be your composer if I might be your friend. Mary's attachment to him now became the source of my greatest happiness. His music and your playing were the attractions on which all the concerts relied. Jack went to these concerts: Mary went with Jack: I followed Mary. We always had an opportunity of speaking to you, thanks to my rival. It was he who encouraged Mary to call on you. It is to him that I owe my freedom from any serious obligation in respect of my long engagement; and hence it is through him also that I dare to come here and beg you to be my wife. Aurélie: I passed the whole of yesterday questioning myself as to the true story of my engagement, in Order that I might confess it to you with the most exact fidelity; and I believe I have told you the truth; but I could devise no speech that can convey to you what I feel towards you. Love does not describe it, it is something new — something extraordinary. There is a new sense — a new force, born in me. There are no words for it in any language:I could not tell you in my own. It —"

"I understand you very well. Your engagement with Miss S-Sutherland — she always pronounced this name with difficulty — "is not yet broken off?"

"Not explicitly. But if you need —"

"Hear me, Monsieur Herbert I will not come between her and her lover. But if you can affirm on your honor as an English gentleman that she no longer loves you, go and obtain an assurance from her that it is so."

"And then?"

"And then — Come back to me; and we shall see. But I do not think she will release you."

"She will. Would I have spoken to you if I had any doubts left? For, if she holds me to my word, I am, as you say, an English gentleman, and must keep it. But she will not."

"You will nevertheless go to her, and renew your offer."

"Do you mean my offer to you — or to her?"

"My God! he does not understand! Listen to me, Monsieur Herbert." Here Aurélie again resorted to the English tongue. "You must go to her and say, 'Marie: I come to fulfill my engagement.' If she reply, 'No, Monsieur Adrian, I no longer wish it,' then — then, as I have said, we shall see. But if she say 'yes,' then you must never any more come back."

"But —"

"No, no, no," murmured Aurélie, turning away her head. "It must be exactly as I have said."

"I will undertake to learn her true mind, Aurélie, and to abide by it. That I promise. But were I to follow your instructions literally, she too would hold herself bound by her word, and would say 'yes,' in spite of her heart. We should sacrifice each other and ourselves to a false sense of honor." Aurélie twisted a button of her chair, and shook her head, unconvinced. "Aurélie," he added gravely: "are you anxious to see her accept me? If so, it would be kinder to tell me so at once. Would you be so cruel as to involve me in an unhappy marriage merely to escape the unpleasantness of uttering a downright refusal?"

"Ah" she said, raising her head again, but still not looking at him, "I will not answer you. You seek to entrap me — you ask too much." Then, after a pause, "Have I not told you that if she releases you, you may return here?"

"And I may infer from that — ?"

She clasped hands with a gesture of despair. "And they say these Englishmen think much of themselves! You will not believe it possible that a woman should care for you!" He hesitated even yet, until she made a sudden movement towards the door, when he seized her hand and kissed it. She drew it away quickly, checked him easily by begging him to excuse her, bowed, and left the room.

He went out elated, and had walked as far as Portland Place before he began to consider what he should say for himself at Cavendish Square, where Mary was staying with Mrs Phipson. At Fitzroy Square he had been helped by the necessity of speaking French, in which language he found it natural and easy to say many things which in English would have sounded extravagant to him. He had kissed Aurélie's hand, as it were, in French. To kiss Mary's hand would, he felt, be a ridiculous ceremony, unworthy of a civilized Englishman. A proposal to jilt her, which was the substance of his business with her now, was not easy to frame acceptably in any language.

When he reached the house he found her with her hat on and a workbag in her hand.

"I am waiting" for Miss Cairns, she said. "She is coming with me on an expedition. Guess what it is."

"I cannot. I did not know that Miss Cairns was in town."

"We have decided that the condition of Mr. Jack's wardrobe is no longer tolerable. He is away at Birmingham today; and we are going to make a descent on his lodgings with a store of buttons and darning cotton, and a bottle of benzine. We shall make his garments respectable, and he will be none the wiser. Now, Adrian, do not look serious. You are worse than an old woman on questions of propriety."

"It is a matter of taste," said Herbert, shrugging his shoulders. "Is your expedition too important to be postponed for half an hour? I want to speak to you rather particularly."

"If you wish," said Mary slowly, her face lengthening a little. She was in the humor to sally out and play a prank on Jack, not to sit down and be serious with Herbert.

"It is possible," he said, noticing this with some mortification, though it strung him up a little, too, "that when you have heard what I have to say, you will go on your expedition with a lighter heart. Nevertheless, I am sorry to detain you."

"You need not apologize," she said, irritated. "I am quite willing to wait, Adrian. What is the matter?"

"Are you quite sure we shall not be disturbed here, even by Miss Cairns?"

"If it is so particular as that, we had better go out into the Square. I cannot very well barricade myself in Mrs Phipson' drawing room. There is hardly anybody in the Square at this hour."

"Very well," said Herbert, trying to repress a sensation of annoyance which he also began to experience. They left the house together in silence, opened the gate of the circular enclosure which occupies the centre of Cavendish Square, and found it deserted except for themselves and a few children. Mary walked beside him with knitted brows, waiting for him to begin.

"Mary: if I were asking you now for the first time the question I put to you that day when we rowed on the Serpentine, would you give me the same answer?"

She stopped, bewildered by this unexpected challenge.

"If you had not put that question before today, would you put it at all?" she said, walking on again.

"For Heaven's sake," he said, angry at at being being parried, "do not let us begin to argue. I did not mean to reproach you,"

Mary thought it better not to reply. Her temper was so far under control that she could suppress the bitter speeches which suggested themselves to her, but she could not think of any soft answers, and so she had either to retort or be silent.

"I have noticed — or at least I fancy so" — he said quietly, after a pause, "that our engagement has not been so pleasant a topic as it once was."

"I am perfectly ready to fulfill it," said Mary steadfastly.

"So am I," said Adrian in the same tone. Another interval of silence ensued.

"The question is," he said then, "whether you are willing as well as ready You would do me a cruel injustice if, having promised me your heart, you were to redeem that promise with your hand alone."

"What have you to complain of, Adrian? I know that you are sensitive; but I have taken such pains to avoid giving you the least uneasiness during the last two years that I do not think you can reasonably reproach me. You agreed with me that my painting was mere waste of time, and that I was right to give it up."

"Since you no longer cared for it."

"I did not know that you felt sore about it."

"Nor do I, Mary."

"Then what is the matter?"

"Nothing is the matter, if you are satisfied."

"And is that all you had to say to me, Adrian?" This with an attempt at gaiety.

Adrian mused awhile. "Mary," he said: "I wish you in the first place to understand that I am not jealous of Mr Jack." She opened her eyes widely, and looked at him. "But," he continued, "I never was so happy with you as when we were merely friends. Since that time, I have become your professed lover; and Mr Jack has succeeded to the friendship which — without in the least intending it — I left vacant. I would willingly change places with him now."

"You ask me to break off the engagement, then," she said, half eager, half cautious.

"No. I merely feel bound to offer to release you if you desire it."

"I am ready to keep my promise," she rejoined stubbornly.

"So you say. I do not mean that you will not keep your word, but that your assurance is not given in a manner calculated to make me very happy. I often used to warn you that you thought too highly of me, Mary. You are revenging your own error on me now by letting me see that you do not think me worthy of the sacrifice you feel bound to make for me."

"I never spoke of it as a sacrifice," said Mary turning red, "I took particular care — I mean that you are groundlessly jealous of Mr Jack. If our engagement is to he broken off, Adrian, do not say that I broke it."

"I do not think that *I* have broken it, Mary," said Herbert, also reddening.

"Then I suppose it holds good," she said. A long silence followed this. They walked once across the grass and half way back. There she stopped, and faced him bravely. "Adrian," she said: "I have been fencing unworthily with you. Will you release me from the engagement, and let us be friends as we were before?"

"You do wish it, then," he said, startled.

"I do; and I was hoping you would propose it yourself, and so be unable to reproach me with going back from my word. That was mean; and I came to my senses during that last turn across the square. I pledge you my word that I only want to be free to remain unmarried. It has nothing to do with Mr Jack or any other man. It is only that I should not be a good wife to you. I do not think I will marry at all. You are far too good for me, Adrian."

Herbert, ashamed of himself, stood looking at her, unable to reply.

"I know I should have told you this frankly at first," she continued anxiously. "But my want of straightforwardness only shows that I am not what you thought I was. I should be a perpetual disappointment to you if you married me. I hope I have not been too sudden. I thought — that is, I fancied — Well, I have been thinking a little about Mlle Szczympliça. If you remain friends with her, you will soon feel that I am no great loss."

"I hope it is not on her account that —"

"No, no. It is solely for the reason I have given. We are not a bit suited to one another. I assure you that I have no other motive. Are you certain that you believe me, Adrian? If you suspect me of wanting to make way for another attachment, or of being merely huffed and jealous, you must think very ill of me."

Herbert's old admiration of her stirred within him, intensified by the remorse which he felt for having himself acted as she was blaming herself for acting. He was annoyed too, because now that circumstances had tested them equally, she had done the right thing and he the wrong thing. He had always been sincere in his protests that she thought too highly of him; but he had never expected to come out of any trial meanly in comparison with her. He thought of Aurélie with a sudden dread that perhaps she saw nothing more in him than this situation had brought out. But he maintained, by habit, all his old air of thoughtful superiority as he took up the conversation.

"Mary," he said, earnestly: "I have never thought more highly of you than I do at this moment. But whatever you feel to be the right course for us is the right course. I have not been quite unprepared for this; and since it will make you happy, I am content to lose you as a wife, provided I do not lose you as a friend."

"I shall always be proud to be your friend," she said, offering him her hand. He took it, feeling quite noble again. "Now we are both free," she continued, and I can wish for your happiness without feeling heavily responsible for it. And, Adrian: when we were engaged, you gave me some presents and wrote me some letters. May I keep them?"

"I shall be very much hurt if you return them; though I suppose that you have a right to do so if you wish."

"I will keep them then." They clasped hands once again before she resumed in her ordinary tone, "I wonder has Miss Cairns been waiting for me all this time."

On the way to the house they chatted busily on indifferent matters, The servant who opened the door informed them that Miss Cairns was within. Mary entered; but Herbert did not follow.

"If you do not mind," he Said, "I think I had rather not go in." This seemed natural after what had passed. She smiled, and bade him goodbye.

"Goodbye, Mary," he said. As the door closed on her, he turned towards Fitzroy Square; a feeling of being ill and out of conceit with himself made him turn back to a restaurant in Oxford Street, where he had a chop and glass of wine. After this, his ardor suddenly revived; and he hurried towards Aurélie's residence by way of Wells Street. He soon lost his way in the labyrinth between Great Portland and Cleveland Streets, and at last emerged at Portland Road railway station. Knowing the way thence, he started afresh for Fitzroy Square. Before he had gone many steps he was arrested by his mother's voice calling him. She was coming from the station and overtook him in the Euston Road, at the corner of Southampton Street.

"What on earth are you doing in this quarter of the town?" he said, stopping, and trying to conceal how unwelcome the interruption was.

"That is a question which you have no right to ask, Adrian. People who have 'Where are you going?' and 'What are you doing?' always in their mouths are social and domestic nuisances, as I have often told you. However, I am going to buy some curtains in Tottenham Court Road. Since you have set the example, may I now ask where you are going?"

"I? I am not going anywhere in particular just at present."

"I only asked because you stopped as if you wished to turn down here. Do not let us stand in the street."

She went on; and he accompanied her. Presently she said: "Have you any news?"

"No," he replied, after pretending to consider. "I think not. Why?"

"I met Mary Sutherland with Miss Cairns in High Street as I was coming to the train; and she said that you had something to tell me about her."

"It is only that our engagement is broken off."

"Adrian!" she exclaimed, stopping so suddenly that a man walking behind them stumbled against her.

"Beg pwor'n, mum," said he, civilly, as he passed on.

"Pray take care, mother," remonstrated Herbert. "Come on."

"Do not be impatient, Adrian. My dress is torn. I believe English workmen are the rudest class in the world. Will you hold my umbrella for *one* moment, *please*?"

Adrian took the umbrella and waited, chafing. When they started again, Mrs Herbert walked quickly, taking short steps.

"It is thoroughly disheartening," she said, "to find that you have undone the only sensible thing you ever did in your life. I thought your news would be that you had arranged for the wedding. I think you had better see Mary as soon as you can, and make up your foolish quarrel. She is not a girl to be trifled with."

"Everything of that kind is at an end between Mary and me. There is no quarrel. The affair is broken off finally — completely — whether it pleases you or not."

"Very well, Adrian. There is no occasion for you to be angry. I am content, if you are. I merely say that you have done a very foolish thing."

"You do not know what I have done. You know absolutely —" He checked himself and walked on in silence.

"Adrian," said Mrs. Herbert, with dignity: "you are going back to your childish habits, I think. You are in a rage."

"If I am," he replied bitterly, "you are the only person alive who takes any pleasure in putting me into one. I know that you consider me a fool."

"I do not consider you a fool."

"At any rate, mother, you have such an opinion of me me, that I would rather discuss my private affairs with any stranger than with you. Where do you intend to buy the curtains?"

Mrs. Herbert did not help him to change the subject. She remained silent for some time to compose herself; for Adrian's remark had hurt her.

"I hope," she said at last, "that these musical people have not brought about this quarrel — or breach, or whatever it is."

"Who are 'these musical people'?"

"Mr Jack."

"He had nothing whatever to do with it. It was Mary who proposed to break the engagement: not I."

"Mary! Oh! Well, it is your own fault: you should have married her long ago. But why should she object now more than another time? Has Mademoiselle — the pianist — anything to do with it?"

"With Mary's withdrawing? No. How could it possibly concern Mademoiselle Szczympliça — if it is of her that you are speaking?"

"It is of her that I am speaking. I see she has taught you the balked sneeze with which her name begins. I call her Stchimpleetza, not having had the advantage of her tuition. Where does she live?"

Herbert felt that he was caught, and frowned. "She lives in Fitzroy Square," he said shortly.

"A-ah! Indeed!" said Mrs. Herbert. Then she added sarcastically, "Do you happen to know that we are within a minute's walk of Fitzroy Square?"

"I know it perfectly well. I am going there — to see her."

"Adrian," said his mother quickly, changing her tone: "you don't mean anything serious, I hope?"

"You do not hope that I am trifling with her, do you, mother?"

Mrs. Herbert looked at him, startled. "Do you mean to say, Adrian, that you have thrown Mary over because —"

"Because it's well to off with the old love, before you you are on with the new? You may put that construction on it if you like, although I have told you that it was Mary, and not I, who ended the engagement. I had better tell you the whole truth now, to avoid embittering our next meeting with useless complaints. I am going to ask Mademoiselle Szczympliça to be my wife."

"You foolish boy. She will not accept you. She is making a fortune, and does not wish to marry."

"She may not need to. She wishes to: that is enough for me. She knows my mind. I am not going to change it."

"I suppose not. I know of old your obstinacy when you are bent on ruining yourself. I have no doubt that you will marry her, particularly as she is not exactly the sort of person I should choose for a daughter=in-law. Will you expect me to receive her?"

"I shall trouble your house no more when I am married than I have done as a bachelor."

She shrank for a moment, taken by surprise by this blow; but she did not retort. They presently stopped before the shop she wished to visit and as they stood together near the entry, she made an effort to speak kindly, and even put her hand caressingly on his arm. "Adrian: do not be so headstrong. Wait a little, I do not say 'give her up.' But wait a little longer. For my sake."

Adrian bent his brows and collected all his hardness to resist this appeal. "Mother," he said: "I never had a cherished project yet that you did not seek to defeat by sarcasms, by threats, and failing those, by cajolery." Mrs. Herbert quickly took her hand away, and drew back. "And it has always turned out that I was right and that you were wrong. You would not allow that I could ever be a painter; and yet I am now able to marry without your assistance, by my success as a painter. I took one step which gained your approval — my engagement to Mary. Had I married her, I should be this day a wretched man. Now that I have the happiness to be loved by a lady whom all Europe admires, you would have me repudiate her, for no other reason that I can see under Heaven than that you make it your fixed principle to thwart me in everything. I am sorry to have to tell you plainly that I have come to look upon your influence as opposed to my happiness. It has been at the end of my tongue often; and you have forced me to let it slip at last."

Mrs. Herbert listened attentively during this speech and for some seconds afterwards. Then she roused herself; made a gesture of acquiescence without opening her lips; and went into the shop, leaving him still angry, yet in doubt as to whether he had spoken wisely. But the interview had excited him; and from it and all other goading thoughts he turned to anticipations of his reception by Aurélie. Short though the distance was he drove to her in a hansom.

"Can I see Miss Szczympliça again?" he said to the servant, who now received him with interest, guessing that he came courting.

"She's in the drawingroom, sir. You may go in."

He went in and found Aurélie standing near the window in a black silk dress. which she had put on since his visit in the morning.

"Mr Erberts, mum;" said the servant. Lingering at the door to witness their meeting. Aurélie turned; made him a stately bow, and by a gesture, invited him to sit also. He obeyed; but when the door was shut, he got up and approached her.

"Aurélie, she begged me to break off the engagement, although, as you bade me, I offered to fulfill it. I am perfectly free — only for the instant, I hope." She rose gravely. "Mademoiselle Szczymplic" he added, changing his familiarly eager manner to one of earnest politeness,"will you do me the honor to become my wife?"

"With pleasure, Monsieur Herbert, if my mother approves."

He was not sure what he ought to do next. After a moment, he stooped and kissed her hand. Catching a roguish look in her face as he looked up, he clasped her in his arms and kissed her repeatedly.

"Enough Monsieur," she said, laughing and disengaging herself. He then sat down, thinking that she had behaved with admirable grace, and he himself If with becoming audacity. "I thought you would expect me to be very cold and ceremonious," she said, resuming her seat composedly. "In England one must always be solemn, I said to myself. But indeed you have as little self-command as anyone. Besides, you have not yet spoken to my mother."

"You do not anticipate any objection from her, I hope."

"How do I know? And your parents, what of them? I have seen your mother: she is like a great lady. It is only in England that such handsome mothers are to be seen. She is widowed, is she not?"

"Yes. I have no father. I wish to Heaven I had no mother either."

"Oh, Monsieur Herbert! You are very wrong to say so. And such a gracious lady, too! Fie!"

"Aurélie: I am not jesting. Can you not understand that a mother and son may be so different in their dispositions that neither can sympathize with the other? It is my great misfortune to be such a son. I have found sympathetic friendship, encouragement, respect, faith in my abilities and love —" here he slipped his arm about her waist; and she murmured a remonstrance — "from strangers upon whom I had no claim. In my mother I found none of them: she felt nothing for me but a contemptuous fondness which I did not care to accept. She is a clever woman, impatient of sentiment, and fond of her own way. My father, like myself, was too diffident to push himself arrogantly through the world; and she despised him for it, thinking him a fool. When she saw that I was like him, she concluded that I, too, was a fool, and that she must arrange my life for me in some easy, lucrative, genteel, brainless, conventional way. I hardly ever dared to express the most modest aspiration, or assert the most ordinary claims to respect, for fear of exciting her quiet ridicule. She did not know how much her indifference tortured me, because she had no idea of any keener sensitiveness than her own. Everybody commits follies from youth and want of experience; and I hope most people humor and spare such follies as tenderly as they can. My mother did not even laugh at them. She saw through them and stamped them out with open contempt. She taught me to do without her consideration; and I learned the lesson. My friends will tell you that I am a bad son — never that she is a bad mother, or rather no mother. She has the power of bringing out everything that is hasty and disagreeable in my nature by her presence alone. This is why I wish I were wholly an orphan, and why I ask you, who are more to me than all the world besides, to judge me by what you see of me, and not by the reports you may hear of my behavior towards my own people."

"Oh, it is frightful. My God! To hate your mother! If you do not love her, how will you love your wife?"

"With all the love my mother rejected, added to what you have yourself inspired. But I am glad you are surprised. You must be very fond of your own mother."

"That is so different," said Aurélie with a shrug, "Mother and son is a sacred relation. Mothers and daughters are fond of each other in an ordinary way as a matter of course. You must ask her pardon. Suppose she should curse you."

"Parental curses are out of fashion in England," said Adrian, amused, and yet a little vexed. "You will understand us better after a little while. Let us drop the subject of my old grievances. Are you fond of pictures, Aurélie?"

"You are for ever asking me that. Yes, I am very fond of some pictures. I have seen very few."

But you have been in Dresden, in Munich, in Paris?"

"Yes. But I was playing everywhere — I had not a moment to myself. I intended to go to the gallery in Dresden; but I had to put it off. Are there any good pictures at Munich?"

"Have you not seen them?"

"No. I did not know of them. When I was in Paris, I went one day to the Louvre; but I could only stay half an hour; and I did not see much. I used to be able to draw very well. Is it hard to paint?"

"It is the most difficult art in the world, Aurélie."

"You are laughing at me. Why, there are not a dozen players — real players — in Europe; and every city is full of painters."

"*Real* painters, Aurélie?"

"Ah! perhaps not. I suppose there are secondrate painters, just like secondrate players. Is it not so, Me — Meestare Adrian?"

"You must not call me that, Aurélie. People who like each other never say 'Mister.' You say you used to draw?"

"Yes. Soldiers, and horses, and people whom we knew. Shall I draw you?"

By all means. How shall I sit? Profile?"

"You need not sit for me. I am not going to copy you: I am only going to make a little likeness. I can draw dark men as well as fair. You shall see."

She took a piece of music, and set to work with a pencil on the margin. In a minute she shewed him two scratchy sketches, vilely drawn, but amusingly like Herbert and Jack.

"I can just recognize myself, " he said, examining them them; "but that one of Jack is capital. Ha! ha!" Then he added sadly, "Professed painter as I am, I could not do that. Portraiture is my weak point. But I would not have left Dresden without seeing the Madonna di San Sisto."

"Bah! Looking at pictures cannot make me draw well, no more than listening to others could make me play. But indeed I would have gone to the gallery had I foreseen that I should meet you. My God! Do not kiss me so suddenly. It is droll to think how punctilious and funereal you were the other day; and now you have less manners than a Cossack. Are you easily offended, Monsieur Adrian?"

"I hope not," he replied. taken aback by a change in manner as she asked the question."If you mean easily offended by you, certainly not. Easily hurt or easily pleased, yes. but not offended, my darling."

"Mäi — mä —" what is that you said in English?

"Nothing. You can look it up in the dictionary when I am gone. But what am I to be offended at?"

"Only this. I want you to go away."

"So soon!"

"Yes. I have not said anything to my mother yet. She will question me the moment she sees me in this dress. You must not be here then. Tomorrow you will call on her at four o'clock; and all will be well. Now go. I expect her every moment."

"May I see you before tomorrow afternoon?"

"Why should you? I go tonight to play at the house of a great dame, Lady Gerald line Porter, who is the daughter of a nobleman and the wife of a baronet. My mother loves to be among such people. She will tell you all about our ancestry tomorrow."

"Aurélie: I shall meet you there. Lady Geraldine is mother's cousin and close friend, on which account I have not sought much after her. But she told me once that she would waste no more invitations on me — I never accepted them — but that I was welcome to come when I pleased. I shall please tonight, Aurélie. Hurrah!"

Heaven! you are all fire and flame in a moment. You will remember that at Lady Geraldine's we are to be as we were before today. You will behave yourself?"

"Of course."

"Now go, I beg of you. If you delay, you will — what is the matter now?"

"It has just come into my mind that my mother may be at Lady Geraldine's. If so, would you mind — In short, do not let Madame Szczympliça speak to her of our engagement. Of course you will say nothing yourself."

"Not if you do not wish me to," said Aurélie, drawing back a step.

"You see, my darling, as I have not yet spoken to your mother, it would be a great breach of etiquette for you or Madame to pretend to know my intentions. That is nonsense, of course; but you know how formal we are in this country."

"Oh, is that the reason? I am glad you told me; and I shall be very careful. So will my mother. Now go quickly. *Au revoir* "

CHAPTER XII

At that time, Jack was richer than he had ever been before. His works were performed at the principal concerts: He also gave lessons at the moderate rate of fifteen guineas a dozen, and had more applications for lessons at that rate than he had time to accept: publishers tempted him with offers of blank cheques for inane drawing room ballads with easy accompaniments. Every evening he went from his lodging in Church Street to some public entertainment at which he had to play or conduct, or to the house of some lady of fashion who considered her reception incomplete without him; for "society" found relief and excitement in the eccentric and often rude manner of the Welsh musician, and recognized his authority to behave as he pleased. At such receptions he received fresh invitations, some of which he flatly declined. Others he accepted, presenting himself duly, except when he forgot the invitation. When he did forget, and was reproached by the disappointed hostess, he denied all knowledge of her entertainment, and said that had he been asked he should have come as he never forgot anything. He made no calls, left no cards, and paid little attention to his dress.

One afternoon he went to the house of Mr Phipson, who had been of service to him at the Antient Orpheus. Among the guests there was Lady Geraldine Porter, Mrs Herbert's friend, whom Jack did not know. She was a lady of strong common sense, resolutely intolerant of the eccentricities and affectations of artists. No man who wore a velveteen jacket and long hair had a chance of an introduction to or an invitation from Lady Geraldine. These people, she said, can behave themselves properly if they like. We have to learn manners before we go into society: let them do the same, since they are so clever. As to Jack, he was her pet aversion. Society, in her opinion, had one clear duty to Jack — to boycott him until he conformed to its reasonable usages. And she set an unavailing example, by refusing all intercourse with him in the drawing rooms where they frequently found themselves together.

When the inevitable entreaty from Mrs Phipson brought Jack to the piano, Lady Geraldine was sitting close behind him and next to Mrs Herbert. There was a buzz of conversation going on; and he struck a few chords to stop it. Those who affected Jack-worship h'shed at the talkers, and assumed an expression of enthusiastic expectation. The buzz subsided, but did not quite cease. Jack waited patiently, thrumming the keyboard. Still there was not silence. He turned round, and saw Lady Geraldine speaking earnestly to Mrs Herbert, heedless of what was passing in the room. He waited still, with his body twisted towards her and his right hand behind him on the keys, until her unconscious breach of good manners, becoming generally observed, brought about an awful pause. Mrs Herbert hastily warned her by a stealthy twitch. She stopped; looked up; took in the situation; and regarded Jack's attitude with marked displeasure.

"You mustn't talk," he said, corrugating his nose. "You must listen to me."

Lady Geraldine's color rose slightly, a phenomenon which no one present had ever witnessed before. "I beg your pardon," she said, bowing. Jack appreciated the dignity of her tone and gesture. He nodded approvingly — to her disappointment, for she had intended to abash him$mdash;and, turning to the piano, gave out his theme in the form of a stately minuet. Upon this he improvised for twenty-five minutes, to the delight of a few genuine amateurs present. The rest, though much fatigued, were loud in admiration of Jack's genius; and many of them crowded about him in the hope of inducing him to give a similar performance at their own houses.

"Oh, how I adore music!"said one of them to him later on, when he came and sat by her. If I were only a great genius like you!" Instead of replying he looked indignantly at her. "I really don't see why I am not supposed capable of appreciating anything," she continued, "I am very fond of music."

"Nobody says you're not," said Jack. "You are fond enough of music when it walks in its silver slippers — as Mr By-ends was fond of religion."

The lady, who was a born Irish Protestant, a Roman Catholic by conversion, a sort of freethinker, after the fashionable broad-church manner, by habit, by conviction nothing at all, and very superstitious by nature, always suspected some personal application in allusions to religion. She looked askance at him, and said pettishly, "I wonder you condescend to converse with me at all, since you have such a low opinion of me."

"I like talking to you — except when you go into rhapsodies over music. Do you know why?"

"I am sure I don't," she said, with a little laugh and a glance at him. "Why?"

"Because you are a chatterbox," said Jack, relishing the glance. "Don't think, madame, that it is because you are a kindred spirit and musical. I hate musical people. Who is that lady sitting next Mrs Herbert?"

"What! You don't know! That explains your temerity. She is Lady Geraldine Porter; and you are the first mortal that ever ventured to rebuke her. It was delicious."

"Is that the lady who would not have me at her house?"

Yes. You have revenged yourself, though."

Plenty of fools will say so; and therefore I am sorry I spoke to her. However. I cannot be expected to know trifles of this kind, though I am in the confidence of pretty Mrs Saunders. Have you any wicked stories to tell me to-day?"

"No. Except what everybody knows, and what I suppose you knew before anybody — about your friend Miss Sutherland and Adrian Herbert."

"What about them? Tell me nothing about Miss Sutherland unless you are sure it is true. I do not want to hear anything unpleasant of her."

"You need not be so cross," said Mrs. Saunders coolly. "You can ask her for the particulars. The main fact is that Mr Herbert, who was engaged to her, is going to marry Szczympliça, the pianist."

"Pshaw! That is an old story. He has been seen speaking to her once or twice; and of course —"

"Now, Mr Jack, let me tell you that it is not the old story, which was mere gossip. I never repeat gossip. It is a new story, and a true one. Old Madame Szczympliça told me all about it. Her daughter actually refused Mr Herbert because of his former engagement; and then he went straight to Mary Sutherland, and asked her to give up her claim — which of course she had to do, poor girl. Then he went back to the Sczympliça, and prevailed with her. Miss Sutherland, with all her seriousness shewed that she knows her *métier* as well as the most frivolous of her sex — as myself, if you like; for she set to work at once to express her remorse at having jilted *him*. How transparent all our little artifices are after all Mr Jack."

"I don't believe a word of it."

"You shall see. I did not believe it myself at first. But Miss Sutherlan told me in this very room the day before yesterday that Mr Herbert was no longer engaged to her, and that she particularly wished it to be understood that if there was any blame in the matter, it was due to her and not to him. Of course I took in the situation at once. She said it admirably, almost implying that she was magnanimously eager to shield poor Adrian Herbert from my busy tongue. Poor Mary! she is well rid of him if she only knew it. I wonder who will be the next candidate for the post he has deserted *Mrs. Saunders, as she wondered, glanced at Jack's eyes.*

"Why need she fill it at all? Every woman's head is not occupied with stuff of that sort." Jack spoke gruffly, and seemed troubled, After a few moments, during which she leaned back lazily, and smiled at him, he rose. "Goodbye," he said. "You are not very amusing to-day. I suppose you are telling this fine story of yours to whoever has time to listen to it."

"Not at all, Mr Jack. Everybody is telling it to me. I am quite tired of it."

Jack uttered a grunt, and left her. Meeting Mrs Herbert, he made his bow, and asked where Miss Sutherland was.

"She is in the conservatory," said Mrs Herbert, hesitating. "But I think she will be engaged there for some time." He thanked her, and wandered through the rooms for five minutes. Then, his patience being exhausted, he went into the conservatory, where he saw Lady Geraldine apparently arguing some point with Mary, who stood before her looking obstinately downward.

"It is quixotic nonsense," Lady Geraldine was saying as Jack entered. "He has behaved very badly; and you know it as well as I do, only you feel bound to put yourself in a false position to screen him."

"That is where I disagree with you, Lady Geraldine. I think my position the true one; and the one you would have me take, the false one."

"My dear, listen to me. Do you not see that your efforts to exculpate Adrian only convince people of his meanness? The more you declare you deserted him, the more they are certain that it is a case of sour grapes, and that you are making the common excuse of girls who are jilted. Don't be angry with me — nothing but brutal plain speaking will move you. You told Belle Woodward — Belle Saunders, I mean — that the fault was yours. Do you suppose she believed you?"

"Of course," said Mary, vehemently, but evidently shocked by this view of the case.

"Then you are mistaken," said Jack, advancing. "She has just given me the very version that this lady has so sensibly put to you."

Lady Geraldine turned and looked at him in a way that would have swept an ordinary man speechless from the room.

Mary, accustomed to him, did not think of resenting his interference, and said, after considering distressedly for a moment, "But it is not my fault if Mrs Saunders chooses to say what is not true. I cannot adapt what has really happened to what she or anybody else may think."

"I don't know what has really happened," said Jack. "But you can hold your tongue; and that is the proper thing for you to do. It is none of their business. It is none of yours, either, to whitewash Herbert, whether he needs it or not. I beg your pardon, ma'am," he added, turning ceremoniously to Lady Geraldine. "I should have retired on seeing Miss Sutherland engaged, had I not accidentally overheard the excellent advice you were giving her." With that he made his best oldfashioned bow, and went away.

"Well, really!' said Lady Geraldine, staring after him, "Is this the newest species of artistic affectation, pray? It used to be priggishness, or loutishness, or exquisite sensibility. But now it seems to be outspoken common sense; and instead of being a relief, it is the most insufferable affectation of all. My dear: I hope I have not distressed you."

"Oh, this world is not fit for any honest woman to live in," cried Mary, indignantly. "It has some base construction to put on every effort to be just and tell the truth. If I had done my best to blacken Adrian after deserting him, I should be at no loss now for approval and sympathy. As it is, I am striving to do what is right; and I am made to appear contemptible for my pains."

"It is not a very honest world, I grant you," said Lady Geraldine quietly, "but it is not so bad as you think. Young people quarrel with it because it will not permit them to be heroic in season and out of season. You have made a mistake; and you want to be heroic out of season on the strength, or rather the weakness of that mistake. I, who know you well, do not suppose, as Belle Saunders does, that you are consciously making a virtue of a necessity; but I think there is a little spiritual pride in your resolution not to be betrayed into reproaching Adrian. In fact, all Quixotism is tainted with spiritual vainglory; and that is the reason that no one likes it, or even admires it heartily, in real life. Besides, my dear, nobody really cares a bit how Adrian behaved or how you behaved: they only care about the facts; and the facts, I must say, are plain enough. You and Adrian were unwise enough to enter into a long engagement. You got tired of one another — wait till I have finished; and then protest your fill. Adrian went behind your back and proposed to another woman, who was more honorable than he, and refused to let him smuggle her into your place. Then, instead of coming to demand his freedom straightforwardly, he came to fish for it — to entrap you into offering it to him; and he succeeded. The honest demand came from you instead of from him."

"But I fished, too," said Mary, piteously. "I was only honest when he drove me to it."

"Of course," said Lady Geraldine, impatiently. "You are not an angel; and the sooner you reconcile yourself to the few failings which you share with the rest of us, the happier you will be. None of us are honest in such matters except when our conscience drives us to it. The honestest people are only those who feel the constraint soonest and strongest. If you had held out a little longer, Adrian might have forestalled you. I say he *might*; but, in my opinion, he would most probably fastened a quarrel on you — about Jack or somebody else — and got out of his engagement that way."

"Oh, no; for he spoke about Mr Jack, and said expressly that he did not mind him at all; but that if he had brought about any change in my feelings, I need not feel bound by the eng — There: I know that is additional proof of his faithlessness in your eyes."

"It is a proof of what a thorough fool a man must be, to expect you to take such a bait. Please release me, Mr Herbert, that I may gratify my fancy for Mr Jack.' That is such a likely thing for a woman to say!"

"I hope you are not in earnest about Mr Jack, Lady Geraldine."

"I am not pleased about him, Mary. These friendships stand in a girl's way. Of course I know you are not in love with him — at least, accustomed as I am to the folly of men and women about one another, even I cannot conceive such infatuation; but, Mary, do not flourish your admiration for his genius (I suppose he has genius) in the faces of other men."

"I will go back to Windsor, and get clear of Mr Jack and Mr Herbert both. I wish people would mind their own business."

"They never do, dear. But it is time for us to go. Have I dashed your spirits very much?"

"Not at all," replied Mary absently.

"Then, if you are quite gay, you need not object to come somewhere with me this evening."

"You mean to go out somewhere? I cannot, Lady Geraldine. I should only be a wet blanket. I am not in the vein for society to-day. Thank you, all the same, for trying to rescue me from my own thoughts."

"Nonsense, Mary. You must come. It is only to the theatre. Mrs Herbert and we two will make a quiet party. After what has passed you cannot meet her too soon; and I know she is anxious to shew that she does not mean to take Adrian's part against you."

"Oh, I have no doubt of that. So far from it, that I am afraid Adrian will think I am going to her to complain of him. There," she added, seeing that this last doubt was too much for Lady Geraldine's patience; "I will come. I know I am very hard to please; but indeed I did not feel in the humor for theatregoing."

"You will be ready at half-past seven?"

Mary consented; sighed; and left the conservatory dejectedly with Lady Geraldine, who, on returning to the drawingroom had another conference with Mrs Herbert.

Meanwhile Jack, after chatting a while with Mrs Saunders, prepared to depart. He had put off his afternoon's work in order to be at Mr Phipson's disposal; and he felt indolent and morally lax in consequence, stopping as he made his way to the door, to speak to several ladies who seldom received even a nod from him. On the stairs he met the youngest Miss Phipson; and he lingered a while to chat with her. He then went down to the hall, and was about to leave the house when he heard his name pronounced sweetly behind him. He turned and saw Lady Geraldine at whom he gazed in unconcealed surprise.

"I forgot to thank you for your timely aid in the conservatory," she said, in her most gracious manner. "I wonder whether you will allow me to ask for another and greater favor."

"What is it?" said Jack, suspiciously.

"Mrs Herbert," replied Lady Geraldine, with a polite simulation of embarrassment," is going to make use of my box at the theatre this evening; and she and has asked Miss Sutherland there. We are very anxious that you should accompany us, if you have no important engagement. As I am the nominal owner of the box, may I beg you to come with us."

Jack was not satisfied. The invitation was unaccountable to him, as he knew perfectly well what Lady Geraldine thought of him. Instead of answering, he stood looking at her in a perplexity which expressed itself unconsciously in hideous grimaces.

"Will you allow me to send my carriage to your house," she said, when the pause became unbearable.

"Yes. No. I'll join you at the theatre. Will that do?"

Lady Geraldine, resenting his manner, put strong constraint on herself, as, with careful courtesy she told him the name of the theatre and the hour of the performance. He listened to her attentively, but gave no sign of assent. When she had finished speaking, he looked absently up the staircase; shewed his teeth; and hammered a tune on his chin with the edge of his hat. The strain on Lady Geraldine's forbearance became very great indeed.

"May we depend on your coming?" she said at last.

"Why do you want me to come?" he exclaimed suddenly. "You don't like me."

Lady Geraldine drew back a step. Then, losing patience, she said sharply, "What answer do you expect me to make to that, Mr. Jack?"

"None," said he with mock gravity. "It is unanswerable. From Capharsalama on eagle wings I fly." And after making her another bow, he left the house chuckling. As he disappeared, Mrs Herbert came downstairs and joined Lady Geraldine.

"Well," she said. "Is Mary to be made happy at our expense?"

"Yes," said Lady Geraldine. "I bearded the monster here, and got what I deserved for my pains. The man is a savage."

"I told you what to expect."

"That did not make it a bit pleasanter. You had better come and dine with me. Sir John is going to Greenwich; and we may as well enjoy ourselves together up to the last moment."

That evening Mary Sutherland reluctantly accompanied Mrs Herbert and Lady Geraldine to the theatre, to witness the first performance in England of a newly translated French drama. When she had been a few minutes seated in their box, she was surprised by the entry of Jack, whose black silk kerchief, which he persisted in wearing instead of a necktie, was secured with a white pin, shewing that he had dressed himself with unusual care.

"Mr Jack!" exclaimed Mary.

"Just so, Mr Jack," he said, hanging his only hat, which had suffered much from wet weather and bad use on a peg behind the door. "Did you not expect him?"

Mary, about to say no, hesitated, and glanced at Lady Geraldine.

"I see you did not," said Jack, placing his chair behind hers. "A surprise, eh?"

"An agreeable surprise," said Mrs Herbert smoothly, with her fan before her lips.

"An accidental one," said Lady Geraldine. "I forgot to tell Miss Sutherland that you had been good enough to promise to come."

Mrs Herbert is laughing at me," said Jack, goodhumoredly. "So are you. It was you who were good enough to ask me, not I who was good enough to come. Listen to the band. Those eighteen or twenty bad players cost more than six good ones would, and are not half so agreeable to listen to. Do you hear what they are playing? Can you imagine anyone writing such stuff?"

"It certainly sounds exceedingly ugly; but I am notoriously unmusical, so my opinion is not worth anything."

"Still, so far as you can judge, you don't like it?"

"Certainly not."

I am beginning to like it," said Mrs Herbert, coolly. "I am quite aware that it is one of your own compositions — or some arrangement of one."

"Ha! ha! *Souvenirs de Jack* , they call it. This is what a composer has to surfer whenever he goes to a public entertainment, Lady Geraldine."

"In revenge for which, he ungenerously lays traps for others, Mr Jack."

"You are right," said Jack, suddenly becoming moody. "It was ungenerous; but I shared the discomfiture. There they go at my fantasia. Accursed be the man — Hark! The dog has taken it upon himself to correct the harmony." He ceased speaking, and leaned forward on his elbows, grinding his teeth and muttering. Mary, in low spirits herself, made an effort to soothe him.

"Surely you do not care about such a trifle as that," she began. "What harm —"

"You call it a trifle," he said, interrupting her threateningly.

"Certainly," interposed Lady Geraldine, in ironically measured tones. "A composer such as you can afford to overlook an ephemeral travesty to which nobody is listening. Were I in your place, I would not suffer a thought of resentment to ruffle the calm surface of my contempt for it."

"Wouldn't you?" said Jack, sarcastically. "Tell me one thing. You are very rich — as rich in money as I am in music. Would you like to be robbed of a sovereign?"

"I am not fond of being robbed at all, Mr Jack."

"Aha! Neither am I. You wouldn't miss the sovereign — people would think you stingy for thinking about it. Perhaps I can afford to be misrepresented by a rascally fiddler for a few nights here as well as you could afford the pound. But I don't like it."

"You are always unanswerable," said Lady Geraldine, good humoredly.

Jack stood up and looked round the theatre. "All the world and his wife are here tonight," he said. That whitehaired gentleman hiding at the back of the balcony is the father of an old pupil of mine — a man cursed with an ungovernable temper. His name is Brailsford. The youth with the eyeglass in the stalls is a critic: he called me a promising young composer the other day. Who is that coming into the box nearly opposite? The Sczympliça, is it not' I see Madame's top-knot coming in through the inner gloom. She takes the best seat, of course, just as naturally as if she was a child at her first pantomime. There is a handsome gentleman with a fair beard dimly visible behind. It must be Master Adrian. He has a queer notion of life — he added, forgetting that he was in the presence of "that chap's" mother.

Mrs Herbert looked round gravely at him; and Lady Geraldine frowned. He did not notice them: he was watching Mary, who had shrunk for a moment behind the curtain, but was now sitting in full view of Herbert, looking at the stage, from which the curtain had just gone up.

Nothing more was said in the box until, at a few words words pronounced behind the scenes by a strange voice. Jack uttered an inarticulate sound and stood up.

Then there came upon the stage a lady, very pretty, very elegantly dressed, a little bold in her manner, a little over-rouged, fascinating because of these slight excesses, but stamped by them as foreign to the respectable society into which she was supposed to have intruded.

"Absurd!" said Mary suddenly, after gazing incredulously at the actress for a moment. "It cannot be. And yet I verily believe it is. Lady Geraldine: is not that Madge Brailsford?"

"I really think it is," said Lady Geraldine, using her opera glass. "How shockingly she is painted! And yet I don't believe it is, either. That woman is evidently very clever, which Madge never was, so far as I could see. And the voice is quite different."

"Oho!" said Jack. "It was I who found that voice for her."

"Then it is Madge," said Mary.

"Of course it is. Rub your eyes and see for yourself." Mary looked and looked, as if she could hardly believe it yet. At the end of the act, the principal performers, including Magdalen, were called before the curtain and heartily applauded. Jack, though contemptuous of popular demonstrations, joined in this, making as much noise as possible, and impatiently bidding Mary take off her gloves, that she might clap her hands with more effect. A moment afterwards, there was a hasty knocking at the door of the box. Mary looked across the theatre; saw that Adrian's chair was vacant; and turned red. Jack opened the door, and admitted, not Adrian, but Mr Brailsford, who hurried to the front of the box; shook Lady Geraldine's hand nervously; made a hasty bow right and left to Mary and Mrs Herbert; and, after making as though he had something particular to say, sat down in Jack's chair and said nothing. He was greatly agitated.

"Well, Mr Brailsford, said Lady Geraldine, smiling. "Dare I congratulate you?"

"Not a word — not a word," he said, as if he were half-suffocated. "I beg your pardon for coming into your box. I am a broken man — disgraced by my own daughter. My favorite daughter, sir — madame — I beg your pardon again. You can tell this young lady that she was my favorite daughter."

"But you must not take her brilliant success in this way," said Lady Geraldine gently, looking at him with surprise and pity. "And remember that you have other girls."

"Psha! Whish-h-h!" hissed the old gentleman, throwing up his hand and snapping his fingers. "They arc all born fools — like their mother. She is like me, the only one who is like me. Did you ever see such impudence? A girl brought up as she was, walking out of a house in Kensington Palace Gardens onto the stage, and playing a Parisian — a French — God bless me, a drab! to the life. It was perfection. I've seen everybody that ever acted — years before your ladyship was born. I remember Miss O'Neill, aye, and Mrs Jordan; Mars, Rachel, Piccolomini! she's better than any of them, except Miss O'Neill — I was young in her time. She wouldn't be kept from it. I set my face against it. So did her mother — who could no more appreciate her than a turnip could. So did we all. We locked her up; we took her money from her; I threatened to disown her — and so I will too; but she had her way in spite of us all. Just like me: exactly like me. Why, when I was her age, I cared no more for my family than I did for Buonaparte. It's in her blood. I should have been on the stage myself only it's a blackguard profession; and a man who can write tragedy does not need to act it. I will turn over some of my old manuscripts; and she shall show the world what her old father can do. And did you notice how self-possessed she was? I saw the nerves under it. I felt them. Nervousness always played the devil with me. I tell you, madame — and I am qualified to speak on the subject — that she walks the stage and gives out her lines in the true old style. You don't know these things, Miss Mary: you are too young: you never saw great acting. But I know. I had lessons from the great Young: Edmund Kean was a mountebank beside him. I was the best pupil of Charles Mayne Young, and of little Dutch Sam — but that was another matter. No true lady would paint her face and make an exhibition of herself on a public stage for money. Still, it is a most extraordinary thing that a young girl like that, without any teaching or preparation, should walk out of a drawing room onto the stage, and take London by storm."

"But has she not had some little experience in the provinces?" said Mary.

Certainly not," said Mr Brailsford impatiently. Strolling about with a parcel of vagabond pantomimists is not experience — not proper experience for a young lady. She is the first Brailsford that ever played for money in a public theatre. She is not a Brailsford at all. I have forbidden her to use the name she's disgraced."

"Come," said Lady Geraldine. "You are proud of her. You know you are."

"I am not. I have refused to see her. I have disowned her. If I caught one of her sisters coming to witness this indecent French play of which she is the life and soul — what would it be without her, Lady Geraldine? Tell me that."

"It would be the dullest business imaginable."

"Hal ha:" cried Brailsford, with a triumphant gesture: "I should think so. Dull as ditch-water. Her voice alone would draw all London to listen.

Perhaps you think that I taught her to speak. I tell you, Mrs. Herbert, I would have slain her with my own hand as soon as trained her for such a profession. Who taught her then? Why — ?"

"I did," said Jack. Mr Brailsford, who had not noticed his presence before, stared at him, and stiffened as he did so.

"I believe you are already acquainted with Mr Jack." said Lady Geraldine, watching them with some anxiety.

"You see what she has made of herself," said Jack, looking hard at him. "I helped her to do it: you opposed her. Which of us was in the right?"

"I will not go into that question with you, sir," said Mr Brailsfod, raising his voice and waving his glove. I do not approve of my daughter's proceedings." He turned from Jack to Mrs Herbert, and made a brave effort to chat with her with a jaunty air. "A distinguished audience, tonight I think I saw somewhere in the house, your son, not the least distinguished of us. Painting is a noble art. I remember when painters did not stand as well in society as they do now; but never in my life have I failed in respect for them. Never. A man is the better for contemplating a great picture. Your son has an enviable career before him."

"So I am told."

"Not a doubt of it. He is a fine young man — as he indeed could not fail to be with such an inheritance of personal graces and mental endowments."

"He is very like his father."

"Possibly, madame," said Mr. Brailsford, bowing. "But I never saw his father."

"Whatever his career may be, I shall have little part in it. I did not encourage him to become an artist. I opposed his doing so as well as I could. I was mistaken, I suppose: it is easier than I thought to become a popular painter. But children never forgive such mistakes."

"Forgive!" exclaimed Mr. Brailsford, his withered cheek reddening faintly. "If you have forgiven him for disregarding your wishes, you can hardly believe that he will be so unnatural as to cherish any bad feeling towards you. Eh?"

"It is not unnatural to resent an unmerited wound to one's vanity. If I could honestly admire Adrian's work even now, I have no doubt he would consent to be reconciled to me in time. But I cannot. His pictures seem weak and sentimental to me. I can see the deficiencies of his character in every line of them. I always thought that genius was an indispensable condition to success."

"Ha! ha!" said Jack. "What you call success is the compensation of the man who has no genius. If you had believed in his genius, and yet wanted success for him, you might have opposed him with better reason. Some men begin by aiming high, and they have to wait till the world comes up to their level. Others aim low, and have to lift themselves to success. Happy follows like Mr Adrian hit the mark at once, being neither too good for the Academy people nor too bad for the public."

"Probably you are right," said Mrs Herbert. "I should have borne in mind that worse painters than he enjoy a fair share of toleration. However, I must abide by my error now."

"But surely," said Mr Brailsford, harping anxiously on the point, "You do not find that he persists in any little feeling of disappointment that you may have caused him formerly. No, no: he can't do that. He must see that you were actuated by the truest regard for his welfare and — and so forth."

"I find that his obstinacy, or perseverance rather, is as evident in his resentment against me as it was in his determination to make himself an artist in spite of me."

Mr Brailsford, troubled, bit his nail, and glanced at Mrs Herbert twice or thrice, without speaking. Lady Geraldine watched him for a moment, and then said: "There is a difference between your case and Mrs Herbert's."

"Of course," he said, hurriedly. "Oh, of course. Quite different I was not thinking of any such —"

"And yet, continued Lady Geraldine, "there is some likeness too. You both opposed your children's tastes. But Mrs Herbert does not believe in Adrian's talent, although she is glad he has made a position for himself. You, on the contrary, are carried away by Magdalen's talent; but you are indignant at the position it has made for her."

"I am not carried away. You entirely misapprehend my feelings. I deeply deplore her conduct. I have ceased to correspond with her even, since she set my feelings at defiance by accepting a London engagement."

"In short," said Lady Geraldine, with goodhumored raillery, "you would not speak to her if she were to walk into this box."

Mr. Brailsford started and looked round; but there was no one behind him: Jack had disappeared. "No," he said, recovering himself. "Certainly not. I cannot believe that she would venture into my presence."

The curtain went up as he spoke. When Madge again came on the stage, her business was of a more serious character than in the first act, and displayed the heartless determination of the adventuress rather than her amusing impudence. Lady Geraldine, admiring a certain illustration of this, turned with an approving glance to Mr. Brailsford. He was looking fixedly at the stage, no longer triumphant, almost haggard. He seemed relieved when the actress, being supposed to recognize an old lover, relented, and showed some capacity for sentiment. When the act was over, he still sat staring nervously at the curtain. Presently the box door opened; and he again looked round with a start. It was Jack, who, returning his testy regard with a grim smile, came close to him; stretched an arm over his head; and pulled over one of the curtains of the box so as to seclude it from the house. Mr Brailsford rose, trembling.

"I absolutely refuse —" he began.

Jack opened the door; and Madge, with her dress covered by a large domino cloak, hurried in. She threw off the cloak as soon as the door was closed, and then seized her father and kissed him. He said with difficulty, "My dear child," sat down; and bent his head, overpowered by emotion for the moment. She stood with her hand on his shoulder, and bowed over him in a very self-possessed manner to Mary, whom she addressed as "Miss Sutherland," and to the others.

"I have no business to be here," she said, in a penetrating whisper. "It is against the rules. But when Mr Jack came and told me that my father was here, I could not let him go without speaking to him."

Lady Geraldine bowed. She and her companions had been prepared to receive Madge with frank affection, but her appearance and manner quite disconcerted them. They recollected her as a pretty, petulant young lady: they had actually seen her as one only two minutes before on the stage. Yet here she was, apparently grown during those two minutes not only in stature but in frame. The slight and elegant lady of the play was in the box a large, strong woman, with resonant voice and measured speech. Even her hand, as she patted her father's shoulder, moved rhythmically as if the gesture were studied. The kindly patronage with which Lady Geraldine had been willing to receive an impulsive, clever young girl, was forgotten in the midst of respect, disappointment, and even aversion inspired by the self-controlled and accomplished woman. Mary was the first to recover herself.

"Madge," she said, " — that is, if one may venture to call you Madge."

"Indeed you may," said Madge, nodding and smiling gracefully.

"You are a great deal more like yourself on the stage than off it."

"Yes," said Madge. "For the last two and a half years, I have not taken a single holiday."

Mr Brailsford now sat upright; coughed; and looked severely round. His lip relaxed as his gaze fell on Magdalen; and after an apprehensive glance at her, he lost his assurance even more obviously than the others.

"You have grown a good deal, I think, my child," he said nervously.

"Yes. I hardly expected you to know me. You are looking better than ever. How are the girls?"

"Quite well, thank you, my dear. Quite well."

"And mother?"

"Oh, she is well. A little rheumatism, of course; and — a —"

I shall come and see you all tomorrow, at one o'clock. Be sure to stay at home for me, won't you?"

"Certainly. Certainly. We shall be very glad to see you."

"Now I must run away; and I shall not see you again tonight except across the footlights, Mr Jack: my domino." Jack put the cloak upon her shoulders. "Is the corridor empty?" Jack looked out and reported it empty. "I must give you one more kiss, father." She did so; and on this occasion Mr Brailsford did not exhibit emotion, but merely looked dazed. Then she bowed as sweetly as before to Lady Geraldine and Mrs. Herbert.

"Good night, Madge," said Mary, putting up her spectacles, and peering boldly at her.

Good night, dear," said Madge, passing her arm round Mary's neck, and stooping to kiss her. "Come tomorrow; and I will tell you all the news about myself. May I fly now, Mr Jack?"

"Come along," said Jack; and she tripped out, whisking her domino dexterously through the narrow door, and revealing for an instant her small foot.

There was an awkward silence in the box for some moments after she left. It was broken by the chuckling of Jack, who presently said aside to Mary, "When I first saw that young lady, she was a helpless good-for-nothing piece of finery."

"And now," said Mary, she is an independent woman, and an accomplished artist. How I envy her!"

"Why?" said Jack.

"Because she is of some use in the world."

"If you will allow me," said Mr Brailsford, rising suddenly, "I will return to my own place, I am incommoding your friend, doubtless. Good night. "He offered a trembling hand to Lady Geraldine; made a courtly demonstration toward Mary and Mrs Herbert, and turned to go, On his way to the door, he stopped; confronted Jack, and made him a grave bow, which was returned with equal dignity. Then he went out slowly, like an infirm old man, without any sign of his habitual jauntiness.

"Poor devil." said Jack.

"I beg your pardon?"said Lady Geraldine sharply.

"He finds his pet baby changed into a woman; and he doesn't like it," said Jack, not heeding her remonstrance. "Now, if she were still the cream-colored, helpless little beauty she used to be, quite dependent on him, he would be delighted to have such a pretty domestic toy to play with."

"Perhaps so," said Lady Geraldine. "But there is such a thing as parental feeling; and it is possible that Mr Brailsford may not be philosopher enough to rejoice at a change which has widened the distance between her youth and his age."

"He need not be alarmed," said Jack. "If he cannot make a toy of her any longer, she can make a toy of him. She is thinking already of setting up a white haired father as part of her equipment: I saw the idea come into the jade's head whilst she was looking down at him in that chair. He looked effective. This family affection is half sense of property, and half sense of superiority. Miss Sutherland — who is no use in the world, poor young lady — had not such property in Miss Brailsford as her father expected to have, and no such comfortable power of inviting her to parties and getting her married as you look forward to. And consequently, she was the only one who bore the change in her with a good grace, and really welcomed her."

"I am not conscious of having been otherwise than perfectly friendly to her."

"Ain't you?" said Jack, sceptically. Lady Geraldine reddened slightly; then smiled in spite of her vexation, and said, "Really, Mr. Jack, you are a sort of grown up *enfant terrible,* I confess that I was a little overpowered by her staginess. I can understand actors being insufferably stagey on the boards, and quite natural in a room; but I cannot make out how an actress can be perfectly natural on the boards, and stagey in private."

"Acting has become natural to her; and she has lost the habit of your society; that is all. As you say, acting never becomes natural to bad actors. There she comes again."

"The charm is considerably weakened." said Lady Geraldine, turning toward the stage, She does not seem half so real as she did before."

The play ended as successfully as it had begun. The translators responded to calls for the author; and Miss Madge Lancaster took the lion's share of the rest of the applause. Then the pit and galleries emptied themselves into the street with much trampling of stairs. The occupants of the more expensive places made their way slowly through the crush-room, one step at a time: the men sliding their feet forward at every advance: the women holding warm head wrappings with one hand, and hanging awkwardly on to the arms of gentlemen with the other. Lady Geraldine got a glimpse of Mr Brailsford as she descended; but he hurried away, as if desirous to avoid further conversation. Jack who had amused her by showing some emotion at the pathetic passages in the play, and who had since been silent, walked gloomily beside Mary. They were detained for some minutes in the vestibule, Lady Geraldine's footman not being at hand.

"Come,"said Jack sulkily, "Here is somebody happy at last."

Mary looked and saw Herbert coming down the stairs with Aurélie. who was, like Jack, the subject of some whispering and pointing.

"Yes," said Mary. "He is happy. I do not wonder at it: she is very gentle and lovely. She is a greater artist than Madge: yet she has none of Madge's assurance, which would repel Adrian."

"She has plenty of assurance in music, which is her trade. Miss Madge has plenty of assurance in manners, which are her trade."

I am just thinking, Geraldine," said Mrs Herbert, of the difference between Adrian and that girl — Madge Brailsford. She, capable, sensible, able to hold her own against the world. She is everything, in short, that Adrian is not, and that I have often wished him to be. Yet her father seems as far from being united to her as Adrian is from me. Query then: is there any use in caring for one's children? I really don't believe there is."

"Not the least, after they have become independent of you," said Lady Geraldine, looking impatiently towards the door. "Where is Williams? I think he must have gone mad."

At this moment Aurélie, recognizing Mrs Herbert, made as though she would stop, and said something to Adrian which threw him into trouble and indecision at once. Apparently she was urging him, and he making excuses, taking care not to look towards his mother. This dumb show was perfectly intelligible to Mrs Herbert, who directed Lady Geraldine's attention to it.

"It is all Williams's fault," said Lady Geraldine. We should have been out of this five minutes ago. You had better take the bull by the horns at once, Eliza. Go and speak to him — the vacillating idiot!"

"I will not, indeed," said Mrs Herbert. "I hope he will have the firmness to make her go away."

The question was settled by the appearance of Lady Geraldine's servant, who hurried in, and began to explain the delay.

"There. I do not want to hear anything about it," said Lady Geraldine. "Now, where is Mary. Mary was already hastening out with Jack. Herbert saw them go with a sensation of relief. When he reached his lodgings he was disagreeably relieved from some feelings of remorse at having avoided Mary. On the table lay a parcel containing all his letters and presents to her, with a note — beginning "Dear Mr Herbert" — in which she said briefly that on second thoughts she considered it best to follow the usual course, and begged him to believe that she was, sincerely his, Mary Sutherland.

CHAPTER XIII

Next day, in the afternoon, Jack left the room, the establishment of a celebrated firm of pianoforte manufacturers, where he gave his lessons, and walked homeward across Hyde Park. Here he saw approaching him a woman, dressed in light peacock blue, with a pale maize colored scarf on her neck and shoulders, and a large Spanish hat. Jack stood still and looked gloomily at her. She put on a pair of eye glasses; scrutinized him for a moment; and immediately shook them off her nose and stopped.

"You have finished work early to-day," she said, smiling.

"I have not finished it," he replied: "I have put them off. I want to go home and work: I cannot spend my life making money — not that I am likely to have the chance. Four lessons — five guineas — lost."

"You wrote to them, I hope."

"No. They will find out that I am not there when they call; and then they can teach themselves or go to the devil. They would put me off sooner than lose a tennis party. I will put them off sooner than lose a good afternoon's work. I am losing my old independence over this moneymaking and society business — I don't like it. No matter. Are you on your way to Cavendish Square?"

"Yes. But you must not turn back. You did not sacrifice your teaching to gad about the park with me. You want to compose. I know by your face."

"Are you in a hurry"

"*I* am not; but —"

"Then come and gad about, as you call it, for a while. It is too fine a day to go indoors and grind tunes."

She turned; and they strolled across the plain between the Serpentine and the Bayswater Road, crossing a vacant expanse of sward, or picking their way amongst idlers who lay prone on the grass, asleep, or basked supine in the sun. It was a warm afternoon and the sky was cloudless.

"You would not suppose, seeing the world look so pleasant that it is such a rascally place as it is," said Jack, when they had walked some time in silence.

"It is not so very bad, though, after all, If you were a little of a painter, as I am, this sunlit sward and foliage would repay you for all the stupidities of people who have eyes, but cannot use them."

"Äye, And painters suppose that their art is an ennobling one. Suppose I held up a lying, treacherous, cruel woman to the admiration of the painter, and reviled him as unimaginative if he would not accept her blue eyes, and silky hair, and fine figure as a compensation for her corrupt heart: he would call me names — cynical sensualist and so forth. What better is he with his boasted loveliness of Nature? There are moments when I should like to see a good hissing, scorching shower of brimstone sear the beauty out of her false face."

"Oh! What, is the matter to-day?"

"Spleen. I am poor. It is the source of most people's complaints."

"But you are not poor. Recollect that you have just thrown away five guineas, and that you will make ten tomorrow."

"I know."

"Well?"

"Well, are guineas wealth to a man who wants time and freedom from base people and base thoughts? No: I have starved out the first half of my life alone: I will fight through the second half on the same conditions. I get ten guineas a day at present for teaching female apes to scream, that they may be the better qualified for the marriage market. That is because I am the fashion. How long shall I remain the fashion? Until August, when the world — as it calls itself — will emigrate, and return next spring to make the fortune of the next lucky charlatan who makes a bid for my place. I shall be glad to be rid of them, in spite of their guineas: teaching them wastes my time, and does them no good. Then there is the profit on my compositions, of which I get five per cent, perhaps, in money, with all the honor and glory. The rest goes into the pockets of publishers and concert givers, some of whom will go down halfway to posterity on my back because they have given me, for a symphony with the fruits of twenty years' hard work in it, about one-fifth of what is given for a trumpery picture or novel everyday. That fantasia of mine has been pirated and played in every musical capital in Europe; and I could not afford to buy you a sable jacket out of what I have made by it."

"It is very hard, certainly. But do you really care about money?"

"Ha! ha! No, of course not. Music is its own reward. Composers are not human: they can live on diminished sevenths; and be contented with a pianoforte for a wife, and a string quartette for a family. Come," he added boisterously, "enough of grumbling. When I took to composing, I knew I was bringing my pigs to a bad market. But don't pretend to believe that a composer can satisfy either his appetite or his affections with music any more than a butcher or a baker can. I daresay I shall live all the more quietly for being an old bachelor."

"I never dreamt that you would care to marry."

"And who tells you that I would now?"

"I thought you were regretting your enforced celibacy," she replied, laughing. He frowned; and she became serious. "Somehow," she added, "I cannot fancy you as a married man."

"Why?" he said, turning angrily upon her. "Am I a fish, or a musical box? Why have I less right to the common ties of social life than another man?"

"Of course you have as much right." she said, surprised that her remark should have hurt him. "But I have known you so long as you are at present —"

"What am I at present?"

"A sort of inspired hermit," she replied, undaunted. "It seems as if marriage would he an impossible condescension on your part. That is only a fancy, I know. If you could find any woman worthy of you and able to make you happy, I think you ought to marry. I should be delighted to see you surrounded by a pack of naughty children. You would never be an ogre any more then."

"Do you think I am an ogre, then? Eh?"

"Sometimes. To-day, for instance, I think you are decidedly ogreish. I hope I am not annoying you with my frivolity. I am unusually frivolous to-day."

"Hm! You seem to me to be speaking to the point pretty forcibly. So you would like to see me married?"

"Happily married, yes. I should be glad to think that your lonely, gloomy lodging was changed for a cheerful hearth; and that you had some person to take care of your domestic arrangements, which you are quite unfit to manage for yourself. Now that you have suggested the idea, it grows on me rapidly. May I set to work to find a wife for you?"

"Of course it does not occur to you," he said, with unabated ill humor, "that I may have chosen for myself already — that I might actually have some sentimental bias in the business, for instance."

Mary, much puzzled, put on her spectacles, and tried to find from his expression whether he was serious or joking. Failing, she laughed, and said, "I don't believe you ever gave the matter a thought."

"Just so. I am a privileged mortal, without heart or pockets. When you wake up and clap your hands after the coda of Mr Jack's symphony, you have ministered to all his wants, and can keep the rest to yourself, love, money, and all."

She could no longer doubt that he was in earnest: his tone touched her. "I had no idea —" she began. "Will you tell me who it is; or am I not to ask?"

He grinned in spite of himself. "What do you think of Mrs Simpson?" said he.

Mary's mood had taken so grave a turn that she was for a moment unable to follow this relapse into banter.

"But," she said, looking shocked, "Mr Simpson is alive."

"Hence my unhappiness." said Jack, with a snarl, disgusted at her entertaining his suggestion.

"I suppose," she said slowly, after a pause of some moments, "that you mean to make me feel that I have no business with your private affairs. I did not mean —"

"You suppose nothing of the sort," said he, losing his temper. "When have I concealed any of my affairs from you?"

"Then you do not really intend to — I mean, the person you said you were in love with, is a myth."

"Pshaw! I never said I was in love with anyone."

"I might have known as much if I had thought for a moment. I am very dull sometimes."

This speech did not satisfy Jack. "What do you mean by that," he said testily. "Why might you have known? I never said I was in love, certainly. Have I said I was not in love?

"Come," she said gaily. "You shall not play shuttlecock with my brains any longer. Answer me plainly. Are you in love?"

"I tell such things as that to sincere friends only."

Mary suddenly ceased to smile, and made no reply.

"Well, if you are my friend, what the devil do you see in my affairs to laugh at? You can be serious enough with other people."

"I did not mean to laugh at your affairs."

"What are you angry about?"

"I am not angry. moment ago you reproached me because I thought you wished to repel my curiosity. The reproach seemed to me to imply that you considered me a friend worthy of your confidence."

"So I do."

"And now you tell me that I am an insincere friend."

"I never said anything of the kind."

"You implied it. However, there is no reason why you should tell me anything unless you wish to. I do not complain, of course; your affairs are your affairs and not mine. But I do not like to be accused of insincerity. I have always been as sincere with you as I know how to be."

For the next minute Jack walked on in silence, with his hands clasped behind him, and his head bent towards the ground. They were crossing a treeless part of the park, unoccupied save by a few sooty sheep. The afternoon sun had driven the loiterers into the shade; and there was no sound except a distant rattle of traffic from the north, and an occasional oar-splash from the south. Jack stopped, and said without looking up: "Tell me this. Is all that business between you and Herbert broken off and done with?"

"Completely."

"Then listen to me," he said, taking an attitude in which she had seen him once or twice before, when he had been illustrating his method of teaching elocution. "I am not a man to play the part of a lover with grace. Nature gave me a rough frame that I might contend the better with a rough fortune. Nevertheless I have a heart and affections like other men; and those affections have centred themselves on you." Mary blanched, and looked at him in terror. "You are accustomed to my ardent temper; but I do not intend that you shall suffer from bad habits of mine, engendered by a life of solitude and the long deferring of my access, through my music, to my fellow creatures. No: I am aware of my failings, and shall correct them. You know my position; and so I shall make no boast of it. You may think me incapable of tenderness, but I am not: you will never have to complain that your husband does not love you." He paused and looked at Mary's face.

She had never had a thought of marrying Jack. Now that he had asked her to do so she felt that refusal would cause a wound she dared not inflict: she must must sacrifice herself to his demand. To fill the empty place in Jack's heart seemed to her a duty laid on her. She summoned all her courage and endurance to say yes with the thought that she would not live long. Meanwhile, Jack was reading her face.

"I have committed my last folly," he said, in a stirring voice, but with. his habitual abruptness. "Henceforth I shall devote myself to the only mistress I am fitted for, Music. She has not many such masters."

Mary, yielding to an extraordinary emotion, burst into tears.

"Come," he said: "it is all over. I did not mean to to frighten you. I have broken with the world now; and my mind is the clearer and the easier for it. Why need you cry?"

She recovered herself, trying to find something to say to him. In her disquietude she began to speak before her agitation had subsided. "It is not," she said with difficulty, "that I am ungrateful or insensible. But you do not know how far you stand beyond other —"

"Yes, yes," he said soothingly. "I understand. You are right: I have no business in the domestic world, and must stick to music and Mrs Simpson to the end of the chapter. Come along; and think no more of it. I will put you into a cab and send you home."

She turned with him; and they went together towards the Marble Arch: he no longer moody, but placid and benevolent: she disturbed, silent, and afraid to meet his gaze. It was growing late. One of the religious congregations which hold their summer meetings in the park had assembled; and their hymn could be heard, softened by distance. Jack hummed a bass to the tune, and looked along the line of trees that shut out the windows of Park Lane, and led away to the singular equestrian statue which then stood at Hyde Park Corner.

"This is a pretty place, after all," he said. "There is enough blue sky and green sward here to compensate for a good deal of brick and mortar. Down there in the hollow there is silver water with white swans on it. I wonder how the swans keep themselves white. The sheep can't."

"Yes, it is an exquisite day," said Mary, trying hard to interest herself in the scene, and to speak steadily, "There will be a fine sunset."

"There is a good view of the Duke of Wellington here."

"Happily, I cannot see so far. But I can imagine the monster swimming sooty in the ether."

"Leave him in peace," said Jack. "He is the only good statue in London: that is why no one has the courage to say a word in his defence. His horse is like a real horse with real harness. He is not exposed bareheaded in the weather, but wears a hat as any other man in the street does. He is not a stupid imitation of an antique bas-relef. He is characteristic of the century that made him; and he is unique, as a work of art should be. He is picturesque too, The — Come, come, Miss Mary, You have no more cause to to be unhappy than those children swinging on the rail there. What are those tears for?"

"Not because I am unhappy," she replied in a broken voice. "Perhaps because I have such a reason to be proud. Pray, do not mind me. I cannot help it."

They were now close to the Marble Arch; and Jack hurried on that she might the sooner escape the staring of the loungers there. Outside he called a cab and assisted her to enter.

"You will never be afraid of me any more, I hope." He said, pressing her hand. She attempted to speak; gulped down a sob; and nodded and smiled as gaily as she could, her tears falling meanwhile. He watched the cab until it was no longer distinguishable among the crowd of vehicles on Oxford Street, and then reentered the Park and turned to the West, which was now beginning to glow with the fire of evening. When he reached the bridge at which the Serpentine of Hyde Park is supposed to turn into the Long Water of Kensington Gardens, he stopped to see the sun set behind the steeple of Bayswater Church, and to admire the clear depths of hazel green in the pools underneath the foliage on the left bank. "*I hanker for a wife*" he said, as he stood bolt upright, with his knuckles resting lightly on the parapet. *I grovel after money*! What dogs appetites have this worldly crew infected me with! No matter, I am free: I am myself again. Back to the holy garret, oh my soul." And having stared the sunset out of countenance, which is soon done by a man old enough to have hackneyed the sentimentality it inspires, he walked steadfastly away, his mood becoming still more tranquil as the evening fell darker.

On reaching Church Street, he called for Mrs Simpson; gave her a number of postage stamps which he had just purchased; and ordered her to write in his name to all his pupils postponing their lessons until he should write to them again. Being an indifferent speller and a slovenly writer, she grumbled that he was risking his income by treating his pupils so cavalierly. It was his custom to meet her remonstrances, even when he acted on them, with oaths and abuse. This evening he let her say what she wished, meanwhile arranging his table to write at. His patience was so far from appeasing her that she at last ventured to say that she would not write his letters and turn good money away.

"You will do as you are told," he said; "for the devils also believe and tremble." And with that explanation, he bade her make him some coffee, and put her out of the room.

Whilst Mary was being driven home from the park, she was for some time afraid that she must succumb publicly to a fit of hysterics. But after a few painful minutes, her throat relaxed; a feeling of oppression at her chest ceased; and when the cab stopped at Mr Phipson's house she was able to offer the fare composedly to the driver, who refused it, saying that the gentleman had paid it in advance. She then went upstairs to her own room to weep. When she arrived there, however, she found that she had no more tears to shed. She went to the mirror, and stood motionless before it. It shewed her a face expressing deep grief. She looked pityingly at it; and it looked back at her with intensified dolor. This lasted for more than a minute, during which she conveyed such a profundity of sadness into her face that she had no attention to spare for the lightening of her heart which was proceeding rapidly meanwhile. Then her nostrils gave a sudden twitch; she burst out laughing, and the self-reproach which followed this outrage on sentiment did not prevent her from immediately laughing all the more.

"After all," she said, seizing a jug of cold water and emptying it with a splash into a basin, "it is not more ridiculous to laugh at nothing than to look miserable about it." So she washed away the traces of her tears and went down to dinner as gaily as usual.

A fortnight elapsed, during which she heard nothing of Jack, and sometimes thought that she had done better when she had cried at his declaration, than when she had laughed at her own emotion. Then, one evening, Mr Phipson announced that the Antient Orpheus Society were about to make an important acquisition — "one, said he, looking at Mary, "that will specially interest you."

"Something by old Jack?" said Charlie, who was dining there that day.

"A masterpiece by him, I hope," said Mr. Phipson. "He has written to say that he has composed music to the *Prometheus Unbound* of Shelley: four scenes with chorus, a dialogue of Prometheus with the earth, an antiphony of the earth and moon, an overture, and a race of the hours."

"Shelley!" exclaimed Mary incredulously.

"I should have thought that Dr. Johnson was the proper poet for Jack," said Charlie.

"It is a magnificent subject," continued Mr Phipson; "and if he has done justice to it, the work will be the crowning musical achievement of this century. I have no doubt whatever that he has succeeded; for he says himself that his music is the complement of the poetry, and fully worthy of it. He would never venture so say so if he were not conscious of having done something almost stupendous."

"Modesty never was one of his failings," remarked Charlie.

"I feel convinced that the music will be — will be —" said Mr. Phipson, waving his hand, and seeking an expressive word, "will be something apocalyptic, if I may use the term. We have agreed to offer him five hundred pounds for the copyright, with the exclusive privilege of performance in the British Isles; and we have reason to believe that he will accept this offer. Considering that the music will doubtless be very difficult, and will involve the expense of a chorus and an enlarged band, with several rehearsals, it is a fairly liberal offer. Maclagan objected, of course; and some of the others suggested three hundred and fifty; but I insisted on five hundred. We could not decently offer less. Besides, the Modern Orpheus will try to snatch the work from us. The overture is actually in the hand the copyist, and the rest will be complete in a month at latest."

"Certainly you must have more money than you know what to do with, if you to pay five hundred pounds for a thing you have never seen," said Mrs Phipson.

"We shall pay it without the least mistrust," said Mr Phipson, pompously "Jack is a great composer; one whose rugged exterior conceals a wonderful gift, as pearl is protected by an oyster shell."

"But he cannot possibly have composed the whole work in a fortnight." said Mary.

"Of course not. What makes you suggest a fortnight?"

"Nothing," said Mary. "At least I heard that he had given no lessons during the past fortnight."

"He has been planning it for a long time, you may depend upon it. Still, there are instances of extraordinary expedition in musical composition. The Messiah was completed by Handel in twenty-one days; and Mozart —"

Mr Phipson went on to relate anecdotes of overtures and and whole acts added to operas in a single night. He was a diligent concert-goer and always read the analytical programs carefully, so he had a fund of such tales, more or less authentic, to relate. Mary, who had heard most of them before, looked attentive and let her thoughts wander.

Some days later, however, when Mary asked for further news of *Prometheus Unbound,* she found his tone changed. On being pressed he admitted that he had induced the Antient Orpheus Society to make a doubtful bargain. The overture and two of the scenes had been completed and delivered to the society by Jack; and no one, said Mr Phipson, had been able to contradict Maclagan's verdict that "the music, most fortunately, was inexecutable." A letter had been carefully drawn up to inform Jack as gently as possible of the fate of his work. "So prodigious," it said, "were the technical difficulties of the work; so large and expensive the forces required to present it adequately; and so doubtful the prospect of its acceptance by a miscellaneous audience in the existing condition of public taste, that the Committee were obliged to confess, with deep regret, that they dared not make arrangements for its early production. If Mr. Jack had by him any more practicable composition, however short it might fall of the *Prometheus* in point of vastness of design, they would be willing to permit of its being substituted without prejudice to those conditions in their agreement which had been inserted in the interest of the composer."

To this Jack had replied that they should have *Prometheus* or nothing; that there was not a note in the score which was not practicable with a reasonable degree of trouble; that he could find no precedents on which to base the slightest regard for the sagacity of the Society; that he cared not one demi-semi-quaver whether they held to their bargain or not, as he would find no difficulty in disposing of his work; and that he insisted on their either returning the score at once, or paying the first installment of five hundred pounds for it, as agreed upon. He added in a postscript that if they accepted the work, he should require strict fulfillment of the clause binding the Society to one public performance of it in London. The Society, which was old enough to have shelved certain works purchased from Beethoven for similar reasons those given to Jack, hesitated, quarreled internally, and at last resolved to hold a private rehearsal of the overture before deciding. Manlius made earnest efforts to comprehend and like this section of the work, which was to occupy half an hour in performance, and was, in fact, a symphony. He only partially succeeded, and he found the task of conducting the rehearsal unusually disagreeable. The players, confident and willing, did wonders in the estimation of Maclagan, but the first repetition broke down twice, and those who who were at fault lost temper and cursed mutinously within hearing of Manlius, who was himself confused and angry. When it was over at last, a dubious murmur rose from the stalls Where the Committee sat in judgment, and a few of the older members protested against a second trial. They were overruled, and the overture was repeated, this time without any stoppage.

"Certainly," said Mr Phipson, describing his sensations to Mary, "It contained grand traits. But these were only glimpses in the midst of chaos, I had to give in to Maclagan, acknowledging that the most favorable account I could give of it was that it impressed me as might the aberrations of a demented giant. He was quite frantic about it, and fairly talked us down with examples of false relations and incorrect progressions from every bar of the score. Old Brailsford, who is one of the old committee, turned up for the first time in years expressly to support Jack's interests. He said it was the most infernal conglomeration of sounds he had ever listened to, and I must say many of us privately agreed with him.

This conversation took place at the dinner table, and was prolonged by Mrs Phipson, who taunted her husband with his disregard of her warning not to pay five hundred pounds for what she termed a pig in a poke. She was a talkative woman, shallow, jolly, and unscrupulous, with a shrewd and selfish side to her character which indulgent people never saw. Mary saw it clearly; and as, to her taste, Mrs Phipson was vulgar, she was not very fond of her, and often felt indignant at her ridicule of her husband's boastful but sincere love of music. On this occasion, seeing that Mr Phipson was getting sulky, and that his wife was perversely minded to make him worse, she left the table quietly without waiting for her hostess, and went upstairs alone to the drawingroom. There, to her surprise, she found a strange man, lounging on a sofa with an album in his hands.

"I beg your pardon," said Mary, retreating.

"Not at all," said the man, rising in disorder. "I hope I'm not in the way. Miss Sutherland, perhaps."

"Yes," said Mary coldly; for she could not see him distinctly, and his manner of addressing her, though a little confused, struck her as being too familiar.

"Very happy to make your acquaintance, Miss Sutherland. Nanny wrote me word that you were staying here. I recognize you by your photograph too. I hope I don't disturb you." He added this doubtfully, her attitude being still anything but reassuring.

"Not at all," said Mary, taking the nearest seat, which happened to be a piece of furniture shaped like the letter S, with a seat in each loop, so that the occupants, placed opposite one another, could converse at their ease across the rail. She then settled her glasses deliberately upon her nose and looked at him with a certain hardihood of manner which came to her whenever she was seized with nervousness, and was determined not to give way to it. He was a tall, jovial looking man, not yet quite middleaged, stout, or florid, but, as she judged, within five years of being all three. He had sandy hair and a red beard, cleft into two long whiskers of the shape formerly known to fashion as "weepers." His expression was goodnatured and, at this moment, conciliatory, as though he wished to disarm any further stiffness on her part. But she thought she saw also saw admiration in his eyes and she continued to gaze at him inflexibly. He looked wistfully at the conversation chair but sat down on the sofa, leaning forward with his elbows on his knees.

"This is a very convenient neighborhood, isn't it?" he said.

"Very."

"Yes. T am sure you must find it so. You are within easy distance of both the parks, and all the theatres. Kensington is too far out of the way for my fancy. How long does it take to go from here to Covent Garden Market now, for instance?"

"I am sorry I cannot tell you," said Mary calmly, looking at him with unflinching eyes: "I never go there."

"Indeed! I wonder at that. You can get tremendous bargains in flowers, I believe, if you go there early in the morning. Do you like flowers?"

"I do not share the fashionable mania for cut flowers. I like gardening."

"I quite agree with you, Miss Sutherland. I often think, when I see every little vase or knickknack in a room stuffed with tulips and lilies and things, what a want of real taste it shews. I was looking at that beautiful painting over the music stand just before you came in. May I ask is it one of yours?"

"Yes. If you look closely at it you will see my name written in large vermilion letters in the left hand corner."

I saw it. That's how I knew it to be yours. It's a capital picture: I often regret that I never learned to paint, though I know I should never have done it half as well as you. It's a very nice occupation for a lady. It is mere child's play to you, I suppose."

"I have given it up because I find it too difficult."

"But nobody could do it better than you. However, it runs away with your time, no doubt. Still, if I were you, I wouldn't give it up altogether."

"You are fond of pictures, I presume."

"Yes. I have a great taste for them. I go to the National Gallery whenever I come to London, to have a look at Landseer's pictures. I sometimes see young ladies copying the pictures there. Did you ever copy one of Landseer's?"

"No. Strange as it may appear to you, there are some pictures there which I prefer to Landseer's."

"You understand the old masters, you see. I don't, unfortunately. I should like to be able to talk to you about them; but if I tried it on, you would find out in no time that I know nothing about it. Put me into a gallery, and I can tell you what pictures I like: that's about as far as I can go."

"I wish I could go as far."

"I am afraid you are chaffing me, Miss Sutherland."

Mary did not condescend to reply. The strange man, now somewhat discomfited, rose and stood with his back to the fireplace, as if to warm himself at the Japanese umbrella that protruded from it.

"Beautiful weather," he said after a pause.

"Very beautiful indeed." she replied, gravely. Then, to prevent herself from laughing at him, "Have you been long in London?"

"Arrived yesterday." he said, brightening. "I came straight from New York via Liverpool. I'm always traveling. Have you ever been to the States?"

"No."

You should go there and see what real life is. We're all asleep here. I only left England last March; and I've started six branches of our company since that, besides obtaining judgment against two scoundrels who infringed our patent. Quick work, that."

"Is it?"

"I should think so. It would have taken two years to do here. More: five years perhaps. The Americans can't resist a new thing as we do. But no matter, unless they look alive here, they will be driven out of the market by foreign manufacturers using our cheap power."

"Your cheap power! What is that?"

"I thought you knew. Why, the Conolly electro-motor, which will drive any machinery at half — aye, at a quarter of the cost of steam. You have heard of it, of course."

"I think so. I have met Mr. Conolly. He does not seem like a man who could do anything badly."

"Badly! I should think not. He's an amazing man. They talk of Seth Jones's motor; and Van Print claims to be the original inventor of Conolly's commutator. But they are a couple of thieves. I can shew you the report of Conolly versus the Pacific —"

"Johnny!" exclaimed Mrs. Phipson, entering. "I thought it was your voice."

"How d'ye do, Nan?" said he. "How are the bairns?"

"Oh, we're all first rate. Have you been here long?"

"It seems only half a minute, Miss Sutherland has been entertaining me so pleasantly." And he winked and frowned at Mrs Phipson, to intimate that he desired to be introduced.

"Then you know each other already," she said. "This is my brother, Mr Hoskyn. I hope you have not been bothering Mary with your electro business."

"Mr Hoskyn was giving me a most interesting account of it when you came in," said Mary.

"You can finish it some other time," said Mrs Phipson. "Inflict it on the next person who has the misfortune to get shut into a railway carriage with you. When did you come back?"

Mr Hoskyn glanced apprehensively at Mary, and did not seem to like his sister's remark, though he laughed goodhumoredly at it. The conversation then turned upon his recent movements; the length of time he expected to remain in London; and so forth.

Mary gathered that he had invested money in the Conolly Electro-Motor Company, and that he occupied himself in traveling to countries where the electro-motor was yet unknown, establishing companies for its exploitation; and making them pay for the right to use it. Mrs. Phipson was evidently tired of the subject, and made attempts to prevent his dwelling on it; but, in spite of her, he boasted a good deal of the superiority of Connely's invention, and predicted ruin for certain other companies which had been set on foot to promote rival projects. He was effectually interrupted at last by the appearance of the younger children, who were excited by the arrival of Uncle Johnnie, and, Mary thought, looked forward to being the richer for his visit. Mr Hoskyn's attention to them, however, flagged after the first few minutes; and Mrs Phipson, who was always impatient of her children's presence, presently bade them to go and tell their father that Uncle Johnnie had come. They were, she added, on no account to return to the drawingroom. Their faces lengthened at this dismissal; but they did not venture to disregard it. Then Mr Phipson came; and his brother-in-law said much to him of what he had said before. Mary took no part in the conversation; but she occupied a considerable share of Mr Hoskyn's attention. Whenever he pronounced an opinion, or cracked a joke, he glanced at her to see whether she approved of it, and always found her in the same attitude, self-possessed, with her upper lip lifted a little from her teeth by the poise of her head, which she held well up in order to maintain her glasses in their position; and by a slight contraction of her brows to shade her eyes from the superfluous rays.

"I need hardly ask whether Miss Sutherland sings," he said, when he had repeated all his news to Mr Phipson.

"Very seldom," replied his sister. Now Mary had a powerful and rather strident contralto voice, which enabled her to sing dramatic music with startling expression and energy. Mrs Phipson, who did not like these qualities, said "Very seldom," in order to deter her brother from pressing his suggestion. But Mr Phipson, who relished Mary's performances, and was also fond of playing accompaniments, immediately went to the piano, and opened it.

"I would give anything to hear you," said Hoskyn, "if you will condescend to sing for such an ignorant audience as me."

"I had much rather not," said Mary, shewing signs of perturbation for the first time. "I sing nothing that would amuse you."

"Of course not," said he. "I know you don't sing ballads and such trash. Something Italian, I should like to hear."

"Come," said Mr. Phipson. "Give us *Che faro senza Euridice,* And he began to play it.

Mary, after a moment's hesitation, resigned herself, and went to the instrument. Mrs Phipson sighed. Hoskyn sat down on the ottoman; leaned attentively forward; and smiled continuously until the song was over, when he cried with enthusiasm: "Bravo! Splendid, splendid! You are quite equal to any professional singer I ever heard, Miss Sutherland. There is nothing like real Italian music after all. Thank you very much: I cannot remember when I enjoyed anything half so well"

"It is not Italian music," said Mary, resuming her former attitude in the causeuse. "It is German music With Italian words."

"It might as well be Chinese music fur all he knows about it." said Mrs Phipson spitefully.

"I know that I enjoyed it thoroughly, at any rate," said Hoskyn. "I have taken such a fancy to that picture on the wall that I should like to see some of your sketches, if you will favor me so far."

Mary felt bound to be civil to Mrs Phipson's brother: else she might have lost patience with Mr Hoskyn. "My sketches are in that book," she said, pointing to a portfolio. "But they are not intended for show purposes, and if you have no real curiosity to see them, pray do not be at the trouble of turning them over. I do not paint for the sake of displaying an extra accomplishment."

"I quite understand that. It is as natural to you to do all these things as it is for me to walk or sleep. You can hardly think how much pleasure a song or a sketch gives me, because, you see, they are everyday things with you, whereas I could no more paint or sing in Italian than little Nettie upstairs. So, if you'll allow me, I'll take a peep. If I bring them over here, you can show them to me better." And, on this pretext, he got into the *causeuse* with her at last.

"Fool!" commented Mrs. Phipson through her teeth to Mr Phipson, who smiled and strummed on the piano. Hoskyn meanwhile examined the sketches one by one; demanded a particular account of each; and, when they represented places at which he had been, related such circumstances of his visit as he could recollect, usually including the date, the hotel charges, and particulars of his fellow travelers; as, for instance, that there were two Italian ladies staying there; or that a lot of Russians took the whole of the first floor, and were really very polite people when you came to know them. Mary answered his questions patiently, and occasionally, when he appealed to her for confirmation of his opinions, gave him a cool nod, after each of which he grew more pleased and talkative. He praised her drawings extravagantly; and she, seeing that the worst satisfied him as well as the best, made no further attempt to deprecate his admiration, listening to it with self-possessed indifference. Mrs Phipson yawned conspicuously all the time. Failing to move him by this means, she at last asked him whether he would take supper with them, or return at once to wherever he was staying. He replied that he was staying round the corner at the Langham Hotel, and that he would wait for supper, to which Mrs Phipson assented with a bad grace. Just then Mary, hearing screams from the nursery pretended that she wished to see what was the matter, and left the room. She did not return; and Hoskyn, on going down to supper, was informed, to his heavy disappointment, that she never partook of that meal.

"So you might have saved yourself the trouble of staying, after all," said Mrs Phipson. "Will you have a wing or a bit of the breast?"

"Anything, please. On my soul, Phipson, I think she is the nicest girl I ever met. She is really very handsome."

"Handsome!" cried Mrs Phipson, indignantly. Don't be a fool, Johnny."

"Why? Don't you think she is?"

"She isn't even plain: she is downright ugly."

"Oh come, Nanny! That is a little too much. What fault can you find with her face?"

"What fault is there that I cannot find? To say nothing of her features, which even you can hardly defend, look at her coarse black hair and thick eyebrows. And then she wears spectacles."

"No. Not spectacles. Only nosers, Nanny. They are quite the fashion now."

"Well, whatever you choose to call them. If you consider a *pince-nez ornamental*, your taste is peculiar."

"I agree with you, John," said Mr Phipson. "I admire Mary greatly."

"*If she were twice as handsome," interposed Mrs Phipson, as Hoskyn's eyes brightened triumphantly, "it would be none the better for you. She is engaged."

Hoskyn looked at her in dismay. Mr Phipson Seemed surprised.

"Engaged to Adrian Herbert, the artist," continued Mrs Phipson, "who can talk to her about high art until she fancies him the greatest genius in England: not like you, who think yourself very clever when you have spent an hour in shewing her that you know nothing about it."

"My dear," remonstrated Mr Phipson: "that business with Herbert is all broken off. You should be a little careful. He is going to be married to Sczympliça."

"You may believe as much of that as you please," said Mrs Phipson. "Even supposing that she really is done with Herbert, there is Jack. A nice chance you have Johnny, with the greatest lion in London for a rival."

"Annie," said Mr Phipson: "you are talking recklessly. There is no reason to suppose that there is anything between Mary and Jack. Jack is not — in that sense, at least — a ladies' man."

"As to that," said Hoskyn, "I will take my chance beside any artist that ever walked on two legs. They can talk to her about things that I may not be exactly *au fait* at; but, for the matter of that, if *I* chose to talk shop, I could tell her a few things that she would be a long time finding out from them. No, Nanny: the question is, Is she engaged? If she is, then I'm off; and there's an end of the business. If not, I guess I'll try and see some more of her, in spite of all the painters and musicians in creation. So, which is it?"

"She is quite free," said Mr. Phipson. "She was engaged to Herbert; but it was an old arrangement, made when they were children, I believe; and at all events it was given up some time ago. I think there will be a little money too, John. And I fancy from her manner that she was struck with you." Mr Phipson winked at his wife, and laughed.

"I don't know about that," said Hoskyn; "but I am out-and-out struck with her. As to money, that needn't stand in the way, though I shan't object to take whatever is going."

"You are so particularly well suited to a girl who cares for nothing but fine art crazes of which you don't even know the names," said Mrs Phipson sourly, "that she will jump at your offer, no doubt. It is no wonder for her to be shortsighted, she reads so much. And she knows half the languages of Europe."

"I should think so," said Hoskyn. "You can see intellect in her face. That's the sort of woman I like. None of your empty headed wax dolls. I'm not surprised that you don't approve of her, Nanny. You are sharp enough, but you never knew anything, and never will."

"I don't pretend to be clever. And I don't disapprove of her; but I disapprove of you, at your age, thinking of a girl who is, in every way, unfit for you."

"We shall see all about that. I am quite content to take my chance, if she is. She can't live on high art, and I expect she is sensible enough in everyday matters. Besides, I shall not interfere with her. The more she paints and sings, the better pleased I shall be."

"Hear, hear," said Mr Phipson. "Let us about a license at once. The season will be over in three weeks and, of course, you Would prefer to be married before then."

"Chaff away," said Hoskyn, rising. "I must be off now. You may expect to see me pretty soon again, and if you don't hear people wondering ring next season how Johnny Hoskyn managed to get such a clever wife — why, I shall be worse disappointed than you. Good night."

CHAPTER XIV

During the remaining weeks of the season, Mary witnessed a series of entertainments of a kind quite new to her. Since her childhood she had never visited the Crystal Palace except for the Saturday afternoon classical concerts. Now she spent a whole day there with Mr Hoskyn, his sister, and the children, and waited for the display of fireworks. She saw acrobats, conjurers, Christy Minstrels, panoramas, and shows of cats, goats, and dairy implements; and she felt half ashamed of herself for enjoying them. She went for the first time in her life to a circus, to a music hall, and to athletic sports at Lillie Bridge. After the athletic sports, she went up the river in a cheap excursion steamer to Hampton Court, where she hardly looked at the pictures, and occupied herself solely with the other objects of interest, which she had neglected on previous visits. Finally she went to Madame Tussaud's.

Hoskyn had proposed all these amusements on behalf of the children; and it was supposed that Mary and Mrs Phipson, on going to them, were goodnaturedly co-operating with Uncle Johnny to make the little Phipsons happy. In the character of Uncle Johnny, Hoskyn frequented the house in Cavendish Square at all hours, and was soon on familiar terms with Mary. He was goodhumored, and apparently quite satisfied with himself. In arranging excursions, procuring and paying for vehicles, spying out and pushing his way to seats left accidentally vacant in the midst of packed audiences, looking after the children, and getting as much value as possible for his money on every occasion, he was never embarrassed or inefficient. He was very inquisitive, and took every opportunity of entering into conversation with railway officials, steamboat captains, cab-men, and policemen, and learning from them all about their various occupations. When this habit of his caused him to neglect Mary for a while, he never pestered her with apologies, and always told her what he had learnt without any doubt that it would interest her. And it did interest her more than she would have believed beforehand, although sometimes its interest arose from the obvious mendacity of Hoskyn's informants: he being as credulous of particulars extracted bu casual pumping as he was sceptical of any duly authorized and published statement. In his company Mary felt neither the anxiety to appear at her best with which Herbert's delicate taste and nervous solicitude for her dignity had always inspired her, nor the circumspection which she had found necessary to avoid offending the exacting temper of Jack. In their different ways, both men had humbled her. Hoskyn admired her person, and held her acquirements to awe, without being himself in the least humbled, although he exalted her without stint. She began to feel too, that she, by her apprenticeship to the two artists, had earned the right to claim rank as an adept in modern culture before such men as Hoskyn. When they went to the Academy, he was quite delighted to find that she despised all the pictures he preferred. In about an hour, however, both had had enough of picture seeing and they finished the day by the trip to Hampton Court.

When the season was over, it was arranged that Mr Phipson should take his family to Trouville for the month of August. Hoskyn, who was to accompany them, never doubted that Mary would be one of the party until she announced the date of her departure for Sir John Porter's country seat in Devonshire. She had accepted Lady Geraldine's invitation a month before. Hoskyn listened in dismay, and instead of proposing some excursion to pass away the time, moped about the house during the remainder of the afternoon. Shortly after luncheon he was alone in the drawing room, staring disconsolately out of window, when Mary entered. She sat down without ceremony, and opened a book.

"Look here," he said presently. "This is a regular sell about Trouville."

"How so? Has anything happened?"

"I mean your not coming."

"But nobody ever supposed that I was coming. It was arranged long ago that I should go to Devonshire."

"I never heard a word about Devonshire until you mentioned it at lunch. Couldn't you make some excuse — tell Lady Porter that you have been ordered abroad for your health, or that Nanny will be offended if you don't go with her, or something of that sort?"

"But why? I want to go to Devonshire and I don't want to go to Trouville."

"Oh! In that case I suppose you will leave us."

"Certainly. I hope you are not going to make a grievance of my desertion."

"Oh no. But it knocks all the fun of the thing on the head."

"What a pity!"

"I am quite in earnest, you know."

"Nobody could doubt it, looking at your face. Can nothing be done to console you?"

"Poking fun at me is not the way to console me. Why do you want to go to Devonshire. It's about the worst climate in England for anyone with a weak chest: muggy, damp and tepid."

"I have not a weak chest, I am glad to say. Have you ever been in Devonshire?"

"No. But I have heard about it from people who lived there for years and had to leave it at last."

"I am going for a month only."

Hoskyn began to twirl the cord of the blind round his forefinger. When he had dashed the tassel twice against the pane Mary interfered.

"Would it not be better to open the window if you wish to let in the fresh air?"

"All I can say is," said he, dropping the tassel, "that you really might come with us."

"Very true, but there are many things I really might do, which I really won't do. And one of them is to disappoint Lady Geraldine."

"Hang Lady Geraldine. At least, not if she is a friend of yours, but I wish she had invited you at any other time."

"I think you have now made quite enough fuss about my going away. I am flattered, Mr Hoskyn, and feel how poignantly you will all miss me. So let us drop the subject."

"When shall I see you again, then?"

"Really I do not know. I hope I shall have the pleasure of meeting you next season. Until then I shall probably be lost to view in Windsor."

"If you mean that we may meet at dances, and that sort of thing, we are likely never to meet at all; for I never go to them."

"Then you had better take lessons in dancing, and change your habits."

"Not I. It is bad enough to be made a fool of by you without making one of myself."

Mary grew nervous. "I think we are going back to the old subject," she said.

"No. I was thinking of something else. Miss Sutherland." here he suddenly raised his voice, which broke, and compelled him to pause and clear his throat — "Miss Sutherland: I hope I am not going to bungle this business by being too hasty — too precipitate, as it were. But if you are really going away, would you mind telling me first whether you have any objection to think over becoming Mrs Hoskyn. Just to think over it, you know."

"Are you serious?" said Mary, incredulously.

"Of course I am. You don't suppose I would say such a thing in jest?"

Mary discomfited, privately deplored her womanly disability to make friends with a man without being proposed to. "I think we had better drop this subject too, Mr. Hoskyn," she replied. Then, recovering her courage, she added, "Of all the arrangements you have proposed, I think this is the most injudicious.'

"We will drop it of you like. I am in no hurry — at least I mean that I don't wish to hurry you. But you will think it over won't you?"

"Had you not better think over it yourself, Mr Hoskyn?"

"I have thought of it — let me see! I guess I saw you first about twenty-one days and two hours ago. Well, I have thinking over it constantly all that time."

"Think better of it."

"I will. The more I think of it, the better I think of it. And if you will only say yes, I shan't think the worse of it in this world. Tell me one thing, Miss Sutherland, did you ever know me to make a mistake yet?"

"Not in my twenty-two days and two hour's experience of you."

"Twenty-one days and two hours. Well, I am not making a mistake now. Don't concern yourself about my prospects: stick to your own. If you can hit it off with me. depend on it, my family affairs are settled to my satisfaction forever. What do you think?"

"I still think we had better abandon the subject."

"For the present?"

"Forever, if you please, Mr Hoskyn."

"For ever is a long word. I've been too abrupt. But you can turn it over in your mind whilst amusing yourself in Devonshire. There is no use in bothering yourself about it now, when we are all separating. Hush. Here's Nanny."

Mary was prevented by the entrance of Mrs Phipson from distinctly refusing Mr Hoskyn's proposal. He, during the rest of the day, seemed to have regained his usual good spirits, and chatted with Mary without embarrassment, although he contrived not to not to be left alone with her. When she retired for the night, he had a short conversation with his sister, who asked whether he had said anything to Mary.

"Yes."

"What did she say?"

"She didn't say much. She was rather floored: I knew I was beginning too soon. We agreed to let the matter stand over. But I expect it will be all right."

"What on earth do you mean by agreeing to let the matter stand over? Did she say yes or no?"

"She did not jump at me. In fact she said no; but she didn't mean it."

"Hoity-toity! I wonder whom she would consider good enough for her. She may refuse once too often."

"She won't refuse me. Though, if she does, I don't see why you should lose your temper on that score, since you have always maintained that I had no chance."

"I am not losing my temper. I knew perfectly well that she would refuse; but I think she may go further and fare worse."

"She hasn't refused. And — now you mind what I am telling you, Nanny — not a word to her on the subject. Hold your tongue; and don't pretend to know anything about my plans. Do you hear?"

"You need not make such a to-do about it, Johnny. I don't want to speak to her. I am sure I don't care whether she marries you or not."

"So much the better. If you give her a hint about going further and faring worse — I know you would like to — it is all up with me."

Mary heard no more about Mr Hoskyn's suit just then. She left Cavendish Square next day, and went with Lady Geraldine to the southwest of Devonshire, where Sir John Porter owned a large white house with a Doric portico, standing in a park surrounded by wooded hills. Mary began sketching on the third day, in spite of her former resolution to discontinue the practice. Lady Geraldine was too busy recovering the management of her house and dairy farm after her season's absence, to interfere with the occupation of her guest; but at the end of the week she remarked one evening with a sigh:

"No more solitude for us, Mary. Sir John is coming tomorrow, and is bringing Mr Conolly as a prisoner of the invading army of autumn visitors. Since Sir John became a director of the Electro-motor company, he become bent on having everything here done by electricity. We shall have a couple of electro-motors harnessed to the pony phaeton shortly."

"Mr Conolly is coming on business then."

"Of course he is coming to pay a visit and make a holiday. But he will incidentally take notes of how the place can be most inconveniently upset with his machinery."

"You are not glad that he is coming."

"I am indifferent. So many people come here in the autumn whom I don't care for that I have become hardened to the labor of entertaining them. I like to have young people about me. Sir John, of course, has to do with men of business and politicians; and he invites them all to run down for a fortnight it in the off season. So they run down; and it is seldom by any means possible to wind them up for conversational purposes until they go away again."

"Mr. Conolly never seems to require winding up. Don't you like him?"

"He never seems to require anything, and it is partly for that reason that I don't like him. I have no fault to find with him — that is another reason, I think. Since I met him I have become ever so much more tolerant of human frailty. I respect the brute; but I don't like him."

This Mr Conolly was known to Mary as a man who, having been an obscure workman, had suddenly become famous as the inventor of something called an electro-motor, by which he had made much money. He had then married a highly born young lady, celebrated in society for her beauty. Not long afterwards she had eloped with a gentleman of her own rank, whom she had known all her life. Conolly had thereupon divorced her, and resumed his bachelor life, displaying so little concern, that many who knew her had since regarded him with mistrust and dislike, feeling that he was not the man to make a home for a young woman accustomed to the tenderest consideration and most chivalrous courtesy in her father's set. Even women, whose sympathy he would not keep in countenance by any pretense of brokenheartedness, had taken his wife's part so far as to say that he ought never to have married her. Mary had heard this much of his history in the course of gossip, and had met him a few times in society in London.

"I don't dislike him," she said, in reply to Lady Geraldine's last remark; "but he is an unanswerable sort of person; and I doubt if it would make the slightest difference to him whether the whole world hated or loved him."

"Just so. Can anything be more unamiable? Such a man ought to be a judge, or an executioner."

"After all, he is only a man; and he must have some feeling," said Mary.

"If he has he ought to show it," said Lady Geraldine. A servant just then entered with letters which had come by the evening mail. There were some for Mary; among them one addressed in a rapid business hand which she did not recognize. She opened them absently, thinking that a little experience of Herbert and Jack would soon remove Lady Geraldine's objection to Conolly's power of selfcontrol. Then she read the letters. One was from Miss Cairns, who was at a hydropathic establishment in Derbyshire. Another was from her father, who was glad she had arrived safely in Devonshire and hoped she would enjoy herself, was sure that the country air would benefit her health, and had nothing more to say at present but would write soon again. The third letter, a long one in a strange hand, roused her attention.

Langham Hotel, London,
W., 10th August

Dear Miss Sutherland — I have returned for a few days from Trouville, where I left Nanny and the children comfortably settled. I was recalled by a telegram from our head office and now that my business there is transacted, I have nothing to do except lounge around this great barrack of a hotel until I take it into my head to go back to Trouville. I miss Cavendish Square greatly. Three or four time day I find myself preparing to go there, forgetting that there is nobody in the house, unless Nanny has left the cat to starve, as she did two years ago. You cannot imagine how lonely I find London. The hotel is full of Americans; and I have scraped acquaintance with most of them; but I am none the livelier for that: somebody or something has left a hole in this metropolis that all the Americans alive cannot fill. Tonight after dinner I felt especially dull. There are no plays worth seeing at this season; and even if there were, it is no pleasure to me to go to the theatre by myself. I have got out of the way of doing so lately; and I don't feel as if I could ever get into it again. So I thought that writing to you would pass the time as pleasantly as anything.

You remember, I hope, a certain conversation we had on the 2nd inst. I agreed not to return to the subject until you came back from Lady Porter's; but I was so flurried by having to speak to you sooner than I intended, that I have been doubtful ever since whether I put it to you in the right way. I am afraid I was rather vague; and though it does not do to be too businesslike on such occasions, still, you have a right to know to a fraction what my proposal means. I know you are too sensible to suppose that I am going into particulars from want of the good oldfashioned sentiment which ought to be the main point in all such matters, or by way of offering you an additional inducement. If you had only yourself to look to, I think I should have pluck enough to ask you to shut your eyes and open your mouth so far as money is concerned; but when other interested parties who may come on the scene hereafter are to be considered, it is not only allowable but right to go into figures.

There are just four points, as I reckon it: 1, I am thirty-five years of age, and have no person depending on me for support. 2, I can arrange matters so that if anything happens to me you shall have a permanent income of five hundred pounds per annum. 3, I can afford to spend a thousand a year at present, without crippling myself. 4, These figures are calculated at a percentage off the minimum, *and far understate what I may reasonably expect my resources to be in the course of* a few years.

I won't go any closer into money matters with you, because I feel that bargaining would be out of place between as. You may trust me that you shall want for nothing, if — !!! I wish you would help me over that if. We got along very well together in July — at least I thought so and you seemed to think so too. Our tastes fit in together to a T. You have genius and I admire it. If I had it myself, I should be jealous of you, don't you see? As it is, the more you sing and paint and play, the more pleased am I, though I don't say that I would not be writing this letter all the same if you didn't know B-flat from a bull's foot. If you will just for this once screw up your courage and say yes, I undertake on my on my part that you shall never regret it.

An early answer will shorten my suspense. Not that I want you to write without taking plenty of time for consideration; but just remember that it will appear cent per cent longer to me than to you. Hoping you will excuse me if I have been unreasonable in following up my wishes, — I am, dear Miss Sutherland,

Sincerely yours,
John Hoskyn.

Mary thrust the letter into its envelope, and knit her brows. Lady Geraldine watched her, pretending meanwhile to be occupied with her own correspondence. "Do you know any of Mrs. Phipson's family?" said Mary slowly, after some minutes.

"No," replied Lady Geraldine, somewhat contemptuously. Then, recollecting that Mr Phipson's daughter was Mary's sister-in-law, she added, "There are brothers in Australia and Columbia who are very rich; and the youngest is a friend of Sir John's. He's in the Conolly Company, and is said to be a shrewd man of business. They all were, I believe. Then there were two sisters, Sarah and Lizzie Hoskyn. I can remember Lizzie when she was exactly like your brother Dick's wife. She married a great Cornhill goldsmith in her first season. Altogether, they are a wonderful family: making money, marrying money, putting each other in the way of making and marrying more, and falling on their feet everywhere."

"Are they the sort of people you like?"

"What do you mean by that, my dear?"

"I think I mean what I say," said Mary laughing. "But do you think, for example, that Mrs. Phipson's brothers and sisters are ladies and gentlemen?"

"Whether Dick's wife's aunts or uncles are ladies and gentlemen, eh?"

"Never mind about Dick. I have a reason for asking."

"Well then, I think it must be sufficiently obvious to everybody that they are not what used to be called ladies and gentlemen. But what has that to do with it? Rich middle class tradespeople have had their own way in society and in everything else as long as I can remember. Even if we could go back to the ladies and gentlemen now, we could not stand them. Look at the county set here — either vapid people with affected manners, or pigheaded people with no manners at all. Each set seems the worst until you try another."

"I quite agree with you — I mean about the Hoskyns, " said Mary. And she changed the subject. But at bedtime, when she bade Lady Geraldine goodnight, she handed her Hoskyn's letter, saying, "Read that; and tell me tomorrow what you think of it."

Lady Geraldine read the letter in bed, and lay awake, thinking of it for half an hour later than usual. In the morning, Mary, before leaving her room, received a note. It ran:

"Sir John will come by the three train. We can chat afterwards — when he and Mr Conolly are settled here and off my mind. —

G. P.

Mary understood from this that she was not to approach the subject of Mr Hoskyn until Lady Geraldine invited her. At breakfast no allusion was made to him, except that once, when they chanced to look at one another, they laughed. But Lady Geraldine immediately after became graver than usual, and began to talk about the dairy farm.

At three o'clock Sir John, heavy, double chinned and white haired arrived with a younger man in a grey suit.

"Well, Mr Conolly," said Sir John, as they passed under the Doric portico, "Here we are at last."

"At home," said Conolly, contentedly. Lady Geraldine, who was there to welcome them, looked at him quickly, her hospitality gratified by the word. Then the thought of what what he had made of his own home hardened her heart against him. Her habitual candid manner and abundance of shrewd comment forsook her in his presence. She was silent and scrupulously polite, and by that Mary and Sir John knew that she was under the constraint of strong dislike to her guest.

Later in the afternoon, Conolly asked permission to visit the farm, and inquired whether there was any running water in the neighborhood. Sir John proposed to accompany him; but he declined, on the ground that a prospecting engineer was the worst of bad company. When he was gone, Lady Geraldine's bosom heaved with relief: she recovered her spirits, and presently followed Sir John to the library, where they had a long conversation together. Having concluded it to her satisfaction, she was leaving the room, when Sir John, who was seated at a writing table, coughed and said mildly:

" My dear."

Lady Geraldine closed the door again, and turned to listen.

"I was thinking, as we came down together," said Sir John slowly, smiling and combing his beard with his fingers, "that perhaps he might take a fancy that way."

"Who?"

"Conolly, my dear."

"Stuff!" said Lady Geraldine sharply. Sir John smiled in deprecation. "At least," she added, repenting, "I mean that he is married already."

"But he is free to marry again."

"Besides, he is not a gentleman."

"Well," said Sir John, good humoredly, "I think we agreed just now that that did not matter."

"Yes, in Hoskyn's case."

"Just so. Now Conolly is a man of greater culture than Hoskyn. Of course, it is only a notion of mine; and I dare say you are quite right if you disapprove of it. But since Mary is a girl with nice tastes — for art and so forth — I thought that perhaps she might not suit a thorough man of business. Hoskyn is only an Americanized commercial traveler."

"Conolly is an American too. But that has nothing to do with it. Conolly treated his wife badly: that is enough for me. I am certain he would make any woman miserable."

"If he really did."

"But, dear," interrupted Lady Geraldine, with restrained impatience, "don't you *know* he did? Everybody knows it."

Sir John shrugged himself placidly. "They say so," he said. "I am afraid he was not all that he should have been to her. She was a charming creature — a great beauty, and, I thought, great rectitude. Dear me! You are right, as usual, Joldie, it would not suit."

Lady Geraldine left the library, and went to dress for dinner, disturbed by the possibility which Sir John had suggested. At dinner she watched Conolly and observed that he conversed chiefly with Mary, and seemed to know more than she on all her favorite subjects. Afterwards, when they were in the drawing room, Mary asked him whether he played the piano. As he replied in the affirmative, Lady Geraldine was compelled to ask him to favor her with a performance. At their request he played some of Jack's music, much more calmly and accurately than Jack, himself played it. Then he made Mary sing, and was struck by her declamatory style, which jarred Lady Geraldine's nerves nearly as much as it had Mrs Phipson's. He next sang himself, Mary accompanying him, and at first soothed Lady Geraldine by his rich baritone voice, and then roused her suspicions by singing a serenade with great expression, which she privately set down as a coldblooded hypocrisy on his part. She at last persuaded herself that he was deliberately trying to engage the affections of Mary, with the intention of making her his second wife. Afterwards, he went out with Sir John, who often smoked cigars after dinner in the portico, and was fond of having a companion on such occasions.

"Thank goodness!" said Lady Geraldine. "Bluebeard has gone; and we can have our chat at last."

"Why Bluebeard?" said Mary, laughing. "His beard is auburn. Has he been married more than once?"

"No. But mark my words, he will marry at least half-a-dozen times; and he will kill all his wives, unless they run away from him, as poor Marian did. However, so long as he does not marry us, he can do as he likes. The question of the day is, what are you going to say to Mr John Hoskyn?"

"Oh!" said Mary, her face clouding. "Let Mr John Hoskyn wait. I wish he were in America."

"And why?" said Lady Geraldine in an obstinate tone.

"Because I want to enjoy my visit here and not be worried by his proposals."

"You can answer him in five minutes, and then enjoy your visit as much as if he actually were in America."

"That is true. Except that it will take much longer than five minutes to devise a letter that will not hurt his feelings too much."

"I could write a sensible letter for you that would not hurt his feelings at all."

"Will you? I shall be so much obliged. I hate refusing people."

"Mary: I hope you are not going to be foolish about this offer."

"Do you mean," said Mary, astonished, "that you advise me to accept it?"

"Most decidedly."

"But you said last night that he was not even a gentleman."

"Oh, a gentleman! Nonsense! What is a gentleman? Who is a gentleman nowadays? Is Mr Conolly, with whom you seem so well pleased" (Mary opened her eyes widely) "a gentleman? Or Mr. Jack?"

"Do you consider Mr. Herbert a gentleman?"

"Yes, I grant you that. I forgot him, but I only conclude from your experience of him that a mere gentleman would not do for you at all. Do you dislike Mr Hoskyn?"

"No. But then I do not absolutely dislike any man; and I know nearly a hundred."

"Is there anyone whom you like better?"

"N–no. Of course I am speaking only of people whom I could marry. Still that is not saying much. If I heard that he was leaving the country for ever, I should be rather relieved than otherwise."

"Yes, my dear, I know it is very annoying to be forced to make up one's mind. But you will gain nothing by putting off. I have been speaking to Sir John about Mr Hoskyn and everything he has told me is satisfactory in the highest degree."

"I am sure of it. Respectable, well off, rising, devotedly attached to me, calculates his figures at a percentage off the minimum, and so forth."

"Mary," said Lady Geraldine gravely: "have I mentioned I even one of those points to you?"

"No," said Mary, taken a little aback. "But what other light can you see him in?"

"In the best of all lights: that of a comfortable husband. I am in dread for you lest your notions of high art should make you do something foolish. When you have had as much experience as I, you will know that genius no more qualifies a man to be a husband than good looks, or fine manners, or noble birth, or anything else out of a story book."

"But want of genius is still less a qualification."

"Genius, Mary, is a positive disqualification. Geniuses are morbid, intolerant, easily offended, sleeplessly self-conscious men, who expect their wives to be angels with no further business in life than to pet and worship their husbands. Even at the best they are not comfortable men to live with; and a perfect husband is one who is perfectly comfortable to live with. Look at the matter practically. Do you suppose, you foolish child, that I am a bit less happy because Sir John does not know a Raphael from a Redgrave, and would accept the last waltz cheerfully as a genuine something-or-other by Bach in B minor? Our tastes are quite different; and, to confess the truth, I was no more romantically in love with him when we were married than you are at present with Mr Hoskyn. Yet where will you find such a modern Darby and Joan as we are? You hear Belle Saunders complaining that she has 'nothing in common' with her husband. What cant! As if any two beings living in the same world must not have more things in common than not; especially a husband and wife living in the same house, on the same income, and owning the same children. Why, I have something in common with Macalister, the gardener. I can find you a warning as well as an example, I knew Mr Conolly's wife well before she was married. She was a woman of whom it was impossible to believe anything bad. In an evil hour she met Conolly at a charity concert where they had both promised to sing. Of course he sang as if he was all softness and gentleness, much as he did just now, probably. Then there was a charming romance. She like you, was fond of books, pictures, and music. He knew all about them. She was very honest and candid: he a statue of probity. He was a genius too; and his fame was a novelty then: everybody talked of him. Never was there such an match. She was the only woman in England worthy of him: he the only man worthy of her. Well, she married him, in spite of the patent fact that with all his genius, he is a most uncomfortable person. She endured him for two years then ran away with an arrogant blockhead who had nothing to recommend him to her except an imposing appearance and an extreme unlikeness to her husband. She has never been heard of since. If she had married man like Hoskyn, she could have been a happy wife and mother today. But she was like you she thought that taking a husband was the same thing as engaging gentleman to talk art criticism with."

"I think I had better advertise, 'Wanted: a comfortable husband. Applicants need not be handsome, as the lady is shortsighted. It sounds very prosaic, Lady Geraldine."

"It *is* prosaic. I told you once before that the world is is not a stage for you to play the heroine on. Like all young people, you want an exalted motive for every step you take."

"I confess I do. However, you have forgotten to apply your argument to Mr. Hoskyn's case. If people with artistic tastes are all uncomfortable, I must be uncomfortable; and that is not fair to him."

"No matter. He is in love with you. Besides, you are not artistic enough to be uncomfortable. You have been your father's housekeeper too long."

"And you really advise me to marry Mr. Hoskyn?"

Lady. Geraldine hesitated. "I think you can hardly expect me to take the responsibility of directly advising you to marry any man. It is one of the things that people must do for themselves. But I certainly advise you not to be deterred from marrying him by any supposed incompatibility in your tastes, or by his not being a man of genius."

"I wonder would Mr. Conolly marry me."

"Mary!"

"It was an unmaidenly remark," said Mary, laughing."

"It is undignified for a sensible girl to play at being silly, Mary. I hope you have no serious intention beneath your jesting. If you have, I shall be very sorry indeed for having allowed Mr. Conolly to meet you here."

"Not the slightest, I assure you. Why, Lady Geraldine, you look quite alarmed."

"I do not trust Mr. Conolly much. Marian Lind was infatuated by him; and another woman may share her fate — unless she happens to share my feeling towards him, in which case she may be regarded as perfectly safe. He is a dangerous subject. Let us leave him and come back to our main business. Is Mr. Hoskyn to be made happy or not?"

"I don't want to marry at all. Let him have Miss Cairns: she would suit him exactly."

"Well, if you don't want to marry at all, my dear, there is an end of it. I have said all I can. You must decide for yourself."

Mary, perceiving that Lady Geraldine felt offended, was about to make a soothing speech, when she heard a chair move, and, looking up saw that Conolly was in the room.

"Do I disturb you?"

Not at all," Said Lady Geraldine with dignity, looking at him rather severely and wondering how long he had been there.

"We were discussing sociology." said Mary.

"Ah!" he said, serenely. "And have you arrived at any important generalizations?"

"Most important ones."

"What about? — if I may ask."

"About marriage." Lady Geraldine stamped hastily on Mary's foot, and looked reproachfully at her.

Mary felt her color deepen, but she faced him boldly.

"And have you come the usual conclusions?" he said, sitting down near them.

"What are the usual conclusions?" said Mary.

"That marriage is a mistake. That men who surrender their liberty, and women who surrender their independence are fools. That children are a nuisance, and so forth."

"We have come to any such conclusions. We rather started in with the assumption that marriage is a necessary evil, and were debating how to make the best of it."

"On which point you differed, of course."

"Why of course?"

"Because Lady Geraldine is married and you are not. Can I help you to arrive at a compromise? I am peculiarly fitted for the task, because I am not married, and yet I have been married."

Lady Geraldine, who had turned her chair so as to avert her face from him, looked round. Disregarding this mute protest, he continued, addressing Mary. "Will you tell me the point at issue?"

"It is not so very important," said Mary, a little confused. "We were only exchanging a few casual remarks. A question arose as to whether the best men make the best husbands. I mean the cleverest men — men of genius, for instance. Lady Geraldine said no. She maintains that a goodnatured blockhead makes a far better husband than a Caesar or a Shakespeare."

"Did you say that?" said Conolly to Lady Geraldine, with a smile.

"No," she replied, almost uncivilly. "Blockheads are never goodnatured. At best, they are only lazy. I said that a man might be a very good husband without any special culture in the arts and sciences. Mary seemed to think that any person who understands as much of painting as an artist, is a person who sympathizes with that artist, and therefore a suitable match for her — or him. I disagree with her. I believe that community of taste for art has just as much to do with matrimonial happiness as community of taste for geography or roast mutton, and no more."

"And no more," repeated Conolly. "You are quite right. Heroes are ill adapted to domestic purposes. That is what you mean, is it not? Perhaps Miss Sutherland will be content with nothing less than a hero."

"No," said Mary. "But T will never admit that a man is not the better for being a hero. According to you, he is the worse. I heartily despise a woman who marries a fool in order that she may live comfortably despotic in her own house. I do not make absolute heroism an indispensable condition — I do not know exactly what heroism means; but I think a man may reasonably be expected to be free from vulgar prejudices against the efforts of artists to make life beautiful; and to have so disciplined himself that a wife can always depend on his selfcontrol and moral rectitude. It must be terrible to live in constant dread of childish explosions of temper from one's husband, or to fear, at every crisis, that he will not act like a man of sense and honor."

Conolly looked at her curiously, and then, with an intent deliberation, that gave the fullest emphasis to his words, leaned a little toward her with his hands upon his knees, and said "Did you ever live with a person whose temper was imperturbable — who never hesitated to apply his principles, and never swerved from acting as they dictated? One who, whatever he might be to himself, was to you so void of petty jealousies, irritabilities and superstitions of ordinary men, that, as far as you understood his view of life, you could calculate his correct behavior beforehand in every crisis with as much certainty as upon the striking of a clock?"

"No," said Lady Geraldine emphatically, before Mary could reply; "and I should not like to, either."

"You are always right," said Conolly. "Yet such a person would fulfill Miss Sutherland's conditions. Like Hamlet," he continued, turning to Mary, "you want a man that is not Passion's slave. I hope you may never get him, for I assure you, you will not like him. He would make an excellent God, but a most unpleasant man, and an unbearable husband. What could you be to a wholly self-sufficient man? Affection would be a superfluity with which you would be ashamed to trouble him. I once knew a lady whom I thought the most beautiful, the most accomplished, and the most honest of her sex. This lady met a man who had learned to stand alone in the world — a hard lesson, but one that is relentlessly forced on every sensitive but unlovable boy who has his own way to make, and who knows that, outside himself, there is no God to help him. This man had realized all that is humanly possible in your ideal of a self-disciplined man. The lady was young, and, unlike Lady Geraldine, not wise. Instead of avoiding his imperturbable self-sufficiency, she admired it, loved it, and married it. She found in her husband all that you demand. She never had reason to dread his temper, or to doubt his sense and honor. He needed no petting, no counsel, no support. He had no vulgar prejudices against art, and, indeed, was fonder of it than she was. What she felt about him I can only conjecture. But I know that she ceased to love him, whilst around her thousands of wives were clinging fondly to husbands who bullied and beat them, to fools, savages, drunkards, knaves, Passion's slaves of many patterns, but all weak enough to need caresses and forgiveness occasionally. Eventually she left him, and it served him right; for this model husband, who had never forfeited his wife's esteem, or tried her forbearance by word or deed, had led her to believe that he would be as happy without her as with her. A man who is complete in himself needs no wife. If you value your happiness, seek for someone who needs you, who begs for you, and who, because loneliness is death to him, will never cease to need you. Have I made myself clear?"

"Yes," said Mary. "I think I understand, though I do not say I agree."

Sir John came in just then, opportunely enough, and he found Conolly quite willing to talk about the prospects of the Company, although the ladies were thereby excluded from any part or interest in the conversation. Mary took the opportunity to slip away, unnoticed save by her hostess. When Conolly's attention was released by Sir John going to the library fore some papers, he found himself alone with Lady Geraldine.

"Mr Conolly," said Lady Geraldine, overcoming, with obvious effort, her reluctance to speak to him: "although you were of course not aware of it, you chose a most unfortunate moment for explaining your views to Miss Sutherland. There are circumstances which render it very undesirable that her judgment should be biased against marriage just at present."

"I hardly follow you," said Conolly, with a benignant self-possession which made Lady Geraldine privately quail. "Are you opposed to the suit of Mr Hoskyn?" She looked at him in consternation." I see you are surprised by my knowledge of Miss Sutherland's affairs," he continued. "But that only convinces me that you do not know Mr Hoskyn. In business matters he can sometimes keep a secret. In personal matters he is indiscretion personified. Everybody in Queen Victoria Street, from the messenger to the Chairman, is informed of the state of his affections."

"But why, if you knew this, did you talk as you did?"

"Because," said he, smiling at her impatience, "I did not then know that you disapproved of his proposal."

"Mr Conolly," said Lady Geraldine, trying to speak politely: "I don't disapprove of it."

"Then we are somehow at cross purposes. I too, approve; and as Hoskyn is not, to my knowledge, likely to be a hero in the eyes of a young lady of Miss Sutherland's culture, I ventured to warn her that he might be all the better qualified to make her happy."

"I told her so myself. But if you want to encourage a young girl to marry, surely it is not a very judicious thing to give such a bad account of your own married life."

"Of my own married life?"

"I mean," said Lady Geraldine, coloring deeply, "of your own experience of married life — what you have observed in others." She stopped, feeling that this was a paltry evasion, and added, "I beg your pardon. I fear I have made a very painful blunder."

"No. An allusion to my marriage — from you — does not pain me. I know your sympathies are not with me; and I am pleased to think that they are therefore where they are most needed and deserved. As to Miss Sutherland, I do not think that what I said will have the effect you fear. In any case, my words are beyond recall. If she refuses Mr Hoskyn, I shall bear the blame. If she accepts him; I will claim to have been your ally."

"She would be angry if she knew that you were aware, all the time you were talking, of her position."

"Angry with me: yes. That does not matter. But if she knew that Mr. Hoskyn had told me, she would be angry with him; and that would matter very much."

Before Lady Geraldine could reply, her husband returned; and Conolly withdrew shortly afterwards for the night.

Next day, Mary received from Hoskyn a second letter begging her to postpone her answer until he had seen her, as he had become convinced that such matters ought to be conducted personally instead of by writing. As soon as he had ascertained which hotel was the near Sir John's house, he would, he wrote, put up there and ask Mary to contrive one long interview. She was not to mention his presence to Lady Geraldine, lest she should think he expected to be asked on a visit. Mary immediately made Lady Geraldine promise that he should not be asked on a visit; and then, to avoid the threatened interview, made up her mind and wrote to him as follows:

Dear Mr. Hoskyn —

I shall not give you the trouble of coming down here to urge what you so frankly proposed in your first letter. 1 trust it will relieve your anxiety to learn that I have decided to accept your offer. However, as the position we are now in is one that we could not properly maintain whilst visiting at the house of a friend, I beg that you will give up all idea of seeing me until I leave Devonshire. My social duties here are so heavy that I can hardly, without seeming rude, absent myself to write a long letter. I suppose you will go back to Trouville until we all return to London. — I am, dear Mr. Hoskyn,

Yours sincerely,
Mary Sutherland.

Mary composed this letter with difficulty, and submitted it to Lady Geraldine, who said, "It is not very loving. That about your social duties is a fib. And you want him to go to Trouville because he cannot write so often."

"I can do no better," said Mary. "But you are right. I will burn it and write him another, refusing him point blank. That will be the shortest."

"No, thank you. This will do very well." And Lady Geraldine closed it with her own hands and sent it to the post. Later in the afternoon Mary said, "I am exceedingly sorry I sent that letter. I have found out my real mind about Mr Hoskyn at last. I detest him."

Lady Geraldine only laughed at her.

BOOK II

CHAPTER I

One evening the concert room in St. James's Hall was crowded with people waiting to hear the first public performance of a work by Mr Owen Jack, entitled *Prometheus Unbound*. It wanted but a minute to eight o'clock; the stalls were filling rapidly; the choristers were already in their seats; and there was a din of tuning from the band. Not far from the orchestra sat Mr John Hoskyn, with a solemn air of being prepared for the worst, and carefully finished at the tie, gloves and hair. Next him was his wife, in a Venetian dress of garnet colored plush. Her black hair was gathered upon her neck by a knot of deep sea green; and her dark eyes peered through lenses framed in massive gold.

On the foremost side bench, still nearer to the orchestra, was a young lady with a beautiful and intelligent face. She was more delicately shaped than Mrs Hoskyn, and was dressed in white. Her neighbors pointed her out to one another as the Szczympliça; but she was now Mrs Adrian Herbert. Her husband was with her; and his regular features seemed no less refined and more thoughtful than those of his wife. Mrs Hoskyn looked at him earnestly for some time. Then she turned as though to look at her husband; but she checked herself in this movement, and directed her attention to the entry of Manlius.

I have counted the band," whispered Hoskyn; "and it's eighty-five strong. They can't give them much less than seven and sixpence apiece for the night, which makes thirty-two pounds all but half a crown, without counting the singers."

"Nonsense," said Mary, after looking round apprehensively to see whether her husband's remark had been overheard. "Five pounds apiece would be nearer the — Hush."

The music had just begun; and Hoskyn had to confine his repudiation of Mary's estimate to an emphatic shake of the head. The overture, anxiously conducted by Manlius, who was very nervous, lasted nearly half an hour. When it was over, there was silence for a moment, then faint applause, then sounds of disapproval, then sufficient applause to overpower these and finally a buzz of conversation. A popular baritone singer, looking very uncomfortable, rose to carry on his part of dialogue between Promethius and the earth, which was the next number of the work. The chorus singers also rose, and fixed their eyes stolidly, but desperately, on the conductor, who hardly ventured to look at them. The dialogue commenced, but the the attention of the audience was presently diverted by the appearance of Jack himself, who was seen to cross the room with an angry countenance, and go out. The conclusion of the dialogue was unbroken silence, in the midst of which the popular baritone sat down with an air of relief.

"I find that the music is beginning to grow upon me, said Mrs Hoskyn.

"Do you?" said Hoskyn. "I wish it would grow quicker. I'm only joking," he added, seeing that she was disappointed. "It's splendid. I wish I knew enough about it to like it; but I can see that it has the real classical style. When those brass things come in, it's magnificent."

Two eminent songstresses now came forward as Asia and Panthea; and the audience prepared themselves for the relief of a pretty duet. But Asia and Panthea sang as strangely as Prometheus, in spite of which they gained some slow, uncertain, grudging applause. The *Race of the Hours*, which followed, was of great length, progressing from a lugubrious midnight hour in E flat minor to a sunrise in A major, and culminating with a jubilant clangor of orchestra and chorus which astounded the audience, and elicited a partly hysterical mixture of hand clapping and protesting hisses.

"How stupid these people are!" exclaimed Mrs Adrian Herbert. "What imbecility! They do not know that it is good music. Heaven!"

"I must confess that, to my ear, there is not a note of music in it," said Adrian.

"Is it possible!" said Aurélie. "But it is superb! Splendid!"

"It is ear splitting," said Adrian. "Your ears are hardier than mine, perhaps. I hope we shall hear some melody in the next part, by way of variety."

"Without doubt we shall. It is a work full of melody."

Herbert was confirmed in his opinion by the final number, entitled, "Antiphony of the Earth and Moon," which was listened to in respectful bewilderment by the audience, and executed with symptoms of exhaustion by the chorus.

"By George," said Hoskyn, joining heartily in some applause which began in the cheaper seats, "that sounded stupendous. I'd like to hear it again."

The clapping, though not enthusiastic, was now general, all being goodnaturedly willing that the composer should be called forward in acknowledgment of his efforts, if not of his success. Jack, who had returned to hear the "Race of the Hours," again arose; and those who knew him clapped more loudly, thinking that he was on his way to the orchestra. It proved that he was on his way to the door; for he went out as ungraciously as before.

"How disappointing."said Mary. "He is so hasty.

"Serves them right,"said Hoskyn. "I like his pluck; and you make take my word for it, Mary, that is a sterling piece of music. It reminds me of the Pacific railroad."

"Of course it is. Even you can see that," said Mary, who did not quite see it herself. "It is mere professional jealousy that prevents the people here from applauding properly, They are all musicians of some kind or another."

"They are going to give us ten minutes law before they begin again. Let us take a walk round, and find what Nanny thinks."

Meanwhile Aurélie was almost in tears. Mr Phipson had just come up to them, shaking his head sadly. "As I feared," he said. "As I feared."

"It is a shame," she said indignantly, "a shame unworthy of the English people. Of what use is it to write music for such a world?"

"It is far above their heads," said Phipson. "I told him so."

"And their insolence is far beneath his feet," said Aurélie. "Oh, it is a scene to plunge an artist in despair."

"It does not plunge me into despair," said Adrian, with quiet conviction. "The work has failed; and I venture to say that it deserved to fail."

"It is unworthy of you to say so," exclaimed Aurélie passionately, throwing herself back in her seat and turning away from him.

"Deserved is perhaps a hard word under the circumstances, Mr Herbert," said Phipson. "The work is a very remarkable one, and far beyond the comprehension of the public. Jack has been much too bold. Even our audiences will not listen with patience to movements of such length and complication. I greatly regret what has happened; for the people who are attracted by our concerts are representative of the highest musical culture in England. A work which fails here from its abstruseness has not the ghost of a chance of success elsewhere. Ah! Here is Mary."

Some introductions followed. Hoskyn shook Adrian's hand cordially, and made a low bow to Aurélie, whom he stole an occasional glance at, but did not at first venture to address. Aurélie looked at Mary's dress with wonder.

"I am greatly annoyed by the way Mr Jack has been treated," said Mary. "An audience of working people could not be more insensible to his genius than the people here have shewn themselves tonight."

My wife is quite angry with me because I, too, am insensible to the beauties of Mr Jack's composition," said Herbert

"You always were," said Mary. "Mr Hoskyn is delighted with Prometheus."

"Is Mr Hoskyn musical?"

"More so than you, it appears, since he can appreciate Mr Jack."

"Phipson then struck in on the merits of the music; and he, Mary, and Adrian, being old friends, fell into conversation together, to the exclusion of the husband and wife so recently added to their circle. Hoskyn, under these circumstances, felt bound to entertain Aurélie.

"I consider that we have had a most enjoyable evening," he said. "I think there can be no doubt that Jack's music is first rate of its kind."

"Ah? Monsieur Jacque's music. You find it goodh."

"Very good indeed,"said Hoskyn, speaking loudly, as if to a deaf person. "Jilitrouvsplongdeed," he added rashly.

"You are right, monsieur," said Aurélie, speaking rapidly in French. "But it seems to me that there is unworthy — something infamous, in the icy stupidity of these people here: Of what use is it to compose great works when one is held in contempt because of them? It is necessary to be a trader here in order to have success. Commerce is the ruin of England. It renders the people quite inartistic.

"Jinipweevoocomprongder," murmured Hoskyn. "The fact is," he added, more boldly, "I only dropped a French word to help you out a little; but you mustn't take advantage of that to talk to me out of my native language. I can speak French pretty well; but I never could understand other people speaking it."

"Ah," said Aurélie, who listened to his English with strained attention. "You understand me not very goodh. It is like me with English. But in this moment I make much progress. I have lesson every day from Monsieur Herbert."

"You speak very well. Vooparlaytraybyang —" tootafaycumoononglays. Jinisoray — I mean I should not know from your speaking that you were a foreigner — oonaytronzhare."

"Vraiment?" cried Aurélie, greatly pleased.

"Vraymong, " said Hoskyn, nodding emphatically.

"It is sthrench. There is only a few months since I know not a word of the English."

"You see you knew the universal language before."

"Comment? La langue universelle?"

"I mean music. Music!" he repeated, seeing her still bewildered.

"Ah, yes," said Aurélie, her puzzled expression vanishing. "You call music the universal language. It is true. You say very goodh."

"It must be easy to learn anything after learning music. Music is so desperately hard. I am sure learning it must make people — spiritual, you know."

"Yes, yes. You observe very justly, monsieur. I am quite of your advice. Understand you?"

"Parfatemong byang, " said Hoskyn, confidently.

Here Mary interrupted the conversation by warning her husband that it was time to return to their places. As they did so, she said:

'You must excuse me for abandoning you to the Szympliça, John. I suppose you could not say a word to one another."

Why not? She's a very nice woman; and we got on together splendidly. I always do manage to hit it off with foreigners, However, it was easy enough in her case; for she could speak broken English and didn't understand it, whereas I could speak French but couldn't understand the way she talked it — she's evidently not a Frenchwoman. So she spoke to me in English; I answered her in French; and we talked as easily as I talk to you."

Meanwhile Adrian could not refrain from commenting on Mary's choice. "I wonder why she married that man," he said to Aurélie. "I cannot believe that she would stoop to marry for money; and yet, seeing what he is, it is hard to believe that she loves him."

"But why?" said Aurélie. "He is a little commercial; but all the English are so. And he is a man of intelligence. He has very choice ideas."

"*You* think so, Aurélie!"

"Certainly. He has spoken very well to me. I assure you he has a very fine perception of music. It is difficult to understand him, because he does not speak French as well as I speak English; but it is evident that he has reflected much. As for her, she is fortunate to have so good a husband. What an absurd dress she wears. In any other part of the world she would be mocked at as a madwoman. Your scientific Mademoiselle Sutherland is, in my opinion, no great things."

Adrian looked at his wife with surprise, and with some displeasure; but the music recommenced just then, and the conversation dropped. Some compositions of Mendelssohn were played; and these he applauded emphatically, whilst she sat silent with averted face. When the concert was over they saw the Hoskyns drive away in a neat carriage; and Herbert, who had never in his bachelor days envied any man the possession of such a luxury, felt sorry that he had to hire a hansom for his wife's accommodation.

Adrian had not yet found a suitable permanent residence. They lived on the first floor of a house in the Kensington Road. Aurélie, who had always left domestic matters to her mother, knew little about housekeeping, and could not be induced to take an interest in house-hunting. The landlady at Kensington Road supplied them with food; and Adrian paid a heavy bill every week, Aurélie exclaiming that the amount was unheard of, and the woman wicked, but not taking any steps to introduce a more economical system.

They reached their lodging at a quarter before twelve; and Adrian, when Aurélie had gone upstairs, turned out the gas and chained the door, knowing that the rest of the household were in bed. As he followed her up, he heard the pianoforte, and, entering the room, saw her seated at it. She did not look round at him, but continued playing, with her face turned slightly upward and to one side — an attitude habitual to her in her musical moments. He moved uneasily about the room for some time; put aside his overcoat; turned down a jet of gas that flared; and rearranged some trifles on the mantelpiece. Then he said:

"Is it not rather late for the pianoforte, Aurélie? It is twelve o'clock: and the people of the house must be asleep."

Aurélie started as if awakened; shrugged her shoulders; closed the instrument softly; and went to an easy chair, in which she sat down wearily.

Herbert was dissatisfied with himself for interrupting her, and angry with her for being the cause of his dissatisfaction Nevertheless, looking at her as she reclined in the chair, and seemed again to have forgotten his existence, he became enamored.

"My darling!"

"Eh?" she said.waking again, "*Qu'est-ce, que c'est?*"

"It has turned rather cold tonight Is it wise to sit in that thin dress when there is no fire?"

"I do not know."

"Shall I get you a shawl?"

"It does not matter: I am not cold." She spoke as if his solicitude only disturbed her.

"Aurélie," he said, after a pause: "I heard tonight that my mother has returned to town." No answer.

"Aurélie," he repeated petulantly. "Are you listening me?"

"Yes. I listen." But she did not look at him.

"I said that my mother was in town. I think we had better call on her.*

"Doubtless you will call on her, if it pleases you to do so. Is she not your mother?"

"But you will come with me, Aurélie, will you not"

"Never. Never."

"Not to oblige me. Aurélie?"

"It is not the same thing to oblige you as to oblige your mother. I am not married to your mother."

Herbert winced. "That is a very harsh speech to English ears," he said.

"I do not speak in English: I speak the language of my heart. Your mother has insulted me; and you are wrong to ask me to go to her. My mother has never offended you; and yet I sent her away because you did not like her, and because it is not the English custom that she should continue with me. I know you did not marry her; and I do not reproach you with harshness because she is separated from me. I will have the like freedom for myself."

"Aurélie," cried Herbert, who had been staring during most of her speech: "you are most unjust. Have I ever failed in courtesy towards your mother? Did I ever utter a word expressive of dislike to her?"

"You were towards her as you were towards all the world. You were very kind: I do not say otherwise."

"In what way can my mother have insulted you? You have never spoken to her; and since a month before our wedding she has been in Scotland."

"Where she went lest I should speak to her, no doubt. Why did she not speak to me when I last met her? She knew well that I was betrothed to you. She is proud, perhaps. Well, be it so. I also am proud. I am an artist; and queens have given me their hands frankly. Your mother holds that an English lady is above all queens. I hold that an artist is above all ladies. We can live without one another, as we have done hitherto. I do not seek to hinder you from going to her; but I will not go."

"You mistake my mother's motive altogether. She is not proud — in that way. She was angry because I did not allow her to choose a wife for me."

"Well, she is angry still, no doubt. Of what use is it to anger her further?"

"She has too much sense to persist in protesting against what is irrevocable. You need not fear a cold welcome, Aurélie. I will make sure, before I allow you to go, that you shall be properly received."

"I pray you, Adrian, annoy me no more about your mother. I do not know her: I will not know her. It is her own choice; and she must abide by it. Can you not go to her without me?"

"Why should I go to her without you'" said Adrian, distressed. "Your love is far more precious to me than hers. You know how little tenderness there is between her and me. But family feuds are very objectionable. They are always in bad taste, and often lead to serious consequences. I wish you would for this once sacrifice your personal inclination, and help me to avert a permanent estrangement."

"Ah yes," exclaimed Aurélie," rising indignantly. "You will sacrifice my honor to the conventions of your world."

"It is an exaggeration to speak of such a trifle as affecting your honor. However, I will say no more. I would do much greater things for you than this that you will not do for me, Aurélie. But then I love you."

"I do not want you to love me," said Aurélie, turning towards the door with a shrug. "Go and love somebody else. Love Madame Hoskyn; and tell her how badly your wife uses you."

Herbert made a step after her. "Aurélie," he said: "if I submit to this treatment from you, I shall be the most infatuated slave in England."

"I cannot help that. And I do not like you when you are a slave. It grows late."

"Are you going to bed already?"

"Already! My God, it is half an hour after midnight! You are going mad, I think."

"I think I am. Aurélie: tell me the truth honestly now: I cannot bear to discover it by the slow torture of watching you grow colder to me. Do you no longer love me?"

"Perhaps," she said, indifferently. "I do not love you tonight, that is certain. You have been very tiresome." And she left the room without looking at him. For some moments after her departure he remained motionless. Then he set his lips together; went to a bureau and took some money from it; put on his hat and overcoat; and took a sheet of paper from his desk. But after dipping a pen in the ink several times, he cast it aside without writing anything. As he did so, he saw on the mantelpiece a little brooch which Aurélie often wore at her throat. He took this up, and was about to put it into his pocket, when, giving way to a sudden impulse, he dashed it violently on the hearthstone. He then extinguished the light, and went out. When he had descended one stair, he heard a door above open, and a light foot fall on the landing above. He stopped and held his breath.

"Adrian, my dear, art thou there?"

"What is it?"

"When thou comest, bring me the little volume which lies on the piano. It is red; and my handkerchief is between the pages for a mark."

He hesitated a moment. Then, saying, "Yes, my darling," me he stole back into the drawing room; undid his preparations for flight; got the red book, and went upstairs, where he found his wife in bed, placidly unconscious of his recent proceedings, with the reading lamp casting a halo on her pillow.

It was Adrian's habit to rise promptly when the servant knocked at his door at eight o'clock every morning. Aurélie, on the the contrary, was lazy, and often left her husband to breakfast by himself. On the morning after the concert he rose as usual, and made as much noise as possible in order to wake her. Not succeeding, he retired to his dressing room and, after a great splashing and rubbing, returned clad in a dressing gown.

"Aurélie." A pause during which her regular breathing was audible. Then, more loudly "Aurélie." She replied with a murmur. He added very loudly and distinctly, "It is twenty minutes past eight."

She moved a little and uttered a strange sound, which he did not understand, but recognized as Polish. Then she said, drowsily in French, "Presently."

"At once, if you please." he said, putting his hand on her shoulder. "Must I shake you?"

"No, no," she rousing herself a little more. "Don't shake me, I implore you." Then, petulantly, "I will not be shaken. I am going to get up. Are there any letters?"

"I have not been downstairs yet."

"Go and see."

"You will be sure not to sleep again."

"Yes, yes. I shall be down almost as soon as you. Bring me up the letters, if there are any."

He returned to his dressing room; finished his toilet; and went downstairs. There were some letters. He looked at them, and went back to Aurélie. She was fast asleep.

"Oh, Anrelie! Aurélie! Really it is too bad. You are asleep again."

"How you disturb me!" she said, opening her eyes, and sighing impatiently. "What hour is it?"

"You may well ask. It is twenty-five minutes to nine."

"Is that all?"

"All! Come, Aurélie, there are three letters for you. Two are from Vienna."

Aurélie sat up, awake and excited. "Quick," she said. "Give them to me."

"I left them downstairs."

"Oh," said Aurélie, disgusted. Adrian hurried from the room lest she should prevail upon him to bring up the letters. He occupied himself with the newspaper for the next fifteen minutes, at the end of which she appeared and addressed herself to her correspondence, leaving him to pour out tea for himself and for her. Nothing was said for some time. Then she exclaimed with emphasis, as though in contradiction of what she read:

"But it is certain that I will go."

"Go where?" said Adrian, turning pale.

"To Vienna — to Prague — to Budapesth, my beloved Budapesth."

"To Vienna!"

"They are going to give a Schumann concert in Vienna. They want me; and they shall have me. I have a specialty for the music of Schumann: no one in the world can play it as I can. And I long to see my Viennese friends. It is so stupid here."

"But, Aurélie, I have my work to do. I cannot go abroad at this season of the year."

"It is not necessary. I did not think of asking you to come. No. My mother will accompany me everywhere. She likes our old mode of life."

"You mean, in short, to leave me," he said, looking shocked.

"My poor Adrian," she said, leaning over to caress him: "wilt thou be desolate without me? But fret not thyself: I will return with much money, and console thee. Music is my destiny, as painting is thine. We shall be parted but a little time."

Adrian was pained, but could only look wistfully at her and say, "You seem to enjoy the prospect of leaving me, Aurélie."

"I am tired of this life. I am forgotten in the world; and others take my place."

"And will you be happier in Vienna than here?"

"Assuredly. Else wherefor should I desire to go? When I read in the journals of all the music in which I have no share, I almost die of impatience."

"And I sometimes, when I am working alone in my studio, almost die of impatience to return to your side."

"Bah! That is another reason for my going. It is not good for you to be so loving."

"I fear that it too true, Aurélie. But will it be good for you to have no one near you who loves you?"

"Oh, those who love me are everywhere. In Vienna there is a man — a student — six feet high, with fair hair, who gets a friend to make me deplorable verses which he pretends are his own. Heaven, how he loves me! At Leipzig there is an old professor, almost as foolish as thou, my Adrian. Ah, yes: I shall not want for lovers anywhere."

"Aurélie, are you mad, or cruel, or merely simple, that you say these things to me?"

"Are you then jealous? Ha! ha! He is jealous of my fairhaired student and of my old professor. But fear nothing, my friend. For all these men my mother is a veritable dragon. They fear her more than they fear the devil, in whom, indeed, they do not believe."

"If I cannot trust you, Aurélie, I cannot trust your mother."

"You say well. And when you do not trust me, you shall never see me again. I was only mocking. But I must start the day after tomorrow. You must come with me to Victoria, and see that my luggage is right. I shall not know how to travel without my mother."

"Until you are in her hands, I will not lose sight of you, my dear treasure," said Adrian tenderly. "You will write often to me, will you not, Aurélie?"

"I cannot write — you know it, Adrian. Mamma shall write to you: she always has abundance to say. I must practise hard; and I cannot sit down and cramp my fingers with a pen. I will write occasionally — I am sure to want something."

Adrian finished his breakfast in silence, glancing at her now and again with a mixture of rapture and despair.

"And so," he said, when the meal was over, "I am to lose you, Aurélie."

Go, go," she replied: "I have much preparation to make; and you are in my way. You must paint hard in your studio until very late this evening."

"I thought of giving myself a holiday, and staying at home with you, dearest, as we are so soon to be separated."

"Impossible," cried Aurélie, alarmed. "My God, what a proposition! You must stay away more than ever, I have to practise, and to think of my dresses: I must absolutely be alone" Adrian took up his hat dejectedly. "My soul and my life, how I tear thy heart!" she added fondly, taking his face between her hands and kissing him. He went out pained, humiliated, and ecstatically happy.

Aurélie was busy all the morning. Early in the afternoon she placed Schumann's concerto in A minor on the desk of the pianoforte, arranged her seat before it, and left the room. When she returned, she had changed her dress and was habited in silk. She bore her slender and upright figure more proudly before her imaginary audience than she usually ventured to do before a real one, and when had taken her place at the instrument, she played the concerto as she was not always fortunate to play it in public. Before she had finished the door was thrown open, and a servant announced "Mrs Herbert." Aurélie started up frowning, and had but just time to regain her thoughtful expression and native distinction of manner when her motherin-law entered, looking as imposing as a wellbred Englishwoman can without making herself ridiculous.

"I fear I disturbed you," she said, advancing graciously.

"Not at all. I am very honored, madame. Please to sit down."

Mrs Herbert had intended to greet her son's wife with a kiss. But Aurélie, giving her hand with dignified courtesy, was not approachable enough for that. She was not distant; but neither was she cordial. Mrs Herbert sat down, a little impressed.

Is it a long time, madame, that you are in London?"

I only arrived the day before yesterday," replied Mrs. Herbert in French, which, like Adrian, she spoke fluently. "I am always compelled to pass the winter in Scotland, because of my health."

"The climate of Scotland, then, is softer than that of England. Is it so?"

"It is perhaps not softer; but it suits me better," said Mrs. Herbert, looking hard at Aurélie, who was gazing pensively at the fireplace.

"Your health is, I hope, perfectly re-established?"

"Perfectly, thank you. Are you quite sure I have not interrupted you? I heard you playing as I came in; and I know how annoying a visit is when it interferes with serious employment."

"I am very content to be entertained by you, madame, instead of studying solitarily."

"You still study?"

"Undoubtedly."

"You are very fond of playing, then?"

"It is my profession."

"Since I am Adrian's mother," said Mrs. Herbert with some emphasis, as if she thought that fact was being overlooked, "will you allow me to ask you a question?"

Aurélie bowed.

"Do you study with a view to resuming your public career at some future time?"

"Surely. I am going to play next week at Vienna."

Mrs Herbert bent her head in surprised assent to this intelligence. *I thought Adrian contemplated your retirement into private life," she said. "However, let me hasten to add that I think you have shewn wisdom in overruling him. Will he accompany you abroad?"

"It is not necessary that he should. I shall travel, as usual, with my mother."

"Your mother is quite well, I hope?"

"Quite well, thank you, madame."

Then there was a gap in the conversation. Mrs Herbert felt that she was being treated as a distinguished stranger in her son's home; but she was uncertain whether this was the effect of timidity, or the execution of a deliberate design on Aurelie's part. Inclining to the former opinion, she resolved to make an advance.

"My dear," she said, may I ask how your friends usually call you?"

"Since my marriage, my friends usually call me Madame Sczympliça"

"I could not call you that," interposed Mrs Herbert, smiling. "I could not pronounce it."

"It is incorrect, of course" continued Aurélie, without responding to the smile; "but it is customary for artists to retain, after marriage, the name by which they have been known. I intend to do so. My English acquaintances call me Mrs Herbert."

"But what is your Christian name?"

Aurélie. But that is only used by my husband and my mother — and by a few others who are dear to me."

"Well," said Mrs. Herbert, with some impatience, "as it is quite impossible for me to address you as Mrs Herbert, I must really ask you to let me call you Aurélie."

"Whatever is customary, madame," said Aurélie, bending her head submissively. "You know far better than I."

Mrs. Herbert watched her in silence after this, wondering whether she was a knave or fool — whether to attack or encourage her.

"You enjoyed your voyage in Scotland, I hope." said Aurélie, dutifully making conversation for her guest.

"Very much indeed. But I grew a little tired of it, and shall probably remain in London now until August. When may I expect to see you at my house?"

"You are very good, madame: I am very sensible of your kindness. But — Mrs Herbert looked up quickly — I set out immediately for Vienna, whence I go to Leipzig and many other cities. I shall not be at my own disposal again for a long time."

Mrs. Herbert reflected for a moment, and then rose. Aurélie rose also.

"Adieu," said Mrs. Herbert suavely, offering her hand.

"Adieu, madame," said Aurélie, saluting her with earnest courtesy. Then Mrs. Herbert withdrew. On reaching the street she hailed a hansom, and drove to her son's studio in the Fulham Road. She found him at his easel, working more rapidly and less attentively than in the old days.

"How d'ye do, mother," he said, "Sit down on the throne." The throne was a chair elevated on a platform for the accommodation of live models. "We should have gone to see you; but Aurélie is going abroad. She has not a moment to spare."

"No, Adrian, that is precisely what you should not have done, though you might have done it. It was my duty to call on your wife first; and I have accordingly just come from your house."

"Indeed?" said Adrian eagerly, and a little anxiously. "Did you see Aurélie?"

"I saw Aurélie."

"Well? What did you think of her?"

"I think her manners perfect, and her dress and appearance above criticism."

"And was there — did you get on well together?"

"Your wife is a lady, Adrian, and I am a lady. Under such circumstances there is no room for unpleasantness of any kind. It is quite understood, though not expressed, that I shall not present myself at your house again, and that your wife's engagements will prevent her from returning my visit."

"Mother, are you serious?"

"Quite serious, Adrian. I have come here to ask you whether your wife merely carries out your wishes, or whether she prefers for herself not to cultivate acquaintances in your family."

"Pshaw! You must have taken some imaginary offence."

"Is that the most direct and sensible answer you can think of?"

"There is no lack of sense in the supposition that Aurélie, being a foreigner, may not understand the English etiquette for the occasion. You may have mistaken her. Even you are fallible, mother."

"I have already told you that your wife's manners are perfect. If you assume that my judgment is not to be relied on, there is no use in our talking to one another at all. What I wish to know is this. Admitting, for the sake of avoiding argument, that I am right in my view of the matter, did your wife behave as she did by your orders, or of her own free will?"

"Most certainly not by my orders," said Adrian, angrily. "I am not in the habit of giving her orders. If I were, they should not be of that nature. If Aurélie treated you with politeness, I do not see what more you had any right to expect. She admired you greatly when she first saw you; but I know she was hurt by your avoidance of her after our engagement became known, even when you were in the same room with her."

"She has not the least right to feel aggrieved on that account. It was your business to have introduced her to me as the lady you intended to marry."

"I did not feel encouraged to do so by what had passed between us on the subject," said Adrian, coldly.

"Well we need not go over that again. I merely wish to ask you whether you expect me to make any further concessions. You have lately acquired a habit of accusing me of various shortcomings in my duty to you; and I do not wish you to impute any estrangement between your wife and me to my neglect. I have called on her; and she did not ask me to call again. I endeavored to treat her as one of my family: she politely insisted on the most distant acquaintanceship. I asked her to call on me and she excused herself. Could I have done more?"

"I think you might, in the first instance."

"Can I do more now?"

"You can answer that yourself better than I can."

I fear so, since you seem unable to give me a straightforward or civil answer. However, if you have nothing to suggest, please let it be understood in future that I was perfectly willing to receive your wife, that I made the usual advances, and that they came to nothing through her action, not through mine.

"Very well, though I do not think the point will excite much interest in the world."

"Thank you, Adrian. I think T will go now. I hope you treat your wife in a more manly and considerate way than you have begun to treat me of late."

"She does not complain, mother. And I never intended to treat you inconsiderately. But you sometimes attack me in a fashion which paralyses my constant wish to conciliate you. I am sorry you have not succeeded better with Aurélie."

"So am I. I did not think she was long enough married to have lost the wish to please you. Perhaps, though, she thought she she would please you best by holding aloof from me."

"You are full of unjust suspicion. The fact is just the contrary. She knows that I have a horror of estrangements in families."

"Then she doesn't study very hard to please you."

Adrian reddened and was silent.

"And you? Are you still as infatuated I as you were last year?"

"Yes, " said Adrian defiantly, with his cheeks burning. "I love her more than ever. I am longing to be at home with her at this moment. When she goes away, I shall be miserable. Of all the lies invented by people who never felt love, the lie of marriage extinguishing love is the falsest, as it is the most worldly and cynical."

Mrs. Herbert looked at him in surprise and doubt. "You are an extraordinary boy," she said. "Why then do you not go with her to the Continent?"

"She does not wish me to," said Herbert shortly, averting his face, and pretending to resume his work.

"Indeed!" said Mrs. Herbert. "And you will not cross her, even in that?"

"She is quite right to wish me to stay here. I should only be wasting time; and I should be out of place at a string of concerts. I will stay behind — if I can."

"If you can?"

"Yes, mother, if I can. But I believe I shall rejoin her before she is absent a week. I may have been an indifferent son; and I know I am a bad husband; but I am the most infatuated lover in the world."

"Yet you say you are a bad husband!"

"Not to her. But I fall short in my duty to myself."

Mrs. Herbert laughed. "Do not let that trouble you," she said. "Time will cure you of that fault, if it exists anywhere but in your imagination. I never knew a man who failed in taking care of himself. Goodbye, Adrian."

"Goodbye, mother."

"What an ass I am to speak of my feelings to her!" he said to himself, when she was gone. "Well, well: at least if she does not understand them, she does not pretend to do so, she has not sympathy enough for that. She did not even ask to see my pictures. That would have hurt me once. At present I have exchanged the burden of disliking my mother the heavier one of loving my wife." He sighed, and resumed his work in spite of the fading light.

CHAPTER II

One moonlit night, in an empty street in Paris, a door suddenly opened; and three persons were thrust violently out with much scuffling and cursing. One of them was a woman, elegantly dressed, but flushed with drink and excitement. The others were a loose-jointed, large-boned, fair young Englishman of about eighteen or twenty, and a slim Frenchman with pointed black moustaches and a vicious expression. The Englishman, like the woman, was heated and intoxicated: his companion was angry, but had not lost his selfcontrol. The moment they passed the threshold, the door was slammed; and the younger man, without heeding the torrent of foul utterance to which the woman promptly betook herself, began kicking the panels furiously.

"Bah!" said the woman, recovering herself with a shrill laugh. "Come, Anatole." And she drew away her compatriot, who was watching the door-kicking process derisively.

"Hallo!" shouted the Englishman, hurrying after them. "Hallo, you! This lady stays with me, if you please. I should think that she has had about enough of you, you damned blackleg, since she has been pitched out of a gambling hell on your account. You had better clear out unless you want your neck broken — and if you were anything like a fair match for me, I'd break it as soon as look at you."

"What does he say, Nata " whispered the Frenchman, keeping his eye on the other as if he guessed his meaning.

The woman. with an insolent snap of her fingers, made a perfunctory translation of as much of the Englishman's words as she understood.

"Look, you, little one, said the Frenchman, advancing to within a certain distance of his adversary, "the night air is not right for you. I would counsel you to go home and put yourself to bed, lest I should have to give your nurse the trouble of carrying you thither."

"You advise me to go to bed, do you? I'll let you see all about that." retorted the young man, posing himself clumsily in attitude of an English pugilist, and breathing scorn at his opponent. Anatole instantly dealt him a kick beneath the nose which made him stagger. The pain of it was so intolerable that he raised his right hand to his mouth. The moment he thus uncovered his body, the Frenchman turned swiftly, and, looking back at his adversary over his shoulder, lashed out his toe with the vigor of a colt, and sent it into the pit of the young man's stomach, flinging him into the roadway, supine, gasping, and all but insensible.

"Ha!" said Anatole, panting after this double feat. "*Prrr'lotte!* So much for thy English boxer, Nata."

"*Cre'matin!* What a devil thou art, Anatole. Come, let us save ourselves."

A minute later the street was again as quiet, and, except for the motionless body on the roadway, solitary as before. Presently a vehicle entered from a side street. It was a close carriage like an English brougham, and contained one passenger, a lady with a white woolen shawl wrapped about her head, and an opera cloak over her rich dress. She was leaning back in a deep reverie when the horse stopped so suddenly that she was thrown forward; and the coachman uttered a warning cry. Recovering herself, she looked out of the window, and, saw, with a sickening sensation, a man stagger out on his hands and knees from between the horse's feet, and then roll over on his back with a long groaning sigh.

"My God!" exclaimed the lady, hastily opening the carriage door, and alighting. "Bring me one of the lamps. It is a young gentleman. Pray God he be not dead."

The coachman reluctantly descended from his box, and approached with a lamp. The lady looked at him impatiently, expecting him to lift the insensible stranger; but he only looked down dubiously at him, and kept aloof.

"Can you not rouse him, or help him to stand up?" she said indignantly.

"I am not such a fool as that," said the man. "Better not meddle with him. It is an affair for the police."

The lady pouted scornfully and stooped over the sufferer, who lifted his eyes feebly. Seeing her face, he opened his eyes widely and quickly, looking up at her with wonder, and raising his hand appealingly. She caught it without hesitation, and said anxiously:

"You are better now, monsieur, are you not? I hope you are not seriously hurt."

"Wha's matter?" said the young man indistinctly. "Are you hurt?" she repeated in English.

"Nor'at all," he replied, with drunken joviality.

Then he attempted to laugh, but immediately winced, and after a flew plunges, staggered to his feet. The coach man recoiled, but the lady did not move.

"Where is he," he continued, looking round. "Yah! You'll kick, will you? Come out, you coward. Come out and shew yourself. Yah! Kick, then run away and hide! I'll slog the kicking out of you. Will you face me with your fists like a man?" He uttered the last sentence with an accession of fury, and menaced the coachman, who retreated. The stranger struck at him, but the blow, reaching nothing, swung the striker round until he was face to face with the lady, whom he regarded with astonishment.

"I beg your par'n," he said, subsiding into humbleness. "I really beg your par'n. The fellow gave me a fearf' kick in the face, and I barely know where I am yet. 'Pon my soul," he added, with foolish glee, "it's the mos'extor'nary thing. Where has he gone?"

"Of whom do you speak" said the lady in French.

"Of — of — je parle d'polisson qui m'a donne un affreux coup de pied under the nose. J'ai un grand desir dénfoncer ce lâche maudit."

"Unhappily, monsieur, it was my horse that hurt you. I am in despair —"

"No, no. I tell you it was a fellow named Annatoal, a card sharper. If I ever catch him again, I'll teach him the English version of the *savate*. I'll kick him from one end of Paris to the other." As he spoke he reeled against the carriage, and, as the horse stirred uneasily, clutched at the door to save himself from falling.

"Madame," said the coachman, who had been looking anxiously for the approach of the police: "do you not see that this is a sot? Better leave him to himself."

"I am not drunk," said the young man earnestly "I have been drinking; but upon my solemn word I am not drunk. I have been attacked and knocked about the head; and I feel very queer. I can't remember how you came here exactly, though I remember your picking me up. I hope you won't leave me."

The lady, moved by his boyish appearance and the ingenious faith with which he made this appeal, was much perplexed, pitying, but not knowing what to do with him. "Where do you live?" she said. "I will drive you home with pleasure."

He became very red. "Thanks awfully," he said; "but the fact is, I don't live anywhere in particular. I must go to some hotel. You are very kind; but I won't trouble you any further. I am all right now." But he was evidently not all right; for after standing a moment away from the carriage, shamefacedly waiting for the lady to reply, he sat down hastily on the kerbstone, and added, after panting a little, "You must excuse me, Mrs Herbert. I can't stand very well yet. You had better leave me here: I shall pick myself up presently."

"Tiens, tiens, tiens! You seem to know me, monsieur. I, too, recollect your face, but not your name."

"Everybody knows you. You may have seen me at Mrs. Phipson's, in London. I've been there when you were there. But really you'd better drive on. This house is a gambling den; and the people may come out at any minute. Don't let your carriage be seen stopping here."

"But I hardly like to leave you here alone and hurt."

"Never mind me: it serves me right. Besides, I'd rather you'd leave me, I would indeed."

She turned reluctantly toward the carriage, put her foot on the step, and looked back. He was gazing wistfully after her. "But it is inhuman!" she exclaimed, returning. "Come, monsieur, I dare not leave you in such a condition: it is the fault of my horse. I will bring you where you shall be taken care of until you are restored."

"It's awfully good of you" he murmured, rising unsteadily and making his way to the carriage door, which he held whilst she got in. He followed, and was about to place himself bashfully on the front seat, when the coachman, illhumoredly using his whip, started the vehicle and upset him into the vacant space next Aurélie. He uttered an imprecation, and sat bolt upright for a moment. Then, sinking back against the cushion, and moving his hand until it touched her dress, he said drowsily, "It's really mos'awfully good of you," and fell asleep.

He was aroused by a shaking which made his head ache. An old and ugly woman held him by one shoulder, and the coachman, cursing him for a besotted pig, was about to drag him out by the other. He started up and got out of the carriage, the two roughly saving him from stumbling forward. In spite of his protests that he could walk alone they pulled him indoors between them. He struggled to free himself, but the woman was too strong for him: he was hauled ignominiously into a decent room, where sofa had been prepared for him with a couple of rugs and a woman's shawl. Here he was forced to lie down, and bidden to be quiet until the doctor came. The coachman, with a parting curse, then withdrew; and his voice, deferentially pitched, was audible as he reported what he had done to the lady without. There was another person speaking also; but she spoke in a tone of vehement remonstrance, and in a strange language.

"Look here, ma'am," said the young man from the sofa. "You needn't trouble sending for a doctor. There's nothing the matter with me."

"Silence, great sot," chattered the old woman."I have other things to do than to listen to thy gibberish. Lay thyself down this instant."

"Will I, by Jove!" he said, kicking off the rug and sitting up. "Can you buy soda water anywhere at this hour?"

"Ah, ingrate! Is it thus that thou obeyest the noble lady who succored thee. Fie!"

"What is the matter, madame," said Aurélie, entering.

"I was only asking her not to send for a doctor. I have no bones broken; and a doctor is no use. Please don't fetch one. If I could have a little plain water — or even soda water — to drink, I should be all right." Whilst he was speaking, an old lady appeared behind Aurélie. She seemed to suffer from a severe cold; for she had tied up her face in a red handkerchief, which gave her a grim aspect as she looked resentfully at him.

"I shall bring you some drink," said Aurélie quietly. "Mamma," she added, turning to the older lady; "pray return to your bed. Your face will be swollen again if you stand in the draught. I have but to get this young gentleman what he asks for."

"The young gentleman has no business here," said the lady. "You are imprudent, Aurélie, and frightfully self-willed." She then disappeared. The stranger reddened and attempted to rise; but Aurélie, also blushing, quieted him by a gesture, whilst the old woman shook her fist at him. Aurélie then left the room, promising to return, and leaving him alone with the woman, who seized the opportunity to recommence her reproaches, which were too voluble to be intelligible to the English ears of the patient.

"You may just as well hold your tongue," he said, as she paused at last for a reply, "for I don't understand a word you say."

"Say then, coquin," repeated the woman, "what wert thou doing in the roadway there when thou gotst beneath the horse's feet?"

"Je m'ètais évanoui."

"How? Ah, I understand, But why? What brought thee to such a pass?"

"N'importe. Cést pas convenable pour une juene femme d'entendre pareilles choses. That ought to fetch you if you can understand it.

"Ah, thou mockst me. Knowest thou, profligate, that thou art in my apartment, and that I have the right to throw you through the door if I please? Eh?"

"Votre discours se fait trés penible, ma mere. Voulez-vous avoir la bonté de shut up?"

"What does that mean?" said the woman, checked by the unknown verb.

'Oh, you are talking too much," said Aurélie, returning with some soda water. "You must not encourage him to speak, madame."

"He needs little encouragement," said the old woman. "You are far too good for him, mademoiselle."

"How do you feel now, monsieur? Better, I hope."

"Thanks very much: I feel quite happy. I have something to shew you. Just wait a —" Here he twisted himself round upon his elbow, and after some struggling with the rug and his coat, pulled from his breast pocket some old letters, which presently slipped from his hand and were scattered on the floor.

"Sot," cried the old woman, darting at them, and angrily pushing back the hand with which he was groping for them. "Here — put them up again. What has madame to do with thy letters, thinkst thou?"

"Don't you be in a hurry, Mrs. Jones," he retorted confidently, beginning to fumble at the letters. "Where the — I'll take my oath I had it this mor — oh, here it is. Did you ever see him before?" he asked triumphantly, handing a photograph to Aurélie.

"*Tiens!* it is Adrian," she exclaimed. "My husband," she added, to the old woman, who received the explanation sardonically. "Are you then a friend of Monsieur Herbert?"

"I have known him since I was a boy, " said the youth. Aurélie smiled: she thought him a boy still. "But this was only taken last week," she said. "I have only just received a copy for myself. Did he send it to you?"

"My sister sent it to me. I suppose you know who I am now."

"No, truly, monsieur. I have seen you certainly; but I cannot recall your name."

"You've seen me at Phipson's, talking to Mr. Jack. Can't you guess?"

Aurélie shook her head. The old woman, curious, but unable to follow a conversation carried on by one party in French and by the other in English, muttered impatiently, "What gibberish! It is a horror."

The youth looked shyly at Aurélie. "Then, as if struck by a new thought, he said, "My name is — Beatty."

Aurélie bowed. "Yes," she said, "I have assuredly heard my husband speak of that name. I am greatly troubled to think that your misfortune should have been brought about by my carriage. Madame: Monsieur Beatty will need a pillow. Will you do me the kindness to bring one from my room?"

Monsieur Beatty began to protest that he would prefer to remain as he was, but he was checked by a gesture from the woman, who silently pointed to a pillow which was on a chair.

"Ah, true. Thank you," said Aurélie, "Now, let me see. Yes, he had better have my little gong,in case he should become worse in the night, and need to summon help. It is on my table, I believe.

The old woman looked hard at Aurélie for a moment, and withdrew slowly.

"Now that that lady is gone," said the patient, blushing, "I want to tell you how grateful I am for the way you have helped me. If you knew what I felt when I opened my eyes as I lay there on the stones, and saw your face looking down at me, you would feel sure, without being told, that I am ready to do anything to prove my gratitude. I wish I could die for you. Not that that would be much; for my life is not worth a straw to me or anyone else. I am old enough to be tired of it."

"Young enough to be tired of it, you mean," said Aurélie, laughing, but pleased by his earnestness. "Well, I do not doubt that you are very grateful. How did you come under my carriage? Were you really knocked down; or did you only dream it?"

"I was really knocked down. I can't tell you how it came about. It served me right; for I was where I had no business to be — in bad company."

"Ah," said Aurélie gravely, approaching him with the pillow. "You must not do so any more, if we are to remain friends."

"I will never do so again, so help me God!" he protested. "You have cured me of all taste for that sort of thing."

"Raise yourself for one moment — so," said Aurélie, stooping over him and placing the pillow beneath his head. His color rose as he looked up at her. Then, as she was in the act of withdrawing, he uttered, a stifled exclamation; threw his arm about her; and pressing his lips to her cheek, was about to kiss her, when he fell back with a sharp groan, and lay bathed in perspiration, and flinching from the pain of his wounded face. Aurélie, astonished and outraged, stood erect and regarded him indignantly.

"Ah," she said. "That was an unworthy act. You, whom I have succored — my husband's friend! My God, is it possible that an English gentleman can be so base!"

"Curse the fellow!" cried the young man, writhing and shedding tears of pain. "Give me something to stop this agony — some chloroform or something. Send for a doctor. I shall go mad. Oh, Lord !"

"You deserve it well," said Aurélie, "Come, monsieur, control yourself. This is childish." As he subsided, exhausted, and only fetching a deep sigh at intervals, she relented and called the old woman who seemed to have been waiting outside for she came at once.

"He has hurt his wound," said Aurélie in an undertone. "What can we do for him?"

The woman shrugged herself, and had nothing to suggest. "Let him make the best of it," she said, "I can do nothing for him."

They stood by the sofa and watched him for some time in silence. At last he opened his eyes, and began to appear more at ease.

"Would you like to drink something?" said Aurélie coldly.

"Yes."

"Give him some soda water," she said to the old woman.

"Never mind," he said, speaking indistinctly in his effort to avoid stirring his upper lip. "I don't want anything. The cartilage of my nose is frightfully tender, but the pain is going off."

"It is now very late, and I must retire, monsieur. Can we do anything further to ensure your comfort?"

"Nothing, thank you." Aurélie turned to go.

"Mrs, Herbert." She paused. "I suppose no one could behave worse than I have. Never mind my speaking before the old lady: she doesn't understand me. I wish you would forgive me. I have been severely punished. You cannot even imagine the torture I have undergone in the last ten minutes."

"If you regret your conduct as you ought," began Aurélie severely.

"I am ashamed of it and of myself; and I will try hard to be sorry — in fact, I am very sorry I was disappointed. I should be more than mortal if I felt otherwise. But I will never do such a thing again."

"Adieu, monsieur," said Aurélie coldly. "I shall not see you again, as you will be gone before I am abroad tomorrow." And she left the room with a gravity that quelled him.

"What hast thou been doing now, rogue?" said the old woman, preparing to follow Aurélie. "What is it thou shouldst regret?"

By way of reply, he leered at her, and stretched out his arms invitingly.

"Thou shalt go out from my house tomorrow," she said threateningly; and went out, taking the lamp with her. He laughed, and composed himself for sleep. But he was thirsty and restless, and his face began to pain him continuously. The moon was still shining; and by its light he rose and prowled about softly in his stockings, prying into drawers and chiffoniers, and bringing portable objects to the window, where he could see them better.

When he had examined everything, he sparred at the mantelpiece, and imagined himself taking vengeance on Anatole. At last, having finished the soda water, he lay down again, and slept uneasily until six o'clock, when he rose and looked at himself in a mirror. His hair was disheveled and dusty; his lip discolored; his eyes were inflamed; but the thought of rubbing his soiled face with a towel, or even touching it with water made him wince. Seeing that he was unpresentable, and being sober enough to judge his last nights conduct, he resolved to make off before any of the household were astir. Accordingly, he made himself as clean as he could without hurting himself. From his vest pockets, which contained fourteen francs, an English half-crown, a latchkey. a lead pencil, and a return ticket to Charing Cross, he took ten francs and left them on the table with a scrap of paper inscribed *Pour la belle propriétaire* — Hommage du misérable Anglais." Then, on another scrap, which he directed to Aurélie, as follows:

"I hope you will forgive me for behaving like an unmitigated cad last night, As I was not sober and had had my sense almost knocked out of me by a foul blow, I was hardly accountable for what I was doing. I can never repay your kindness nor expiate my own ingratitude; but please do not say anything about me to Mr Herbert, as you would get me into no end of trouble by doing so. I am running away early early because I should be ashamed to look you in the face now that I have recovered my senses — Yours, most gratefully —"

He "took several minutes to consider how he should sign this note. Eventually he put down the initial C only. After draining the soda-water bottle of the few flat and sickly drops he had left in it the night before, he left the room and crept downstairs, where he succeeded in letting himself out without alarming the household. The empty street looked white and spacious in the morning sun; and the young man — first looking round to see that no one was at hand to misinterpret his movements — took to his heels and ran until he turned a corner and saw a policeman, who seemed half disposed to arrest him on suspicion. Escaping this danger, he went on until he found a small eating house where some workmen were breakfasting. Here he procured a cheap but plentiful meal,and was directed to the railway station, whither he immediately hastened. A train had just arrived as he entered. As he stood for a moment to watch the passengers coming out, a hand was laid gently on his arm. He turned, and confronted Adrian Herbert, who looked at him with a quiet smile.

"Well, Charlie," he said: "so this is Hounslow, is it? What particular branch of engineering are you studying here?"

"Who told you I was at Hounslow?" said Charlie, with a grin.

"Your father, whom I met yesterday at Mrs. Hoskyn's. He told me that you were working very hard at engineering with a tutor. I am sorry to see that your exertions have quite knocked you up."

"On the contrary, somebody else's exertions have knocked me down. No, I ran over here a few days ago for a little change. Of course I didn't mention it to the governor: he thinks Paris a sink of iniquity. You needn't mention it to him either, unless you like."

"I hope I am too discreet for that. Did you know that Mrs. Herbert is in Paris?"

"Is she? No, I didn't know it: I thought she was with you in Kensington. I hope you will have a good time here. "

"Thank you. How long do you intend to stay?"

"Oh, I am going back directly. If I don't get a train soon, I shall starve; for I have only two or three francs left to keep me in sandwiches during the voyage."

"Draw on me if you are inconvenienced."

Thanks," said Carlie, coloring. "but I can get on well enough with what I have — at least if you could spare me I if you could spare me five franks — Thanks awfully. I have run a rig rather this time; for I owe Mary five pounds already on the strength of this trip. It is a mistake coming to Paris. I wish I had stayed at home."

"Well, at least you have had some experience for your money. What has happened to your lip? Is it a bruise?"

"Yes, I got a toss. It's nothing. I'm awfully obliged for —"

"Not at all. Have you breakfasted yet? What, already! You are an early bird. I was thinking of asking you to breakfast with me. I do not wish to disturb my wife too early, and so will have to kill some time for a while. By the by, have you ever been introduced to her?

"No," "said Charlie hastily; but nothing would induce to me to face her in this trim. I know I look a perfect blackguard. I can't wash my face; and I have a blue and and green spot right here" — touching the hollow of his chest — "which would make me screech if anyone rubbed me with a brush. In fact I shall take it as a particular favor if you wont mention to her that you have met me. Not that it matters much, of course; but still —"

"Very well, I shall not breathe a word of it to anyone. Goodbye.*'

Charlie shook his hand; and they parted. "Now," thought Charlie, looking after him with a grin, and jingling the borrowed money in his pocket, "if his wife will only hold her tongue, I shall be all right. I wish she was my wife." And heaving a sigh, he walked slowly away to inquire about the trains.

Herbert breakfasted alone. When his appetite was appeased, he sat trying to read, and looking repeatedly at his watch. He had resolved not to seek his wife until ten o'clock; but he had miscalculated his patience; and he soon convinced himself that half past nine, or even nine, would be more convenient. Eventually he arrived at ten minutes to nine, and found Madame Szczympliça alone at table in an old crimson bed gown, with her hair as her pillow had left it.

"Monsieur Adrian!" she exclaimed, much discomposed. "Ah, you take us by surprise. I had but just stepped in to make coffee for the little one. She will be enchanted to see you. And I also."

"Do not let me disturb you. I have breakfasted already. Is Aurélie up?"

"She will be here immediately. How delighted she will be! Are you quite well?"

Not badly, madame. And you?" I have suffered frightfully with my face. Last night I was unable to go to the concert with Aurélie. It is a great misfortune for me, this neuralgia."

"I am very sorry. It is indeed a terrible affliction. Are you quite sure that Aurélie is not fast asleep?"

"I have made her coffee, mon cher; and I know her too well to do that before she is afoot. Trust me, she will be here in a moment. I hope it is nothing wrong that has brought you to Paris."

"Oh no. I wanted a little change; and when you came so near, I determined to run over and meet you. You have been all round Europe since I last saw you."

"Ah, what successes, Monsieur Adrian! You cannot figure to yourself how she was received at Budapesth. And at Leipzig too! It was — behold her!"

Aurélie stopped on the threshold and regarded Adrian with successive expressions of surprise, protest and resignation. He advanced and kissed her cheek gently, longing to clasp her in his arms, but restrained by the presence of her mother. Aurélie paused on her way to the table just long enough to suffer this greeting, and then sat down, exclaiming:

"I knew it! I knew it from that last letter! Oh thou silly one! Could not Mrs. Hoskyn console thee for yet another week?"

"How Indifferent she is," said Madame Sczympliça. "She is glad at heart to see you, Mr. Adrian." Now, this interference of his motherin law, though made with amiable intention, irritated Herbert. He smiled politely, and turned a little away from her and towards Aurélie".

"And SO you have had nothing but triumphs since we parted," he said, looking fondly at her.

"What do you know of my triumphs!" she said, raising her head. "You only care for the tunes that one whistles in the streets' At Prague I turned the world upside down with Monsieur Jacques fantasia. How long do you intend to stay here'"

"Until you can return with me, of course."

"A whole week. You will be tired of your life, unless you go to the Louvre or some such stupidity, and paint."

"I shall be content, Aurélie, never fear. Perhaps you will grow a little tired of me."

"Oh no, I shall be too busy for that. I have to practise, and to attend rehearsals, and concerts, and private engagements. Oh, I shall not have time to think of you."

"Private engagements. Do you mean playing at private houses?"

"Yes. This afternoon I play at the reception of the Princess — what is she called, mamma?"

"It does not matter what she is called," said Herbert. "Surely you are not paid for playing on such occasions?"

"What! You do not suppose that I play for nothing for people whom I do not know — whose very names I forget. No, I play willingly for my friends, or for the poor; but if the great world wishes to hear me, it must pay. Why do you look so shocked? Would you, then, decorate the saloon of the Princess with pictures for nothing, if she asked you?"

"It is not exactly the same thing — at least the world does not think so, Aurélie. I do not like the thought of you going into society as a hired entertainer."

Aurélie shrugged herself. "I must go for some reason," she said. "If they did not pay me I should not go at all. It is an artist's business to do such things."

"My dear Mr. Adrian," said Madame Szczympliça, "she is always the most honored guest. The most distinguished persons crowd about her; and the most beautiful women are deserted for her. It is always a veritable little court that she holds."

"It is as I thought," said Aurélie. "You came across the Channel only to quarrel with me." Herbert attempted to protest; but she went on without heeding him. "Mamma: have you finished your breakfast?"

"Yes, my child."

"Then go; and put off that terrible robe of thine. Leave us to ourselves: if we must quarrel, there is no reason why you should be distressed by our bickerings"

"I hope you are not really running away from me," said Herbert, politely accompanying Madame Sczympliça to the door, and opening it for her.

"No, no, *mon cher*," she replied with a Sigh. "I must do as I am bidden. I grow old; and she becomes a greater tyrant daily to all about her."

"Now, malcontent," said Aurélie, when the door was closed, "proceed with thy reproaches. How many thousand things hast thou to complain of? Let us hear how sad it has made thee to think that I have been happy and successful, and that thou hast not once been able to cast my happiness back in my — Heaven wouldst th eat me, Adrian?" He was straining her to his breast and kissing her vehemently.

"You are rightt," he said breathlessly. "Love is altogether selfish. Every fresh account of your triumphs only redoubled my longing to have you back with me again. You do not know what I Buffered during all these weary weeks. I lived in my studio, and tried to paint you out of my head; but I could not paint your out of my heart. My work, which once seemed a wifer thing than my mind could contain, was only a wearisome trade to me. I rehearsed imaginary versions of our next meeting" for hours together, whilst my picture hung forgotten before me. I made a hundred sketches of you, and, in my rage at their badness, destroyed them as fast as I made them. In the evenings, I either wandered about the streets thinking of you"

"Or went to see Mrs. Hoskyn?"

"Who told you that?" said Herbert, discomfited.

"Ah!" cried Aurélie, laughing â€" almost crowing with delight, "I guessed it. Oh, that poor Monsieur Hoskyn! And me also! Is this thy fidelity — this the end of all thy thoughts of me?"

"I wish your jealousy were real," said Herbert, with a sort of desperation. "I believe you would not care if I had gone to Mrs. Hoskyn as her lover. Why did I go to her? Simply because she was the only friend I had who would listen patiently whilst I spoke endlessly of you — she, whose esteem I risked, and whose respect I fear I lost, for your sake. But I have ceased to respect myself now, Aurélie. It is my misfortune to love you so much that you make light of me for being so infatuated."

"Well," said Aurélie soothingly, "you must try and not love me so much. I will help you as much as I can by making myself very disagreeable. I am far too indulgent to you, Adrian."

"You hurt me sometimes very keenly, Aurélie, though you do not intend it. But I have never loved you less for that. I fear your plan would make me worse."

"Ah, I see. You want to be made love to, and cured in that way."

"I am afraid I should go mad then, Aurélie."

"I will not try. I think you are very injudicious to care so much for love. To me, it is the most stupid thing in the world. I prefer music. No matter, my cherished one: I am very fond of thee, in spite of thy follies. Art thou not my husband? Now I must make an end here, and go to practise."

"Never mind practising this morning, Aurdlie. Let us talk."

"Why, have we not already talked? No, when I miss my little half hour of seeking for my fine touch, I play as all the world; and that is not just to myself, or to the Princess, who pays me more than she pays the others. One must be honest, Adrian. There, your face is clouded again. You are ashamed of me."

"It is because I am so proud of you that I shrink from the thought of your talent being marketed. Let us change the subject. Have you met any of our friends in Paris?"

"Not one. I have not heard an English voice since we came here. But I must not stop to gossip." She took his hand, pressed it for an instant against her bosom; and left the room. Herbert, troubled by the effort to enjoy fully the delight this caress gave him, sat down for a moment, panting. When he was calmer, he took his hat and went downstairs, intending to take a stroll in the sunshine. he was arrested at the door of one of the lower rooms by the porter's wife, who held in her shaking hand some money and a scrap of paper, the sight of which seemed to frenzy her; for she was railing volubly at some person unknown to Adrian. lie looked at her with some curiosity, and was about to pass on, when she stepped before him.

"Look you, monsieur," she said. "Be so good as to tell madame that my house is not a hospital for sots. And tell your friend, he whose nose someone has righteously crushed, that he had better take good care not to come to see me again. I will make him a bad quarter of an hour if he does."

"My friend, madame!" said Herbert, alarmed by her shrewishness.

"Your wife's friend, then, whom she brings home drunk in her carriage at midnight, and who kicks my sofa to pieces, and makes shameless advances to me beneath my husband's roof, and flies like a thief in the night, leaving for me this insult." And she held out the scrap of paper to Adrian. "With ten francs. What is ten francs to me!" Adrian, bewildered, looked unintelligently at the message. "Come you, monsieur, and see for yourself that I speak truly," she continued, bringing him by a gesture into the room. "See there, my sofa ripped up and soiled with his heels. See madame's fine rug trampled on the floor. See the pillow which she put under his wicked head with her own hands —"

"What are you talking about?" said Adrian sternly. "For whom do you take me?"

"Are you not Monsieur Herbert?"

"Yes."

"Yes, I should think so. Well, Monsieur Herbert, it is your dear friend, who carries your portrait next his heart, who has treated me thus."

"Really," said Adrian, "I do not understand you. You speak of me — of my wife — of some friend of mine with my portrait —"

"And the nose of him crushed."

" — all in a breath. What do you mean? As you know, I only arrived here this morning."

"Truly, monsieur, you have arrived a day after the fair. All I tell y<>u is that madame came home last night with a drunken robber, a young English sprig, who slept here. He has run away; and heaven knows what he has taken with him. He leaves me this money, and this note to mock me because I scorned his vile seductions. Behold the table where he left it."

Adrian, hardly venturing to understand the woman, looked upon the table, and saw a note which had escaped her attention. She, following his glance, exclaimed:

"What! Another."

"It is addressed to my wife," said Adrian, taking it, and losing color as he did so. "Doubtless it contains an explanation of his conduct. I recognize the handwriting as that of a young friend of mine. Did you hear his name?"

"It was an English name. English names are all alike to me."

"Did he call himself Sutherland?"

"Yes, it was like that, quite English."

"It is all right then. He is but a foolish boy, the brother of an old friend of mine."

"Truly a strong boy for his years. He is your old friend, of course. It is always so. Ah, monsieur, if I were one to talk and make mischief, I could —"

"Thank you," said Adrian, interrupting her firmly. "I can hear the rest from Madame Herbert, if there is anything else to hear." And he left the room. On the landing without, he saw Madame Sczympliça, who, overlooking him, addressed herelf angrily to the old woman.

"Why is this noise made?" she demanded. "How is it possible for Mademoiselle to practise with this hurly-burly in her ears?"

"And why should I not make a noise," retorted the woman, "when I am insulted in my own house by the friends of Mademoiselle?"

"What is the matter?" cried a voice from above. The woman became silent as if struck dumb; and for a moment there was no sound except the light descending footfall of Aurélie. "What is the matter?" she repeated, as she came into their view.

"Nothing at all," muttered the old woman sulkily, glancing apprehensively at Adrian.

"You make a very great noise about nothing at all," said Aurélie coolly, pausing with her hand on the balustrade. "Have you quite done; and may I now practise in peace?"

"I am sorry to have disturbed you," said the woman apologetically, but still grumbling. "I was speaking to Monsieur."

"Monsieur must either go out, or come upstairs and read the journals quietly," said Aurélie.

"I will come upstairs," said Adrian, in a tone that made her look at him with momentary curiosity. The old woman meanwhile retreated into her apartment; and Madame Sczympliça, who had listened submissively to her daughter, disappeared also. Aurélie, on returning to the room in which she practised, found herself once more alone with Adrian.

"Oh, it is a troublesome woman," she said. "All proprietresses are so. I should like to live in a palace with silent black slaves to come and go when I clap my hands. She has spoiled my practice. And you seem quite put out."

"I — Aurélie: I met Mrs. Hoskyn's brother at the railway station this morning."

"Really! I thought he was in India."

"I mean her younger brother."

"Ah, I did not know that she had another."

Herbert Looked aghast at her. She had spoken carelessly, and was brushing some specks of dust from the keyboard of the pianoforte, as to the cleanliness of which she was always fastidious.

"He did not tell me that he had seen you, Aurélie," he said, controlling himself. "Under the circumstances I thought that rather strange. He even affected surprise when I mentioned that you were in Paris."

She forgot the keyboard, and looked at him with wonder and some amusement "You thought it very Strange!" she said. "What are you dreaming of? What else should he say, since he never saw me, nor I him, in our lives — except at a concert? Have I not said that I did not know of his existence until you told me?"

"Aurélie he exclaimed in a strange voice, turning pallid. She also changed color; came to him quickly; and caught his arm, saying, "Heaven! What is the matter with thee?"

"Aurélie," he said, recovering his selfcontrol, and disengaging himself quietly from her hold; "pray be serious. Why should you, even in jest, deceive me about Sutherland? If he has done anything wrong, I will not blame you for it."

She retreated a step, and slowly raised her head and slowly raised her head in a haughtier attitude. "You speak of deceit!" she said. Then, shaking her finger at him, she added indignantly, "Ah, take care, Adrian, take care."

"Do you mean to tell me," he said sternly, "that you have not made the acquaintance of Sutherland here?"

"I do tell you so. And it seems to me that you do not believe me."

"And that he has not passed the night here."

"Oh!" she cried, and shrank a little.

"Aurélie," he said, with a menacing expression which so disfigured and debased his face that she involuntarily recoiled and covered her eyes with her hands: "I have never before opened a letter addressed to you; but I will do so now. There are occasions when confidence is mere infatuation; and it is time, I fear, to shew you that my infatuation is not so blind as you suppose. This note was left for you this morning, under circumstances which have been explained to me by the woman downstairs." A silence followed whilst he opened the note and read it. Then, looking up, and finding her looking at him quite calmly, he said sadly, "There is nothing in it that you need be ashamed of, Aurélie. You might have told me the truth. It is in the handwriting of Charlie Sutherland."

This startled her for a moment. "Ah," she said, "the scamp gave me a false name. But as for thee, unhappy one," she added, as a ray of hope appeared in Herbert's eyes, "adieu *for ever* ." And she was gone before he recovered himself.

His first impulse was to follow her and apologize, so simply and completely did her exclamation that Sutherland had given her a false name seem to explain her denial of having met him. Then he asked himself how came she to bring home a young man in her carriage; and why had she made a secret of it? She had said, he now remembered, that she had not heard any English voice except his own since she had come to Paris. Herbert was constitutionally apt to feel at a disadvantage with other men, and to give credit to the least sign that they were preferred to himself. He did not even now accuse his wife of infidelity; but he had long felt that she misunderstood him, withheld her confidence from him, and kept him apart from those friends of hers in whose society she felt happy and unrestrained. In the thought of this there was for him there was more jealousy and mortification than a coarser man might have suffered from a wicked woman. Whilst he was thinking over it all, the door opened and Madame Sczympliça, in tears, entered hastily.

"My God, Monsieur Adrian, what is the matter betwixt you and Aurélie?"

"Nothing at all,' said Herbert, with constrained politeness. "Nothing of any consequence."

"Do not tell me that," she protested pathetically. "I know her too well to believe it. She is going away and she will not tell me why. And now you will not tell me either. I am made nothing of."

"Did you say she is going away?*

"Yes. What have you done to her? — my poor child!"

Herbert did not feel bound to account for his conduct to his motherin-law: yet he felt that she was entitled to some answer. "Madame Sczympliça, " he said, after a moment's reflexion: "can you tell me under what circumstances Aurélie met the young gentleman who was here last night?"

"That is it, is it? I knew it: I told Aurélie that she was acting foolishly. But there was nothing in that to quarrel about."

"I do not say there was. How did it happen?"

"Nothing in the world but this. I had neuralgia; and Aurélie would not suffer me to accompany her to the concert. As she was returning, her carriage knocked down this miserable boy, who was drunk. You know how impetuous she is. She would not leave him there insensible; and she took him into the carriage and brought him here. She made the woman below harbor him for the night in her sitting room. That is all."

"But did he not behave himself badly?"

"Mon cher, he was drunk — drunk as a beast, with his nose beaten in."

"It is strange that Aurélie never told me of such a remarkable incident."

"Why, you are not an hour arrived; and the poor child has been full of the joy and surprise of seeing you so unexpectedly. It is necessary to be reasonable, Monsieur Adrian."

"The fact is, madame, that I have had a misunderstanding with Aurélie in which neither of us was to blame. I should not have doubted her, perhaps; but I think, under the circumstances, my mistake was excusable. I owe her an apology, and will make it at once."

Wait a little, " said Madame Szczympliça nervously, as he moved towards the door. "You had better let me go first: I will ask her to receive you. She is excessively annoyed."

Herbert did not like this suggestion; but he submitted to it, and sat down at the pianoforte to await Madame Sczympliça's return. To while away the time and and to persuade himself that he was not too fearful of the result of her mission he played softly as much of his favorite Mendelssohnian airs as conld be accompanied by the three chords which exhausted his knowledge of the art of harmonizing. At last, after a long absence, bis motherin-law returned, evidently much troubled.

"I am a most unlucky mother," she said, seating herself, and trying to keep back her tears. "She will not listen to me. Oh, Monsieur Adrien, what can have passed between you to enrage her so? You, who are always so gentle! — she will not let me mention your name."

"But have you explained to her — ?"

"What is the use of explaining? She is not rational."

"What does she say?"

"She says absurd things. Recollect that she is as yet only a child. She says you have betrayed your real opinion of her at last. I told her that circumstances seemed at the time to prove that she had acted foolishly, but that you now admitted your error."

"And then —"

"Then she said that her maid might have doubted her, and afterwards admitted her error on the same ground. Oh, she is a strange creature, is Aurélie. What can one do with such a terrible child? She is positive that she will never speak to you again; and I fear she is in earnest. I can do no more. I have argued — implored — wept; but she is an ingrate, a heart of marble."

Here there was a tap at the door; and a servant appeared.

"Madame Herbert wishes you to accompany her to the pianoforte place, madame. She is going thither to practise."

Herbert only looked downcast; and Madame Szczympliça left the room stifling a sob. Herbert knew not what to do. A domestic quarrel involving the interference of a motherin-law had always seemed to him an incident common among vulgar people, but quite foreign to his own course of life; and now that it had actually occurred to him, he felt humiliated. He found a little relief as the conviction grew upon him that he, and not Aurélie, was to blame. There was nothing new to him in the reflexion that he had been weak and hasty: there would be pleasure in making reparation, in begging her forgiveness, in believing in and loving her more than ever. But this would be on condition that she ultimately forgave him, of which he did not feel at all sure, as indeed he never felt sure of her on any point, not even that she had really loved him.

In this state of mind he saw her carriage arrive, and heard her descend the stairs and pass the door of the room where he was. Whilst he was hesitating as to whether he should go out and speak to her then, she drove away; and the opportunity, now that it was lost, seemed a precious one. He went downstairs, and asked the old woman when she expected Madame Herbert to return. Not until six o'clock, she told him. he resigned himself to eight hours' suspense, and went to the Luxembourg, where he enjoyed such pleasure as he could obtain by admiring the works of men who could paint better than he. It was a long day; but it came to an end at last.

"I will announce you, monsieur," said the old woman hastily, as she admitted him at half-past six.

"No," he said firmly, resolved not to give Aurélie an opportunity of escaping from him. "I will announce myself." And he passed the portress, who seemed disposed, but afraid, to bar his path. As he went up, he heard the pianoforte played in a style which he hardly recognized. The touch was hard and impatient; and false notes were struck, followed by almost violent repetitions of the passage in which they occurred. He stood at the door a moment, listening.

"My child," said Madame Sczympliça's voice: "that is not practice. You become worse every moment: and you are spoiling the instrument."

"Let me alone. It is a detestable piano; and I hope I may break it."

Herbert's courage sank at the angry tone of his wife's voice.

"You let yourself be put out by nothing at all. Do I not tell you that everybody thought you played like an angel?"

"I will not be told so again. I played vilely. I will give up music. I hate it: and I never shall be able to play. I have tried and failed. It was a mistake for me ever to have attempted it."

At this moment Adrian, hearing the footsteps of the old woman, who was coming up to listen at the keyhole, entered the room. Madame Sczympliça stared at him in consternation. He walked quickly across the room, and sat down close to his wife at the pianoforte.

"Aurélie," he said: "you must forgive me."

"Never, never, never," she cried, turning quickly round so as to confront him. "I have this day disgraced myself: and it is your fault."

"My fault, Aurélie?"

"Do not call me Aurélie. Now you smile because you have had your revenge. Am I not unhappy enough without being forced to see and speak to you, who have made me unhappy? Go: disembarrass me, or I will myself seek some other roof. What madness possessed me, an artist, to marry? Did I not know that it is ever the end of an artist's career?"

"You cannot believe, " he said, much agitated, "that I would wilfully cause you a moment's pain. I love —"

"Ah, yes, you love me. It is because you love me that you insult me. It is because you love me that you are ashamed of me and reproach me with playing for hire. It is because you love me that I have failed before the whole world, and lost the fruit of long years of work. You will find my mother's scissors in that box. Why do you not cut off my fingers, since you have paralysed them?"

Adrian, shuddering in every fibre at the suggestion, caught her proffered fingers and squeezed them in his hands. "My darling," he said: "you pain me acutely by your reproaches. Will you not forgive me?"

"You waste your breath," she said obdurately, disengaging herself petulantly. "I am not listening to you." And she began to play again.

"Aurélie," he said presently.

She played attentively, and did not seem to hear him.

"Aurélie," he repeated urgently. No answer. "Do cease that horrible thing, my darling, and listen to me."

This stopped her. She turned with tears in her eyes, and exclaimed, "Yes, it is horrible. Everything that I touch is horrible now." She shut the piano as she spoke. "I will never open it more. Mamma."

"My angel," replied Madame Sczympliça, starting.

"Tell them to send for it tomorrow. I do not want even to see it when I come down in the morning."

"But," said Herbert, "you quite misunderstand me. Can you suppose that I think your playing horrible, or that, if I thought it, I would be so brutal as to say so.

"You do think it horrible. Everyone finds it horrible. So you are right."

"It was only what you were playing"

"I was one of Chopin's studies. You used to like Chopin. You would do better to be silent: every word you utter betrays your real thoughts."

Herbert gently reopened the pianoforte. "If it were the singing of angels, Aurélie, it would be horrible to me as long as it delayed the assurance I am waiting for — of your forgiveness."

"You shall never have it. Nor do I believe that you care for it."

"Never is a long word. You have said it very often this evening, Aurélie. You will never play again. You will never speak to me again. You will never forgive me."

"Do not argue with me. You fatigue me." She turned away, and began to improvise, looking upward at the cornice with a determined expression which gradually faded and vanished. Herbert, discouraged by her last retort, did not venture to interrupt her until the last trace of displeasure had disappeared from her face. Then he pleaded in a low voice. "Aurélie." The frown reappeared instantly. "Do not stop playing. I only wish to assure you that I was not jealous this morning."

"O — h!" she ejaculated, taking her hands from the keyboard, and letting them fall supine in her lap. Herbert, taken aback by the prolonged and expressive interjection, looked at her in silent discomfiture. "Mamma: thou hearest him! He says he was not jealous. Oh, Adrian, how art thou fallen, thou, who wast truth itself! Thou art learning to play the husband well."

"I thought you had deceived me, dearest; but I was not jealous."

"Then you do not love me."

"Let me explain. I thought you had deceived me in your account of — of that wretched boy whom we shall never allude to again —"

"There, there. Do not remind me of it. You were base: you were beneath yourself: no explanation can change that. But my failure at the Princess's is so much greater a misfortune that it has put all that out of my head."

"Aurélie," remonstrated Herbert involuntarily.

"What! you begin to complain already — before I have half relented?"

"I know too well," he replied sadly, "that your art is as much dearer to you than I, as you are dearer to me than mine. Well, well, I plead guilty to everything except want of love for you. Now will you forgive me?"

Instead of replying she began to play merrily. Presently she looked over her shoulder, and said, "You will promise never to commit such a sin again."

"I swear it."

"And you are very sorry?"

"I am desolate, Aurélie."

"Be pardoned, then. If thou art truly penitent, I will accompany thee to the Louvre; and thou shalt shew me the pictures."

She played away without intermission whilst she spoke, disregarding the kiss which he, in spite of Madame Sczympliça's presence, could not refrain from pressing on her cheek.

CHAPTER III

When the novelty of Mrs. Hoskyn's first baby had worn off, she successfully resisted the temptation to abandon it to the care of her servants, as an exacting little nuisance; but her incorrigible interest in art, no longer totally eclipsed by the cradle, retook possession of her mind. This interest, as usual, took the form of curiosity as to what Adrian Herbert was doing. Now that her domestic affections were satisfied and centred by Hoskyn, and that the complete absorption of Herbert's affections by his wife was beyond all suspicion, she felt easier and more earnest in her friendship for him than ever before. Marriage had indeed considerably deepened her capacity for friendship.

One morning, Hoskyn looked up from his paper and said, "Have you looked at the Times. There is something in it about Herbert that he won't like."

"I hope not. The Times always spoke well of him."

Hoskyn, without a word, handed her the sheet he had been reading and took up another.

"Oh John," said Mary, putting down the paper in dismay; "what is to be done?"

"Done! What about?"

"About Adrian."

"I don't know," said Hoskyn, placably. "Why should we do anything?"

"I for one, shall be very sorry if he loses his position, after all his early struggling."

"He won't lose it. Who cares about the Times?"

"But I am greatly afraid that the Times is right."

"If you think so, why, that's another thing. In that case, Herbert had better work a little harder."

"Yes; but he always used to work so hard."

"Well, he must keep at it, you know."

Mary fell amusing; and Hoskyn went on reading.

"Adrian should never have married," she said presently.

"Why not, my dear?"

"Because of that," she replied, pointing to the paper.

"They don't find fault with him for being a married man, though."

"They find fault with him for being what his marriage has made him. He neither thinks nor cares about anything but his wife."

"That needn't prevent his working," said Hoskyn. "*I* contrive to do a goodish deal of work," he added with an amorous glance, "without caring any the less for my wife."

"Your wife does not run away from you to the other end of Europe at a moment's notice, John. She does not laugh at your business and treat you as if you were a little boy who sometimes gets troublesome."

"Still," said Hoskyn reflectively, "she has a sort of fascination about her."

"Nonsense," said Mary, supposing that her husband had been paying her a compliment, whereas he had really referred to Aurel "I feel very much in earnest about this. It is quite pitiable to see a man like Adrian become the slave of a woman who obviously docs not care for him — or perhaps I should not say that; but she certainly does not care for him as he deserves to be cared for. I am beginning to think that she cares for nothing but money."

"Oh, come!" remonstrated Hoskyn. "You're too hard on her, Mary. She certainly doesn't seem to concern herself much about Herbert: but then I fancy that he is rather a milk-and-water sort of man. I know he is a very good fellow, and all that; but there is a something wanting in him — not exactly stamina, but — but something or other."

"There is a great want of worldliness and indifference in him; and I hope there always will be, although a little of both would help him to bring his wife to her senses. Still, Adrian is weak."

"I should think so. For my part," said Hoskyn, scratching his beard, and glancing at his wife as if he were going to make a venturesome remark, "I wonder how any woman could be bothered with him! I may be prejudiced: but that's my opinion."

"Oh, that is absurd," said Mary. "She may consider herself very fortunate in getting so good a man. He is too good for her: that is where the real difficulty lies. He is neglecting himself on her account. Do you think I ought to speak to him seriously about it?"

"Humph!" muttered Hoskyn cautiously. "It's generally rather unwise to mix oneself up with other people's affairs, particularly family affairs. You don't as a rule get thanked for it."

"I know that. But is it right to hold aloof when one might do some good by disregarding considerations of that sort? It is always safest to do nothing. But I doubt if it is generous."

"Well, you can do as you like. If I were in your place, I wouldn't meddle."

"You are running away with an idea that I am going to make mischief, and talk to Adrian about his wife. I only want to give him a little lecture, such as I have given him twenty times before. I am in some sort his fellow student. Don't you think I might venture? I cannot see how I can do any harm by speaking to him about what the Times says."

Hoskyn pursed his lips, and shook his head. Mary, who had made up her mind to exhort Adrian, and wanted to be advised to do so, added, with some vexation, "Of course I will not go if you do not wish me to."

"I! Oh Lord no, my dear: I don't want to interfere with you. Go by all means if you like."

"Very well, John. I think I had better." As she said this as if she were about to go in deference to his wishes, he seemed inclined to remonstrate; but he thought better of it, and buried himself in the newspaper until it was time for him to go to the city.

After luncheon that day, Mary put on her broad hat and cloak — her matronhood had not reconciled her to bonnets — walked and to South Kensington where Herbert still kept his studio. The Avenue, Fulham Road, resembles a lane leading to the gates of the back-gardens of the neighboring houses rather than an artist's courtyard. Except when some plaster colossus, crowded out of a sculptors studio, appears incongruously at the extremity of the short perspective, no person would dream of turning down there in quest of statues or pictures. Disregarding a gigantic clay horse which ramped in the sun, its nostrils carved into a snort of a type made familiar to Mary by the Elgin marbles and the knights in her set of chessmen, she entered at a door on the right which led to a long corridor, on each side of which were the studios. In one of these she found Adrian, with his palette set and his canvas uncovered on the easel, but with the Times occupying all his attention as he sat uncomfortably on the rung of a broken chair.

Mrs. Hoskyn!" he exclaimed, rising hastily.

'Yes, Adrian. Mrs. Hoskyn's compliments; and she is surprised to see Mr. Herbert reading the newspapers which he once despised, and neglecting the art in which he once gloried."

"I have taken to doing both since I established myself as a family man," he replied with a sigh. "Will you ascend the throne? It is the only seat in the place that can be depended upon not to break down."

"Thank you. Have you been reading the Times ever since your breakfast?"

"Have you seen it, Mary?"

"Yes."

Herbert laughed, and then glanced anxiously at her.

"It is all very well to laugh," she said, " — and, as you know, nobody despises newspaper criticism more thoroughly than I, when it is prejudiced or flippant."

"In this instance, perhaps you agree with the Times."

Mary immediately put on her glasses, and looked hardily at him, by which he knew that she was going to say "I do." When she had said it, he smiled patiently.

Adrian," she said, with some remorse: "do you feel it to be true yourself? If you do not, then I shall admit that I am in error."

"There may be some truth in it — I am hardly an impartial judge in the matter. It is not easy to explain my feeling concerning it. To begin with, I am afraid that when I used to preach to you about the necessity of devoting oneself wholly and earnestly to the study of art in order to attain true excellence, I was talking nonsense — or at least exaggerating mere practice, which is a condition of success in tinkering and tailoring as much as in painting, into a great central principle peculiar to art. I have discovered since that life is larger than any special craft. The difficulty once seemed to lie in expanding myself to the universal comprehensiveness of art: now I perceive that it lies in contracting myself within the limits of my profession, and I am not sure that that is quite desirable."

"Well, of course, if you have lost your conviction that it is worth while to be an artist, I do not know what to say to you. You once thought it worth any sacrifice."

"Yes, when I was a boy, and had nothing to sacrifice. But I do not say that it is not worth while to be an artist; for, you see, I have not given up my profession."

"But you have brought the Times down on you."

"True. The Times now sees defects in my work which I cannot see. Just as it formerly failed to see defects in my early work which are very plain to me now. It says very truly that I no longer take infinite pains. I do my best still; but I confess that I work less at my pictures than I used to, because then I strove to make up for my shortcomings by being laborious, whereas I now perceive that mere laboriousness does not and cannot amend any shortcoming in art except the want of itself, which is not always a shortcoming — sometimes quite the reverse. Laboriousness is, at best, only an appeal *ad misericordiam* to oneself and the critics. 'Sir Lancelot' is a bad picture, if you like; but do you suppose that any expenditure of patience would have tortured it into a good one? My dear Mary — I beg Mr Hoskyn's pardon —"

"Beg Mrs Herbert's, rather. Go on."

"Mrs Herbert is a very good example of my next heresy, which is, that earnestness of intention, and faith in the higher mission of art, are impotent to add an inch to my artistic capacity. They rather produce a mental stress fatal to all freedom of conception and execution. I cannot bring them to bear on drawing and painting: they seem to me to be more the concern of clergymen and statesmen. Your husband once told my mother that art was a backwater into which the soft chaps got to be out of the crush in the middle of the stream. He was thinking about me, I suppose — oh, don't apologize, Mary: I quite agree with him. It is a backwater; and faith and earnestness are of no use in it: mere brute skill carries everything before it. You once asked me how I should like to be Titian and a lot of other great painters all rolled into one. At present I should be only too glad to be as good as Titian alone; but I would not pay five years of my life for the privilege: it would not be worth it. What view did Titian take of his mission in life? Simply that he was to paint pictures and sell them. He painted religious pictures when the church paid him to do it; he painted indecent pictures when licentious noblemen paid him to do it; and he painted portraits for the wealthy public generally. Believe me, Mary, out in the middle the stream of life, from the turbulences and vulgarities of which we agreed to hold aloof, there may be many different sorts of men — earnest men, frivolous men, faithful men, cynical men and so forth; for the backwater there are only two sorts of painters, dexterous ones and maladroit ones. I am not a dexterous one; and that is all about it: self-criticism on moral principles, and the culture of the backwater library, won't mend my eyes and fingers. I said that Aurélie's was a case in point. Even the Times does not deny that she is a perfect artist. Yet if you spoke of her being a moral teacher with a great gift and a a great trust, she would not understand you, although she has some distorted fancy about her touch on the piano being a moral faculty. She thinks your husband a most original and profound thinker because he once happened to remark to her that musical people were generally clever. As I failed to be overwhelmed by her account of this, she, I believe, thought I was jealous of him because I had not hit on the observation myself."

"Perhaps she would play still better if she did look upon herself as the holder of a great gift and a great trust."

"Did I paint the *Lady of Shalott* the better because I would have mixed the colors with my blood if the picture would have gained by my doing so? No: I could paint it twice as well now, though I should not waste half as much thought on it. But put Aurélie out of the question, since you do not admire her. Take —"

"Oh, Adrian, I ad —"

" — the case of Jack. You will admit that he is a genius: he has the inexhaustible flow of ugly sounds which constitutes a composer a genius nowadays. I take Aurélie's word and yours that he is a great musician, in spite of the evidence of my own ears. Judging him as a mere unit of society, he is perhaps the most uncouth savage in London. Does he ever think of himself as having a mission, or a gift, or a trust?"

"I am sure he does. Consider how much he endured formerly because he would not write down to the level of the popular taste."

"Depend upon it, either he did not get the chance or he could not. Mozart, I believe, wrote ballets and Masses in the Italian style. If Jack had Mozart's versatility, he would, in similar circumstances, act just as Mozart acted. I do not make a virtue of never having condescended to draw for the illustrated papers, because if anyone had asked me to do it, I should certainly have tried, and probably have failed."

"Adrian," said Mary, coming down from the throne, and approaching him: "do you know that it gives me great pain to hear you talk in this way? If there was one vice more than another which I felt sure could never taint your nature, it was the vice of cynicism."

"You reproach me with cynicism!" he said, with a smile, evidently enjoying some inconsistency in her.

"Why not?"

"There is, of course, no reason why you should not — , except that you seem to have come to very similar conclusions yourself."

"You never made a greater mistake, Adrian. My faith in the ennobling power of Art, and in the august mission of the artist, is steadfast as it was years ago, when you first instilled it into me."

"And that faith has never wavered?*

"Never."

"Not even for a moment"

"Not even for a moment."

A slight shrug was his only comment. He took up his palette and busied himself with it, with a curious expression at the corners of his mouth.

"What do you mean, Adrian?"

"Nothing. Nothing."

"You used to be more candid than that."

"I used to be many that I am not now."

"You admit that you are changed!"

"Surely."

"Then the change in me that you hint at is only a change in your way of looking at me."

"Perhaps so."

A pause followed, during which he put a few touches on the canvas, and she watched him in growing doubt."

"You won't mind my working whilst you are here." he said, presently.

"Adrian: do you remember that day on the undercliff at Bonchurch, when I announced my falling off, in principle, from the austerity of our worship of art?"

"I do. Why do you ask?"

"I little thought, then, which of us would be the first to fall off in practice. If a prophet had shewn you to me as you are now, contemning loftiness of purpose and renouncing arduous work, I should have been at a loss for words strong enough to express my repudiation of the forecast."

"I cannot say that *I* did not suspect then who would be the first to fall off," said Adrian, quietly, though his color deepened a little. "But I should have been as sceptical as you, if your prophet had shewn me you —" He checked himself.

"Well, Adrian?"

"No. I beg your pardon: I was going to say something I have no right to say."

"Whatever it may be, you think it: and I have a right to hear it, so that I may justify myself. How could a prophet have shewn me so as to astonish you?"

"As Mrs Hoskyn," he replied, looking at her steadily for a moment, and then resuming his work.

"I don't understand," said Mary anxiously, after a pause.

"I told you there was nothing to understand," said he, relieved. "I meant that it is odd in the first place that we are both married, and not to one another — I suppose you don't mind my alluding to that. It is still odder that I should be married to Aurélie, who knows nothing about painting. But it is oddest that you should be married to Mr Hoskyn, who knows nothing about art at all."

Mary, understanding him well now, became very red, and for a moment tried hard to keep back a retort which came to her lips. He continued to paint attentively. Then she said indignantly, "Do you conclude that I do not care for my husband because I can still work and think and respect myself — because I am not his slave when he is present, and a slave to my thoughts of him when he is absent?"

"Mary!" exclaimed Herbert, putting down his palette and confronting her with a color as deep as her own. She stood her ground without flinching. Then he recovered himself, and said, "I beg your pardon. I was quite wrong to say anything about your marriage. Have I annoyed you?"

"You have let slip your opinion of me, Adrian."

"And you yours of me, I think, Mary."

After this there was another strained pause, disconcerting to both. This time Mary gained her self-possession first. "I was annoyed just now," she said: "but I did not mean that we should quarrel. I hope you did not."

"No, indeed," he said fervently. "I trust we shall never have any such meaning, whatever may pass between us."

"Then," she rejoined, instinctively responding to his emotion with an impulse of confession, "let me tell you candidly how far you were right in what you said. I married because I discovered, as you have that the world is larger than Art and that there is plenty of interest in it for those who do not even know what Art means. But I have never been in love in the storybook fashion; and I had given up all belief in the reality of that fashion when I cast in my lot with John's, though I am very fond of him, and do not at all regret being Mrs. Hoskyn."

"It is curious that our courses of action should be so similar and our motives so different! My confession is so obvious that it is hardly worth while to make it. I did fall in love in the storybook fashion: and that is the true explanation of what the Times notices in my work. I will not say that I can no longer work, think, or respect myself — I hope I am not so bad as that: but the rest is true. I am a slave to her when she is present, and a slave to my thoughts of her when she is absent. Perhaps you despise me for it."

"I can hardly despise you for loving your wife. It would be rather unreasonable."

"There are many things which are not reasonable, and are yet quite natural. I sometimes despise myself. That occurs when I contrast Aurélie's influence on my work with yours. Before I met her, I worked steadfastly in this studio, thinking of you whenever my work palled on me, and never failing to derive fresh courage from you. I know now, better than I did then, how much of my first success, and of the resolute labor that won it, was due to you. The new influence is a different — a disturbing one. When I think of Aurélie, there is an end of my work. Where in the old time I used to be reinforced and concentrated, I am now excited and distracted; impatient for some vague tomorrow that never comes; capable of nothing but trouble or ecstasy. Imagine, then, how I value your friendship — for you must not think that you have lost your old power over me. Even to-day, because I have had this opportunity of talking with you, I feel more like my old artist self than I have been for a longtime. We understand each other: I could not say the same to Aurélie. Therefore, Mary, will you — however ill I may in your opinion have deserved it — will you still stand my friend, and help me to regain the ground I have lost, as you formerly helped me to win it?"

"Most willingly, "said Mary with enthusiasm, holding out both her hands to him. "I will take your word for my ability to help you, though I know that you used to help yourself by helping me. Now we are fast friends again, are we not?"

"Fast friends," he repeated, taking her hands, and turning her with affectionate admiration and gratitude.

"Aha!" cried a voice. They released each other's hands quickly, and turned, pale and startled, towards the newcomer. Aurélie, in a light summer dress, was smiling at them from the doorway.

"I fear I derange you," she said in English, which she now spoke easily and carelessly, though with a soft foreign accent. "How do you do, Madame Hoskyn? Am I too much? Eh?"

Mary, confused by the surprise of her entry, and still more by the innocent and caressing manner in which she spoke, murmured some words of salutation.

This is a very unusual honor, Aurélie," said Herbert, affecting to laugh.

"Yes, I did not know of it beforehand myself. I got into the wrong train, and was carried to South Kensington instead of to Addison Road. So I said, 'I will give Adrian a surprise.' And so I have."

"You came in at an interesting moment," said Mary, who had now partly regained some of her self-possession, and all her boldness. "Mr Herbert and I have had a serious quarrel; and we are just making it up. English fashion."

"Oh, it is not an English fashion. People quarrel like that everywhere. And you are now greater friends than ever. Is it not so?"

"I hope so," said Mary.

"I knew it," said Aurélie, with a wave of her fingers. "The human nature is the same things throughout the world. Ah yes. What an untidy atelier is this! How can you expect that great ladies will come here to sit for their portraits?"

"I do not desire that they should, Aurélie."

"But it is by portraits that the English artists make great sums of money. Why do you not cure him of these strange notions, Madame? You have so much sense; and he respects you so. He mocks at me when I speak of painting: yet I am sure I am right."

Mary smiled uneasily, not knowing exactly how to reply. Aurélie wandered about the studio, picking up sketches and putting them down without looking at them; peeping into corners; and behaving like a curious child. At last her husband, seeing her about to disturb a piece of drapery, cried out to her to take care.

"What is the matter now?" said she. "Is there somebody behind it? *Ciell!* it is a great doll."

"Please do not touch it," he said. "I am drawing from it; and the change of a single fold will waste all my labor."

"Yes; but that is not fair. You should not copy things into your pictures: you should paint them all out of your head." She went over to the easel. "Is this the great work for next year? Why has that man a bonnet on?"

"It is not a bonnet: it is a helmet."

"Ah! He is a fireman then. Tiens! You have drawn him with long curling hair! There — I know — he is a knight of the round table: all your knights are the same. Of what use are such barbarians? I prefer the Nibelungs and Wotan and Thor — in Wagner's music. His arm is a deal too long, and the little boy's head is not half large enough in proportion to height. The child is like a man in miniature. Madame Hoskyn: will you do me a great favor — that is, if you are disengaged?"

"I have no engagements today, happily," said Mary. You may command me."

"Then you will come back with us to our house, and stay to dinner. Oh, you must not refuse me. We will send a telegram to Mr Hoskyn to come too. *En famille,* you understand. Adrian will entertain you; I will play for you; my mother will shew you the *bambino.* He is a droll child — you shall see if he is not"

"You are very kind," said Mary, wavering. "Mr Hoskyn expects me to dine at home with him; but —" She looked inquiringly at Adrian.

"As Aurélie says, we can ask Mr Hoskyn by telgraph. I hope you will come, Mary."

Mary blushed at his use of her Christian name, accustomed as she was to it. "Thank you," she said. "I will come with pleasure."

"Ah, that is very good," said Aurélie, apparently delighted. "Come then," she added, in French, to Adrian. "Put away thy *sottises* and let us go at once."

"You hear?" he remarked. She calls my canvas and brushes *sottises*" He put them away resignedly, nevertheless. Aurélie, chatting lightheartedly with Mary, meanwhile. When he was ready, they went out together past the white horse, whose shadow was tending at some length eastward, and sallied into the Fulham Road, where they halted to consider whether they should walk or drive, Whilst they stood, a young man with a serious expression, long and curly fair hair, and a velveteen jacket, approached them. He was reading a book as he walked, taking no note of the persons whom he passed.

"Why, here is Charlie," exclaimed Mary. The young man looked up, and immediately stopped and shut his book, exhibiting a remarkable degree of confusion. Then, to the surprise of his sister, he raised his hat, and attempted to pass on.

"Charlie," she said: "are you going to cut us?" At this he stopped again, and stood looking at them discomfitedly.

"How do you do?" said Adrian, offering his hand, which was eagerly accepted. Charlie now ventured to glance at Aurélie, becoming redder as he did so. She was waiting with perfect composure and apparently without interest for the upshot of the encounter.

"I thought you knew Mrs Herbert," said Mary, puzzled. "My brother, Mrs Herbert," she added, turning to Aurélie.

Charlie removed his hat solemnly, and received in acknowledgement what was rather a droop of the eyelids than a bow.

Herbert, seeing that an awkward silence was likely to ensue, interposed goodhumoredly. "What is your latest project?" he said. "If you are an engineer still your exterior is singularly unprofessional. Judging by appearances, I should say that I must be the engineer and you the artist."

Oh, I've given up engineering," said Charlie. It's a mere trade. The fact is, I have come round at last to your idea that there is nothing like Art. I have turned my attention to literature of late."

"Poetry, I presume," said Herbert, drawing the book from beneath his arm and looking at the title.

"I wish I had the least scrap of genius to make me a poet. In any ease I must give up the vagabond life I have been leading, and settle down to some earnest pursuit. I may not ever be able to write a decent book; but I at least can persevere in the study of Art and literature and — and so forth."

"Persevere in literature:" repeated Mary. "Oh, Charlie! How many novels and tragedies have you begun since we went to live at Beulah? and not one of them ever got to the second chapter."

"I shewed my good sense in not finishing any of them. What has become of the pictures you used to work so hard at, and of the great compositions that were to have come of your studies with Jack?

"I think," said Herbert jocularly, "that if we wait here until you and Mary agree on the subject of your perseverance, our dinner will be cold. Mrs. Hoskyn is coming to dine with us this evening, Charlie. Suppose you join us."

"Thank you," he said, hastily: "I should like it of all things; but I am not dressed; and —"

"You can hardly propose to dress for dinner on my account at this late stage of our acquaintance: and Mrs. Herbert will excuse you, I think."

"You shall be the welcome, monsieur," said Aurélie, who had been gazing abstractedly down the vista at the white h<>rse.

"Thanks, very much indeed," said Charlie. This decided, it was arranged that they should go by train to High Street, and walk thence to Herbert's lodging: for he had never fulfilled his intention of taking a house, his wife being only nominally more at home in London than in the other European capitals. They accordingly moved towards the railway station, Adrian going first with Mary, and Charlie following with Aurélie, who seemed unconscious of his presence, although his uneasiness, his frequent glances sidelong at her, and his occasional dumb efforts to hazard some commonplace remark, were much more obvious than he suspected. In this way they came within a hundred yards of the South Kensington station without having exchanged a word, his dismay increasing at every step. He stole another look at her, and this time met her eye, which fixed him as if it had been that of the ancient mariner: and the longer she looked, the redder and more disconcerted he became.

"Well Monsieur Beatty," she said composedly.

He glanced apprehensively at Adrian, who was within earshot. "I hardly know how to tell you," he said: "but my name is not Beatty."

"Is it possible! I beg your pardon, monsieur: I mistook you for a zhentleman of that name, whom I met at Paris. You resemble him very much."

"No, I assure you," said Charlie eagerly. "I am not in the least like him. I know the fellow you mean: he was a drunken wretch whom you rescued from being run over or robbed in the street, and who made a most miserable ass of himself in return. He is dead."

"*Jesu Christ!* " ejaculated Aurélie with an irrepressible start: "do not say such things. What do you mean?"

"Dead as a doornail," said Charlie, triumphant at having shaken her composure, but still very earnest. "He was killed, scotched, stamped out of existence by remorse, and by being unable to endure the contrast between his worthlessness and your — your goodness. If you would only forget him, and not think of him whenever you see me, you would confer a great favor on me — far greater than I deserve. Will you do this please, Mrs Herbert?"

"I believe you will make great success as poet," said Aurélie, looking oddly at him. "You are — what you call clever. Ach! This underground railway is a horror."

They said nothing more to one another until they left the train at High Street, fromm which they walked in the same order as before. Charlie again at a loss for something to say, but no longer afraid to speak. His first effort was:

"I hope, Madame Sczympliça is quite well."

"Thank you, she is qute well. You will see her presently."

"What! Is she staying with you?"

"Yes. You are glad of that?"

"No, I'm not," he said bluntly."How could I be glad? She remembers that vagabond of whom we were speaking. What shall I do?"

Aurélie shook her head gravely. "Truly, I do not know," she replied. "You had better prepare for the worst."

"It is very easy for you to make a jest of the affair, Mrs Herbert. If you had as much cause to be ashamed of meeting her as I have, you would not laugh at me. However, since you have forgiven me, I think she may very well do so."

Madame Sczympliça did, in fact, receive him without betraying the slightest emotion. She did not remember him. All her attention was absorbed by other considerations, which led her to draw her daughter into a private conversation on the stairs whilst their guests supposed her to be fetching the baby.

"My child: have you brought home dinner as well as guests? What are they to eat? Do you think that the proprietress can provide a double dinner at a moment's notice?"

"She must, *maman* . It is very simple. Let her go to the shops — to the pastrycooks. Let her go wherever she will, so that the dinner be ready. Perhaps there is enough in the house."

"And how —"

"There, there. She will manage easily. If not, how can I help it? I know nothing about such things. Go for the bambinotelegraph; and do not fret about the dinner. All will be well, depend upon it." And she retreated quickly into the drawingroom. Madame Szczympliça raised her hands in protest; let them fall in resignation; and went upstairs, whence she presently returned with a small baby who looked very sad and old.

"Behold it!" said Aurélie, interlacing her fingers behind her back, and nodding from a distance towards her child. "See how solemn he looks! He is a true Englishman." The baby uttered a plaintive sound and stretched out one fist. "Aha! Knowest thou thy mother's voice, rogue? Does he not resemble Adrian?"

Mary took the infant gently; kissed it; shook its toes, called it endearing names; and elicited several inarticulate remonstrances from it. Adrian felt ridiculous, and acknowledged his condition by a faint smile. Charlie kept cautiously aloof. Mary was in act of handing the child carefully hack to Madame Sczympliça, when Aurélie interposed swiftly; tossed it up to the ceiling; and caught it dexterously. Adrian stepped forward in alarm; Madame uttered a Polish exclamation; and the baby itself growled angrily. Being sent aloft a second time, it howled with all its might.

"Now you shall see," said Aurélie, suddenly placing it supine and screaming, on the pianoforte. She began to play the Skater's Quadrille from Meyerbeer's opera of The Prophet. The baby immediately ceased to kick, became silent, and lay still with the bland expression of a dog being scratched, or a lady having her hair combed.

"It has a vile taste in music," she said, when the performance was over. "It is old fashioned in everything. Ah Monsieur Sutherland: would you kindly pass the little one to my mother?"

Madam Madame Sczympliça hastily advanced to forestall Charlie's compliance with this request, made purposely to embarrass him. But he lifted the baby very expertly, and even gave it a kiss before he handed it to the old lady, who watched him as if he were handling a valuable piece of china.

"There. Take it away," said Aurélie. "You would make a good nurse, monsieur."

"What a mother!" whispered Madame Szczympliça. "Poor infant!" and she indignantly carried it away.

"I wish he would grow up all at once," said Aurélie. "By the time he is a man, I shall be an old woman, half deaf, with gout in my fingers. He will go to hear the new players, and wonder how I got my reputation. Ah, it is a stupid world! One may say so before you, madame, because you are a philosopher."

Madame Szczympliça soon returned, and was of much service in maintaining conversation, as she was not, like the other three, unable to avoid keeping a furtive watch on her daughter. At dinner, Aurélie, when she found that the talk would go on without her help, said no more, eating but little, and drinking water. In her abstraction, she engaged their attention more than ever. Mary, trying to puzzle out the real nature of Adrian's wife, considered her carefully, but vainly. The pianist's character appeared as vaguely to her mind as the face did to her shortsighted eyes. Even Herbert, though he ate with the appetite of a husband, often glanced along the table with the admiration of a lover. Charlie did not dare to look often; but he sought for distorted images of her face in glass vessels and bowls of spoons, and gazed at them instead. At last Mary, oppressed by her silence, determined to make her speak.

"Is it possible that you never drink wine?" she said: "you, who work so hard!"

"Never," said Aurélie, resuming her volition instantly. "I have in the tip of every finger a sensation of touch the most subtle, the most delicate, that you can conceive. It is a — *chose* — a species of nervous organization. One single glass of wine would put all those little nerves to sleep. My fingers would become hammers, like the fingers of all the world; and I should be excited, and have a great pleasure to hammer, as all the world has. But I could no longer make music."

"Aurélie has rearkable theories of what she calls her fine touch," said Herbert. "Practically, I find that when she is in a musical humor, and enjoys her own playing, she says she has 'found her fingers'; but when only other people enjoy it, then the touch is gone; the fingers are like the fingers of all the world; and I receive formal notice that Mlle Sczympliça is about to retire from the musical profession.

"Yes, yes, you are very wise. You have not this fine touch; and you do not understand. If you had, ah, how you would draw! You would greater than no matter what artist in the world."

Mary burned with indignation at Aurélie, knowing how it hurt Herbert to be reminded that he was not a firstrate artist. Aurélie, indifferent to the effect of her speech, relapsed into meditation until they left the table, when she seated herself at the pianoforte and permitted Charlie to engage her in conversation, whilst Herbert became engrossed by a discussion with Mary on painting. and Madame Sczympliça sat still in a corner, knitting.

"What!" said Aurélie, when Charlie had been speaking for some time: "were you at that concert too?"

"Yes."

223

"Then you have been at every concert where I have played since I returned to London. Do you go to *all* concerts?"

"To all of those at which you play. Not to the others."

"Oh, I understand. You pay me a compliment. I am very — very recognizant, do you call it? — of your appreciation."

"I am musical, you know. I was to have been a musician, and had lessons from old Jack in the noble art. But I gave it up, I am sorry to say."

"What presumption! It does not become you to speak of a great man in that fashion, Monsieur Charles."

"True, Mrs Herbert. But then nobody minds what I say."

"Tiens!" said Aurélie, with a light laugh. "You are right. You know how to make everything gay. And so you gave up the music, and are now to be a poet. Can you think of no more suitable profession than that?"

"It's the only one left to me, except the army; and that is considered closed to me because my brother — Phipson's daughter's husband, you know — is there already. First I was to be a college don — a professor. Then I took to music. Then I tried the bar, the medical, engineering, the Indian civil service, and got tired of them all. In fact I only drew the line at the church."

"What is that? You drew a line at the church!"

"It is what you very properly call an idiotisme. I mean that I would not condescend to be a parson."

"What a philosopher! Proceed."

"I am now — if the poetry fails, which it most likely will — going into business. I shall try for a post in the Conolly Electro-Motor Company."

"I think that will suit you best. I will play you something to encourage you."

She began to play a polonaise by Chopin. Herbert and Mary ceased speaking, but presently resumed their conversation in subdued tones. Charlie listened eagerly. When the polonaise was finished, she did not stop, but played on, looking at the ceiling, and occasionally glancing at Charlie's face.

"Aurélie," said Herbert, raising his voice suddenly: "where are those sketches that Mrs. Scott left here last Tuesday?"

"Oh, I say!" said Charlie, in a tone of strong remonstrance, as the music ceased. Herbert, not understanding, looked inquiringly at him. Aurélie rose, took the sketches from her music stand; and handed them silently to Mary.

"I am afraid we have interrupted you," said Mary, coloring. Aurélie deprecated the apology by a gesture and sat down in a loww chair near the window.

"I wish you'd play again, if you're not tired, Mrs Herbert," said Charlie timidly.

She shook her head.

"It is hard that I should have to suffer because my sister has a wooden head with no ears on it," he whispered, glancing angrily not at Mary, but at Adrian. I was comfortably settled in in heaven when they interrupted you. I wish Jack was here. He would have given them a piece of his mind."

"Mr Herbert does not like Monsieur Jacques."

"Monsieur Jacques doesn't like Mr Herbert either. There is no love lost between them. Adrian hates Jack's music; and Jack laughs at Adrian's pictures."

"Maman: ring the bell. Tell them to bring some tea."

"Yes, my angel."

"The conversation now became general and desultory. Mary, fearing that she had already been rudely inattentive to her hostess, thought it better not to continue her chat with Adrian. "I see our telegram is of no avail, " she said. "Mr. Hoskyn has probably dined at his club."

"The more fool he," said Charlie, morosely.

"What is that for?" said Mary, surprised by his tone. He looked sulkily at the piano, and did not reply. Then he stole a glance at Aurélie, and was much put out to find that she was tendering him her empty teacup. He took it, and replaced it on the table in confusion.

"And so," she said, when he was again seated near her, "you have succeeded in none of your professions."

This sudden return to a dropped subject put him out still more. "I — you mean my — ?"

"Your metiers — whatever you call them. I am not surprised, Monsieur Charles. You have no patience."

"I can be patient enough when I like."

"Do you ever like?"

"Sometimes. When you play, for instance, I could listen for a year without getting tired."

"You would get very hungry. And I should get very tired of playing. Besides —"

A thud, followed by babyish screams, interrupted her. She listened for a moment, and left the room, followed by her mother. Mary and Adrian, accustomed to such incidents, did not stir. Charlie, reassured by their composure, took up the book of sketches.

Adrian," said Mary in a low voice: "do you think Mrs Herbert is annoyed with me?"

"No. Why"

"I mean, was she annoyed — to-day — in the studio?"

"I should not think so. N — no. Why should she annoyed with you?"

"Not perhaps with me particularly. But with both of us. You must know what I mean, Adrian. I felt in an excessively false position when she came in. I do not mean exactly that she might be jealous: but —"

"Reassure yourself, Mary," he replied, with a sad smile. She is not jealous. I wish she were."

"You wish it!"

"Yes. It would be proof of love. I doubt if she is capable of jealousy.

"I hope not. She must have thought it very odd; and, of course, we looked as guilty as possible. Innocent people always do. Hush! here she is. Have you restored peace to the nursery, Mrs Herbert?

"My mother is doing so." said Aurélie. "It is a very unlucky child. It is impossible to find a cot that it cannot fall out of. But do not rise. Is it it possible that you are going?"

Mary, who in spite of Herbert's assurance was not comfortable, invented unanswerable reasons for returning home at once. Charlie had to go with her. He tried to bid Aurélie good night unconcernedly, but failed. Mary remarked to Herbert, who accompanied them to the door, that Charlie had behaved himself much less awkwardly a boy than he did now as a man. Adrian assented; let them out; stood for a moment to admire the beauty of the evening; and returned to the drawingroom, where Aurélie was sitting on an ottoman, apparently deep in thought.

"Come!" he said spiritedly: "does not Mrs Hoskyn improve on acquaintance? Is she not a nice woman?"

Aurélie looked at him dreamily for a moment, and then said, "Charming."

"I knew you would like her. That was a happy thought of yours to ask her to dinner. I am very glad you did."

"I owed you some reparation, Adrian."

"What for?" he said, instinctively feeling damped.

"For interrupting your tete-a-tete."

He laughed. "Yes," he said. "But you owe me no reparation for that. You came most opportunely."

"That is quite what I thought. Ah, my friend, how much more I admire you when you are in love with Mrs. Hoskyn than when you are in love with me! You are so much more manly and thoughtful. And you abandoned her to marry me! What folly!"

Adrian stood openmouthed, not only astonished, but anxious that she should perceive his astonishment. "Aurélie," he exclaimed: "is it possible — it is hardly conceivable — that you are jealous?"

"N — no," replied she, after some consideration. "I do not think I am jealous. Perhaps Mr. Hoskyn will be, if he happens upon another tete-a-tete. But you do not fight in England, so it does not matter."

"Aurélie: are you serious?"

"Wherefore should I not be serious?" she said, rousing herself a little.

"Because," he answered, gravely, "your words imply that you have a vile opinion of Mrs. Hoskyn and of me."

"Oh, no, no," she said, carelessly reassuring him. "I not think that you arc a wicked gallant, like Don Juan. I know you would both think that a great English sin. I suspect you of nothing except what I saw in your face when you had her hands clasped in yours. You could not look at me so."

"What do you mean?" said he, indignantly.

"I will shew you," she replied calmly, rising and approaching him. "Give me your hands."

"Aurélie: this is chil —"

"Both your hands. Give them to me."

She took them as she spoke, he looking foolish meanwhile.

"Now, she aid. taking a step back so that they were nearly at arms length. "behold what I mean. Look into my eyes as you looked at hers, if you can." She waited; but his face expressed nothing bn1 confusion. "You cannot," she added, attempting to loose his hands. But he grasped her tightly, drew her towards him, and kissed her. "Ah," she said, disengaging herself quietly, "I did not see that part of it. I was only at the door for a moment before I spoke."

"Nonsense, Aurélie, I do not mean that I kissed Mrs. Hoskyn."

"Then you should have. When a woman gives you both her hands, that is what she expects."

"But I pledge you my word that you are mistaken. We were simply shaking hands on a bargain: the commonest thing possible in England."

"A bargain?"

"An agreement — a species of arrangement between us."

"*Eh bien!* And what was this agreement that called such a light into your eyes?"

Adrian, about to reply confidently, hesitated when he realized the impression which his words would probably convey. "It is rather difficult to explain," he began.

"Then do not explain it; for it is very easy to understand. I know. I know. My poor Adrian: you are in love without knowing it. Ah! I envy Mrs Hoskyn."

"If you really mean that," he said eagerly, "I will forgive you all the rest."

"I envy her the power to be in love," rejoined Aurélie, sitting down again, and speaking meditatively. "I cannot love. I can feel it in the music — in the romance — in the poetry; but in real life — it is impossible. I am fond of mamman, fond of the bambino, fond of you sometimes; but this is not love — not such love as you used to feel for me — as she feels now for you. I see people and things too clearly to love. Ah well! I must content myself with the music. It is but a shadow. Perhaps it is as real as love is, after all."

"In short, Aurélie, you do not love me, and never have loved me."

"Not in your way."

"Why did you not tell me this before?"

"Because, whilst you loved me, it would have wounded you."

"I love you still; and you know it. Why did you not tell me so before we were married?"

"Ah, I had forgotten that. I must have loved you then. But you were only half real: I did not know you. What is the matter with you?"

"You ask me what is the matter, after — after —"

"Come and sit by me, and be tranquil. You are making grimaces like a comedian. I do more for you than you deserve; for I still cherish you as my husband, whilst you make bargains, as you call it, with other women."

"Aurélie," he said, sternly: "there is one course, and only one, left to us. We must separate."

"Separate! And for why?"

"Because you do not love me. I suspected it before: now I know it. Your respect for me has vanished too. I can at least set you free: I owe that much to myself. You may not see the necessity for this; and I cannot make you see it. None the less, we must separate."

"And what shall I do for a husband? Do you forget your duty to me and to my child? Well, it does not matter. Go. But look you, Adrian, if you abandon your home only to draw that woman away from hers, it will be an infamy — one that will estrange me from you forever. Do not hope, when you tire of her — for one tires of all pronounced people, and she, in face and character, is very pronounced — do not hope to console yourself with me. You may be weak and foolish if you will; but when you cease to be a man of honor, you are no longer my Adrian."

"And how, in heaven's name, shall I be the worse for that, since already I am no longer your Adrian? You have told me that you never cared for me —"

"Chut! I tell thee that I am not of a nature to fall in love. Becalm ; and do not talk of separation, and such silly things. Have I not been good to her and to you this day?"

"Upon my soul," cried Adrian despairingly, "I believe you are either mad or anxious to make me mad."

"He is swearing!" she ejaculated, lifting her hands.

"I am not in love with Mary," he continued. "It is a gross and absurd libel on both of us to say so. If anyone be to blame, you are — yes, you, Aurélie. You have put the vilest construction on a perfectly innocent action of mine; and now you tell me with the most cynical coolness that you do not care for me.

Aurélie, implying by a little shrug that she gave him up, rose and went to the piano. The moment her fingers touched the keys, she seemed to forget him. But she stopped presently, and said with grave surprise, "*What* did you say, Adrian?"

"Nothing," he replied shortly.

"Nothing!" she repeated incredulously.

"Nothing that was intended for your ears. Since you overheard me, I beg your pardon. I do not often offend you with such language; but tonight I do say with all my soul, 'Damn that pianoforte.'"

"Without doubt you have often said so before under your breath," said Aurélie, closing the instrument quietly.

"Are you going?" he said anxiously, as she moved toward the door. "No," he exclaimed, springing forward, and timidly putting his arm about her, "I did not mean that I disliked your playing. I only hate the piano when you make me jealous of it — when you go to it to forget me."

"It does not matter. Be tranquil. I am not offended," she said coldly, trying to disengage herself.

"You are indeed, Aurélie. Pray do not be so quick to —"

"Adrian: you are worrying me — you will make me cry; and then I will never forgive you. Let me go."

At the threat of crying he released her, and stood looking piteously at her.

"You should nut make scenes with me," she said plaintively. "Where is my handkerchief? I had it a moment ago."

"Here it is, my darling." he said humbly, picking it from the floor where it had fallen. She took it without thanking him. Then, glancing petulantly at him, and seeing him dejected and wistful, she relented and stretched out her arms for a caress.

"*Mon âme,*" she whispered, as she rested her face against his.

"*Ma vie,*" he said fervently, and clasped her with a shudder of delight to his breast.

CHAPTER IV

Early in the afternoon of the following day, which was Sunday, Charlie Sutherland presented himself at Church Street, Kensington and asked Mrs Simpson, who opened the door, if Mr Jack was within.

"No, sir," said Mrs. Simpson, gravely. "He is not in just at present."

On being pressed as to when he would be in, Mrs. Simpson became vague and evasive, although she expressed sympathy for the evident disappointment of the visitor. At last he said he would probably call again, and turned disconsolately away. He had not gone far when, hearing a shout, he looked back, and saw Jack, uncombed, unshaven, in broken slippers, and a stained and tattered coat, running after him, bareheaded.

"Come up — come back," cried Jack, his brazen tones somewhat forced by loss of breath. "It's all a mistake. That jade — come along." He seized Charlie by the arm, and began to drag him back to the house as he spoke. The boys of the neighborhood soon assembled to look with awe at the capture of Charlie, only a few of the older and less reverent venturing to ridicule the scene by a derisive cheer. Jack marched his visitor upstairs to a large room, which occupied nearly the whole of the first floor. A grand pianoforte in the centre was covered with writing materials, music in print and manuscript, old newspapers, and unwashed coffee cups. The surrounding carpet was in such a state as to make it appear that periodically, when the litter became too cumbrous, it was swept away and permitted to lie on the floor just it chanced to fall. The chairs, the cushions of which seemed to have been much used as pen-wipers, were occupied, some with heaps of clothes, others with books turned inside out to mark the place at which the reader had put them down, one with a boot, the fellow of which lay in the fender, and one with a kettle, which had been recently lifted from the fire which, in spite of the season, burnt in the grate.

Black, brown and yellow stains of ink, coffee, and yolk of egg were on everything in the place.

"Sit down," said Jack, impetuously thrusting his former pupil into the one empty chair, a comfortable one with elbows, shiny with constant use. He then sought a seat for himself, and in so doing became aware of Mrs Simpsom, who had come in during his absence with the hopeless project of making the room ready for the visitor.

"Here," he said, "Get some more coffee, and some buttered rolls. Where have you taken all the chairs? I told you not to touch anything in this — why, what the devil do you mean by putting the kettle down on a chair?"

"Not likely, Mr Jack said the landlady, "that I would do such a thing. Oh dear! and one of my yellow chairs too. It's too bad."

"You must have done it: there was nobody else in the room. Be off: and get the coffee."

"I did not do it," said Mrs Simpson, raising her voice; "and well you know it. And I would be thankful to you to make up your mind whether you are to be in or out when people call, and not be making a liar of me as you did before this gentleman."

"You are a liar ready made, and a slattern to boot," retorted Jack. "Look at the state of this room."

"Ah," said Mrs. Simpson, with a sniff. "Look at it indeed. I ask your pardon, sir," she added, turning to Charlie, "but what would anybody think of me if they was told that this was my drawing room?"

Jack, his attention thus recalled to his guest, checked himself on the verge of a fresh outburst, and pointed to the door. Mrs. Simpson looked at him scornfully, but went out without further ado. Jack then seized a chair by the back, shook its contents on to the floor, and sat down near Charlie.

"I should not have spoken as I did just now," he said, with compunction. "Let me give you a word of advice, Charles. Never live in the house with an untidy woman."

"It must be an awful nuisance, Mr Jack."

"It is sure to lead to bad habits in yourself. How is your sister, and your father?"

"Mary is just the same as ever; and so is the governor. I was with him at Birmingham last autumn. We heard the Prometheus. By Jove, Mr Jack, that is something to listen to! The St Matthew Passion, the Ninth Symphony, and the Nibelung's Ring, are the only works that are fit to be put behind it. The overture alone is something screeching."

"You like it? That's right, that's right. And what are you doing at present? Working hard, eh?"

"The old story, Mr Jack. I have failed in everything just as I failed at the music, though I stuck to that better than any of the rest, whilst I had you to help me."

"You began everything too young. No matter. There is plenty of time yet. Well, well. What's the news?"

"I'm going to an at-home at Madge Lancaster's — the actress, you know. She made me promise I'd call on my way and mention casually where I was going. She thought that you'd perhaps come with me — at least I expect that was her game."

"She, asked me to come some Sunday; and I told her I would. Is this Sunday?"

"Yes, Mr. Jack, I hope you won't think it cool of me helping her to collar you in this way."

Jack made some inarticulate reply; pulled his coat off; and began to throw about the clothes which were heaped on the chairs. Presently he rang the bell furiously, and, after waiting for about twenty seconds for a response, went to the door and shouted for Mrs Simpson in a stunning voice. This had no more effect than the bell; and he returned, muttering execrations, to resume his search. When he had added considerably to the disorder, Mrs Simpson entered with ostentatious unconcern, carrying a tray with coffee and rolls.

"Where would you wish me to put these things, sir?" she said with a patient air, after looking in vain for a vacant space on the pianoforte.

"What things? What do you mean by bringing them? Who asked for them?"

"You did, Mr Jack. Perhaps a you would like to deny it to this gentleman's face, who heard you give the order."

"Oh!" said Jack, discomfited. "Charles: will you take some coffee whilst I am dressing. Put the tray on the floor if you can't find room for it elsewhere."

Mrs Simpson immediately placed it at Charlie's feet.

"Now," said Jack, looking malignantly at her, "be so good as to find my coat for me; and in future, when I leave it in a particular place, don't take it away from there."

"Yes, sir. And where did you leave it last, if I may make bold to ask?"

"I left it on that chair," said Jack violently. "Do you see? On that chair."

"Indeed," said Mrs. Simpson, with open scorn. "You gave it out to me yesterday to brush; and a nice job I have had with it: it took a whole bottle of benzine to fetch out the stains. It's upstairs in your room; and I beg you will be more careful with it in future, or else send it to the dyers to be cleaned instead of to me. Shall I bring it to you?"

"No. Go to the — go to the kitchen; and hold your tongue. Charlie: I shall be back presently, my boy, if you will wait. And take some coffee. Put the tray anywhere. Confound that — that — that — that woman." He left the room then, and after some time reappeared in a clean shirt and a comparatively respectable black frock coat.

"Where does she live?" he said.

"In the Marylebone Road. Her athomes are great fun. Her sisters don't consider it proper for a young unmarried woman to give athomes on her own hook; and so they never go. I believe they would cut her altogether, only they can't afford to, because she gives them a new dress occasionally. It will be a regular swagger for me to go in with you. Next to being a celebrity oneself, the best thing is to know a celebrity."

Jack only grunted, and allowed Charlie to talk until they arrived at the house in the Marylebone Road. The door was opened by a girl in a neat dress of dark green, with a miniature mob-cap on her head.

"I feel half inclined to ask her for a programme, and tip her sixpence," whispered Charlie, as they followed her upstairs. "We may consider that she is conducting us to our stalls. Mr Jack and Mr Charles Sutherland," he added aloud to the girl as they reached the landing.

"Mr Sutherland and Mr Charles Sutherland," she answered, coldly correcting him.

Jack, meanwhile had advanced to where Madge stood. She wore a dress of pale blue velvet, made in Venetian style imitated from old Paul Veronese. Round her neck was a threefold string of amber beads, and she was shod with slippers of the same hue and material as her dress. Her complexion, skilfully put on, did not disgust Charlie, but rather inspired him with a gentle regret that it was too good to be genuine. The arrangement of the room was as remarkable as the costume of the hostess. The folding doors had been removed, and the partition built into an arch with a white pillar at each side. A curtain of silvery plush was gathered to one of side of this arch. The walls were painted a delicate sheeny grey, and the carpet resembled a piece of thick whitey-brown paper. The chairs of unvarnished wood, had rush seats, or else cushions of dull straw color or cinnamon. In compliance with a freak of fashion which prevailed just then, there were no less than eight lamps distributed about the apartments. These lamps had monstrous stems of pottery ware, gnarled and uncouth in design. Most of them represented masses of rock with strings of ivy leaves clinging to them. The ceiling was of a light maize color.

Magdalen, surprised by the announcement of Mr Sutherland, was looking towards the door for him over the head of Jack, than whom she was nearly a head taller.

"How d'ye do?" he said, startling her with his brassy voice.

"My dear master," she exclaimed, in the pure, distinct tone to which she owed much of her success on the stage. "So you have come to me at last."

"Aye, I have come at last," he said, with a suspicious look. "I forgot all about you; but I was put in mind of your invitation by Charles. where's Charles?"

Charles was behind him, waiting to be received.

"I am deeply grateful to you," said Magdalen, pressing his hand. Charles, rather embarrassed than gratified, replied inarticulately; vouched for the health of his family; and retreated into the crowd.

"I had ceased to hope that we should ever meet again," she said, turning again to Jack. "I have sent you box after box that you might see your old pupil in her best parts; but when the nights came, the boxes were empty always."

"I intended to go — I should have gone. But somehow I forgot the time, or lost the tickets, or something. My landlady mislays things of that sort; or very likely she burns them."

"Poor Mrs Simpson! How is she?"

"Alive, and mischievous, and long tongued as ever. I must leave that place. I can stand her no longer. Her slovenliness, her stupidity, and her disregard of truth are beyond belief."

"Dear, dear! I am very sorry to hear that, Mr. Jack." Magdalen turned her eyes upon him with an expression of earnest sympathy which had cost her much study to perfect. Jack, who seldom recollected that the subject of Mrs Simpson's failings was not so serious to the rest of the world as to himself, thought Magdalen's concern by no means overstrained, and was about to enlarge on his domestic discomfort, when the servant announced "Mr Brailsford."

Jack slipped away, and his old enemy advanced, as sprucely dressed as ever, but a little more uncertain in his movements. Magdalen kissed him with graceful respect, as she would have kissed an actor engaged to impersonate her father for so many pounds a week. When he passed on and mingled with the crowd like any other visitor, she forgot him, and looked round for Jack. But he, in spite of his attempt to avoid Mr Brailsford, had just come face to face with him in a remote corner whither chance had led them both. Jack at once asked him how he did.

"How de do," said the old gentleman with nervous haste. "Glad to — I am sure." Here he found his eyeglass, and was able to distinguish Jack's features.

"Sir," said Jack: "I am an ill-mannered man on occasion; but perhaps you will overlook that and allow me to claim your acquaintance."

"Sir," replied Brailsford, tremulously clasping his proffered hand: "I have always honored and admired men of genius, and protested against the infamous oppression to which the world subjects them. You may count upon me always."

"There was a time," said Jack, with a glance at the maize-colored ceiling, "when neither of us would have believed that we should come to make two in a crowd of fashionable celebrities sitting round her footstool."

"She has made a proud position for herself, certainly. Thanks, as she always acknowledges, above all things to your guidance."

"Humph," said Jack doubtfully. "I taught her to make the best of such vowels as there are left in our spoken language; but her furniture and her receptions are her own idea."

"They are the most ridiculous absurdities in London," whispered Brailsford with sudden warmth. "To you, sir, I express my opinion without reserve. I come here because my presence may give a certain tone — a sanction — you understand me?" Jack nodded. "But I do not approve of such entertainments. I am at a loss to comprehend how the actress can so far forget the lady. This room is not respectable, Mr Jack: it is an outrage on taste and sensibility. However, it is not my choice: it is hers; and *de gustibus non est disputandum*. You will excuse my quoting my old school books. I never did so, sir, in my youth, when every fool's mouth was full of scraps of Latin."

"There is a bad side to this sort of thing," said Jack. "These fellows waste their time coming here; and she wastes her money on extravagances for them to talk about. But after all, there is a bad side to everything: she might indulge herself with worse follies. Now that she is her own mistress, we must all stand further off. Her affairs are not our business."

The old gentleman nodded several times in a melancholy manner. "There you have hit the truth, sir," he said in a low voice. "We must all stand further off — I as well as others. A very just observation."

This dialogue, exceptionally long for a crowded afternoon reception in London, was interrupted by Magdalen coming to invite Jack to play, which he peremptorily refused to do, remarking that if the company were in a humor to listen to music, they had better go to church. The rebuff caused much disappointment; for Jack's appearances in society, common as they had been during the season which preceded the first performance of Promethius, had since been very rare. Stories of his eccentricity and inaccessible solitude had passed from mouth to mouth until they became too stale to amuse or too exaggerated to be believed. His refusal to play was considered so characteristic that some of the guests withdrew at once in order that they might be the first to narrate the circumstances in artistic circles, which are more "at home" on Sundays than those of the more purely fashionable ones which have nothing particular to do on week days. Jack was about to go himself when the blue velvet sleeve touched his arm, and Magdalen whispered:

"They will all go in a very few minutes now. Will you stay and let me have a moment with you alone? It is so long since I have had a word of advice from you."

Jack again looked suspiciously at her; but as she looked very pretty, he relented, saying good humoredly, "Get rid of them quickly, then. I have no time to waste waiting for them."

She set herself to get rid of them as well as she could, by pretending to mistake the purpose of men who came up to converse with her, and surprising them with effusive farewells. To certain guests with whom she did not stand on ceremony she confided her desire to clear the room; and they immediately conveyed her wishes to their intimate friends, besides setting an example to others by taking leave ostentatiously, or declaring in loud whispers that it was shamefully late; that dear Madge must be tired to death; and that they were full of remorse at having been induced by her delightful hospitality to stay so long. In fifteen minutes the company was reduced to five or six persons, who seemed to think, now that the crowd was over, that the time had come for enjoying themselves. A few of them, who knew each other, relaxed their ceremonious bearing; raised their voices; and entered into a discussion on theatrical topics in which they evidently expected Magdalen to join. The rest wandered about the rooms, and made the most of their opportunity of having a good look at the great actress and the great composer, who was standing at a window with his hands clasped behind him, frowning unapproachably. Mr Brailsford also remained; and he was the first to notice the air of exhaustion with which his daughter was mutely appealing to her superfluous guests.

"My child," he said: "are you fatigued?"

"I am worn out," she replied, in a whisper which reached the furthest corner of the room. "How I long to be alone!"

"Why did you not tell me so before," said Brailsford, offended. "I shall not trouble you any longer, Magdalen. Good evening."

"Hush," she said, laying her arm caressingly on his, and speaking this time in a real whisper. "I meant that for the others. I want you to do something for me. Mr Jack is waiting to go with you; and I particularly want to speak to him alone — about a pupil. Could you slip away without his seeing you? *Do,* dear old daddy; for I may never have another chance of catching him in a good humor. Magdalen knew that her father would be jealous of having to leave before Jack unless she could contrive to make him do so of his own accord. The stratagem succeeded and Mr Brailsford left the room with precaution, glancing apprehensively at the musician, who still presented a stolid back view to the company. The group of talkers, warned by Madge's penetrating whisper, submissively followed him, leaving only one young man who was anxious to go and did not know how to do it. She relieved him by giving him her hand, and expressing a hope that she should see him next Sunday, He promised earnestly, and departed.

"Now," said Jack, wheeling round the instant the door closed. "What can I do for you? Your few minutes have spun themselves out to twenty."

"Did they seem so very long?" she said, seating herself upon an ottoman and throwing her dress into graceful folds.

"Yes," said Jack, bluntly.

"So they did to me. Won't you sit down?"

Jack pushed an oaken stool opposite to her with his foot, and sat upon it, much as, in a Scandinavian story, a dwarf might have sat at the feet of a princess. "Well, mistress," he said. "Things have changed since I taught you. Eh?"

"Some things have."

"You have become great; and so — in my small way — have I."

"*I* have become what you call great," she said. But you have not changed. People have found out your greatness, that is all."

"Well said," said Jack, approvingly. "They starved me long enough first, damn them. Used I to swear at you when I was teaching you?"

"I think you used to. Just a little, when I was very dull."

"It is a bad habit — a stupid one, as all low habits are. I rarely fall into it. And so you stuck to your work, and fought your way. That was right. Are you as fond of the stage as ever?"

"It is my profession," said Madge, with a disparaging shrug. "One's profession is only half of one's life. Acting in London, where the same play runs for a whole season, leaves one time to think of other things. "

"Sundays at home, and fine furniture, for instance."

"Things that they vainly pretend to supply. I have told you that my profession is only half my life — the public half. Now that I have established that firmly, I begin to find that the private and personal half, the half which is concerned with home and — and domestic ties, must be well established too, or else the life remains incomplete, and the heart unsatisfied."

"In plain English, you have too much leisure which you can employ no better than in grumbling."

"Perhaps so; but am I much at fault? When I entered upon my profession, its difficulties so filled my mind with hopes and fears, and its actual work so fully occupied my time, that I forgot every other consideration and cut myself off from my family and friends with as little hesitation as a child might feel in exchanging an estate for a plaything. Now that the difficulties are overcome, the hopes fulfilled (or abandoned) and the fears dispelled — now that I find that my profession does not suffice to fill my life, and that I have not only time, but desire, for other interests, I find how thoughtless I was when I ran away from all the affection I had unwittingly gathered to myself as I grew."

"Why? What have you lost? You have your family still."

"I am as completely estranged from them by my profession as if it had transported me to another world."

"I doubt if they are any great loss to you. The public are fond of you, ain't they?"

"They pay me to please them. If I disappeared, they would forget me in a week."

"Why shouldn't they? How long do you think they should wear mourning for you? Have you made no friends in your own way of life?"

"Friends? Yes, I suppose so."

"You suppose so! What is the matter, then? What more do you want?"

Magdalen raised her eyelids for an instant, and looked at him. Then she said, "Nothing," and let the lids fall with the cadence of her voice.

"Listen to me," said Jack, after a pause, drawing his seat nearer to her, and watching her keenly. "You want to be romantic. You won't succeed. Look at the way we cling to the stage, to music, and poetry, and so forth. Why do you think we do that? Just because we long to be romantic, and when we try it in real life, facts and duties baffle us at every turn. Men who write plays for you to act, cook up the facts and duties so as to heighten the romance; and so we all say 'How wonderfully true to nature!' and feel that the theatre is the happiest sphere for us all. Heroes and heroines are to be depended on: there is no more chance of their acting prosaically than there is of a picture in the Royal Academy having stains on its linen, or blacks in its sky. But in real life it is just the other way. The incompatibility is not in the world, but in ourselves. Your father is a romantic man; and so am I; but how much of our romance have we ever been able to put into practice?"

"More than you recollect, perhaps," said Madge, unmoved (for constant preoccupation with her own person had made her a bad listener), "but more than I shall ever forget. There has been one piece of romance in my life — a very practical piece. A perfect stranger once gave me, at my mere request, all the money he had in the world."

"Perhaps he fell in love with you at first sight. Or perhaps — which is much the same thing — he was a fool."

"Perhaps so. It occurred at Paddington Station some years ago."

"Oh! Is that what you are thinking of? Well, that is a good illustration of what I am saying. Did any romance come out of that? In three weeks, time you were grubbing away at elocution with me at so much a lesson."

"I know that no romance came out of it — for you."

"So you think," said Jack complacently; "but romance comes out of everything for me. Where do you suppose I get the supplies for my music? And what passion there is in that! — what fire — what disregard of conventionality! In the music, you understand: not in my everyday life."

"Your art, then, is enough for you," said Madge, in a touching tone.

"I like to hear you speak," observed Jack: "you do it very well. Yes: my art is enough for me, more than I have time and energy for occasionally. However, I will tell you a little romance about myself which may do you some good. Eh? Have you the patience to listen?"

"Patience!" echoed Madge, in a low steady voice. "Try whether you can tire me."

"Very well: you shall hear. You must know that when, after a good many years of poverty and neglect, I found myself a known man, earning over a hundred a year, I felt for a while as if my house was built and I had no more to do than to put it in repair from time to time — much as you think you have mastered the art of acting, and need only learn a new part occasionally to keep your place on the stage. And so it came about that I — Owen Jack — began to languish in my solitude; to pine for a partner; and, in short, to suffer from all those symptoms which you so admirably described just now." He gave this account of himself with a derision so uncouth that Madge lost for the moment her studied calm, and shrank back a little. "I was quite proud to think that I had the affections of a man as well as the inspiration of a musician; and I selected the lady; fell in love as hard as I could; and made my proposals in due form. I was luckier than I deserved to be. Her admiration of me was strictly impersonal; and she nearly had a fit at the idea of marrying me. She is now the wife of a city speculator; and I have gone back to my old profession of musical student, and quite renounced the dignity of past master of the art. I sometimes shudder when I think that I was once within an ace of getting a wife and family."

"And so your heart is dead?"

"No: it is marriage that kills the heart and keeps it dead. Better starve the heart than overfeed it. Better still to feed it only on fine food, like music. Besides, I sometimes think I will marry Mrs Simpson when I grow a little older."

"You are jesting: you have been jesting all along. It is not possible that a woman refused your love."

"It is quite possible, and has happened. And," here he rose and prepared to go, "I should do the same good service to a woman, if one were so foolish as to persuade herself on the same grounds that she loved me."

"You would not believe that she could love you on any deeper and truer grounds?" said Madge, rising slowly without taking her eyes off his face.

"Stuff! Wake up, Miss Madge; and realize what nonsense you are talking. Rub your eyes and look at me, a Kobold — a Cyclop, as that fine woman Mrs Herbert once described me. What sane person under forty would be likely to fall in love with me? And what do I care about women over forty, except perhaps Mrs. Herbert — or Mrs. Simpson I like them young and beautiful, like you."

Madge, as if unconsciously, raised her hand, half offering it to him. He took it promptly, and continued humorously, "And I love you, and have always done so. Who could know such a lovely woman and fine genius as you without loving her? But," he added, shaking her fingers warningly, "you must not love me. My time for playing Romeo was over before you ever saw me; and Juliet must not fall in love with Friar Lawrence, even when he is a great composer."

"Not if he forbids her — and she can help it," said Madge with solemn sadness, letting her hand drop as he released it.

"Not on any account," said Jack. "Come, he added, turning to her imperiously: "we are not a pair, you and I. I know how to respect myself: do you learn to know yourself. We two are artists, as you are aware. Well, there is an art that is inspired by nothing but a passion for shamming; and that is yours, so far. There is an art which is inspired by a passion for beauty, but only in men who can never associate beauty with a lie. That is my art. Master that and you will be able to make true love. At present you only know how to make scenes, which is too common an accomplishment to interest me. You see you have not quite finished you lessons yet. Goodbye."

"Adieu," said Madge, like a statue.

He walked out in the most prosaic manner possible; and she sank on the ottoman in an attitude of despair, and — finding herself at her ease in it, and not understanding him in the least — kept it up long after he, by closing the door, had, as it were, let fall the curtain. For it was her habit to attitudinize herself when alone quite as often as to other people, in whose minds the pleasure of attitudinizing is unalloyed by association with the labor of breadwinning.

Jack, meanwhile, had let himself out of the house. It had become dusk by this time; and he walked away in a sombre mood, from which he presently roused himself to shake his head at the house he had just left, and to say aloud, "You are a bold-faced jade." This remark, which was followed by muttered imprecations, was ill-received by a passing woman who, applying it to herself, only waited until he was at a safe distance before retorting with copious and shrill abuse, which soon caused many persons to stop and stare after him. But he, hardly conscious of the tumult, and not suspecting that it had anything to do with him, walked on without raising his head, and was presently lost to them in the deepening darkness.

All this time, Charlie, who had been among the first to leave Madge's rooms, was wandering about Kensington in the neighborhood of Herbert's lodging. He felt restless and unsatisfied, shrinking from the observation of the passers-by, with a notion that they might suspect and ridicule the motive of his lurking, there. He turned into Campden Hill at last, and went to his sister's. Mary usually had visitors on Sunday evenings; and some of them might help him to pass away the evening pleasantly in spite of Hoskyn's prose. Perhaps even — but here he shook off further speculation, and knocked at the door.

"Anyone upstairs?" he asked carelessly of the maid, as he hung up his hat.

"Only one lady, sir. Mrs Herbert."

Something within him s make a spring at the name. He glanced at himself in the mirror before going into the drawing room, where, to his extreme disappointment, he found Mary conversing, not with Herbert's wife, but with his mother. She had but just arrived, and was explaining to Mary that she had returned the day before, from a prolonged absence in Scotland. Charlie never enjoyed his encounters with Mrs Herbert; for she had known him as a boy, and had not yet got out the of habit of treating him as one. So, hearing that Hoskyn was in another room, smoking, he pleaded a desire for a cigar, and went off to join him, leaving the two ladies together.

"You were saying — ?" said Mary, resuming the conversation which his entrance had Interrupted.

"I was saying," said Mrs Herbert, "that I have never been able to sympathize with the interest which you take in Adrian's life and opinions. Geraldine tells me that I have no maternal instinct; but then Geraldine has no sons, and does not quite know what she is talking about. I look on Adrian as a failure, and I really cannot take an interest in a man who is a failure. His being my son only makes the fact disappointing to me personally. I retain a kind of nursery affection for my boy; but of what use that to him, since he has given up his practice of stabbing me through it? I would go to him if he were ill; and help him if he were in trouble; but as to maintaining a constant concern on his account, really I do not see why I should. You, with your own little dear one a fresh possession — almost a part of yourself still, doubtless think me very heartless; but you will learn that children have their separate lives and interests as completely independent of their parents as the remotest strangers. I do not think Adrian would even like me, were it not for his sense of duty. You will understand some day that the common notion of parental and filial relations are more unpractical than even those of love and marriage."

Mary, who ^had already made some discoveries in this direction, did not protest as " she would have done in her maiden time. "What surprises me chiefly is that Mrs Herbert should have been rude to you," she said. "I doubt whether she is particularly fond of me: indeed, I am sure she is not; but nothing could be more exquisitely polite and kind than her manner to me, especially in her own house."

"I grant you the perfection of her manners, dear. She was not rude to me. Not that they are exactly the manners of good society; but they are perfect of their kind, for all that. Hush! I think — did I not hear Adrian's voice that time?"

Adrian was, in fact, speaking in the hall to Hoskyn, who had just appeared there with Charlie on his way to the drawing room. Aurélie was with her husband. They all went for a moment into the study, which served on Sunday evenings as a cloak room.

"I assure you, Mrs. Herbert," said Hoskyn, officiously helping Aurélie to take off her mantle, "I am exceedingly glad to see you."

"Ah, yes," said Aurélie; "but this is quite wrong. It is you who should render me a visit in this moment, because I ask you to dine with me; and you do not come."

"You have turned up at a very good time,' said Charlie mischievously. "Mrs. Herbert is upstairs."

"My mother!" said Adrian, in consternation.

"Shall we go upstairs?" said Hoskyn, leading the way with resolute cheerfulness.

Adrian looked at Aurélie. She had dropped the lively manner in which she had spoken to Hoskyn, and was now moving towards the door with ominous grace and calm.

"Aurélie," he said, detaining her in the room for a moment: "my mother is here. You will speak to her — for my sake — will you not?"

She only raised her hand to signify that she was not to be troubled, and then, without heeding his look of pain and disappointment, passed out and followed Hoskyn to the drawingroom, where Mary and Mrs Herbert, having heard her foreign voice, were waiting, scarcely less disturbed than Adrian by their fear of how she might act.

"Mrs Herbert junior has actually condescended to pay you a visit, Mary," said Hoskyn.

"How do you do?" said Mary, with misgiving. "I am so very glad to see you."

"So often have I to reproach myself not to have called on my friends," said Aurélie in her sweetest voice, "that I yielded to Adrian at the risk of deranging you by coming on the Sunday evening." A pause followed, during which she looked inquisitively around. "Ah!" she exclaimed, with an air of surprise and pleasure, as she recognized Mrs. Herbert, "is it possible? You are again in London, madame."

She advanced and offered her hand. Mrs Herbert, who had sat calmly looking at her, made the greeting as brief as possible, and turned her attention to Adrian. Nevertheless, Aurélie drew a chair close to hers, and sat down there.

"You are looking very well, mother," said Adrian. "When did you return?"

"Only yesterday, Adrian." There was a brief silence. Adrian looked anxiously at Aurélie; and his mother mutely declined to look at her.

"But behold what is absurd!" said Aurélie. "You, madame, who are encore so young — so beautiful — here Mrs. Herbert, who had turned to her with patient attention, could not hide an expression of wonder&mdash"you are already a grandmother. Adrian has what you call a son and heir. It is true."

"Yes, I am aware of that," said Mrs. Herbert coolly.

A slight change appeared for an instant in Aurélie's face; and she glanced for a moment gravely at her husband. He, with disgust only half concealed, said, "You could not broach a subject less interesting to my mother," and turned away to speak to Mary.

"Adrian," began Mrs. Herbert, who found herself unexpectedly disturbed by the implied imputation of want of feeling: "I do not think —" Then, as he was not attending to her, she turned to Aurélie and said, "You really must not accept everything that Adrian says seriously. Pray tell me all about your boy — my grandson, I should say."

"He is like you," said Aurélie, trying to conceal the chill which had fallen upon her. "Perhaps you will like to see him. If so, I shall bring him to you, if you will permit me."

"I shall be very glad," said Mrs. Herbert, rather surprised. "Let me say that I have been expecting you to call on me for some time."

"You are very good," said Aurélie. "But think of how I live. I am always voyaging; and you also are seldom in London. Besides, when one is an artist one neglects things. Forget, I pray you, my — my — ach! I do not know how to say it. But I will come to you with Monsieur Jean Sczympliça Herbert. That reminds me: I know not your address.

Mrs Herbert supplied the information; and the conversation then proceeded amicably with occasional help from Hoskyn and Charlie. Mary and Adrian had withdrawn to another part of the room, and were engrossed in a discussion. In the course of it Mary remarked that matters were evidently smooth between the two Mrs Herberts.

"I am glad of it," said Adrian, not looking glad. "I was disposed to think Aurélie in fault on that point; but I see plainly enough now how the coolness was brought about. I should not have blamed Aurélie at all if she had repaid my mother's insolence — I do not think that at all too strong a word — in kind. Poor Aurélie! I have been all this time secretly thinking hardly of her for having, I thought, rebuffed my mother. Unjust and stupid that I am not to have known better from my lifelong experience of the one, and my daily observation of the other! Aurélie has conciliated her tonight solely because I begged her to do so as we came upstairs. You cannot deny that my wife can be perfectly kind and selfsacrificing whenever there is occasion for it."

"I cannot deny it! Adrian: you speak as though I were in the habit of disparaging her. You are quite wrong. No one can admire her more than I. My only fear is that she is too sweet, and may spoil you. How could I resist her? Even your mother, prejudiced as she certainly was against her, has yielded. You can see by her face that she has given up the battle. I think we had better join them. We have a very rude habit of getting into a corner by ourselves. I am sure, in spite of all you say, that Mrs Herbert is too fond of you to like it."

"Mrs Herbert is a strange being," said Adrian, rising. "I no longer pretend to understand her likes and dislikes."

Mary made a mental note that Aurélie had probably had more to say on the subject of what she saw in the studio than Adrian had expected. The general conversation which ensued did not run on personal matters. Aurélie was allowed to lead it, as it was tacitly understood that the interest of the occasion in some manner centred in her. Mrs Herbert laughingly asked her for the secret of managing Adrian; but she adroitly passed on to some other question, and would not discuss him or in any way treat him more familiarly than she did Hoskyn or Charlie.

Later on, Hoskyn proposed that they should go downstairs to a room which communicated with the garden by a large window and a small grassy terrace. As the night was sultry, they readily agreed, and were soon seated below at a light supper, after which Hoskyn strolled out into the garden with Adrian to smoke another cigar and to shew a recently purchased hose and lawn mower, it being his habit to require his visitors to interest themselves in his latest acquisitions, whether of children, furniture or gardening implements. Mrs Herbert, who, despite the glory of the moon, could not overcome her belief that fresh air, to be safely sat in, should tempered by a roof, did not venture beyond the carpet; and and Mary felt bound to remain in the room with her. Aurélie walked out to the edge of the terrace, clasped her hands behind her, and became rapt in contemplation of the cloudless sky, which was like a vast moonlit plain. Her attention was recalled by the voice of Charlie beside her.

"Awfully jolly night, isn't it, Mrs Herbert?"

"Yes, it is very fine."

"I suppose you find no end of poetry in all those stars."

"Poetry! I am not at all poetic, Monsieur Charles."

"I don't altogether believe that, you know. You look poetic."

"It is therefore that people mistake me. They are very arbitrary. They say 'Madamoiselle Sczympliça has such and such a face and figure. In our minds such a face and figure associate with poetry. Therefore must she be poetic. We will have it so; and if she disappoints us, we will be very angry with her.' And I do disappoint them. When they talk poetically of music and things I am impatient myself to be at home with *mamma*, who never talks of such things, and the bambino, who never talks at all. What, think you, do I find in those stars? I am looking for Aurélie and Thekla in what you call Charles's wain. Aha! I did not think of that before. You are Monsieur Charles, to whom belongs the wain."

"Yes, I have put my hand to the plough and turned back often enough. What may Aurélie and Thekla be?"

"Aurélie is myself; and Thekla is my doll. In my infancy I named a star after every one whom I liked. Only very particular persons were given a place in Charles's wain. It was the great chariot of honor; and in the end I found no one worthy of it but my doll and myself. Behold how I am poetic! I was a silly child; for I forgot to give my mother a star — I forgot all my family. When my mother found that out one day, she said I had no heart. And, indeed, I fear I have none."

"Heaven forbid!"

"Look you, Monsieur Charles," she said, with a sudden air of shrewdness, unclasping her hands to shake her finger at him: "I am not what you think me to be. I am the very other things of it. I have the soul commercial within me."

"I am glad of that," he said eagerly; "for I want to make a business proposal to you. Will you give me lessons?"

'Give you lesson! Lesson of what?"

"Lessons in playing. I want awfully to become a good pianist, and I have never had any really good teaching since I was a boy."

"Vraiment? Ah! You think that as you persevered so well in the different professions, you will find it easy to become a player. Is it not so?"

"Not at all. I know that playing requires years of perseverance. But I think I can persevere if you will teach me."

"Monsieur Charles — what shall I call you? You are an ingenious infant, I think."

"Don't make fun of me, Mrs. Herbert. I'm perfectly in earnest." Here, to his confusion, his voice broke with emotion.

"You think I am mocking you!" she said, not seeming to notice the accident.

"I am not fool enough to suppose that you care what I think." he said lamely, losing his self-possession. "I know you won't give me the lessons. I knew it before."

"And wherefore then, did you ask me?"

"Because I love you," he replied, with symptoms of hysterical distress. "I love you."

"Ah," said Aurélie severely, "Do you see my husband there looking at you? And do you not know that it is very wicked to say such a thing to me? Remember, Monsieur Charles, you are quite sober now. I shall not excuse you as I did before."

"I couldn't help it," said Charlie, half crestfallen, half desperate, "I know it's hopeless: I felt it the moment I had said it. But I can't always act like a man of the world. I wish I had never met you."

"And why?"' I Like you very well when you are good. But this is already twice that you forget to be an honest gentleman. Is it not dishonorable thus to envy your friend? If Monsieur Herbert had a fine watch, would you wish to possess it? No, the thought that it was his would impeach — would hinder you to form such a wish. Well, you must look upon me as a watch of his. You must not even think such things as you have just said. I will not be angry with you, Monsieur Sutherland, because you are very young, and you have admirable qualities. But you have done wrong."

Before he could reply, she moved away and joined her husband at the end of the garden. Charlie, with his mouth hanging open, stared at her for some seconds, and then went into the supper room, where he incommoded Mary and Mrs. Herbert by lounging about, occasionally taking a grape [from the table or pouring out a glass of wine. At last he strolled to the drawingroom, where he was found with a book in his hand, pretending to read, by the others when they came upstairs some time after. He did not speak again until he bade farewell to the elder Mrs. Herbert, who departed under Hoskyn's escort. Aurélie, before following her example, went to the nursery with Mary, to have a peep at Master Richard Hoskyn, as he lay in his cot.

"He smiles," said Aurélie. "What a charming infant! The bambino never smiles. He is so *triste,* like Adrian!" As they turned to leave the room, she added, "Poor Adrian! I think of going to America this year; but he does not know. You will take care of him whilst I am away, will you not?"

Mary, seeing that she was serious, was puzzled how to reply. "As far as I can, I will, certainly," she said after some hesitation. Then, laughing, she continued, "It is rather an odd commission."

"Not at all, not at all," said Aurélie, still serious. "He has great esteem for you, madame — greater than for no matter what person in the world."

Mary opened her lips to say, "Except you"; but somehow she did not dare, Instead, she remarked that perhaps Adrian would accompany his wife to America. The trip, she suggested, would do him good.

"No, no," said Aurélie, quickly. "He does not breathe freely in the artists' room at a concert. He is out of place there. My mother will come with me. Do not speak of it to him yet: I know not whether they will guarantee me a sufficient sum. But even should I not go, I shall still be much away. As I have told you, I leave England for six weeks on the first of next month. You will not suffer Adrian to mope; and you will speak to him of his pictures, about which I am so *épouvantably* stupid."

"I will do my best," said Mary, privately thinking that Aurélie was truly an unaccountable person.

Whilst she was speaking, they reentered the drawing room.

"Now, Adrian. I am ready."

"Yes," said Herbert "Good night, Mary."

"I think I heard you say that Mrs Herbert is going off on a long tour," said Charlie, coming forward, and speaking boldly, although his face was very red.

"Yes," said Adrian. "Not a very long tour though, thank goodness."

Then I shall not see her againmdash;at least not for some time. I have made up my mind to take that post in the Conolly Company's branch at Leeds; and I shall be off before Mrs Herbert returns from the continent"

"This is a sudden resolution," said Mary, in some astonishment.

"I hope Mrs. Herbert thinks it a wise one," said Charlie. "She has often made fun of my attempts at settling myself in the world."

"Yes," said Aurélie, "it is very wise, and quite right. Your instinct tells you so. Goodnight and *bon voyage*, Monsieur Charles."

"My instinct tells me that it is very foolish and quite wrong," he said, taking her proffered hand timidly; "but I see nothing else for it under the circumstances. I don't look forward to enjoying myself. Goodbye." Mary then went downstairs with her guests; but he turned back into the room, and watched their departure from the window.

THE END

www.ingramcontent.com/pod-product-compliance
Lightning Source LLC
LaVergne TN
LVHW011933070526
838202LV00054B/4626